THE PRICE OF PANDEMONIUM

BLACK SKIES: BOOK TWO

Sasha A. Linderson

First published in 2024 by Linderson Creations Limited

Paperback ISBN: 978-0-473-70453-7
Epub ISBN: 978-0-473-70454-4
Kindle ISBN: 978-0-473-70455-1
Apple Books ISBN: 978-0-473-70456-8

Linderson Creations Limited
Auckland, New Zealand

www.lindersoncreations.com

To my parents for supporting me in whatever I choose to do.
~ Ashley

In loving memory of my grandma, and the countless afternoons
spent at her kitchen table, learning what 'character' truly is.
~ Sarah

CHAPTER ONE

GRACE

Home was the last place I wanted to be. But here I was. Against my will, and facing down death. My cheek rested on soft green grass as the droning airplane that dropped us back into this picturesque hell faded away.

Levi and I were stranded, alone in a farmer's field with the New Zealand sun bearing down, unrelenting. Blackbirds chirruped happily to a background orchestra of cicadas while the sickly sweet fragrance of wildflowers wafted on the breeze, doing nothing to refresh the stifling summer air. This peaceful façade was a decent cover-up—you could be tricked into thinking the war was over. But I knew better.

"We've got to get out of here," Levi said urgently as he tried to untangle himself from the web of parachute ropes. "Get this bloody parachute off us."

Levi and I were still strapped together from our tandem skydive.

"I'm trying," I muttered, my fingers fumbling with the buckles that attached us to the parachute. But my hands shook uncontrollably, charged with adrenaline from our surprise skydive.

"Hurry up, Grace," Levi said in my ear. "Soldiers could be on us any minute."

"I know, I know."

I was on the verge of tears. I didn't want to be back in this war again. Anywhere was better than this god-forsaken place. My heart thudded loudly in my chest as the panic of being back overtook me. I tried to calm my rapid breathing, to no avail. We were back. Back where Prime Minister Marion could order his soldiers to hunt us down. We had no time to rest or let it soak in. We had to get the hell out of here and find somewhere safe to hole-up.

Finally, the stubborn buckles came free. I rolled off Levi and staggered to my feet. I took a quick glance around our surroundings. Nothing but open, rolling hills dotted with little shrubs. No cover anywhere and no sign of our friends. I'd give anything to see those four people appear over the crest of the hill. The six of us had become family over the last few months, and I couldn't lose them now.

I struggled out of my harness and let it fall to the ground. Our white parachute was stark against the green paddock. If an enemy plane passed overhead, it would be obvious where we landed.

"Come on," Levi said, grabbing my hand. His brown hair was windswept from our jump out of the plane. He ruffled it out of habit and pulled me forward.

"We don't even know where the others are," I said as we ran together. Who knew how far we had drifted. I rubbed at the sharp pain in my thigh from the bullet wound I suffered the last time I was home. Luckily, the nice British medic had stitched it up on our flight. It was the only thing he could do to help us. They knew sending us back here was a death sentence, and they did it anyway. I felt my anger rising, but there was no time to deal with it. We had to get out of here. Now.

"Dylan!" Levi called out. "Jess!"

"Lizzie!" I screamed. "Jennifer!"

No answer.

"Dylan! Jess!" Levi yelled again.

Where were they? Levi and I couldn't wander around aimlessly looking for them. Soldiers would be here soon, and if we didn't run, it wouldn't matter where our friends were. We'd be dead.

"Lizzie!" I called. "Lizzie!"

Then I heard it: A quiet voice floating on the wind.

"Levi?" Jess' voice wafted across the paddock. I looked around and saw Jess and Jennifer running up the hill toward us. Jess' wild copper hair flew around her face. Jennifer looked terrified, her round face pale and fearful.

"Thank God you two are OK," I said, crushing Jennifer in a hug once they reached us.

"I want to get out of here," Jennifer whimpered, trembling against me. Tears spilled down her face, sticking her shoulder-length hair to her cheek.

"Have you seen Lizzie and Dylan?" Levi asked them. They both shook their heads.

I frantically scanned the paddocks and saw a speck of white in the distance. "There." I pointed.

"I see it," Levi said.

"Let's go," Jess said, already running toward it.

We chased after her, clambering over No. 8 wire fences and running through paddocks, the long grass whipping our shins. By the time we reached the speck of white, we were drenched in sweat. Levi's tall, muscular frame stood before me, hunched over to catch his breath. A dark sweat patch spread over his back, and pearls of perspiration snaked down his neck. I pulled at my t-shirt as it clung to my sweat-soaked body.

"Lizzie!" I called out breathlessly.

"Dylan!" Levi shouted out as we continued our approach.

"Over here," Dylan said. "Give us a hand."

I rushed over. Lizzie was still strapped to Dylan, her fair

features masked by a grimace, and her pale skin flushed bright pink as she struggled against the straps binding them together.

"The clips are stuck," Lizzie said. She was getting desperate. Levi and I tried in vain to free them, but true to her word, the clips were stuck fast. Jess and Jennifer kept a fearful eye out for approaching soldiers.

"Hurry up," Dylan said.

"I'm trying," Levi said, pulling at the straps as hard as he could.

Chuff-chuff-chuff. We heard the helicopters before we saw them.

"Guys… incoming!" Jess said.

"Crap," Lizzie said, looking up and scanning for the incoming helicopters. Levi pulled out his utility knife and started sawing at the straps.

"There's a Swiss Army knife in my pocket," Dylan said. I frantically patted him down and triumphantly pulled out his knife. I went to work on the second strap.

"Hurry the hell up," Lizzie said, fear alight in her misty-gray eyes. "They're coming."

"Come on, come on, come on," Jennifer squeaked.

I risked a quick glance behind me. Three helicopters, small black dots in the sky, were looming closer. But the ropes binding Lizzie and Dylan together were thick. I sawed at the ropes as fast as I could, but the knife was slippery in my sweaty hands, and I struggled to keep a firm grip.

"Guys!" Lizzie yelled. "Get a move on!"

"You don't have much time," Jess warned, looking over at our progress.

The whirring of the helicopters hummed louder.

"Finally," Levi said as the first strap came free.

I feverishly hacked at the final few millimeters left. Levi came to help me and ripped the last part of the strap with brute force.

"OK," I yelled. Lizzie didn't even bother to get out of her harness. Dylan pulled the vest attached to the parachute off, and we ran.

"There," Dylan said, pointing at some manuka bushes in bloom. We scurried under the wiry branches. The helicopters were sweeping low now, hovering thirty meters above the pastures. The grass billowed out in ripples as they scoured the landscape for us. I crouched low to the ground as a helicopter flew overhead, sending the little white manuka flowers flying up in a blooming white cloud. The helicopter sat above us for a few tense seconds before buzzing off. I let out a slow breath. We were safe for now. But Marion's soldiers would be back. The helicopters would have spotted the parachutes, and ground troops would be on their way. We didn't have long.

"What do we do?" Jess whispered as she tried to untangle her hair from the mass of spindly branches. I peered through the bushes to try and see the helicopters.

"It looks like they're leaving," Levi muttered.

"We've got to make it back to camp," Dylan said.

Lizzie shook her head. "We have no idea where we are." She was trying to wriggle out of her harness.

"They dropped us near Tauranga. It can't be far. I could see the city from the plane," Dylan said.

Chuff-chuff-chuff. The large military helicopters were back. They rose, desert-green monsters from behind one of the rolling hills. The sun glinted off their tinted windows, flashing across the paddocks as they slowly descended, in unison, a few hundred meters from where we hid.

"We've got to run. They must know we're here," Levi said.

The helicopters landed, and troops began leaping from the doors, dressed in full combat gear. One of the soldiers pointed toward the bushes we hid in.

"Shit," Dylan said.

"We're screwed," Jennifer moaned.

"Run!" Levi yelled.

We scrambled out of the bushes and sprinted in the opposite direction of the soldiers. For a moment, I thought we were home free. Maybe we hadn't been spotted after all. But soon, bullets flew all around us, smashing into the ground and whistling past us, and crashing into the dirt ahead. Welcome home.

"Hurry up, Grace," Levi urged as I lagged behind. But my injured thigh screamed, the stitches pulling at the skin, threatening to rip apart. I screwed my face up in pain but kept running. One foot in front of the other. Run or die. There was no other choice.

The soldiers charged after us, never breaking stride. But we were faster. We had no armor or weapons and managed to get some distance from them. Of course, their bullets could still reach us. And we weren't faster than their helicopters, which were in the air again, tailing us.

"Watch out!" Levi yelled as the helicopters opened fire, their high-caliber machine guns sending dirt and grass flying in all directions. I dove out of the way of a line of gunfire as earth showered down on me. Levi grabbed my arm and pulled me up. I stumbled to my feet and kept running.

"We've got to lose them!" Lizzie shouted as we jumped another wire fence. We needed to get out of sight of the helicopters. We could win a footrace, but outrunning helicopters was impossible.

"Where?" Levi yelled.

"The forest," Jess shouted back. I looked ahead. The forest was far. More than a kilometer away, but we had no choice. I sprinted, my lungs gasping for air and my legs burning. The helicopters were still above us, but we were small moving targets, and their gunfire wasn't accurate. We just had to make it to the forest. Every second, we moved closer and closer. I risked a look over my shoulder. We had put some distance between the soldiers and us on the ground. If we could get out of sight of the helicopters, we might have a chance.

The helicopters opened fire once more as we fled into the bush. The cool forest air was welcoming, but there was no chance to savor it. Bullets crashed through the branches, slamming into trees and ripping up the forest floor.

"Hide," Levi ordered.

I looked around and noticed a river running through the forest. A tree with dense branches overhung it.

"This way," I said to Levi. Without a second thought, I jumped into the river. I plunged into the frigid water, a welcome relief from the sticky, blistering sun. My feet brushed the bottom, and I kicked off strongly toward the overhanging tree. I squinted through the water, watching bullets punch through the surface like miniature torpedoes, drilling through the water before drifting harmlessly to the bottom. I kicked madly and popped up for air, well hidden amongst the tree branches with a good vantage of the approaching soldiers. Levi resurfaced a second later, spluttering and floundering in the water.

"I can't touch!" Levi whispered frantically, his legs uselessly flailing in the water. I grabbed him under his arm and helped keep him afloat.

"It's OK. I've got you," I whispered, guiding him to a sturdy branch. He grabbed it desperately, and we waited.

"Why did I follow you?" he muttered to me as we watched bullets tear up the forest in a furious frenzy.

"Relax," I whispered as I treaded water next to him. Suddenly, the forest dropped into tense silence except for our panting breath echoing in the small chamber. Leaves and pine needles rained down to the forest floor, dislodged from the barrage of helicopter gunfire. But the bullets had stopped. That could only mean one thing: soldiers were coming.

A couple of seconds later, the first soldiers charged through the native bush. Their boots crunched rhythmically as they marched forward. Twigs cracked under their feet as they moved methodically through the undergrowth in a pack. I held my breath as the black muzzles of their assault rifles swept across the forest, seeking any sign of movement.

"Keep moving," a soldier yelled, motioning for his men to keep pursuing forward. "They haven't gone far. Shoot anything that moves."

His soldiers did another cursory sweep of their surroundings before jogging farther into the bush. Thirty soldiers ran past the riverbank and disappeared deep into the forest. A few moments later, their crashing footsteps faded into silence. A wave of relief washed over me. I let out a slow breath and rested my forehead on Levi's shoulder.

"Thank God," I whispered.

"We're not out of the woods yet," Levi warned. "We've got to keep moving. Let's go."

Levi and I swam out from our hiding spot and clambered onto the riverbank. Dylan crawled out from behind a log while Lizzie carefully shuffled down a tree. Jess and Jennifer emerged from some dense brush, their faces marked by fear.

"We better run," Dylan said.

I didn't need telling twice. Levi was already running for the forest's edge, with Lizzie close behind him. Once we reached the tree line, we slowed, carefully checking the soldiers were gone. There was no one in sight. We burst from the safety of the bush and ran in search of a road. The late afternoon sun burned down as we sprinted across more empty paddocks, keeping a wary eye behind us. The last thing we wanted was soldiers to surprise us.

"There!" Jennifer shouted, pointing at a modest farmhouse perched on a hill in the distance.

"Head for it," Levi said.

My legs burned as I used the last of my energy to run for the house. We dashed across the expanse of paddocks between us and the farmhouse, before stumbling exhausted through the splintered door and into a quaint kitchen. As soon as the door shut behind me, I hunched over to catch my breath, sucking the stale air in.

"I think," Levi said, puffing hard, "we lost 'em."

Dylan peeked out the kitchen window to the driveway. "No one's there," he said.

"God, I hate this country," Lizzie said, her porcelain skin

gleaming with sweat. She paced the length of the kitchen with her hands on her petite waist, catching her breath.

"You better check the house," Dylan mentioned to Levi.

"Come on, Grace," Levi said to me. I nodded and followed him cautiously. We walked from the kitchen into a small living room with a tatty love seat and a shaggy rug in front of an empty fireplace. Two large bay windows looked out at the farmland we had just run through. Outside, it was eerily calm. The breeze had dropped, and the long grass lay still and silent. But thick purple storm clouds spilled over the horizon, rolling toward us.

Levi grabbed my hand and pulled me farther into the house. A short hallway came off the lounge and led to two small bedrooms and a bathroom.

"It looks clear," Levi called out to the others as we walked around the second bedroom.

When we returned to the kitchen, Jennifer was perched on a rickety wooden chair and rested her forehead on the dining table.

"Guess the war's still on," Jess muttered as she pulled her thin black cardigan off, discarding it on the floor. She stood in her tight singlet, fanning herself.

"No shit," Levi said, ambling over to the pantry and flinging it open. Dylan kept a watchful eye out the window.

"Anything good?" Dylan asked Levi.

Levi shrugged and began tossing bags of potato chips and biscuits onto the dining table.

"Dinner of champions," Lizzie said as she ripped open a bag of salt and vinegar ones and pulled up a chair. She held the bag out to me. I eagerly grabbed a handful.

"As long as it's food, I don't care," Levi said, munching on a bag of corn chips.

"I'm bloody starving," Dylan said, tearing into a packet of chocolate chip cookies.

"When was the last time we ate?" I mused. The past few days

had merged into a confusing blur.

"Those burgers back in London," Levi said, giving me a small nudge.

London felt like forever ago, but it was only yesterday. Or maybe the day before.

"Before Marion's rocket blew up parliament," Lizzie said, staring distastefully down at her bag of chips.

"Before Uncle Ross died," Jess said, wiping her eyes.

"And all those innocent people were killed," Jennifer said, crossing her arms.

"All because of Prime Minister Marion's sick plan. He killed all those people," Lizzie said.

"We couldn't stop it… we failed," I said.

"We did everything we could. And this"—Lizzie gestured around her—"is how we get rewarded. They send us back here to die."

"No one cares about us," Jennifer said.

"Because anyone who ever did is imprisoned or dead," I said, trying to hold back tears. The events of the past couple of days were catching up with me. Our frantic attempts to warn the US about the impending rocket launch and our last-ditch flight to London to try and tell anyone who would listen that Marion was hijacking an American rocket. When our efforts failed, and the rocket crashed into Parliament, MI5 still didn't believe us. We were illegal wartime refugees, and not only that, we had come from a country that had been in quarantine for months. We were too big of a risk. So, they sent us home… back to where the war began.

"What are we going to do?" Jennifer said, dejected.

"Hide here till morning, and then head straight to our old campsite," Levi said.

"We should go now," Lizzie said.

"What?" I asked. "We're exhausted. We can't make the trek all the way to our old camp."

"It's way too far," Dylan said as he flicked through a pile of mail sitting on the kitchen bench.

"Where are we?" Lizzie asked, snatching the letter from Dylan's hand.

"Te Puke," Dylan said. "Or, somewhere near there."

"It's got to be, what, at least thirty kilometers away from camp?" Levi said.

"Fine," Lizzie said.

"But maybe we can check out town instead?" Dylan suggested.

"I don't know," Jennifer said. "Isn't it a bit soon?"

"I'm not going along with one of your crazy plans, Dylan. Last time you got me shot," I said defensively.

Rain started pinging on the tin roof, small droplets that instantly sapped the humidity from the air. Goosebumps raised on my arms as the temperature plummeted. Now that I wasn't running for my life, my sopping wet clothes were sucking all my warmth, and I started to shiver.

"We need to know what's changed since we've been gone," Lizzie said.

"It's better than waiting for the soldiers to find us here," Jess agreed.

"You can't be serious?" I said.

Thunder grumbled in the distance. A storm was brewing.

"Maybe that's not such a bad idea since we're already out here," Levi said thoughtfully.

"You're siding with them?" I asked Levi, outraged.

Levi pulled me aside, just out of earshot of the others. His hand rested comfortingly against my arm. "You know as well as I do it's not safe to hide out in one of these houses."

"I know," I said. "But it's better than being out there." Thunder cracked right on cue.

"You don't believe that," Levi said, shaking his head. "I know you."

He was right, of course. I hated being cooped up in a house. That's how the soldiers almost captured Lizzie and me at the start of the war. It's where Lizzie's brother was killed. And where Levi and I narrowly avoided arrest a few weeks later.

"We need to know where we stand. We need to know what we're up against," Levi said.

"I think we just saw what the soldiers are capable of," I muttered.

"We'll be quick. In and out," Dylan interrupted, coming over. "And I promise, no tricks this time."

Everyone looked expectantly at me. They had decided, and I would be outvoted, anyway.

"Fine," I said, looking to Levi and Dylan in turn. "But I need some dry clothes before we go anywhere."

"You look frozen," Lizzie said, still munching on her bag of chips.

Dylan shrugged. "We'll see if there's anything else useful here before we head out."

"I should change, too," Levi said. He tucked his hands in his pockets and followed me to the bedrooms to hunt for clothes. His dark hair was matted unglamorously to his head and his clothes clung to him, still soaked from our jump into the river.

"We were lucky," Levi said as he pushed open one of the bedroom doors. "Those soldiers nearly got us."

"I know," I replied, sitting on the dusty double bed. I immediately jumped up again, remembering I was wet. Levi gave me a weak smile and rummaged in the cupboard, pulling out some towels. He tossed one to me and used the other to dry his hair. I felt the adrenaline that had kept me going slowly ebbing away, leaving me cold and shaken. I wrapped the towel around my shoulders and shivered.

I gazed around the cramped bedroom as the afternoon gave way to evening. The days were long right now, and there was still some time before night would truly fall, but the cloud cover shrouded us in dim shadows. Rain drummed heavily on the tin roof, and little rivers of water slithered down the windows looking out into the fields. Soldiers could be out there, I thought.

Silently surrounding the house as we sat unsuspecting inside. Just like when the war first started.

That thought was enough to set me off. Fear rose in my gut, and all at once, the weight of the war we had returned to crashed down on me. I choked back the sudden onset of tears.

"Are you all right?" Levi asked me, his face softening.

"I hate this place," I said, wiping my teary face with the towel. Every minute we had been back was hell, exactly like we left it—an insurmountable mess of fear and destruction.

"This house isn't so bad," Levi said, trying to lighten the situation. "A bit small for my liking." He peeled off his t-shirt, discarding it on the floor, and rummaged through the chest of drawers. In usual circumstances, the sight of Levi's bare chest would stop every one of my thoughts in their tracks. But today, I was too miserable to be distracted.

"That's not what I mean," I said, sniffing, as I tried to cover up my mini-breakdown by toweling my hair dry.

"I know," Levi said as he pulled out a t-shirt. He looked at it quizzically. "I think this might fit you." He tossed it to me. I caught it and laid it on the bed.

"New Zealand's supposed to be our home," I said, licking salty tears from my lips. "Not this waking nightmare."

"It still is," Levi said as he pulled open another drawer, "home."

"How can you say that? Our own army is trying to kill us. We're the enemy in our own country," I said, my voice quivering. I was on the verge of losing any semblance of composure. My edges were fraying, and if I wasn't careful, I would unravel entirely. I wasn't strong like Lizzie or Levi. Or even Jess, for that matter. And if I came undone, I couldn't stitch myself back up. I had too much pain and hurt buried under the surface.

Levi's brow creased with concern, and he walked over to me. He slipped his arm around my shoulders and hugged me close. "We're not the enemy. They are. Marion is," Levi said, his voice calm. "We belong here too."

"We're going to die here," I sobbed, resting my head on his bare shoulder and letting my tears flow.

"I don't plan on dying," Levi whispered. "They'd have to catch me first."

"I'm serious, Levi," I said with a half-hearted laugh. "What are we going to do?"

"Survive," Levi said, looking down at me, serious. "It's all we can do."

Chapter Two

Lizzie

"Who runs a farm without a gun of any sort?" Dylan asked me. We had flung open every cupboard in the small farmhouse and hadn't found a gun safe or a weapon.

"Hippies, maybe," I said, flopping back on the bed. A puff of dust erupted from the forgotten mattress.

"I thought a farmhouse was a shoo-in, at least for a .22," Dylan said, scowling. It was true. We always found a gun of some sort at the farmhouses we raided. My family even had a couple of .22s floating around at our farm. We used them mostly for pest control, possums, and the like.

"Just our luck," I said as I stared up at the stucco ceiling. Before the war, I wouldn't think of using a gun for defense because nothing ever happened in New Zealand. Until it did. And now, the thought of venturing into town without protection of any kind made me nervous.

Actually, the whole prospect of being back here made me nervous. I acted tough, but I was just as afraid as everyone else. Usually, I was hellbent on scrapping it out for everything we had lost. But I wasn't feeling like myself since being back. I talked the big talk; fight, fight, fight. But all I wanted to do was run. Maybe our brief taste of freedom had sensitized me to the war. And maybe it was affecting me more than it used to? Whatever it was, I didn't like it.

"I'm not keen on going to town unarmed," Dylan said as he stared intently into the bedroom closet, like he was trying to will a gun into existence with his mind.

"We don't have another option," I said, rubbing at my sleep-heavy eyes. "Unless you know somewhere we can magically get more guns."

"No," Dylan admitted with a sigh.

"We'll just have to use whatever we can find."

Dylan sniggered. "What, like a kitchen knife? What are you going to do with that? Throw it at a soldier if he gets close enough?"

"If that's all we have, then yeah."

Dylan laughed and then hung his head. His blond hair was growing out, hanging down over his eyes. He slammed the closet door shut. "This place is shit. So shit."

"It wasn't so bad before the war," I said, trying to bring good memories to the surface. But the instant I started to mentally rewind time, I landed on the moment the war began: my brother getting shot in front of me.

"Don't kid yourself, Lizzie," Dylan said, looking up and running his hand through his hair. "It's been a shithole for years."

"At least I had my family before the war," I said stubbornly.

"The good days are long gone. They died when the pandemic rolled in. The war was just the cherry on top," Dylan said. "This is our future."

I sat up and crossed my arms. "I refuse to believe that. We'll get our country back."

"How?" Dylan asked, meeting my eyes. "We're a bunch of teenagers. We can't make a difference."

"Stop being defeatist, Dylan," I accused, a spark of defiance igniting inside me.

"I'm not defeatist. I'll fight till the bitter end. But I'm a realist. The chances of us being the ones to end this are non-existent."

"We can try," I said. We had to. Fighting was all we had left. Marion's war took everything else. Our families, our homes, and our freedom.

"And we will," Dylan said, his blue eyes fierce. "Until the end. Whenever that may be."

I sighed and lay back down on the bed. "You're probably right— about not being the ones to end the war."

Dylan flopped down next to me. "I don't want to be," Dylan admitted with a sigh.

"I just want it all to be over. There was a part of me hoping the war had ended in our absence. We'd get back, and my parents would be free, looking for me."

"Me too," Dylan said.

"Does that make us weak?" I asked.

"No, it makes us human, Lizzie," Dylan said with a hollow laugh. "We're not maniacs. No one willingly lives like this."

"I know, I know. But sometimes it feels like we're the only ones who can do anything."

"Stop putting the whole war on your shoulders," Dylan said, giving me a gentle nudge. "We've only been back for like five minutes. You'll have plenty of time to wage war. You're allowed to take a minute to catch your breath."

Grace interrupted our conversation. "We're ready," she called out from what sounded like the kitchen.

I looked over at Dylan, who was lying next to me and staring up at the ceiling.

"Looks like we better get going," Dylan muttered.

"This was your idea," I reminded him.

"I know, but I don't enjoy being here any more than you do," Dylan said, walking to the door. I got up and followed him to the kitchen, where the others were waiting.

Grace finally looked more like herself. She was out of her sopping clothes and now wore an oversized black t-shirt that hid her slim frame, and a pair of black leggings. Her long brown hair was tied in a high ponytail, a determined look set on her face.

"So, we're defenseless?" Levi asked, noting the absence of a gun.

"Looks that way," Dylan said with a shrug.

"Let's just go," Jennifer said, nervously wringing her hands. "I hate this part. The waiting."

Jess walked to the front door and opened it. The smell of wet grass wafted inside, along with the pattering of rain. Jess stood at the door, looking out at the rain splashing on the driveway. She looked over her shoulder at us, her wild locks firmly secured in a bun.

"What are we waiting for?" she asked before stepping out into the storm. We all followed her. Grace was the last one outside. She hesitated at the doorstep, trying to build up the courage to enter the war again.

"Come on," Levi encouraged her.

"I'm coming," she said, feigning annoyance before stepping briskly into the rain.

The rain fell relentlessly, drowning out our footsteps and blurring the landscape around us. Perfect conditions for sneaking around, I thought. We followed the long driveway out to the main road.

Levi looked around and then glanced up at the street sign. "Oh, I know where we are," he called out over the downpour. "We're way closer to town than I thought. This way," he said, pointing down the road.

We took off at a jog. It was only a few minutes before my legs were tired, dead from our earlier escape from the soldiers. But soon, I broke into my familiar rhythm. Left, right, left, right, left, right. The burning was gone, and I felt invigorated, ready for whatever the soldiers threw at me.

The rain whipped around my head, and I pulled my sopping hair into a ponytail with the band I carried habitually around my wrist. My breathing echoed in my ears in a steady pattern, reminding me to keep calm.

Time merged into a blur, and the minutes no longer felt like hours. We eventually made it over a hill that overlooked our city. It was early evening, and a valley of fog spread out below us. The only lights that blinked in the distance came from the direction of the hospital. The odd army truck crawled through the streets, their lights hazy in the rain. A chilly wind gusted, lashing rain against my face.

"At least we know the war's not over yet," Dylan offered. He had a knack for stating the obvious.

"We already knew that," Grace muttered. "Soldiers don't chase and shoot for no reason."

Levi sniggered.

"What's the plan?" Jess asked.

"I want to go closer and see what's going on," I said, wringing the water from my ponytail. Now that we were out here, I felt the desire to do something. I wanted to see what had become of our town—I wanted to get a real feel for the place. My hunger for action was back.

"Lead the way," Grace said to me. We made our way down the hill and traversed across the paddocks. The rain had eased to a fine mist by the time we reached the industrial sector on the outskirts of town. It was as if we had never left, the streets empty and silent.

Alone, I walked forward and gazed at a half–knocked–over sign. "It never seems real," I whispered to no one in particular.

This little town was the first real set of shops on the way into the city. In summer, flowers blossomed in the centers of roundabouts, and the streets were packed with kids strolling to and from the ice cream store. Teenage girls wore skimpy shorts and tank tops as they traipsed from shop to shop, and the guys drove by nice and slow with their music blaring, wolf-whistling out the window. Now there was nothing left but an empty shell of what had been.

I kicked the sign in an outburst of bottled-up frustration. It gave a horrible creak before toppling over with an echoing crash.

"Nice. Now the whole world knows we're here," Jess said as we heard shouts from around the corner.

My legs sprang into action, and before I even noticed I was running, we were ducking into the shelter of a large warehouse. There were a couple of sporadic bullets fired, then silence.

Grace's face was flushed red. "Did you have to kick the sign?"

"I'm sorry," I whispered. There was nothing else to say. Dylan and Levi were pacing the inner perimeter of the building, peeking through windows to spy on the soldiers.

"There's nothing we can do about it now," Jennifer said. She leaned against a gas cylinder bracketed to the wall, trying to catch her breath.

"What if we die because of me?" I voiced my biggest fear.

"No one's going to die," Jess said as she touched a hand to my shoulder.

I held my breath as the sounds of voices and footsteps echoed along the empty streets. The noises stopped. Were we safe?

"Move!" Dylan's voice was too loud. They must have found us then. I couldn't see where he was. There was barely time to turn before bullets shattered the glass window. I started for the back of the building, with Grace and Jess hot on my tail and Jennifer not far behind.

As I ran, a deafening explosion rocked the ground. It was like being hit by a train. The noise. The sudden impact. The force of it tossed me against the wall. For a moment, I lay there stunned, my senses fragmented. My ears rang, and everything sounded far away. Heavy black smoke filled my lungs as I struggled to breathe.

"Lizzie!" Jess coughed beside me. "Are you OK?"

I opened my eyes slowly and shielded them from the blaze of fire springing up around us. I tried to sit up. There was something wrong with my legs. I was scared to look at them, but when I next tried to move, they thankfully obeyed. I pushed myself to my feet and wobbled like a newborn calf. I saw Jess' smoky shape at my side as she got to her feet.

A shadow emerged and steadied me with a hand on my arm. "Run, Lizzie!" Dylan shouted over the crackle of the fire. "Get out of here now!" He gave me a small shove toward the door.

I shook my head, trying to rid myself of the fog dulling my senses. The air felt too close, suffocating—the fire was devouring all our oxygen. I looked around for Jess, but she had gone.

"Come on!" Grace said and held out a trembling hand. As usual,

Grace refused to leave me. Her face was caked with ash, and a trail of blood slipped down her cheek from a nasty gash on her hairline. Her eyes were bright with terror, and her clothes singed from the fire. I grabbed hold of her hand, and she pulled me, stumbling through the warehouse, both of us struggling to keep our balance.

I chanced a look behind me. "Jennifer!"

Everything melted away in that moment. Through the fiery haze, I could see Jennifer trapped under a fallen beam. Jennifer's eyes locked with mine, pleading with me to do something. The flames danced around her, taunting me, mocking my helplessness.

Grace left my side and started toward Jennifer. I wasn't sure what we could do, but we couldn't leave her to die. I shielded my face from the fire and tried to get to her. My skin burned, the heat too intense to bear.

The solid forms of Levi and Dylan appeared in front of us. "Get out now!"

"But, Jennifer…" My voice was nothing but a dry croak.

"The place is going to blow!" Dylan yelled as he dragged me away.

"No, Dylan… please… Jennifer's back there!" I screamed at him. Dylan didn't seem to hear me. I yelled in pain as another beam fell with a shower of sparks, scalding my back. The images in front of me blurred as the smoke billowed thicker and thicker. Then there was blackness.

MY HEAD WAS THICK and groggy. I tried to open my eyes, but my eyelids were too heavy. My lungs strained to get fresh air. With one last-ditch effort, I forced my eyes open.

"Shhh!" Dylan hissed in my ear. I had no energy to make noise anyway.

I glanced around us. We were in another building, maybe a shop of some kind. It had clearly been looted, with shelves tipped over and cardboard boxes ripped open, scattered across the floor. Outside, it had stopped raining. The evening sun filtered through the still-smoggy air, entering through a pair of smashed windows at the back of the shop. An orange haze lit the dusty shop interior.

Dylan crouched beside me. I was lying on my side, with my back against a wall. Grace was propped up against Levi, deeply unconscious. Her head leaned against his shoulder, and Jess was pressing part of her shirt against the deep cut on Grace's head.

My eyes moved between my friends as my mind struggled to stitch together what had happened. The soldiers. The fire. The explosion.

How did we escape? Where were we? And… where was Jennifer? That thought sent my heart racing. Panicked, I looked around again. Grace, Jess, Levi, Dylan… Jennifer wasn't there.

Images of Jennifer's trapped and burning body flashed back to me. The fire consuming the warehouse. The acrid smoke filling my lungs. The heat searing my skin. Frantic, I tried to get up. I had to rescue her from the building.

Dylan saw my feeble attempt to move. He pushed me forcibly back down and brought his face close to mine. I gazed into his eyes. His, too, were brimming with tears. "Stay quiet. Don't move."

She was dead. Dylan didn't even have to say it. The tears began to fall, slowly at first, but soon they became a steady stream. She was gone. Sadness swelled in my chest as tears spilled down my cheeks.

"What—" I started, my voice shaking.

Dylan clamped his hand over my mouth

"…searched a number of nearby buildings, but the rebels must have fled," a soldier's voice floated in through the cracked window.

The voices grew louder as the two men neared our hideout. "They can't have gone far. Keep it up, we'll find 'em. If that girl's body's anything to go by, they got caught bad in the explosion. They could be severely wounded." The voice paused briefly before adding, "Send someone to notify the hospital. They might show up there looking for help."

"Yes, sir."

"And who was it who shot that god-damn gas canister?"

A long pause grew in the stagnant, smoky air. "I did, sir," the first man admitted.

"Hell of a shot, hell of a shot. I'll see you get a commendation for that one. I might even be able to swing a promotion for you if we catch the other rebels."

"And if we don't find them?" The younger soldier was clearly worried his promotion was in jeopardy.

"We'll find them," the more senior of the two asserted. "Dead or alive."

Their voices faded into the distance as they walked away.

I rested my cheek against the cold concrete floor and cried. Even crying hurt. My lungs ached every time I took a breath. Dylan said nothing but took one of my hands in his, trying to comfort me. I drew back with a gasp of pain, and we both stared at my raw, burned flesh. With a deep breath, I used my arm to wipe the tears from my face. I struggled upright and sat against the wall, spent. My vision swam.

"What happened?" I said finally, as things came back into focus.

"I'll tell you later. Maybe now's not such a good time," Dylan said in a soothing voice.

"No, I want to know now." Talking tickled my throat, and I doubled over with a hacking cough.

Dylan and Levi exchanged glances. Levi shrugged. Dylan stared at me critically for a moment. The side of his face was burned, and his blond hair streaked gray with ash and soot.

Finally, Dylan gave in with a heavy sigh. "Levi and I went out the back door to check for soldiers. As we left, we heard gunshots." He took a breath. "It happened so fast. We barely had time to warn you before the gas can exploded." He paused as he tried to clean some of the ash from my face with the sleeve of his jumper.

"We rushed back inside and saw"—he hesitated and looked

over at Levi who gave him an encouraging nod—"and saw Jennifer trapped beneath a beam. You three were knocked practically unconscious at the far wall." Dylan's voice was shaking now. "Levi and I tried to get to Jennifer. We really did. But the flames were too high, and we couldn't get through. That was when Levi saw the other gas bottles in the corner," Dylan said with empty eyes as he recalled the disaster. "There was no way to get Jennifer out. It was hard to leave her there. I promise… we tried our best to save her." He looked away and took a deep, shaking breath. His throat moved as he swallowed hard.

"So then what?"

"The place was going to blow, and we had to get you guys out of there. Jess seemed OK. She got out by herself. I thought you were, too—you seemed to wake up instantly—so I told you to run. When you and Grace didn't leave, we dragged you out. You passed out halfway to the door," Dylan said. "I dragged you here and left Jess with you to make sure you were all right."

"What about Grace?" I asked as I looked over at her worriedly.

"She collapsed while we tried to get you out. Levi had to carry her, but another beam fell and trapped them. After I got you out, I ran back and helped Levi. Somehow we got out before the building blew."

"Will she be OK?" I asked, glancing over at her. My hands started shaking, and I gripped my knees to try and keep them still before I remembered both my hands were burned badly. White-hot pain erupted in them, and I almost bit through my lip.

"She hit her head pretty hard in the blast, and she has a few nasty burns, but we think she'll pull through," Dylan said, sounding as though he was trying to convince himself.

Our situation was dire. My stomach churned when I remembered a crucial fact in the whole episode: I was the one who kicked that bloody sign. I had completely forgotten about it, but now Dylan had finished his tale, that knowledge came back in its entirety.

"We need to get out of here," I said as I tried not to let my emotions overwhelm me. I needed to be strong. I couldn't help Jennifer—I had already done a god-awful job of that—but I could be strong for everyone else.

"We're not going anywhere for a few hours," Dylan said. He pointed to Grace, who was still unconscious. "Even when she wakes up, I don't know how much pain she'll be in. I don't know how much pain you'll be in," he added as he looked unintentionally at my legs.

I followed his gaze. By contrast, the burns across my calves made my hands look mildly sunburned. They didn't look like my legs, and they didn't feel like them either; I felt fine.

"I don't feel any pain."

"You're in shock," Dylan whispered. "Once all of this finally sets in… you're going to wish you were in Antarctica. Jess and I will go get some first aid supplies and food when the search dies down. Then we'll have to wait it out until you two are fit to leave."

I nodded absently.

"Lizzie…" Dylan said and touched my shoulder gently. "I know you're going to think this is your fault. It's not. Just rest, OK?" He forced his concerned face into a fake smile.

He only said that to make me feel better, but it gave me an out. I closed my eyes, hoping sleep would carry me into oblivion.

WHEN I WOKE, I was lying on the ground with Dylan's jumper thrown over me. I tossed the jumper aside and opened my eyes. My legs were on fire. In fact, my whole body felt hot all over. I was a sweaty mess.

Preparing for the worst, I pushed up on my burned hands, but it was my legs that sent me soundlessly back down to the floor, without so much as a whimper. The pain came in waves, rippling through my legs and leaving me shaking and weak. I tried to focus on something else and looked about me. Dylan and Jess were gone, and darkness was stealing into the world, the last few patches of sunlight falling prey to the shadows.

"Are you OK?" Levi asked. He shuffled into my line of vision. "You were twitching and moaning in your sleep."

"It just… hurts." I screwed my face up in pain and tried to get control of myself. I could do this. *Pain is in the mind.* Still, my body screamed at me. I took a deep breath and attempted to ignore it. There was nothing that could be done.

"I'm surprised you're not screaming in pain," Levi commented.

"Trust me, I'm trying to refrain from that urge," I said through clenched teeth. "Is Grace awake yet?"

"Yes, she woke up a few moments ago," Levi said, sounding relieved.

"Is she OK?" I didn't think I could take it if she wasn't.

"I'll live," Grace said quietly. I couldn't manage to turn to her, but I registered her sitting against the wall a few paces away from me. "I have a killer headache, though."

I tried to laugh, but it hurt too much. "Can you help me sit up?" I asked Levi.

"You should probably stay lying down," he said uncertainly.

"I don't care. Help me up," I said again.

He sighed and helped me into a sitting position against the wall.

"You look terrible," I said to Levi, who gave me a reproachful look. He seemed about to say something but then changed his mind and kept his mouth shut. I must have looked truly awful if he didn't give me shit for that.

"Grace will be fine," Levi said. I hoped so.

I looked over at Grace. Her head nodded as she tried to stay awake. The blood was still dripping down her cheek from the cut on her head. "Let me see her cut."

"You really shouldn't move," Levi said as he halted me.

"I know you're trying to be sensitive," I said, wincing as I tried to move my legs, "but please let me see her."

"No."

"When's Jennifer coming back?" Grace said, interrupting us.

My eyes filled with tears, and I looked at Levi. There was a great deal of pain on his face.

He moved over to Grace. "Hey, can't you take it easy for five minutes and rest? Looking after you two is a bloody tough gig," Levi said. I would never forget the look on his face and all the effort it took him to smile.

"Seriously, Levi. Before the explosion happened, she said… or at least I thought she said…" Grace was getting muddled. "It doesn't matter. Just tell me, when is she coming back?" It was obvious that even this short conversation was sapping much of her strength.

I opened my mouth to say something but shut it quickly. I didn't know what to tell her. Was she strong enough to hear the answer I didn't want to give?

"What's wrong, Lizzie?" Grace asked as a look of concern passed over her. "Why are you crying? I'm going to be fine. Don't worry."

Levi caught my eye and shook his head slowly.

"I'm not worried." I tried to smile.

"Good," Grace said, closing her eyes, "you shouldn't be."

"Rest," I said vaguely as Levi gently stroked her head.

"But—"

"Whatever you want to say can wait," Levi said. "You need your strength."

"OK. But when Jennifer gets back…" Grace said as she slowly closed her eyes.

"All right," Levi said, trying to sound strong and sure.

We had no right to keep this from her. Grace deserved to know, but Levi was right, and now was not the time.

"We couldn't tell her now," Levi whispered to me. "We can't do this to her when she's so…" He looked down at Grace.

"But she's going to hate us when she finds out. This isn't

something you keep secret, don't you think we might make it worse?"

"As long as she lives, she can hate me for all I care. But I… I can't lose someone else." Levi cast his eyes down, and his face was troubled.

"Hey, Grace is going to get through this. She'll be back to her normal self real soon." I tried to sound calm and reassuring, but my voice betrayed me. Even to my own ears, I sounded too peppy, too bright.

"I nearly lost you guys. I can't forgive myself. I wasn't sharp enough… I wasn't strong enough," Levi said.

"Don't be stupid. You and Dylan saved our lives. We owe you several times over."

"That doesn't change the facts: Jennifer is dead, Grace is practically dying in my lap, and your legs are burned beyond recognition," Levi said as he put his head in his hands and ruffled his fingers through his messy brown hair.

"Levi," I said, trying to get him to look at me. "Don't talk like that. If anyone is to blame, it's me. Don't try and tell me it was you who failed in saving us because it was me who got us into this mess." Whatever anyone tried to tell me, it made no difference.

The facts spoke for themselves. I was responsible for all of this. Levi didn't deny it.

I started getting shivery despite the heat raging through my body, and I was beginning to regret tossing Dylan's jumper aside—I was too helpless to reach for it. But no, it wasn't the cold bothering me, I thought. What was sending me into shivers was the shock of it, and the grief. Jennifer was dead. Another life snuffed out. Just like that, she was gone. And, it was an awful way to go. I had always thought death by fire would be the most horrific way to go. It was rare that I regretted being right.

Chapter Three

Jess

"Do you think paracetamol is strong enough?" Dylan asked as he rummaged through yet another house's first aid supplies. I shook my head as I stood guard at the kitchen window, a rifle held shakily in my hands.

This was the fourth house we'd raided tonight, and already it didn't sound like a winner. So far, the best luck we'd had was finding the gun. We discovered it in the second house we'd raided, stored in an old closet. The fragile lock broke easily when Dylan aimed a sturdy kick at it, but it was barely worth the effort. A rifle was one thing, but ammo was another. A few slugs rattled around in an almost empty box, and that was it. Enough for five shots.

My head spun, and I had long ago given up on trying to hold back tears. There was a tremor in my hand that, no matter how hard I tried, wouldn't ease. I glanced out the window. Darkness had finally fallen. Soldiers' torch beams flashed past, and I ducked low. Hours had passed, and we had expected the search to die down, but the soldiers continued relentlessly.

"OK, what about extra-strength paracetamol?" Dylan asked as

he shoved bandages and burn cream into a black knapsack.

"Is that all there is?"

Dylan shrugged. "That's it."

"It will have to do. There's no way we can get any morphine or codeine."

We were interrupted as a soldier stalked close to the window I was crouched under. Dylan stepped back into the shadows as the soldier flicked his torch beam around the room before moving on. I let out a breath. Dylan was already back at the cupboard, and I saw him pause before taking a bottle of something and jamming it into his bag.

"What's that?" My voice was barely a whisper. Too scared that the soldier might come back. Though I didn't say it, I hoped this would be our last stop. Every soldier that slunk by the house had my hairs standing on end.

"It's nothing. Just something that might help." But the look on his face told me he still wasn't satisfied with our pickings. Dylan shifted his weight from foot to foot, trying to decide what to do. "We could go to the hospital and get some morphine or something," he finally said, his voice desperate.

"I'm drawing the line there. You heard the soldiers. They have orders to monitor the hospital."

"They're in pain. And they need antibiotics too. They might die without it."

I shook my head in refusal. "We'll get caught the second we show up there. I know you want to save Lizzie and Grace, but doing something stupid won't help anyone, no matter how desperate you are."

Dylan studied me.

"Dylan, please," I said. "You know how dangerous that is. Please."

"Fine," he said. "But if they die…"

"They won't," I said with finality. I sounded surer than I felt, but the perpetual frown between Dylan's brow seemed to ease up. Apparently, I was better at convincing Dylan of it than I was at convincing myself.

"If you're sure…"

"I am," I snapped.

"Are you not upset about all of this?"

Another lump threatened to clog up my throat, and I swallowed it down while the tears gathered like a storm. I closed my eyes, but a few fat drops escaped and splashed down my cheeks, nonetheless. Several deep breaths later, I opened my eyes again. Dylan faced away from me with his arms folded, his shoulders shaking. He brought a hand up and rubbed at his eyes. I hesitantly touched him on the shoulder. I wasn't very good at comforting people.

"Of course I'm upset," I said, my voice heavy. "But I want to do this job cleanly. I don't want to get caught or shot. They need our help, and we're more useful alive than dead. Jennifer is sitting there in the back of my mind, reminding me of the reasons to keep holding on."

Dylan turned to face me. "I'm scared," he admitted. His face was torn with fear. "I'm scared I won't be able to save them."

"You can't save anyone without saving yourself first." I returned to that moment only months ago, after my friend Leah died. I had tried to end my life and convinced myself I would never escape my depression. It was a deep pit lined with lies, and I scrambled to the surface to find the truth: I was good enough. I wasn't going back there. Jennifer's death was a devastating accident, and there was nothing we could do about it now. There were still people we could help, and until they were OK, I had no time for mourning.

Dylan's face was pale. "I know, I do, but I can't believe how close I was to losing everyone who's ever meant something to me."

"Not everyone," I said. I gave his shoulder a friendly squeeze.

"It was damn close," he said, shaking his head.

"Yes, it was close but… look… we can have this emotional rant later? Right now, we need to get out of here," I whispered as the soldiers circled past again. "Man up, boy." I punched him playfully on the shoulder. I was too fragile to talk about this now. I had to put on a brave face and get the job done.

"Ouch." Dylan glared at me. "I'm burned there."

"Sorry."

The shouts of soldiers from one house over brought Dylan back to his senses. "You're right. We should go." Dylan crawled off below the windows and out of sight of the incoming soldiers. I quickly followed.

"Gun," Dylan said, grabbing the air with his hand. I handed it forward to him. "There's a soldier out there. I'm going to have to shoot him."

"Seriously? If that's not stupid, I don't know what is." I grabbed his arm firmly, not allowing him to move.

"Those bastards killed Jennifer. They deserve it," Dylan whispered as he lined up the sights.

"You shoot, and they'll know where we are," I said in his ear. "Please, wait."

Dylan looked at me. The vein by his temple throbbed faintly, his jaw clenched tight. "You have no idea how much I want to get back at those soldiers."

"I know exactly how much you do, but now is not the time," I said. "You shoot now, they'll never call the search off. Right now, they think we're dead. If you shoot, we'll never get out of here alive."

He flashed me an annoyed look but allowed me to take the gun off him. The soldier stood there scanning with night vision goggles. I ducked back behind the door.

"This is going to be a mission," I whispered.

"You think? It would be so much easier to shoot him," Dylan said, only half-joking.

"I said no."

Dylan sighed. Warm relief spread through me as the soldier walked off.

"Now!" Dylan hissed.

We stood up and sprinted across the open road. We ran through the front lawn of a respectable colonial villa before disappearing behind it. Dylan and I crept through the orchard trees dotting the huge backyard. I clutched the gun tightly, trying to gain courage from its mere presence.

"Shhh," Dylan warned as we crouched behind a huge walnut tree.

Soldiers were pacing down the yard toward us, their lights illuminating parts of the lawn in flashes. I pressed hard against the tree trunk. They walked slowly past me with lights sweeping the ground in wide arcs. I closed my eyes and held my breath. They continued on in silence. Dylan's cold hand yanked on my arm, pulling me around the other side of the tree. Before I could stop myself, I let out an involuntary yelp of surprise. Dylan mouthed an array of violent profanities.

"Did you hear that?" a soldier said, his voice too close, his torch beam hovering only a few feet away. Fear jumped up in my stomach.

"Hear what?" a female soldier asked.

"Where do we go?" I mouthed to Dylan, panicked.

Dylan shook his head. "Stay here," he mouthed back. He put a finger to his lips and peered around the tree. I followed suit, leaning shakily against the trunk. The rough bark scratched at my fingers.

"I swear I heard a noise," the male soldier said. It was surprising to me that he sounded scared. Not all the soldiers were brave and ruthless.

But the woman sounded more confident. "From where?" she asked.

The man pointed toward our tree, and they approached. They stalked around it, and in unison, we silently circled around the other side. My heart hammered so loudly in my ears, I was sure it would give us away.

"There's nothing here," the woman muttered from the opposite side of the tree. I could have reached around the trunk and touched her.

"It could be one of those guerrillas," the man said. His flashlight waved around erratically. I couldn't breathe. Dylan and I stared at each other. Our faces were calm, but I could see the terror in my eyes reflected in his.

"They're all dead in that building," the woman said. "They know this search is pointless, but the orders came from the top. Brigadier Cameron wants us to make damn sure they're dead."

The man was growing more reckless now that there was no sign of us. "So, we're supposed to indulge their paranoia?" he said daringly.

"You have no idea how much trouble those kids have caused. The word is they nearly ruined one of Marion's most important missions," the woman said.

"Where is he, anyway?" the soldier grumbled. "We're here chasing down some kids while he has a bloody vacation—"

"It's not a vacation, and he'll be back in due time," the woman chastised him. "Here's some advice—don't ask questions. Or you'll find yourself dead like those kids."

"Yes, ma'am. Sorry, ma'am," the soldier replied in a meek voice as they began walking away.

We stood there for a few moments, too afraid to move.

Dylan shot me an exasperated glance. "Why do you have to make so much noise?" he finally said as he walked off. "You nearly got us killed."

"Trust me, I know," I muttered to myself as I followed him.

We got to the end of the large property and scaled the fence. I put my leg over the top and dropped to the ground.

"Not too far now," Dylan said. We turned onto a street lined with shops. Our hideout was visible now, only half a block away, and I resisted the urge to run to it. We walked as quickly as we dared, glued to the shadows of the sheltered storefronts. I breathed a sigh of relief when Dylan eased the door to our hiding spot open.

"Did Grace wake up?" I asked as Dylan shut the door behind

us. My eyes slowly adjusted to the dark shop. Grace was exactly where we had left her—slumped against the wall with Levi next to her. Levi twisted his mouth into a smile and nodded.

"Thank God," Dylan said, relieved.

"But…" Lizzie said slowly. Lizzie looked awful. Her usually rosy face was frighteningly pale, and her eyes had lost their brightness. She was sitting awkwardly with her legs stretched in front of her.

"But what?" I asked, dreading the answer.

"She doesn't remember. She's asking for Jen," Lizzie said tearfully.

"Oh," was all I managed.

"Obviously, you told her about what happened," Dylan said and looked expectantly at Lizzie.

"Not exactly," she said, her shoulders tensed.

"You didn't tell her." Dylan sighed and turned to face Levi. "Why the hell not, Levi?"

Levi didn't answer. He stared sullenly at Dylan.

"Oh great," Dylan muttered. "So, who's going to tell her?"

"I think Levi has to do it," Lizzie said slowly, not meeting his eyes.

Levi looked up at Lizzie, panic on his face. "I can't do that… no one should have to do that." He looked around at each of us, hoping someone would step forward. None of us did. I couldn't blame him for not wanting to be the bearer of bad news. How was this fair? We shouldn't be expected to tell our friend someone close to her had died. All I knew was I didn't want that responsibility on my shoulders.

"You're the one who didn't tell her in the first place," Lizzie voiced as she glared at him.

I didn't know what to do or say.

"You were here too," Levi retorted. But I could see it in his eyes; he knew it was his duty.

"We brought painkillers," I interrupted, trying to change the subject. Lizzie looked at Levi in annoyance, but she quickly turned her attention to me.

"You're a lifesaver," Lizzie said, her shoulders sagging with relief.

"It's not anything to get too excited about," Dylan warned and looked at her with concern. "It's really hurting then?"

"Understatement of the year," Lizzie said.

I rummaged through the knapsack on Dylan's back and handed the paracetamol to Lizzie.

"What! Extra strength paracetamol? You've got to be kidding me. This isn't going to do a thing," Lizzie said. She tossed the package aside.

"We couldn't risk breaking into the hospital to get anything stronger," I said.

"What about a pharmacy?" Lizzie said, exasperated. "You could have grabbed some codeine or something. Anything would be better than this!"

The tips of Dylan's ears were going red in shame. "Sorry, we didn't think of that."

"Yeah, that's right, you didn't think!"

I supposed Lizzie's attitude could be overlooked, given her current state, but it didn't stop a ball of anger from forming in the pit of my stomach. We had risked our lives for her. She could at least be grateful.

"Please stop yelling, you're killing my head," Grace said softly from beside Levi. Everyone shut up. "If you're talking about painkillers... I'd love some right now."

Lizzie shut her mouth.

"I'm not dying. It's safe to talk," Grace said with a strained smile. There was no way I was telling Grace about Jennifer. I quickly grabbed a drink bottle from Dylan's knapsack and tossed it to Levi, who grabbed the packet of paracetamol Lizzie had discarded and helped Grace swallow two tablets.

"Anyway, where's Jennifer?" Grace asked. "I need to talk to her."

Dylan and I stared hard at Levi, who shook his head in violent protest.

"Hello? Is anyone listening to me?" Grace rubbed her head to ease the pain.

"Yeah," Levi muttered.

"So? Wasn't she with you guys?" Grace asked Dylan and me as she struggled to push herself more upright.

"Grace, Jennifer is gone," Levi said slowly and kindly.

"Where'd she go?" Grace asked absentmindedly. "Doesn't seem like her to go off alone."

I registered the pain in Levi's eyes. He was holding back tears, and suddenly I felt guilty. We had shunned this onto Levi because we were too weak to admit the truth to Grace.

"She's gone," Levi said, his face serious.

A confused look crossed Grace's eyes as she sensed something was wrong. "I don't understand."

Levi bit his lip hard.

"What's wrong, Levi?" Grace asked.

I felt tears welling in my own eyes.

"Jess...? What? What is it you're trying to say?" Her breath began coming in spurts. "Is she...?"

"Grace, she's... dead," Levi finally managed to say.

"I thought... I thought..." Grace said as tears began spilling down her cheeks. "I th-th-thought she was w-with you," Grace finally managed to say as she looked at Dylan and me.

The most I could manage was the tiniest shake of my head.

"Dylan and I tried to save her," Levi said honestly. "We tried, but... there was no way."

Grace's face was screwed up in pain. She brought up a shaky hand and tried to wipe away her tears.

Levi gently tucked her hair behind her ears. "Everything will be OK," Levi soothed.

Grace shook her head. "Why didn't you tell me before?" she said, her voice thick with tears.

Levi couldn't answer.

"Why?" Grace demanded.

"Because we were afraid you couldn't handle it. We thought you might die too," Lizzie said as she let out a sob.

"You were in on this?" Grace said, sounding betrayed.

"I wasn't in on anything," Lizzie said, shaking her head. "We were only trying to protect you."

"Protect me from what?" Grace asked as she licked a tear from her top lip. "Protect me from the truth? You had no right to keep this from me." She sounded weak and swayed slightly where she was sitting.

"I know," Levi said, his face apologetic.

"Grace, I think you should rest," I said, trying to calm her.

"I don't need rest," Grace said as she tried to get up. Levi pushed her back down. Lizzie turned away and wiped her tears on her sleeve. Dylan stood still, just watching, unable to move or say anything. Grace was too weak to say anything else. Her head lolled unwillingly onto Levi's shoulder, and she lost consciousness.

Lizzie leaned back against the wall and cried. We all did. Eventually, Lizzie attempted to regain her composure. With a loud sniff, she wiped her red-rimmed eyes and looked at Dylan.

"Pass me a bandage," she demanded, her voice still clogged with grief. Dylan robotically got one from his bag and passed it to her. She stood up. "OK, give me some paracetamol," she said, wincing. Levi handed her the box. She grabbed and took two pills without water.

Dylan got up and wet a cloth with some water, then began cleaning Grace's face. He gently wiped the dark trails of blood, revealing Grace's glowing skin. Then Lizzie limped over and crouched next to Grace. Lizzie silently analyzed Grace's wound and wrapped the bandage firmly around her head. She lightly rolled up Grace's sleeve.

I winced as I saw the large burn on her shoulder. "That looks bloody painful."

"Now you know how I feel," Lizzie commented.

Dylan tried to awkwardly clean the burn.

"Give it here," Levi said, holding out his hand. Dylan passed him the cloth. Levi tenderly dabbed the burn clean of soot. Lizzie applied burn cream soothingly on top.

"Please tell me you guys remembered plastic wrap," Lizzie said. Dylan nodded. "At least you aren't completely hopeless," said Lizzie, attempting to make a joke. She then tightly wrapped Grace's burn.

"Your turn," Dylan said to Lizzie.

"I'm perfectly fine," Lizzie protested.

"You are not fine," Dylan said. "Sit."

Lizzie rolled her eyes at him and sat. "OK, mother."

"Jess, I might need your help," he whispered to me.

I crawled over and looked down at Lizzie's legs. I attempted to hide my shock, but I was sure Lizzie saw it in my eyes.

"They're not pretty," Lizzie said, apparently unbothered by my reaction. But after knowing her for several months, I was beginning to see through the act. They were more painful than she was letting on. And she was right, they weren't pretty. Up close, Lizzie's legs looked terrible. It was like someone had peeled back the top layer of skin. What was left was raw and red, darkened with patches of soot and dirt. I looked at Lizzie sympathetically.

"We need to clean them. This is really going to hurt," Dylan said.

"Can't you knock me out?" Lizzie said seriously. She bit her lip in anticipation.

Dylan shook his head and fetched a bottle of whiskey from his bag. "No, but this might help," he suggested, holding it up.

"You can't be serious," Lizzie said.

"Deadly."

"I'm not drinking that."

"Whatever," Dylan said, shrugging. "I'll leave it beside you just in case."

Dylan handed me a fresh cloth he had wet. My hand hovered over Lizzie's leg before I gently reached down and dabbed it.

She immediately drew back with a gasp, and I jerked my hand away.

"Shit, that hurts!" Lizzie exclaimed as tears quickly formed in her eyes. She grabbed the bottle of whiskey off the floor and chugged a fair amount of it. Dylan and I looked at her, stunned.

"OK, I'm ready," she said, spluttering.

"Are you sure?" I asked.

"Just do it."

I hesitantly dabbed her leg again. She winced but said nothing else, and took comfort in the whisky bottle. Half an hour later, Dylan and I had cleaned and dressed Lizzie's wounds.

"We're done," Dylan said.

Lizzie giggled and let the now half-empty bottle tip over. I grabbed it before it could spill all over the floor. "You're so handsome," Lizzie said to Dylan. She giggled again as she tried to crawl over to Dylan.

"I knew the whiskey was a bad idea," Dylan said. He sighed as he made Lizzie sit back down.

"It was your idea," I reminded him.

Levi smirked and gave Dylan an annoying wink.

"It's not funny," Dylan said.

"It's hilarious," Levi said, trying not to laugh.

Dylan held Lizzie at arm's length as she attempted to pinch his cheeks.

"Your face is so perfect. Let me touch it," Lizzie insisted.

"At least she's not in pain," Dylan managed to say as he fended off another attack.

"She will be tomorrow," Levi said, sniggering. "Her headache's going to rival Grace's."

"Do you want to know something?" Lizzie sang as she conducted an invisible orchestra with her finger.

"Not really," Dylan said back, unimpressed.

"You," she said, pointing at him, "saved my life."

Dylan didn't know what to say. I smiled to myself.

"It's so heroic," Lizzie said as she gazed absently at the

ceiling. "I think the room's spinning," she added. A loud hiccup escaped her, and she dissolved into laughter.

Dylan stared at her. He looked like he didn't know whether to be amused or alarmed.

"Maybe you should sleep," I suggested, intervening.

"I agree," Dylan said quickly. "Sleep's a good idea. You should sleep now."

"Are you trying to get rid of me?"

"Yes," Dylan said, sounding scared.

"I don't bite," Lizzie said.

Dylan raised his eyebrows. "You never know."

I helped Lizzie lie down, and she promptly fell asleep.

Dylan breathed a sigh of relief. "Remind me to never give Lizzie whiskey again."

Levi threw his head back and laughed.

"At least she was nice," I said, trying to be helpful.

Dylan ignored me, and silence fell. For a minute, treating Lizzie had distracted us, and we had almost managed to put Jennifer's death out of our minds. But the memory came rushing back. I breathed deeply, trying to keep a breakdown at bay.

Dylan caught my eye and frowned. "We need to get out of here," he said finally. "Staying holed up forever isn't going to work. Eventually, they're going to find us, and there's nowhere to go."

"I know," Levi said. "But no one is in any shape to go anywhere."

"We can't stay here," Dylan countered.

I knew he was right. And judging by the look on Levi's face, so did he. If we waited until Grace and Lizzie were strong enough, we would be caught for sure. Levi cast his eyes over the sleeping forms of Lizzie and Grace.

"I don't"—Levi ran a hand through his hair—"I don't know how we're going to move them."

"Maybe we can stay here for one more night," Dylan relented as he looked over at Lizzie's helpless form, "but no longer. We're lucky no one has come in here yet. We need to go, the sooner the better."

Levi sighed, leaned his head back against the wall, and closed his eyes. "OK, we'll leave tomorrow. Let's hope they can handle it."

"We might have to carry them out if it comes to it," Dylan said, stifling a huge yawn.

"You two sleep. I'll take watch," I said.

"Are you sure?" Dylan asked as he rubbed his eyes.

"Yeah, I'm sure. I don't think I'd be able to sleep anyway."

Levi opened his eyes and gave me a critical look. "Don't beat yourself up over what happened," he said carefully.

I studied them both for a moment before I responded, "You know I wouldn't. Not now. Don't you two beat yourselves up either."

"All right," Dylan replied. "But if you feel—"

"I'm not going to kill myself," I said plainly.

"OK," Levi said and closed his eyes.

Dylan handed me the rifle and settled himself beside Lizzie. I knew they meant well, but I was different now. I padded toward the door, perched myself on an upturned box, and peered out into the night. The streets were silent and empty. I wished things were back the way they were.

The longer I sat alone in the dark with my thoughts, the more my grief began to bubble to the surface. I couldn't help but feel we were all to blame for Jennifer's death. We had taken things too casually. We had forgotten what it took to survive in this place. We let ourselves slip.

Lizzie would be cursing herself for kicking the sign and drawing the soldiers in, while Dylan and Levi agonized over leaving Jennifer behind. Grace would be fretting over keeping us here in even more danger. We were all blaming ourselves for something, yet all this guilt would fix nothing.

I knew that for a fact.

For some reason, everyone close to me in this war had died.

First, it was Leah. She was my strength to get through the war. Then it was Uncle Ross. He wasn't a part of this, and he didn't deserve to die. He died trying to keep us safe. Now it was Jennifer. We were all friends, but Dylan had known Levi since childhood. Lizzie and Grace had been friends for years. And for a brief while, I had Jennifer.

I thought back, and my thoughts lingered over our time in America. Jennifer had been furious when I voiced how jealous I was of the others. I told her I wanted to find my person. I was an idiot. She was there and wanted to be my friend, but I pushed her away.

Now, with Jennifer gone, I was truly alone. Would I ever find my person now?

CHAPTER FOUR

DYLAN

A SCRABBLE OF MOVEMENT roused me, and I clutched at the empty space where I usually kept my gun. But it was only Jess, her light hand on my shoulder, her hair dark and falling in front of her face as she bent down to my ear.

"Change of plans." She didn't have to say more. Soldiers.

I rubbed the sleep out of my eyes and glanced around.

Levi was already waking Grace. "Where to?" Levi whispered to Jess and me.

"Toward our old camp," I said. I turned to the sleeping form of Lizzie next to me and touched her arm, "Lizzie," I whispered. She usually slept lightly, jumping at the slightest touch, but not today.

"Dylan, go away," Lizzie slurred into the sweater she had rolled into a pillow. She was still drunk.

"Lizzie, seriously, you have to get up." I roughly shook her shoulder. "Soldiers are coming."

"We have to leave, now!" Jess whispered as she kept a nervous eye on the door she had come through.

But Lizzie had no interest in moving.

"You might have to carry her," Jess said, coming over to see what was taking so long. She crouched down beside Lizzie, who was now mumbling indistinctly. Jess squeezed Lizzie's shoulder a few times before giving up and saying, "There's no time. Carry her, Dylan."

Jess was right, the soldiers would be on us any minute. "Give me a hand," I said. Between the two of us, we managed to lift Lizzie up and sling her across my back.

"Are you taking me for a piggyback ride?" Lizzie mumbled, giggling.

"Yeah. That's what this is. A piggyback ride," I muttered.

I stared out the window, and through the hazy night, I could see the soldiers marching down the road, systematically checking each and every building. They weren't far from our hideout.

Jess had seen them too. "Hurry!" she pleaded.

Grace wobbled to her feet with about as much elegance as Bambi.

"The backdoor," I said, nodding toward it as I hitched Lizzie farther up. She was heavy for someone who looked no bigger than a pixie. She hung onto my shoulders with a death grip.

Jess opened the door quietly and poked her head outside. "Looks clear," she whispered and moved forward.

I glanced over my shoulder, watching Levi support Grace, who walked gingerly out the door and followed us into the next building.

"My head is seriously spinning," Grace said.

"Mine too," Lizzie said, quite cheerfully.

"I'm not surprised," I retorted.

Jess walked back outside and peeked around the building. From the look on her face, I knew the soldiers were coming closer. "We have to keep moving," Jess urged.

We stumbled from building to building, trying to keep ahead of the soldiers despite our slow progress.

"I don't think I can walk anymore," Grace said as she nearly fell over for the tenth time.

Levi caught her, again. "You aren't walking. I'm practically dragging you," said Levi, grunting with effort.

"You'd do better if you were actually carrying her," I pointed out.

"Yeah, maybe," Levi admitted.

"Seriously, my legs won't go any farther," Grace said again.

Levi sighed. "Here," he directed and hoisted Grace into a piggyback the same way I was carrying Lizzie.

"Giddy-up, Dylan, we have to keep going," said Lizzie, clearly still tipsy. "If we stop, the soldiers are going to come and blast our heads to pieces," she said as she nodded dramatically. "And I would be so upset if that happened to you. Your face is so—"

"Perfect? Yeah, you may have already mentioned that," I said. My 'perfect' face was turning redder by the second. "If you don't shut up, the soldiers will definitely come and blast our heads to pieces," I said in an embarrassed whisper and started forward again.

Jess peeked out the window. "It seems like we're safe for the moment. We've gained some distance. If we can make it out of these buildings before the soldiers come, we might get to the forest... to safety."

Levi paused for a moment's rest. "How far away do you think we are?" he asked.

I let Lizzie down for a moment. She swayed but seemed to recover and managed to stand by herself. I glanced out the window in the same way Jess had.

"Not far," I answered. "If I'm remembering right, there's a small suburb ahead. And then some empty farmland before we make it to the bush."

"That's doable," Levi agreed. "Come on, Grace, we're nearly there."

"Can't we just let the soldiers find us?" she moaned as her head lolled to the side. She jerked it upright again. She'd slipped down, and Levi hitched her back up, his face determined.

"That's not an option on my watch," Levi said. "It's only a little farther."

I wasn't sure if he was trying to encourage Grace or himself. Her arms slackened around his neck.

"Grace, hang in there," I said, squeezing her arm. She looked at me and nodded, but it was clear if we didn't get to safety soon, she'd pass out altogether.

"OK, come on, Lizzie," I said.

Lizzie shook her head. "I can walk," she said. "I'll be fine."

"OK, but you have to keep up."

"Try and stop me. No soldier will have the satisfaction of catching me," she said, except her words were mushed together, and 'satisfaction' sounded more like 'salisfashion'. I shrugged and let it be. After all, I couldn't force her to cooperate.

As we passed through the last of the industrial sector, we eventually stumbled into a rundown residential area. We passed by the abandoned houses, letterboxes crooked on their posts. Rusting cars sat untouched in the driveways, weeds creeping ever closer from the untended lawns. The housing became sparse as we approached the fringes of town. I kept my eyes ahead, fixed on our goal. Soon, we would have to brave the empty fields to make it to the forest.

Grace constantly slumped forward, only half-conscious, and it was all we could do to catch her and stop her from falling off Levi's back. Lizzie had it lucky… if that was at all possible. She wouldn't remember this in the morning, and she was so drunk that she wasn't feeling much pain. If I thought I could catch a break now that I wasn't piggybacking her anymore, I was wrong. Despite knowing the soldiers were after us, she kept trying to burst into conversation, and I was continually hushing her.

We were disorganized, slow, and noisy. I couldn't believe we'd made it as far as we had. We had one gun with five bullets in it. If we made it to safety, it would be a miracle. We huddled in a shed around the back of a house to catch our breaths. I could see a wire fence leading to a small paddock a few yards away that separated the backyard from the adjoining farmland.

"We're getting close. Just a few paddocks before the forest," Jess whispered nervously. Levi and I nodded.

Lizzie stared blankly around. "Why is it so dark?"

"Because it's night," I said, frustration seeping into my voice. I was thoroughly sick of drunken Lizzie, and I wanted smart, sober Lizzie back. "If you don't want me to gag you, you need to shut up for five seconds."

"Don't be so mean," she said as she began to cry.

Jess, Levi, and Grace started leaving the shed, but Lizzie wouldn't go. She continued sobbing noisily, and stubbornly refused to move.

Crap.

Jess sighed. "Now look what you've done."

"What I've done?" Like it was my fault. Jess glared at me, and I took her point. Apologize now or apologize later in a prison camp, provided we had the chance before soldiers executed us one at a time. I turned to Lizzie. "I'm sorry."

Drunk as she was, Lizzie still saw straight through it. "You don't mean that." Another tear dribbled down her face. I lifted a finger and wiped it away awkwardly.

"Of course I do," I said, more genuine this time. It wasn't my fault, but it wasn't really Lizzie's either.

"Truth?" Lizzie asked, her eyes still shining with tears.

"Yeah, it's the truth. I'm sorry," I said again. I turned away from her under the mistaken impression the conversation was at its end and tugged on her arm.

Lizzie was still rooted to the ground. "Dylan, will you keep me safe?" she asked in a small voice. I had never seen Lizzie so vulnerable and frightened, and that scared me.

I remembered my little sister had asked me that same question, a long time back. Rosie had begged Mom and Dad for a pony, but when they finally relented and bought her one, she was too scared to ride it. She made me promise to walk beside her so she wouldn't fall, but a plastic bag flew out of nowhere and terrified the living daylights out of both of them. The pony ripped the reins out of my hands and took off at a gallop. Rosie fell and broke her arm. I would always feel guilty about that, especially now. I had no clue where Rosie was or how she was doing. All I had left were memories of a promise I never kept.

I looked Lizzie in the eye. She wouldn't remember this, but I would. "I'll always keep you safe," I swore to her. It was a hard thing to promise. I knew that. I wasn't sure if it was a promise I could keep. I would die trying—there was no doubt about that—but I was scared because there were no guarantees.

On our way out, I pushed the shed door shut as gently as possible. The last thing we needed was a door banging in the wind. I peered into the night, relieved to see the coast was clear. I waved the others on. We made it over the fence using a well-placed stile and shuffled across the paddock. Jess took up the tail with her gun raised and ready to shoot.

Levi tripped and nearly fell, Grace's weight tipping him off balance.

Grace shrieked, abruptly silencing her surprise. Levi swore.

"Over there!" a voice shouted. The wire fence squeaked as the soldiers hurdled it, chasing after us.

"Run!" I yelled. Levi adjusted his hold on Grace, and we stumbled forward, trying to force our destroyed bodies to run one more race. Levi and Grace were drifting behind, and fear fluttered uncomfortably in my stomach as the soldiers closed the gap.

I glanced at the expansive field ahead. It was the last one before the forest. We had been so close. Even if we managed to stay ahead of them, we would still be leading them straight to our hideout. I couldn't risk that. Jess popped a couple of shots at the approaching soldiers that disappeared into the night without reaching their target.

"This way!" I called and darted to the left of an approaching fence line.

"Where are we going?" Jess called.

"I don't know, but we can't lead them into the forest," I shouted back. Bullets crashed around us, splintering the fencing batons. There was a twang as one skimmed across a wire. I flung open a rickety gate, and Lizzie and Jess raced through. There was a rush of noise as we disturbed a flock of sheep, and suddenly there were masses of them stampeding alongside us. I dropped back to where Levi was struggling to carry Grace forward. Her head kept lolling to the side, and I could tell she was slipping in and out of consciousness. Her bandage had already soaked through with blood.

"Let me take her for a bit," I said.

Somehow, still moving, Levi managed to hoist Grace over my shoulder. I grasped at her legs, put my head down, and powered forward in a rugby charge. The soldiers had gained more ground, and gunshots sliced through the air, too close for my liking.

Then there were shouts of surprise, and more gunfire lit the night. The soldiers slowed. A grenade detonated, and I heard someone scream behind us. The scream went on and on before another gunshot rang out, plunging us into sudden silence.

"What's happening?" Jess asked. I paused, breathing heavily as Jess looked through the rifle sights. Lizzie vomited on a patch of grass and weakly wiped at her mouth.

Grace let out a moan. "Are we safe yet?" she asked.

"Nowhere is safe, Grace," Lizzie said, bent over with her hands on her knees. She was breathing fast from the sprinting, and her fair skin was a sallow white.

"We'll find somewhere," Levi promised them both. He wiped the sweat from his brow.

"I can't see anything," Jess said. She peered through the rifle sight again. "I can't see any of them anymore."

"I think someone killed the soldiers," Lizzie said. She seemed to be sobering up now.

"Yeah, and I think whoever killed them is watching us right now," Jess said as she glanced nervously around us, not sure where to aim her gun.

"Do we run?" I asked. A prickle of fear crawled up my spine.

No one had a chance to reply. The men rose up through the dark more silently than the night itself.

"Put your hands up!" a voice ordered.

They stepped forward with frightening coordination, like they had practiced this moment thousands of times before. They hulked over us with black combat vests broadening their already muscular frames. One of them motioned for Jess to drop her gun. She put it carefully on the ground and pushed it forward with her foot. She stepped back with her hands in the air.

The man nearest to me raised a black-gloved hand with a small radio device. "We've got them," he said.

The device crackled as the reply came through. "Bring them in," a female voice replied.

Grace was grabbed roughly from my shoulders, and cuffs were slapped unceremoniously around my wrists.

"Be careful, she's hurt," Levi warned as he and Jess submitted to being cuffed as well.

I looked at Lizzie. Her hair was messy, and the cling film we had wrapped around her legs was barely holding in place. I could only imagine how painful they were, but Lizzie looked ready to fight. I caught her eye, and she looked at me with that familiar wildfire.

"Please, Lizzie," I whispered, looking back at her as the men pushed me forward. These men had killed the soldiers. We didn't know what they would do with us. I had to hope they had rescued us for a reason. Lizzie stood up as tall as she could manage and offered her wrists to be cuffed. I let out a breath. I didn't want to watch her die for nothing. Once we were all safely shackled, we were forced to stumble onward into the never-ending night.

I FOCUSED ON PUTTING one foot in front of the other. At least one man guarded each of us as we walked, and if I slowed, he occasionally pulled me forward with my cuffs. Levi tried to engage our captors in conversation, but they remained silent. We didn't know who they were or where they were taking us.

Eventually, a glow in the distance indicated the imminent arrival of the sun, and I could hardly believe we were alive. Yet here we were—a little damaged, both inside and out, but still here, still breathing. This thought gave me some strength, like our very breathing was defiance. We valued our freedom over all else. Now, that too had been taken from us. As if enough hadn't been taken from us already.

The soldiers had taken Jennifer.

And just like that, my throat began to close up. I blinked away tears that kept trying to creep their way into existence. It was easier to pretend like it didn't hurt. It would be easier if I couldn't remember Jennifer's screams as the fire took her. The horrid stench of burning flesh was seared so thoroughly into my memory, I could still smell it. I envied Grace and Lizzie, who would never have that memory. They were lucky.

Though I knew we had done our best, I played that moment where Levi and I turned away over and over again in my head. She was reaching out for help, and we turned away. We left her there, without a word of comfort. I couldn't even say sorry or explain myself. We turned away to save Lizzie and Grace, and it had been a conscious decision. That was what I couldn't wrap my mind around. My friend was screaming for help and, clinically, I had examined the situation. I found no other solution than to look her in the eyes, turn around without a word, and leave her to die. Jennifer was another person who I had failed.

I watched Lizzie walk in front of me. Her dirtied blond hair hung in a scraggly mess down her back. I was sure she was as exhausted as the rest of us, but she was back to her usual self, standing as tall as her five-foot-three would allow. I could still hear her voice in my ears. *Dylan, will you keep me safe?* I had promised yes, I would. Even if it was against her wishes. I would keep her safe, and maybe one day, that would be my redemption.

A HAND PRESSED AGAINST my shoulder, and my feet obediently stopped.

"We're here," a man said. I'd heard the accent before, but it seemed out of place. The day was waking, and the light flickered across his features. He wasn't from here.

"You're American," Jess said at once.

The man shrugged. He reached for his radio. "The birds are back at the nest," he said.

I heard several locks clunk, and a woman with jet-black hair opened the door. Her hand rested on a pistol holstered on her hip. She, too, was swathed in black combat clothes.

The dark-skinned man who carried Grace pushed forward. "This one's hurt. We need a medic," he said as he carried Grace inside. The woman stepped aside to let him pass. She appraised us all with one intelligent sweep of her brown eyes.

"You can take the cuffs off," she said. "They're not prisoners. But... I wouldn't try to run," she warned us. The man who had been walking with me unlocked my cuffs, and I massaged some feeling back into my hands.

"Who are you?" Lizzie asked.

"We're a special ops group from the CIA," the woman replied. "Welcome to our base."

Chapter Five

Levi

"Where's Grace?" I demanded. Tamzin pushed her jet-black hair behind her ears and looked at me kindly. She finished thumbing some information into a high-tech hand-held device and then sat down in her roller chair facing me. While we weren't exactly in chains, we weren't free, either. We were kept in isolation, and being split up made me uneasy.

I had gone out by myself to find Grace. The doors weren't locked inside the building, but as soon as I left my area, one of the agents caught me and shepherded me back, with some bullshit excuse to keep me contained. The last I saw of Grace, she was unconscious. And I was terrified I would never see her again.

We had spent all those months together hiding out in the bush, and I never found the courage to tell her how I felt. I had figured there would always be time later. I should have known that in war, there is no 'later'. Enough people from our group had died for me to know that. What if I had missed my chance? She knew I liked her. But she didn't know how deep it ran. I would do anything for her. Anything.

I ran my fingers through my greasy hair, but my hands wouldn't stop shaking. I settled for shoving them into my pockets. I didn't want the CIA to see how nervous I was. Confidence. An illusion of confidence was needed right now. That's what Dad would have said. Show no weakness.

"Where's Grace?" I demanded again. I hated being apart from everyone. They told us it was only a precaution, and soon they would lift the security, but we weren't stupid. We were being interrogated, and I was sure they were seeing if our stories lined up. And, although we were allowed to eat and move around unshackled, it didn't mean we weren't prisoners.

"Grace is fine. She's recovering well, but she needs rest," Tamzin said. "Now, let's run through this again."

I sighed. "I don't know what else I can tell you. We were running from the soldiers, and we managed to climb onto Marion's private jet to hide. That was how we first heard of his plan to launch the rocket."

"Tell me again about the conversation between the Prime Minister and his associate," Tamzin pressed.

I tried to recall the exact words he had used, but drew a mental blank. "Look, I don't see how this helps at all," I said instead. "The rocket already crashed, there's nothing more to do."

"The United States of America requires answers. We cannot let a heinous act of terrorism occur using US technology go unpunished. The President is demanding the truth. That's why we're here," Tamzin said for the tenth time with a surprising amount of patience behind her voice. I expected the CIA to be brutal, but so far, that hadn't been my experience. I wondered if they were playing nice because we were kids.

"You have to admit, it sounds far-fetched," she continued. "You lot show up without warning, break through security into the Pentagon, and insist a rocket is going to launch from our country and crash into the United Kingdom."

"When you put it like that…"

"Do you know how many people have ever broken into the Pentagon?"

"No," I said sulkily.

"None. It has never happened before. Sure, some people have hacked into servers. But a physical break-in? You can see why you look suspicious." Tamzin leaned back on the roller chair and pushed herself away from the desk. "Do you want a coffee?"

It was like she'd never left her office. All she'd done was transport it to New Zealand. That's not to say they weren't alert. Their eyes were constantly watchful, always looking out for a new threat. Tamzin's brown eyes roved once around the room before coming back to meet mine. Her sleek black bob was combed perfectly in a way that made me think she was all business. She wasn't the type to let others push her around. The only other woman on the CIA team was an African American woman named Shannon, who was equally intimidating. I guess in their line of work, they had to be.

"Ezra! Get us a drink, would you? Two coffees. You know how I like it," she barked. A minute later and a steaming mug of coffee was pushed toward me. Tamzin took her own coffee and sipped it, eyeing me curiously over the brim.

"Thanks," I muttered. "So, you think we caused the rocket to crash?"

The direction the conversation was going was beginning to piss me off. We did everything we could to make these people open their eyes, but nothing worked. We'd been ignored, and eventually, people like them had shipped us back to New Zealand because they were too stupid to listen. Now, they were following us and demanding answers. But the damage was already done. What did they expect to achieve?

"No," Tamzin surprised me by saying. "We don't. We don't know what to think at the moment. That's why we're here. The President needs us to get to the bottom of this, and I think there was more to that conversation you overheard. So, as repetitive as all this is, I need you to tell me again."

"I'll do you a deal," I said.

"You're not in a position to make a deal," Tamzin said, narrowing her eyes.

I ignored her. "I tell you what happened, and you let me see Grace and the others."

A smile escaped Tamzin's lips. "You seem to care a lot about Grace."

"What's it to you?" I said, crossing my arms.

Tamzin shrugged. "Just an observation."

"Keep your observations to yourself."

Tamzin leaned back in her seat, studying me.

"So, are you going to take the deal or not?" I was getting frustrated now. I wanted to see Grace. I wanted to see the others. And I was sick of being interrogated.

Tamzin looked down at her watch before answering me. "You know what, Levi... I'll take your deal. But you tell me every detail. Leave nothing out."

"Every detail," I repeated obediently.

"And start from the beginning," Tamzin said.

"And then you'll let me see Grace," I said.

"Yes," Tamzin said with a sigh. "Then I'll take you to Grace."

I took a deep breath and told her everything.

"LEVI!" GRACE'S FACE LIT up as she saw me, and she tried to get out of the army cot she lay in. At the sight of her, I couldn't stop smiling. It didn't matter what we'd been through. She was alive and staring back at me in a way that made my heartbeat race and my palms sweat. I wanted to pull her into my arms, but we weren't alone. Plus, I was never quite sure whether she felt the same way.

The dark-skinned agent who had brought Grace in the day earlier pushed her gently back down. I briefly remembered Tamzin calling him Luke.

"You're supposed to be resting," he said gruffly.

"Hey," I said as I approached the cot, acting casual. I put a hand on her shoulder. "He's probably right. Go easy," I said.

"I thought I'd never see you again," Grace said, her eyes welling with tears.

"There's no way I'd let that happen."

Luke strolled away and stood guard at the window, looking alertly for any soldiers. "What's going on?" Grace whispered.

"They're trying to get information about the rocket," I briefly filled her in.

"Don't they realize it was all Marion's doing?" Grace asked. "After all, we did try and tell them."

I frowned. "I'm not sure they believe us, but they're trying to figure out what's going on. There's definitely a lot they're not telling us yet."

"Oh," Grace said, leaning disappointedly against the pillows.

"Levi, Grace?" I heard Jess' voice.

Lizzie, Dylan, and Jess were standing at the doorway.

"Guess it's visiting hours at the local hospital," Luke said, rolling his eyes and staring out the window. He reached for his radio. "Ezra, we're gonna need some extra coverage over here."

Did they ever relax? I supposed not. I briefly wondered how they remained on high alert every waking moment. Maybe it was a habit, like learning to drive. At first, you try to concentrate on everything all at once. Then, slowly, your brain starts making the connections without it being a conscious decision. The CIA agents moved in a way that was both practiced and natural. They didn't have to think about it. They acted. But they did it with caution and skill.

"Can we have some privacy?" Lizzie shot at Luke.

Luke's dark brown eyes assessed us all. "I'm not supposed to do that," he said simply. He scratched behind his ear. His hair was shaved so close to his scalp that he was almost bald.

"Then ask whoever gives orders and get an OK from them. We've been through enough, and we don't need you gawking at our reunion," Lizzie said, folding her arms.

"You're a brat," Luke said, but he didn't appear annoyed. Just bored. "Don't you know we're here to keep you safe? Where would you be if we hadn't stepped in and saved your sorry asses?"

He then pulled out his radio before Lizzie had a chance to respond. "Tammy, they want alone time," he said into his radio.

On the other end of the line, Tamzin sighed, and it crackled through the tiny speaker. "Give it to them. They can have five minutes."

"You heard what she said. Five minutes," Luke told us as he walked swiftly from the room.

Everyone started trying to talk to each other at once.

"Have they been interrogating you like they have been me?" Dylan asked.

"I think they've been interrogating us all," Lizzie said.

"Not me," Grace said, "they stitched my head, though." Grace pulled her fringe to the side and revealed a neat line of stitches holding her head wound together.

"Lucky you," said Lizzie dryly. "Meanwhile, the rest of us have been quizzed on 101 questions about the rocket launching."

"Levi was filling me in before you came," Grace said.

"What do you think they'll do once they're done questioning us?" Dylan asked.

The same question was on my mind.

"I don't think they'll harm us," Jess said slowly.

"They might," Lizzie said. "I mean, let's face it, how many civilians get pulled into CIA ops and come back without either being recruited or killed?"

"Or recruited and killed," I joked.

"This isn't funny, Levi," Lizzie said, glaring at me.

I shrugged. "I'm with Jess. They want our help to figure out why Marion attacked England. That's in line with our own goals, right?"

"I suppose..." Lizzie faltered.

"I say we wait it out," Dylan said. "Let's not be too trusting. After all, we're basically prisoners at the moment. But it doesn't hurt to see where this leads, at least for now."

Jess sat on the ground and leaned up against Grace's cot. "I don't think we'd be able to escape even if we wanted to," she said. "These guys aren't amateurs."

"You got that one right," Luke said as he reentered the room. "Five minutes is up."

Ezra, one of the CIA guys, came in behind him.

"It's a little too crowded in here," he said with a thick southern American accent. "Y'all need to go back to your rooms now."

Silently, we obeyed. I caught Dylan's eye before I walked back to my room. I hoped he was right about seeing where this was going. Because we could've missed our only chance to escape.

I ALWAYS HATED BEING alone. I think it had something to do with my absent father. Or maybe it was because I was an only child. I remember sitting in my room as a kid, crying as I listened to my parents fight. They were good fights too; broken plates, screaming, and slamming doors. Eventually, mom kicked him out for good.

Whatever my reason was, I despised time alone. It left too much time for thinking. And it wasn't long before the guilt and grief came clawing back. I was still finding a way to cope with Jennifer's death, and as soon as I was alone, staring at the wall, the memories came rushing back to me.

Jennifer's shrill scream was etched in my memory. I knew it wasn't my fault, but I couldn't let it go. My mind insisted I was to blame. I told myself over and over it was a lie. But the guilt wouldn't leave.

Is this how the rest of the war would go? Our lonely group of friends getting picked off one by one until no one was left? I felt a tear slip down my face. I barely ever let myself cry. I could hear my dad scolding me: *Hold it together, Levi. Real men don't cry.* He was wrong, of course. Always had been, always would be. But that was the way he dealt with the hard stuff. Turn a blind eye, and everything would work out fine.

Would my life have been better if he had been a better dad?

I guess I'll never know. I didn't blame Mom for divorcing him. I didn't want to be like my dad. But after years of him embedding his doctrine into my mind, sometimes, it was tricky to shake.

Another tear crawled down my face as I thought about Mom. I hoped she was OK.

"Hey," Shannon said. The CIA agent barged her way into the room and sat down on the floor beside me. "Are you OK?"

I sniffed and wiped the tear away, not facing her. It was embarrassing being caught crying.

"We're not total monsters, you know. I know we're keeping you here, but we have our reasons," she said.

I nodded absently. I didn't want to talk.

"Speaking of… Tamzin wants to see you all. We've been through every angle of this, and now it's time for action," Shannon said. Her black afro was combed into a wild ponytail, and her high cheekbones gave her face an angular look. She looked at me through intelligent eyes. Her words might have been comforting, but her hand on her hip piece told me they didn't trust us. I blinked several times, hoping it wouldn't show I had been crying, and followed her to a large room in the center of the factory.

Several cold-looking metal chairs were arranged in a semicircle in the wide-open space. The others were already seated, looking like they were ready for some bizarre conference to proceed. Shannon pointed to my seat. She took her place next to Tamzin while other agents prowled around the perimeter of the building, looking for movement outside. I still hadn't figured out exactly how many agents there were here. Ten? Twelve? I'd only met a few, and it was impossible to tell how big this operation was.

Tamzin stood front and center.

"From the information you have given us, I take it you have

no further intelligence beyond the point where you were forced to return here," Tamzin clarified.

"No," Dylan said, speaking for us all. "They forced us out of the plane a couple days ago, and then we ran into you."

"The crashed rocket is an international tragedy. People are, understandably, demanding answers, and the UK government is blaming a group of teenagers with radicalized views. A group of teenagers who wanted to make a statement," she said.

"What!" Lizzie yelled, outraged. "They're blaming us?" She leaped out of her chair, furious. Ezra immediately stood up with his hand on his weapon, ready to defuse the situation.

"She's right," Dylan said. His eyes blazed with anger, and his cheeks flushed red. "They can't do that! We tried to warn them… we tried to warn all of you, and this is the thanks we get?"

"Sit down, Elizabeth," Tamzin said calmly, "Dylan." I had never heard Lizzie called by her full name before.

"It's Lizzie," she hissed through clenched teeth but she sat anyway.

"We had to be sure it wasn't you. I've already explained why." Tamzin's eyes rested on each of us thoughtfully as she paused.

"Because we knew it was going to happen? But that doesn't prove anything," Grace said stubbornly with her brown eyes glaring. She was propped up on a chair, but it looked like it was draining her of the little energy she had.

I wasn't sure how I felt. We had known what we were doing was illegal—we knew there was a chance we would be called terrorists. But I never thought that would actually happen. The war here would shelter us from the international media, or so I thought.

I expected my anger to be explosive like Lizzie's and Dylan's —another trait I'd inherited from my dad. Instead, it bubbled away underneath the surface.

"But that's in the past. We know it wasn't you now. Besides, where would you have gained the resources for something like that?" Tamzin said with a dismissive wave of her hand. "That's beyond the capabilities of a group of teenagers."

I wanted to jump in a say they had no idea what we were capable of, but Jess got in first.

"Then you'll make sure the rest of the world knows," Jess said.

"We can do that. Eventually. But right now, it would compromise our mission."

"And what's that?" I asked.

"To bring down Marion. Someone has to pay for what happened," Tamzin said.

The pieces were coming together.

"We're being recruited," Grace said slowly. "You want our help."

Tamzin nodded, and we all considered this in silence. The only sounds were the agents' boots as they trod from one vantage point to another.

"You don't have to say yes yet," Tamzin said as none of us spoke.

"We're not saying yes, yet," Jess retorted.

We had just lost a friend on a stupid visit to town. We weren't going to agree to anything without talking it over. I shifted in my chair.

"If we were to agree, what information do you have on him so far?" Lizzie asked cautiously.

"Not much, but we're getting there. Frankly, we can't share anything until we have a definitive answer from you." Tamzin eyed us expectantly.

We all looked at each other. I took in the tired faces of my friends. Jess' small oval face was furrowed in thought, and her copper hair was dirty and tangled. The familiar fire that burned within Lizzie was close to being put out, but she stared defiantly at the Americans, her chin raised. Dylan looked on with perplexed blue eyes. I could tell he still hadn't let go of the anger of being painted as a terrorist. Dylan always hated being made out to be the bad guy.

Lastly, I looked at Grace. She was exhausted, with deep lavender shadows under her soft brown eyes. Her chestnut hair hung limply from her head and remnants of the soot and blood clung to her tanned skin. She looked back into my eyes, and in hers, I found my answer: Grace needed me. Saying no to helping the CIA didn't make us bad people. Right now, more than anything, we needed a break. We needed to look after ourselves. We needed to find some peace after Jennifer's death.

"We can't give you the answer you want right now. We've just lost one of our friends," I said. "We need time. We need to go… home."

Chapter Six

Grace

We were alone again. One moment, the CIA agents were standing next to us. The next, they melted into the trees and were gone. I was exhausted. Even standing sapped my energy. My mind was a foggy haze I struggled to think through. I ran my finger along the stitches across my head.

Why was it me who kept getting injured?

First, it was the gunshot wound. And now, a head wound and a concussion. As if this war wasn't bad enough. At least I wasn't dead, I thought.

We stood in a small clearing, the trees looming dizzyingly overhead, a mass of forest with no discerning features. The agents told us they dropped us near our old campsite, but I was disorientated. It felt familiar to me, but I didn't recognize anything. It didn't help that the forest seemed to twirl in my vision. I pressed my hand against a nearby tree to steady my balance.

"This way," Dylan said knowingly.

I didn't know how he knew where we were, but I stumbled after him nonetheless.

Levi was immediately at my side, grabbing my hand for support. "You have a concussion. Be careful."

The dizziness came in waves. I would feel perfectly fine, but then a wave of nausea would overtake me, the world would spin, and it would take all of my willpower not to collapse.

"We'll take it slow," Levi said, guiding me through the undergrowth.

Ahead of me, Lizzie was also struggling. Her legs had nasty burns, and the strong painkillers they gave her made her woozy. She swayed along next to Dylan, who kept a firm hand under her elbow to help her along. It was slow going, but after an hour of agonizing progress, we made it.

As soon as we arrived at our campsite, I recognized it. The big kauri tree where we always talked. The stream bubbling away— my sanctuary. The little grassy knolls. The thick underbrush. The clearing where our shelter used to stand. New Zealand didn't feel like home anymore, but this place did. Our little haven in the forest. Relief washed over me, and I sank to the ground. It had been a few days since the British army dropped us back in hell. But finally, we were home.

Dylan helped Lizzie down next to me, and we sat amicably next to each other as we watched the others set up our camp. Lizzie stretched her legs out in front of her, leaning back against a tree.

The summer sun shone strong and bright through the trees. Jess and Levi dug up all our old gear while Dylan sorted it out. I let my head rest back against the tree and closed my eyes. It was a relief to sit after our hike here. The dizziness had abated, and I felt more like myself. Except for the pesky headache. But it would heal with time, or so I was told. Lizzie seemed more like her old self, as well. She promptly started issuing orders about how the camp should be set up.

"It should go over there," Lizzie said, directing Dylan, who'd laid out the old tarpaulin.

"Here?" Dylan asked. His face was streaked with dirt, and his blond hair lay flat on his head. Sweat glistened on his forehead and rolled down his temples.

"A little to the left," Lizzie said, pointing. Dylan dragged the tarpaulin in the requested direction.

"Better?" he asked with a sigh, wiping his brow.

"Much. Don't you think so, Grace?" Lizzie asked, seeking my opinion.

"Much better," I agreed.

Lizzie smiled in satisfaction. We were home.

A COUPLE OF HOURS later, the campsite looked like it had before we left. Levi even had a small fire going, and he'd found the old logs we used as seating. "It will do," he said with a boyish grin. His eyes met mine, and I couldn't help but smile back.

The sun was going down, sending a golden glow over our rebuilt home. The last rays of light shimmered through the trees, casting shadows across the forest floor. The CIA had given us a bag of food to tide us over until we could venture out and raid our own, and Jess was already boiling some water in a pot over the fire to make rice.

Levi came over and offered me his hand. "Come on. I'll help you up."

I reached up and grabbed it. His hand wrapped around mine, warm and comforting. We may have been back in hell, but at least we had each other. Levi pulled me to my feet and guided me unsteadily toward the fire. We perched on one of the logs together. He kept my hand in his for a moment longer, long enough for me to know he held it on purpose. "I'm glad you're OK," he whispered in my ear before letting my hand go.

"Me too," I whispered back. I knew how fragile life here could be. My thoughts drifted to Jennifer, and I pushed them away. I didn't want to cry. Not again.

We watched the fire for a while and let the sounds of the forest lull us back to safety. Eventually, My eyes were drawn to the little black box lying discarded on a bed of ferns—the CIA's parting gift to us. A radio to contact them with if we changed our minds. I was sure they knew the effect it would have on us. As we ate our dinner around the fire, our gazes would frequently flick over to it.

"Ignore it," Levi said, tossing his jumper over the radio.

"Maybe we should call it," Lizzie said.

Dylan glared at her. "We've been here for five minutes. Give it a rest."

"But—"

Dylan shook his head. "You're in no state to be fighting at all. You need to heal… we all need to heal," Dylan said, looking into the fire.

I was too tired to think about fighting. It had been hard to come back here, to New Zealand, and even harder to lose Jennifer.

"Our group feels so small," I said, looking around the fire.

Levi had moved off the log next to me and now leaned back against it, his legs outstretched. He frowned and pushed the food around his plate. Dylan's plate lay discarded on the ground as he stared blankly into the fire. Somehow, Lizzie had her signature stubborn determination in her gray eyes. I admired her. Nothing got her down. She would make it to the end, fighting for every inch of her freedom. Jess sat, hunched over, her hair frizzy and disheveled. Her eyes teared up as she looked at the empty space next to her. It would have been Jennifer's seat, if she had been here. If she was still alive.

My eyes welled with tears again. It wasn't fair. Jennifer didn't deserve to die. It was another blow, another death. How many more could I take before I broke entirely? Frankly, I was surprised I had lasted this long. The demons from my past didn't usually let me suffer in peace. But so far, throughout this war, they hadn't bothered me. My past stayed put, and I prayed it would stay that way.

LEVI BANNED US FROM talking about the radio for an entire week. It was more important for us to heal, physically and mentally, before we made any sort of decision. At least, that was his excuse. The radio sat, untouched in our makeshift tent, always watching. It was there when we went to sleep and still there at daybreak. When the week was finally over, the radio was the only thing anyone could think about.

"Should we call it?" Lizzie asked, succumbing to the pressure. We were all sitting in the shelter, trying to stay out of the sun. It was sweltering hot in the stuffy shelter, the sun notoriously strong. It was late summer, but that didn't stop the days from being stifling hot. Dylan had already been sunburned twice. I was lying back on my sleeping bag, watching the shadows of branches sway across the roof.

"I don't know," I said carefully.

"I can't sit here and do nothing," Lizzie said, crossing her arms. "I've been doing that for an entire week already." Lizzie, predictably, wanted to fight. She was still battered and burned, but the fire in her raged fiercely.

"This is something we should discuss," Levi said diplomatically.

"There's no need to discuss it," Lizzie said, looking at each of us. "I know we all want to fight. So that should settle it."

"Some of us need to think things through for ourselves," Jess said.

"We had a whole week to think about it," Lizzie said.

"I spent the week trying to get over Jennifer. I tried not to think about the radio," I said, glaring at it.

"We don't even know what the CIA wants us to do," Dylan said.

"Even more reason to call it," Lizzie said.

No one knew what the CIA wanted us to do, but it had to be something huge. Why else keep it a secret from us? What if it was something horrible? Was I prepared for that? My eyes were drawn back to the radio. The chatter of the others melted into white noise as I thought about what the CIA might get us to do. My breath quickened, and the stuffy tent threatened to suffocate me. I had to get out of there. I needed space to think. Alone. "I need some air," I said as I stood and walked out of the shelter.

I found it hard to be in the same vicinity as the radio. It sounded strange, but I wasn't sure how I felt about it. I couldn't decide what I wanted more—to smash it into pieces or use it to beg the CIA to help us. I began to walk down to the stream. I always felt safe there. It was somewhere I could air my thoughts. I sat on my favorite rock and let my legs hang into the cold, flowing water. All I wanted was for the war to end. And I didn't care how it happened. I wanted to see my mom again, and I would do anything to have that chance. But how far was I willing to go?

Sometimes I felt the same way Lizzie did—nothing would satisfy me more than being a part of something big. Our own mission. But I wasn't strong like the others. Most days, I barely held myself together. Could I really bring myself to go all the way if I had to? I didn't know, and it scared me to think about it.

I closed my eyes and let myself get lost in the sounds of the forest. They were soothing, allowing my mind to wander freely. I thought about the last time I saw my mom: in the car on the way to Lizzie's place a few hours before the war started. We never saw it coming.

I sat in the passenger seat singing along to *I Don't Want to Miss a Thing* by Aerosmith. Mom always loved that song. It was one of Dad's favorites. Mom rolled the window down, letting the air gush in. I remembered the floral smell of Mom's favorite perfume swirling around the car. I could almost smell it now. She rarely wore it after Dad passed away. She never said anything, but I knew it was because Dad gave it to her as a birthday gift just before he died. Maybe she avoided it because the smell made her sad, or maybe because she didn't want to use it up. It was probably both.

For a moment, I let myself drift in the memory, dramatically screaming the lyrics out the window. Mom looked over at me and smiled, a dimple denting her cheek, her long black hair flowing around her shoulders. She reached over and grabbed my hand, her dainty hand holding mine tight.

I broke down into tears as I realized how much I missed her.

A twig snapped behind me. I looked around me, the trance

broken.

"Grace?" Levi said as he approached. I was somehow standing now, staring at the gurgling water as it bubbled over the stones. I turned around to face Levi, tears flowing down my cheeks and my breathing coming in gasps. He took one look at me and crushed me in a hug. It wasn't the same as one of Mom's hugs. But he had his own healing powers over me, and eventually, I managed to quiet my sobbing.

"I miss... I miss..." I tried to say.

"Jennifer?" Levi whispered into my hair.

I cried again. Oh, God, I missed Jen too. There were too many people to miss and not enough space in my heart to miss them all. There wasn't enough time either. For all I knew, we would die tomorrow. What then? There would be no one left to remember.

"I miss everyone," I tried to explain, sniffling. "Sometimes, it's all too much."

"It's OK, Grace, it's OK," Levi soothed as I buried my teary face in his shoulder.

"No, it's not! Our friend is dead, Levi. She's gone. How many more of us w-w-will die before this war ends?" I cried, pulling away from the hug. I stared up at Levi. It was an impossible question, but I wanted the answer. Levi stared back at me. His face was pained. He wanted to tell me what I desired to hear: No one. But he knew that was a lie. Though we had pulled back from the hug, his hands still rested on my shoulders. He reached up and pushed my chestnut hair back behind my ear.

"I don't know, Grace," Levi said finally. "And I can't promise anything. That's just the way it is."

I sniffled. "I know."

"I can't see the future. We have to have some faith that we will make it to the end," Levi said with a weak smile.

I shook my head. I wasn't convinced by words like 'faith' and 'believe'. There was enough trauma in my life for me to be realistic. Faith and belief meant nothing when it came down to it.

They were words we used to try and comfort ourselves. My faith disappeared the moment my family died, and nothing had happened since to convince me otherwise. But I knew Levi was different. Despite everything, he maintained an unfailing hope that everything would work out OK. I wasn't as sure.

"What if all of us die, Levi?" I asked, as the thought came to the forefront of my mind. If we did nothing, our friends' lives would have been lost for nothing. This whole war would be for nothing.

"Someone's going to make it. I can feel it."

"You can't be sure," I said, shaking my head.

"No, I can't, Grace," Levi said. "But what do you want me to do about it?"

"I want to do something to be remembered. I don't want to be forgotten," I said, now convinced about what I wanted to do. We could die tomorrow just lazing around the camp. Or we could die doing something memorable. Something to try and make a difference in the war.

"We won't be forgotten, Grace. Our families—"

"We don't even know if they're alive, Levi!" I said, raising my voice.

"Well... then... our diaries," Levi said, searching for something to calm my train of thought. "You're still writing in yours, aren't you? I am. And I know the others are, too."

"If they win this war, Levi, no one will know. No one will care, and if soldiers find the diaries, they'll be burned."

"Well, what then? What would you do?" Levi asked me.

He brought his face down close to mine, and I could see the spark in his brown eyes. His faith in me and in the world. I saw every groove in Levi's skin—every frown-line the war had gifted him as it stole his youth. A fresh stubble was growing around his mouth. Having him so close was muddling up all my thoughts.

"I... I would..."

"You would...?"

I shook my head to clear it. "I would hold them accountable

for what they've done to you… to me… and to everyone. I want to make a difference. And for that, I think we need the Americans. I want to call the CIA."

"Then that's what we do," Levi said. He didn't question me or try to change my mind. He accepted it. We were still inches from each other, and I could feel Levi's breath against my cheek. He brought his hand up and cupped my cheek gently in his palm, turning my face up to look into his eyes.

"Grace…" he whispered.

My heart thudded loudly. We had been skirting around our feelings for a long time now. He brought his face close to mine, his breath warm and soft against my lips. Was now the right time? My eyes were drawn to his slightly parted lips, and I wondered what it would be like to kiss them. I wanted to let him, but I was afraid. People always left me.

Plus, "It would make everything awkward," I said, thinking aloud. Levi let his forehead rest against mine.

"I thought I was going to lose you," he breathed.

What was I supposed to say to that? I wanted to go through with it, but what if it ruined everything? So much was changing at once, and I wanted to hold on to this feeling. I didn't want anything to change between us. Not yet, at least.

"I'm sorry," I said, pulling away.

"Don't be," Levi said, his eyes downcast. But he smiled at me. "This doesn't change anything. You know I'm always here for you, no matter what." He took his hand away from my face and squeezed my fingers.

"I know." I trusted Levi. Maybe I struggled to find meaning in the universe, but Levi was always right beside me to hold on to my hope until I could find my way.

SUNLIGHT FLITTERED THROUGH THE trees, silhouetting Dylan and Levi sitting together on a log. I watched them anxiously from a distance—Levi was going to talk to Dylan about calling the CIA and waging war. We had discussed launching an attack on the soldiers countless times. We had even gone on missions to gather intel. But we hadn't quite worked up the courage to make it happen. This time, it felt different.

Maybe it was because I wanted to go through with it—Lizzie wasn't beating the war drum alone. And, with the help of the CIA, we might actually do something meaningful. I felt a new determination rising inside me. And now that I had made my decision, I couldn't wait to get out there. The soldiers had taken too much, and it was time we took something from them.

But first, we all needed to agree.

I was furious at Lizzie and Dylan for tricking us into action last time. They didn't think it through, and it nearly killed me. But, as much as it upset me I had to admit that, ultimately, it led us to this moment. Strangely, I was now grateful for that. If it had never happened, maybe we would be trapped in a prison camp. Maybe, we would be dead.

My attention was drawn to Dylan, who tensed and then waved his hands angrily at Levi. He raised his voice, "Getting revenge is stupid!"

Levi shook his head and gestured frantically back. Levi must have mentioned something about Jennifer because Dylan turned away, clearly upset. He saw me watching. I couldn't let Levi take all the fallout from my idea. I walked up to them, expecting Dylan to yell at me.

"He told you I want to fight back, right," I said to Dylan.

Dylan wiped his teary eyes. "He didn't say it was you behind it."

I pretended not to notice, and Levi squeezed my arm.

"We've talked about this over and over. Usually, Lizzie brings it up. Sometimes me. Sometimes even you," Levi said, looking Dylan in the eye. "How many times do we have to bring this up before we finally get the courage to do something?"

"We've tried. It never works out," Dylan said, defeated.

"We've never planned it properly," I said. "Every time we go, we have some crazy idea that it will be easy. It's not. And this time, we have the CIA to back us."

Dylan shoved his hands in his pockets and looked skyward. "I'm not sure I can justify the type of killing you're talking about."

Lizzie and Jess heard the commotion and made their way over from the shelter.

"What's going on?" Lizzie asked, sensing the tension between us.

"Grace wants to use the radio and call the CIA," Dylan said.

"To fight?" Lizzie asked. Her gray eyes sparked with renewed hope.

"Why else?" I said.

"Grace is right. I'm tired of Marion deciding our fate. Don't we get a say in our own future?" Lizzie asked.

No one answered. The future was one topic we avoided discussing because anything in the future was on hold. If we ignored the future, we wouldn't be disappointed about never having one. But it was time to face our questions and make our own answers.

"I don't know," Jess said, her lips pursed.

"What do you guys want? Because I know what I want. I want my life back." My lip trembled, and I bit it gently between my teeth to steady it. "I want things to go back to the way they were before. We can't sit here and hope the war will come to a peaceful end."

Dylan shrugged. "I want the same. To walk around without looking over my shoulder every second. To have a job. A life."

"And how do you think we're going to get that future?" Lizzie asked, standing with her hands on her hips. "I don't want to be remembered as a terrorist like the rest of the world is painting us. We don't deserve that. I want our names to be cleared, and the CIA has the power to do that."

Dylan sighed. It was a big move with a lot of risks. "So we call the CIA, and then what?"

"They help us stage an attack that will actually make a

difference," Levi said.

"What is wrong with you people?" Jess finally burst out. "You're talking of willingly going out there to get yourselves killed. Am I the only one who sees the problem here?"

"Jess, I'm so tired," I said plainly. "I'm tired of our lives being controlled, and I'm exhausted, constantly pretending everything is going to be OK. Nothing ever is. I want to turn the tables. I want them to be the ones hiding, running, and watching their friends die one by one." I took a deep breath as my emotions threatened to get the better of me.

"Look who's all pro-killing," Jess said.

"What's wrong with you?" Lizzie snapped at Jess. "Just let off."

"Why? Am I the only one who has a problem with this?" Jess asked.

"I'm not convinced," Dylan muttered, "but I'm not insulting everyone to prove my point."

Jess sighed and threw her hands up into the air in frustration. "I can't do this right now," she said abruptly and stalked off.

"That was awkward," Levi said.

"You all agree, right? We can't sit here anymore. The longer we wait, the more we lose our grip on our future," I said. "If we die, we will be remembered as the kids who crashed a rocket into England. I don't want us to be remembered like that. After everything we've been through, we deserve more. Jennifer deserves more."

Lizzie nodded.

"We can't do anything if Jess doesn't agree," Dylan said, casting his eyes down.

"You didn't seem to have a problem with that last time," I said, irritated. For once, I was the one bringing up the idea of fighting, and it felt like everyone was against me. Every other time, I was expected to go along with it.

"That's exactly why," Lizzie said. She took a breath and blinked away the tears that threatened. "We were wrong last time. We should never have tricked you… and… I don't think I've ever apologized for that," Lizzie said. She looked at Dylan, and he nodded.

"We're sorry," he said.

"It's fine," Levi said as he kicked a stone that danced across the ground and disappeared into the undergrowth.

"I think we're over it," I agreed. "I shouldn't have brought it up."

"But it was horrible. You were shot," Dylan said with regret in his eyes. "That's why this time, everyone has to be on board. We all deserve that choice."

We looked at the ground in silence. Dylan was right.

"Someone should talk to Jess," Dylan hinted.

No one volunteered.

"Someone has to," Lizzie pointed out, "and we all know how crap I am at those types of conversations."

No one could argue with that.

"Maybe you should, Grace," Levi said.

It was always me.

"Levi's right," Lizzie backed him.

"Fine," I said, marching off into the forest. As I veered from the campsite, I was once again enclosed by the silence and tranquility of the woods.

"Jess," I called out.

"Go away," I heard her voice wail somewhere to my right.

My mind flashed back to the day I found Jess with a gun, about to commit suicide. She said she would never try again, but I wasn't so sure. She had been really upset when she stormed off. And with Jennifer's death still at the forefront of all our minds, my stomach twisted in anxiety as I thought about what Jess might do. It didn't help that her uncle had died helping us in England. Or that being back here would surely bring back memories of Leah's death from the start of the war, the event that triggered Jess in the first place.

"Jess. Are you OK?" I asked as I approached her. She was

sitting up against the trunk of the weathered kauri tree. She glared up at me, her pale skin mottled pink with tears.

"Of course, I'm not OK. Do I look OK to you?" she shouted, her voice thick with emotion. "Didn't you hear me before? I said, go away. What part of wanting to be alone do you people not understand?" She folded her arms and refused to look at me.

"Jess, I'm not going anywhere until you tell me what's wrong. We look out for each other. This is me looking out for you."

"Looking out for me by forcing me to fight. What a great friend," she muttered. But she wasn't scaring me off that easily. I walked up to her and sat on one of the gigantic tree roots that erupted from the ground.

"Fine, I'll sit here until you're ready to talk. You have to talk to me at some point."

I stared at the rustling leaves. When that got boring, I stared at the blowing grass. Surprisingly, that was less interesting than the first option, so I began making shapes out of the clouds. Half an hour passed before Jess finally said, "You're not going to leave, are you."

I shook my head.

Jess sighed and glanced up at the canopy. "Fine." She took a deep breath. "I have a problem with getting revenge."

"I think all of us do. I don't want to hurt anyone. I don't even know if I can go through with it."

"The Bible tells us to 'love thy enemy.'" Jess looked away, embarrassed.

I had forgotten Jess was religious. I stared at Leah's cross hanging around her neck. We never talked about religion. I scoffed at Levi when he told me to have hope, but for Jess, faith was all she had.

"How can you possibly love them?" I asked, but even as I said that, I knew it wouldn't help.

"They're people too."

"So are we. We have a right to walk around without getting shot at, and live our lives free from fear," I said. "They took our freedom."

"But we have to kill," Jess said, "and not only in defense."

"Jess… this doesn't have to be about revenge. For me, it's about protecting the people I love," I said, tears blurring my vision as I thought about Mom. She was out there somewhere. I could feel it.

Jess stared at the ground and gathered her knees to her chest. Her face was conflicted, and she sat in silence for a moment. "I know what you're saying, but it doesn't feel right for us to be serving out justice. Who gave us the right to decide?"

I looked up at the towering canopy. I thought of my dad and what he would tell me. He'd tell me to never lose sight of what was important. That justice was worth fighting for, and wars are won one battle at a time. But my dad was strong, and I wasn't sure I had it in me. Still, I had to try.

"They gave us that right the day they stormed our houses," I said. "Everyone has a right to their own opinions on religion or politics or whatever else. But when you start violating the lives of others, you can't expect people to take it on the chin. We've let them run this war for too long. They have no respect for what is ours."

I stared at Jess, willing her to understand. Her copper hair fell forward, covering her face.

"I can't sit idle anymore," I pressed. "We must stand up for what's ours. And it's not only our blood. Think about all those people in London… like Ross. That's the soldiers' fault. But, it was blamed on us." The anger was back and burned within me. My hands shook.

Jess tucked her hair behind her ear and sighed. She looked confused. I knew what she was thinking—I had been there, too. Her internal compass had her questioning everything. I, too, still had questions. I wondered if we were right. But I was finished debating over the ethics of our situation. Sometimes, action was the only option.

"Ross doesn't deserve to be remembered as a terrorist," I

insisted, "and neither do we. The CIA can change that."

"What if the CIA is using us?" Jess asked. "They know we're desperate and have nowhere to go. We're stuck in this. They're free."

I hadn't thought of that. I sat silently, questioning myself. Did it change anything? What if they were using us? But this war had to end somehow. Someone had to step up to the plate. Why not us?

"Then we negotiate," I said with sudden hope bursting forth. "We agree to fight. They agree to help us free our families." The hope emanating from me was infectious. I could see the fire blaze in Jess' eyes too, and I knew I had finally reached her. We were all in.

Chapter Seven

Lizzie

THE REVELATION THAT THE world thought of us as terrorists hit me hard. I knew the risks we took when we broke into the Pentagon. I knew the trouble we were asking for. But I had plowed ahead, convinced what we were trying to do was right. And I thought everyone else would see it that way. I had hoped we could stop the war or at least garner some support. But instead... here we were. Some reward, I thought bitterly.

I sat on the ground, slowly beheading daisies as I made a chain and let my mind wander. It wasn't fair. I knew it was childish to think that. What was fair about any of this? It could be worse. I could be locked up in a camp, with no hope of escape. Like our families were. Instead I was free. So what if the world thought we were terrorists? For all it mattered, we could be on a different planet. Or a whole other universe. We weren't governed by the same rules as the rest of the world, and it shouldn't have made a difference. But it mattered to me. And I was ready to do something about it.

Yesterday, after Grace had talked Jess around to contacting the CIA, we sat crosslegged in a circle, our faces dim in the torchlight and the shelter shutting out the gentle chirrup of crickets in the night. Levi took the black box in his palm, and hovered a finger over the button.

"Do it," Grace encouraged him. He turned it on. First, a crackle of static buzzed through the still air. Nerves fluttered in my belly and I wondered if the radio was in working order. What would we do if it was broken?

"Hello?" Dylan said, clearing his voice loudly. "Uh… we need to talk."

There was silence.

"Roger that. I hear you loud and clear," Tamzin replied. We looked at each other, our faces equal parts terrified and excited.

"We've decided. We want to join you," Grace said eagerly.

"OK. Don't talk any more on this line. It's not secure," Tamzin said clearly through the radio. "It would be better to talk in person. Meet you at 2100 tomorrow night at the drop zone." Again, static hummed. Levi turned the radio off with a click, and silence strained the air.

Jess was the first to speak. "What's the drop zone?" she asked, confused.

"Maybe where they dropped us off in the bush," Dylan said.

"Oh." Jess had almost looked disappointed at not immediately diving into action. I didn't blame her. All of us were hyped up, especially when Grace said she wanted to negotiate with the CIA and free our families. It was anticlimactic to wait another day.

A harsh wind gusted through the trees, bringing me back to the present. I reached for my jumper and draped it around my shoulders. I was excited to fight. I always was, but the others took it for granted. If there was a fight to be had, you could count on Lizzie. Dylan, Levi, and Jess didn't know the Lizzie from before the war. That Lizzie had been so different. I'd been a bit awkward then. I'd gotten over it, mostly, but I didn't have the confidence I had now.

My dreams had been simple enough. To go to college and

become a nurse. Find myself a real job and try and fix the ones who were hurting. I'd always felt a strong sense of justice, but now, the war had hardened my heart, and I knew I sometimes lacked compassion. Even for those closest to me. I hadn't been like that before. The war had changed me, and not entirely for the better.

I plucked another daisy and squeezed the stem on the end of the chain to form a tiny hole. The watery green juice stained the tips of my fingers as I pushed the new daisy through the opening. It broke, and I sighed in annoyance, throwing the chain onto the ground. A tiny ant crawled up to it and stared at it curiously.

I looked up to see Grace sitting at another of the many trees surrounding our campsite. I stood and brushed the dirt off my pants before joining her. The skin on my legs was still healing, and anytime I walked, it pulled painfully. I tried not to grimace as I reached Grace.

"Hey, can I sit?" I asked.

"Sure," she replied, motioning beside her. Her bronzed skin glowed in the afternoon sun, and she looked content, watching the birds fly between the branches in the canopy.

I gratefully sat, leaning against the tree next to her. "Funny to see you sitting all by yourself," I commented.

"What do you mean?" she asked absently. She had been thinking hard about something and had a faraway look in her eyes before she brought them back to me.

I shrugged. "Usually, you and Levi are inseparable."

Her cheeks flared red. "We aren't," she said immediately.

"You are, and you know it." I examined her more closely. "Did something happen between you two?"

"No," she said shortly.

Her eyes flicked sideways, betraying the lie. I knew something had happened. Did Levi finally make a move? About time, I thought. But I needed details. "Come on, please tell me?" I wheedled.

"I'll tell you later," Grace said, her cheeks rosy pink. "I doubt my love life was the real reason you came over here. What did you want, anyway?" Grace said, steering the conversation away from her. I didn't press her, though my curiosity was killing me.

"Can't I spend some time with my bestie?" I said in a lighthearted tone. Grace wasn't buying it. She gave me a half-hearted smile.

"Not you, Lizzie. There's always an agenda."

That sort of cut, but I bit my tongue.

"OK. I really need to ask you something."

"Shoot," Grace said, turning to me.

"Why did you suddenly decide we needed to do this?"

"Do what?" she asked.

"You know, contact the CIA."

"Why does it matter?" she said with a shrug and glancing away. "You know as well as I do. We can't sit around here forever."

"No, we can't," I said, suspiciously eyeing her, "but there was a time when you liked to pretend we could. And with everything that has happened recently—"

"I'm tired of pretending, Lizzie," Grace said. "If you're here to talk me out of going tonight, you're wasting your time. I don't know why you would, though, unless you're simply determined to disagree."

"I'm not," I said. The hurt dug deeper, but I knew she didn't mean it. I had always been the one to look out for Grace, and I felt like I had done a crappy job of it lately. We were all grieving, but I could see cracks beginning to show in Grace. The same as when her family had been killed by a drunk driver.

I thought back to the day in court when the driver had been sentenced. He was young, barely older than us. A better person would have understood the gravity of his mistake. But he hadn't learned from it. He was remorseless, and I was angry at him for taking Grace's happiness. To make it worse, because he was so young, all the judge gave him was community service and a meager fine his parents would pay. He destroyed a family but paid a pittance.

In the weeks that followed, Grace had cried. She had been angry, too. A quiet, simmering fury. And then she was silent. That was when her foundations broke, and she tumbled into darkness. It had been over a year since their deaths, and though she had patched over the wounds in her heart, I knew she was still raw from it.

"I wanted to see how you are. You've been really quiet lately," I said.

"I miss Jennifer," Grace whispered.

"I know. I do too." I gave Grace a warm hug.

"You smell like daisies," Grace said.

I laughed. "That makes a change from sweat and mud."

"Yeah," Grace said, smiling and stretching out on the grass. She wriggled her bare toes toward the sky.

"I haven't been the only quiet one since coming back," she said. The sunlight flickered through the trees, lighting up her face as the trees shifted in the wind.

"Who... me?"

"If you want me to spill about what happened with Levi, you need to come clean first." She gave me a critical look. "What's happening with you and Dylan? Usually, you two are as thick as thieves," Grace said.

"Oh... that." Heat crept up around my neck and flooded into my cheeks. "Jess told me everything I said that night while we were trying to escape from the soldiers."

"So?"

"It's embarrassing how drunk I was." I looked down at my legs. They were a constant reminder of that night. The CIA had been a godsend. They'd given me some extra burn cream and some serious painkillers, but there wasn't much else to be done. I had wrapped them all over with cling film and bandages, but supplies quickly ran low. I was using the tablets sparingly but I only had a few doses left. The breakthrough pain was far from pleasant.

"You know I would never get that wasted in any other scenario," I said to Grace. I felt like I was begging for her forgiveness. We had promised each other after the crash we would always be responsible with alcohol.

"Of course I know," Grace said and smiled at me. She didn't hold it against me, but that was Grace. She was the understanding type. I was grateful to have a friend like her. It was harder to be forgiving toward myself. If I had never kicked the sign… everything would've been different. I tried to stop myself from thinking about that. I knew *if I'd never* were a dangerous group of words.

"It's OK, you know," Grace said.

"What is?" It didn't feel like anything was OK.

"To be vulnerable sometimes. Take it from someone who knows."

"Is that what you were with Levi? Vulnerable?" I asked in a teasing tone.

Grace gave me a playful shove. "Don't do that."

"Do what?"

"Make this about me."

"You said you'd spill if I did. So?" I asked, taking the conversation in full circle.

"Maybe another time," Grace said, flashing me a rare smile. There she was, I thought. There was the old Grace. "I'm serious. You need to let down your walls sometimes," she lectured.

"Yeah. Vulnerable isn't me," I said with a lump forming in my throat. I swallowed it back down. "Thanks, though."

I WALKED DOWN TO the creek to clear my head. In a matter of hours, we would hike out to the meeting point to talk to the CIA. I wondered what they had planned for us. It would be dangerous, that much was certain. But would we be willing to go through with it?

Jess thought they only wanted to use us—another expendable

resource. Still, it would be worth it if we could free our families and clear our names. As my mind raced, I barely noticed where I was walking, taking my usual path along the bank. No matter how far I wandered, I could never get away from myself. Or Dylan, I thought, as I noticed him stepping across the rocks and making his way toward me. I automatically turned to leave. It was mortifying what I had said. I didn't know how to be around him right now.

I called his face perfect. That's not really that bad, is it? I considered everything Jess had told me about my state and then groaned to myself. It was terrible. Grounds for a non-breakup. Grace and I had coined the term 'non-breakup' when one of our friends, Ashley, went through a tough situation with a guy at school. Ashley thought she was dating Sam, but she was never sure, and it had never been truly official. We weren't really sure why it had turned so bad. Perhaps she came on too strong, or maybe he was never interested in the first place. Whatever the story was, for several weeks, their non-breakup had been the talk of the school.

"Lizzie!" Dylan called.

"Not now, I'm..." I desperately racked my brains for an excuse. There were only so many times you could use the toilet in a day. Unless you wanted it to seem like you had some sort of desperate, embarrassing situation going on down there.

"You're what...?" Dylan asked as he grabbed my arm to prevent me from escaping.

"OK. Fine. What do you want?"

"You're avoiding me."

So it was that obvious, I thought.

"You have been ever since we got back. I want to know why." He let my arm go and studied me with his piercing blue eyes, imploring me to speak.

"Seriously? You haven't worked that one out yet?"

Dylan swiped his messy blond hair out of his eyes. "What did I do?" he said, sighing. "There must have been something."

"You didn't do anything," I said. I sat on one of the larger rocks by the stream and motioned for Dylan to sit beside me. I tried to continue speaking, but the words clogged in my throat. I looked out over the water, my cheeks burning.

"What is it? I've never seen you this way before. Are you sure you're all right?" Dylan said, looking concerned.

"I'm fine," I muttered. "Just… embarrassed, I guess."

Dylan looked confused. "What about?"

I let him mull it over. It was amusing watching his mind tick, trying to pin down the cause. His eyes kept flicking over to me as if catching a quick glance of me would help him work out whatever was bothering me.

"I acted like an idiot. I mean, before the Americans stepped in and saved us from the soldiers," I added for clarification.

"Oh, that's what's been bothering you?" To his credit, Dylan looked genuinely surprised. "Lizzie, you'd been through hell." He glanced down at my bandages, and I felt another ripple of shame. Poor Lizzie's mangled legs. "Honestly, I blame myself for not finding you better pain relief. Or not preventing the explosion in the first place."

I looked into Dylan's eyes. He was nothing but authentic. "You didn't kick the sign, Dylan," I said, pointing out the obvious. I stared down at the stream and flicked a pebble into it from the side of the bank.

"And you didn't force the soldiers to shoot at us," Dylan countered. "Everyone is responsible for their own actions, including the soldiers. Stop taking their actions and labeling them as something you did wrong."

I shrugged. "Maybe you're right."

Dylan grinned. "Can you say that once more?"

I glared at him.

"I want to record it and play it back to myself every time I can't sleep."

His smile was infectious, and I couldn't help but grin too. I punched him playfully on the shoulder. "Not likely."

Dylan laughed softly under his breath. "You were really embarrassed?" he asked, raising an eyebrow.

"Can we drop it already?" I said, turning away.

"Yeah, we can. But before we do, can you answer me one thing?" Dylan asked, his gaze meeting mine and demanding honesty. Damn. I hated how he did that, and I sighed.

"Sure, what is it?"

"Did you mean any of what you said that night?"

"Ugh. Honestly, Dylan, I was so drunk I don't even remember most of that night. And then the morphine blocked out the rest…"

"But you know what you said," he pressed. "I was talking to Grace. She said Jess told you everything."

"Wow. And you didn't think anything got lost in all that gossip?" I asked sarcastically.

"Come on, Lizzie. Please, tell me."

"Which part? About your face being perfect or about you being the handsome hero who saved my life?"

"You asked whether I would keep you safe," Dylan said. His voice shook with emotion. "Jess didn't tell you that part?" He hazarded a lucky guess. His cheeks flushed a delicate pink.

"No, she didn't. But I don't need anyone to keep me safe," I said. It came out crueler than I intended.

Dylan's face fell, and he sighed. "Yeah, I figured you'd say that," Dylan said, his shoulders sagging. He stood up and stretched before walking away, leaving me sitting alone with only the gurgling stream for company.

I SAT BY THE stream all evening and dangled my feet in the cool water. We had made a choice, and soon we would see where that choice would lead us. I stood and waded out to the center of the stream, slimy stones slipping underneath my feet. I bent and washed my face in the water. Any minute we would meet with the CIA. At first glance, we were a ragtag bunch of teens. Wounded from battle and reeking of dirt and sweat, with nothing but the clothes on our back. Despite that, I wanted them to respect us. Even if we were as desperate as we looked, I wanted them to understand we agreed to this because we were warriors, and we would fight for the future we deserved. I pulled my blond hair into a bun and straightened my top.

"Lizzie, it's time to go," Grace said. I looked up at her as she stood at the top of the bank. She had tied her thick brown hair into a high ponytail, and she brushed impatiently at a few wayward strands obscuring her vision. She still limped from the fading gunshot wound to her leg, but she, like me, seemed determined. Unstoppable. I wondered if I was wrong. I had thought she was spiraling into depression again, but here she stood: the strongest person I knew.

"I'm coming," I called to her and walked doggedly up the bank. She disappeared before I could reach the crest, and I caught up to her as we marched northeast toward the outskirts of the forest.

"Do you think it will work?" I asked her.

"You mean whether they'll agree to help us free our families?"

I looked at Grace as she swept her long fringe out of the way again. Her deep brown eyes were alive with hope.

"Yes, I think so. If they really want us to help... it's a fair exchange," she said.

It was hard to think about seeing my parents again. I would have to tell them about Jaden. The thought terrified me. My mom would cry. I hated when Mom cried. Whenever she did, it wrenched my heart in a way nothing else ever could. I knew I was a difficult teenager, and Mom and I butted heads about almost everything. When we had blowups, they ended with us screaming at each other and slamming doors. Despite this, we were close. We were so similar—I knew her inside out. I could divine her every thought. As for Dad, he was the cheery, outgoing type, always trying to keep the peace. And I knew losing his son would shake that optimistic outlook of his.

My mom and dad's faces rose in my mind as I remembered

the last time I had seen them. Mom's clear blue eyes stared at me, and her short bob fell around her face. Gray hairs peeked through the blond. She used to pull them out, but as she grew older, there were too many, and eventually, she gave up. It made her look even more severe as she pursed her lips together in all too familiar disapproval—I hadn't done the laundry as I had promised before Grace came around. I hugged Dad goodbye, his rough stubble rubbing against my cheek.

"See you soon, sweetie," he said to me.

He pulled away, and his crinkly hazel eyes smiled at Jaden, who stood beside Grace and me. "Look after your sister," Dad said as he clapped Jaden on the shoulder. "And be nice to Grace, too. We'll be back before curfew."

Jaden grunted a response. We lived half an hour's drive from the city, and Mom and Dad didn't expect to be away for long—straight to the voting booths and back. It was election day when it all happened. They stepped into the car and trundled out of the drive. Then, my mind tripped over the early part of that evening, until… there I was again. Staring at Jaden's face as the life bled out of him. I tried not to think about my parents because every time, it led me to this. I curled my hands into fists to stop them from shaking.

"Are you OK, Lizzie?" Dylan whispered as we walked through the forest.

Twigs crunched under my shoes, and a ray of moonlight burst through the trees, illuminating Dylan's face. He looked concerned, and he seemed to battle with himself before he touched my arm gently in comfort. His touch set my skin alight.

I was sure Dylan cared about me, but did he like me in that way? Grace always told me I was oblivious when guys were into me. But this time, I was confident. The question was, did I like him back? The lingering sensation from where his hand had been on my arm told me the answer. If we both liked each other, why hadn't we taken it any further? Or, maybe the more important question was: *Should we take it further?*

"I'm fine," I said. I breathed in and out slowly and managed to get my thoughts and emotions under control.

"We're nearly there," Levi whispered from up ahead. I checked my watch. Five minutes to the hour. Jess pressed her hands against her thighs to help herself up a small hill. The rich smell of the forest filled my senses. Earthy, organic matter soft under our feet. I pushed past a small shrub.

"I think it was here," Dylan said as we reached a small clearing.

"Don't ask me," Grace said, gazing around. "I was out of it when they dropped us off."

We weren't far away from the road now. I glanced at my watch again. One minute. I gripped a gun I held tightly at my side. Silence fell as we stared all around us.

A branch snapping broke the quiet of the night. I turned instinctively toward the noise, my hands drifting to the empty space where I usually kept my gun tucked close. I had a pocketknife stashed down the side of my boot, but other than that, we were defenseless.

The hour had passed. Tamzin and her agents emerged from the shadows.

"I knew you would join," Tamzin said confidently as we stepped forward in unison.

"We have some terms," said Dylan.

Chapter Eight

Levi

"I don't know if we can offer you that," Tamzin said doubtfully.

"Then we can't help you," Jess replied, shrugging.

We sat around the clearing, hidden from prying eyes by the thick canopy of trees. The woods offered some protection from the wind, but it was a chilly night. Grace shivered as she sat beside me. She shuffled even closer as another biting breath of wind blew through the trees. I resisted the urge to put my arm around her—I didn't need the Americans to think we were an item. I knew Grace wasn't ready to take our relationship further. Not yet. I chanced a glance over at her petite form, huddled over in the cold. Stray brown hairs gusted around her face with the wind, and she had her arms wrapped around her for warmth. I couldn't put my arm around her, but I could move a bit closer. I inched nearer, and Grace flashed me a grateful smile.

"If you don't agree to help us with our families, then there is nothing in it for us," Lizzie backed Jess.

"We're only a small task force. That's why we need your help in the first place," Tamzin tried to reason. "I don't think we'd have the resources to break your families out of the prison camp.

Even if we did, it would compromise our cover," Tamzin said.

Luke, the dark-skinned agent, grunted in agreement with her. "We're here on a clandestine operation to gather intelligence and act according to our orders. Orders passed on from the CIA headquarters—they don't care about your families or problems."

"If you don't care about us, then why should we care about what you want?" Dylan leveled with them.

"Asides from having a part in ending this war?" Ezra said with a snort. "You'd be getting your names cleared from the fiasco in England, for one."

"That hardly matters here in this hellhole," Lizzie fired back. She was getting more riled up by the minute. Her cheeks flushed bright red, and her eyes held that all too familiar spark.

"We'd be risking our lives to help you. We've put our lives on the line a lot these last few months, and frankly, I'm sick of it," Grace said. She rubbed her hands together, attempting to generate some heat. "We want to help. We want the war to be over, but we're only kids. Please. We would do anything to have our families back."

Tamzin looked around at all of us. Maybe she was inspired by our determination. Or maybe she pitied us. "Look. We'll do what we can, but only after you help us," she finally caved.

The hope those words gave us spread fast. I glanced at Grace and could see it brimming in her eyes. I knew Grace's mom meant more to her than anyone. Tamzin saw it, too. "We can't promise anything," she quickly added. But it didn't quench the fire she'd lit. "You still have that radio?" Tamzin asked. We nodded. "Good. We'll use that to keep in touch. When you've completed the mission, you can contact us, and we will let you know where to meet."

"What exactly is the mission?" Jess asked nervously.

There was a moment of silence as the wind swept through, rustling the leaves on the forest floor. The noise had Luke on edge. His hand tightened around his gun, and he directed the other agents to do a sweep of the area.

"I'm sure y'all know of the Skytower up in Auckland," Ezra said.

"Yeah…" Lizzie said. She glanced at Dylan and me. Were they suggesting we go to Auckland?

"We want you to blow it up," Ezra said.

"You want what?" I said, my eyebrows rising into my hairline. They couldn't be serious. But their faces didn't flinch.

"We want you to bring the Skytower to the ground," Tamzin said. "It's not as crazy as it sounds," she added as we stared at her, dumbfounded. "We've been keeping tabs on Marion since he got back on New Zealand soil. The Skytower has become a major base."

"Great, so we go from being terrorists who crashed a rocket into England's houses of parliament to being the kids who blew up New Zealand's most iconic tower?" I said. "That's a great improvement. Really makes us look good."

Lizzie snorted, and Dylan tried to cover a laugh with a cough.

"I'm serious," Tamzin said, annoyed, as she swept her straight black hair out of her eyes.

"So am I," I said, meeting her stern gaze.

"It's clever, really. A structure with 360° views makes a decent watchtower, and it's easy to defend. The adjoining hotel acts as a damn comfortable barracks, and they even have several restaurants with commercial kitchens to keep them well fed."

"If it's so well-protected, how are we supposed to attack it?" Grace asked. "We're going to end up dead."

"Not if you follow the plan," Tamzin said.

"There's a plan?" Jess asked.

"Of course, there's a plan. There's always a plan," Tamzin said, scowling. She nodded at Shannon, who unslung her assault rifle and directed some of the agents to accompany her into the night.

"Where are they going?" I asked, shivering as another breeze swept through the clearing and raked at the leaves on the ground.

"If you're going to blow up the Skytower, you're going to need some explosives…" Tamzin said, "and… other… assorted items, shall we say."

Shannon returned several minutes later carrying lumpy-looking bags of equipment. She threw them down at our feet, the moon catching her frizzy black hair in a faint blue glow.

"What are these?" Lizzie said as she pulled a futuristic-looking device out of one of the bags.

"That's a microwave drill," Ezra said. "It works silently using radiation and heat to drill holes in concrete. You'll need it to effectively plant the explosives."

"Oh," Lizzie said, looking mystified and tucking the metal contraption back into the bag.

Dylan was already checking out the rifles. There were a few basic hunting rifles, and I spotted the one they took from Jess in the pile. They remembered to return it, apparently. But there were also a couple of new AK47s, along with a pile of ammo.

"Sweet, we'll be able to create some serious carnage with these," Dylan said, holding up the AKs.

Tamzin sighed. I wondered if she was reconsidering using a group of teenagers for this mission. "Just don't get caught with any of this, or they'll know you're part of a bigger op. Those weapons aren't the standard issue here."

But something felt off. Why were they giving us all this stuff? Didn't they need it?

"Why can't you do this? Why us?" Jess asked, cottoning onto the same line of thought.

"Because if the United States is exposed as having a hand in this, there would be severe political ramifications. The consequences would be… significant." Tamzin said.

"So, you won't be coming?" Grace asked.

"No."

Grace looked down at the ground, and Jess stared out into the black. For once, there were others on our side, adults to help us. I wanted to sit back and let them deal with all the hard decisions.

But with the news they wouldn't be accompanying us, I felt my heart sink. We were alone in this. Again. We were always alone.

There was disappointment in Tamzin's dark eyes as a cloud drifted away from the moon and bathed the clearing in light. Tamzin wanted to go to war. It looked like she was upset at missing out on the action. I would give anything to be free of it.

"Here," Shannon said and tossed us each a wad of papers. I jumped. I'd forgotten she was there.

"Read those, memorize them, then give them back. We can't let them fall into the wrong hands." Shannon tossed us each a little black object no bigger than a machine gun casing, and I caught mine deftly with one hand. I opened my fist. It was a tiny keychain flashlight. Not much use for anything. But it gave enough light to read the fuzzy letters scrawled on the first page: *OPERATION DARK TOWER*.

WE WERE ALL QUIET on the way back to camp. Were we really going to do this? It was a good plan. Detailed. Smart. But it was also risky. I could see so many possibilities for it to go off the rails. Were we prepared to go ahead with it, knowing we might never come back?

We trudged through the familiar forest, and I watched Grace up ahead. Her chin was lifted, and her eyes were distant. Was she dreaming of the future? I wasn't sure it was a good thing. The present grounded us, and the 'now' was all we had in this war. Right here, the five of us.

I glanced over at Dylan, and I could tell he was worried, too. A familiar frown deepened the creases on his forehead. I jogged to catch up with him.

"This is big," I said.

"That's what I'm worried about," he agreed. "Do you think it's too big for us?"

I shrugged. We'd done crazy things before: the warehouse attack, sneaking onto Marion's plane, and breaking into the Pentagon in the US. But this felt like one step too far.

"When has that ever stopped us?" I said with a weak laugh.

"It never has," Dylan answered uncomfortably. "And it's not going to this time either."

He was right. We were in this, no matter what. We had already made the decision.

"Who's going to… you know…" he said, talking about the plan. The first step was to hijack a truck, and that meant ambushing some soldiers. "I don't know if any of the girls would be able to. Not up close, not like that."

"I don't know. They're strong, Lizzie might."

"I won't let her," Dylan said, shaking his head. "It would destroy her. Eventually, all of this will catch up with us."

"What about you? Will it destroy you any less?"

"No. But I'd rather carry that burden. I don't want her to have to," Dylan said.

I looked at him, and he pushed his blond hair out of his eyes, troubled.

"Hey," I said, clapping Dylan on the shoulder. "It'll be OK." I could tell the bond between him and Lizzie was deepening. He would carry all her pain if he could. He'd die for her without thinking twice.

"Yeah. Maybe," Dylan said with a lopsided grin.

"I'll have your back too," I said. There was no way I would let Dylan take on a truck full of soldiers without any help.

"You'll be my backup?" Dylan asked me.

"Yup, I'll lurk in the bushes, and if you mess up…" I trailed off.

"You'll finish the bastards off," Dylan said with a strained laugh.

"Exactly," I said, looking sidelong at Dylan.

WE MADE IT BACK to our camp and stared around in silence. The Americans had given us two more weeks to recover. Grace and Lizzie were in no shape to travel any distance. And losing Jennifer had deeply affected us all. They wanted us in our best frame of mind before starting the mission. It was strange calling it a mission. But that's what it was: Operation Dark Tower.

I tried to imagine what Dad would say now. Would he be proud? Probably not. He didn't have it in him. Regardless, in two weeks, we would pack up camp and move out. The last time we left this camp, we thought it was permanent. This time I knew—if we lived—we would see this place again. It was our home.

"I can't believe we're leaving here… again," Jess said, looking around.

"There's still time," Lizzie said quietly. Even Lizzie, despite her tough exterior, was struggling to find the courage to turn her talk into action.

"Two weeks," Grace said simply. For once, Grace looked put together. I had never seen her want something so badly.

"If we're not leaving for another two weeks, we'll need to stock up on supplies," Dylan said practically. He dumped his bag of equipment down on the ground. "I don't know about you guys, but I'm starving."

"I need different clothes," Grace said, looking down at her attire and poking her finger through a hole in her shirt. She was wearing the same black leggings and baggy t-shirt from the farmhouse. They looked good on her, highlighting her athletic figure. But the leggings were ripped at the knees, and her shirt burned with holes, revealing patches of alluring skin.

"Me too," Lizzie agreed as she pulled delicately at the shirt she was wearing. "And this stinks," she added.

"You could wash it," Jess pointed out.

"What, and go naked while I wait for it to dry out?" Lizzie said.

"I wouldn't mind," Dylan said with a wink.

"In your dreams," Lizzie muttered, but her face had turned bright pink. "Let's face it," she continued, getting ahold of herself, "we've never been in worse shape. We need to get ourselves sorted before we go out there."

"Can't this wait till tomorrow?" Grace said, stifling a yawn. "I'm exhausted. Let's let all this information sink in and make plans tomorrow."

"That sounds good to me," Jess said, rubbing at her eyes. "I've had enough for one day." She and Grace crawled into the shelter.

I'd never felt more awake. My mind buzzed with the events of the evening. "I'll keep watch," I offered. Dylan didn't put up any argument, ducking into the shelter after the girls.

Lizzie was the only one left outside with me. I sat down on a log, and Lizzie sat next to me.

"You need sleep," I said to her.

"Not tired," she replied, staring at the fire pit. The fire had died while we were gone, and she busied herself prodding the embers to life. They glowed and then reluctantly sizzled into life as they curled a dry splinter of wood into ash.

"You know, Dylan really cares about you," I said. She had been avoiding Dylan ever since Jennifer died. Dylan hated it when I got involved in his business. But this wasn't just about him. Lizzie was my friend, too. She ignored me and continued piling sticks onto the fire.

"He wants to be the one to hijack the truck," I said.

"I could do it, you know," Lizzie said as she added a more substantial log to the fire now that it had restarted.

"I know. Dylan knows it too. But he doesn't want to put you through that."

"I don't need protection," Lizzie fired back. "I was Daddy's little girl, Jaden's little sister. Even Grace... she worries for me. But they don't need to. I'm not a helpless victim." Lizzie sat back down on the log with a sigh, her blond hair glowing gold in the firelight, and her face creased with frustration.

"I know you're not helpless. But I think Dylan really wants to —"

"I'm not letting him do it alone," Lizzie said, with a defiant lift of her chin. "I'm strong enough, and I'm just as capable as

Dylan."

"The plan only calls for one person," I said, already aware Lizzie was going to be a part of the hijacking. There was no way to stop her. "The CIA said to—"

Lizzie crossed her arms and glared at me. "You don't think I'm up to it."

"Of course you are," I said.

"Then why not two of us?" she said. "There's more chance of it working. We're better as a team."

It was hard to argue with her logic. "If it's something you want to do," I said, shoving my hands into my pockets.

"I'm not a decoy," Lizzie said. "I'm a fighter. I don't need anyone to protect me. Not even Dylan."

Lizzie was right. We had no place telling her what to do. She was her own person, capable of making her own decisions. If she wanted in on the action, who was I to stop her?

"OK," I said.

"OK, what?"

"I'm on board. You've convinced me."

Lizzie poked at the fire with a long stick.

"You might have a harder time convincing Dylan, though," I said. "After the explosion, all he wants to do is keep you safe."

"I know he means well," Lizzie said, her brow furrowing. "But he can't tell me what to do."

"Do you want me to talk to him?" I offered.

"Would it help?" she asked.

I shrugged. "It can't hurt."

"Don't bring it up yet," Lizzie warned me. "Wait till it's closer to the time."

"Why?"

"If he sees me stronger... and not injured from the explosion... there's more of a chance," Lizzie said.

"Fine," I said. "You tell me when."

Lizzie nodded and stared into the fire. I slouched and put my hands over the fire to warm them up.

"I never imagined I'd blow up the Skytower. We're really going to do it, aren't we," she said at last. She looked across at me, the flickering fire lighting her eyes with flame. An omen.

"Yeah. We really are."

Chapter Nine

Dylan

THE TWO WEEKS PASSED quickly and uneventfully. We ventured out toward Lizzie's old township the day after meeting with the Americans. The streets looked like crap. They had looked shit before the war, too, thanks to the economic hardship our country had suffered through. But before, you could see where people tried to make an effort. The road might have been cracked, the houses in disrepair, but some still did what they could: Bright flowers in cheap hanging baskets decorated front porches, and the farms were tended. But now, with no one about, it was worse than ever. Houses were choked in weeds, their doors eerily open to the elements. And everywhere, the familiar muddy footprints of army boots trekked from door to door.

We took what we needed and left in silence. Sometimes it felt like we were robbing the dead.

No one spoke of our mission. We were all letting it sink in, and even Lizzie was quiet about it. It wasn't until the night before leaving that I found out why.

Levi and I were at the stream, washing the dishes from the final dinner at our campsite.

"Lizzie wants in," Levi said to me as he washed a particularly dirty plate.

I remained silent and scrubbed furiously at a pot. I wasn't going to let Lizzie get hurt again.

"Come on, Dylan. She's as capable as you and me," Levi said, trying to sound casual. "She can eliminate one of the soldiers."

"No way," I said, shaking my head. "I don't want anything to happen to her."

"That's not really your decision," Levi said with a sigh.

"You're meddling," I said, discarding the now overly clean pot on the riverbank. "You know I hate when you get involved with my relationships."

"This has nothing to do with your relationship with Lizzie," Levi said.

"Like hell it does."

"Get a grip, Dylan. You can't control her. You don't know what's best for her," Levi said, keeping his voice measured.

"I can speak for myself thanks, Levi," Lizzie said from behind me. I turned to see her leaning against a tree.

"Lizzie—"

"I'm helping you hijack the truck, Dylan," she said, her face stony.

Levi stood up and edged away from us before darting into the forest, leaving Lizzie and me alone.

"I want to help," Lizzie said, her face softening.

"I don't want you to live with it," I said. "The guilt… it's a horrible thing to have to do."

"I can handle it," Lizzie said confidently. That was something I loved about Lizzie. She was so sure of herself. She could conquer anything.

"The plan calls for one person to carry out the attack and one person to act as backup. Levi's already taken that job," I said, trying to come up with a good reason to stop her from getting involved.

"Screw the CIA," Lizzie said, crossing her arms. "Two people can carry out the attack. You and me."

"I don't know," I started.

"You said it yourself, Levi is there for backup if it goes sour," Lizzie said, determined.

I was running out of reasons to stop her.

"Dylan, you need to let me make my own choices. And accept the consequences of my actions. You don't have to keep me safe all the time," she said.

It hurt me to hear that out loud. My mind flashed back to our escape after the explosion, remembering the promise I had made. Most of the time, Lizzie was a one-woman band. She never showed weakness. But, in that moment, she had been vulnerable.

"I'm stronger than you think," Lizzie said with an edge to her voice.

"Then why did you ask me if I'd always keep you safe?" I challenged, irritation seeping into my voice. I couldn't keep the thought to myself anymore.

Lizzie sighed. "Not this again, Dylan. I was drunk. You know this. I didn't mean it."

"You say that, but I have a hard time believing you. It's OK to be vulnerable sometimes."

Lizzie grunted in annoyance. "Why does everyone keep saying that to me? I'm not vulnerable. And I don't need you protecting me."

My heart sank.

"Fine," I said, relenting. Lizzie didn't need me. "If you want in, then you're in."

"Thanks, Dylan," Lizzie said. She turned and started walking away.

"I don't know why I thought I could protect you," I muttered to her back.

Lizzie looked over her shoulder. She was all smiles now. "Because you care."

That was true. I cared about her. A lot.

A COUPLE HOURS LATER, night had wrapped itself around us, and we sat around the fire, savoring the last of its warmth. Levi and Grace were huddled under a blanket together, whispering to each other. Jess stared into the fire, deep in thought. Meanwhile, Lizzie sat across the fire from me, her eyes lit with determination. I was guarded—still raw from the disagreement we'd had earlier.

"Do you think it will work?" Jess asked, pulling her gaze from the fire and looking at the rest of us.

Levi and Grace stopped chatting and pulled the blanket away from their faces.

"It better," Grace said, readjusting her ponytail. "Or you and I are dead meat."

"That's one way to put it," Levi said with a chuckle.

"It's not funny," Jess said. "Grace and I are putting our lives in your hands."

"And we won't let you down," Lizzie said with a confident smile.

"I won't let anything happen to you, Grace," Levi said. "I'd rather forgo the whole mission than let you die."

"Yuck," Jess said. "Romantic much?"

Levi blushed and slouched back on the log he and Grace were leaning against.

"It won't come to that," I said.

"How can you be so sure?" Jess asked.

"For one, the CIA planned this mission. It wasn't one of our dumb ideas," I said.

"That's true," Lizzie said.

"Our ideas aren't dumb," Levi interjected.

"I really don't want to be bait," Jess said, ignoring Levi's comment.

Rain began to fall, splashing and sizzling on the hot stones that ringed our firepit. Grace and Levi looked at the sky before deciding the storm was here to stay. They gathered up their blanket and headed for the shelter.

"Are you guys coming?" Grace asked as she stooped under the entrance.

"Yeah," Lizzie said, chasing after them as the rain began to fall harder. By the time all of us were under the shelter, the rain was pelting down.

Jess snuggled into her sleeping bag and repeated her fear. "I really don't want to be bait."

"You're a distraction, not bait. It's a necessary part of the plan," I said, peeling off my damp hoodie and getting in my sleeping bag.

"You mean a stupid part of the plan," Jess retorted.

I couldn't help but be annoyed with Jess. She didn't have to kill any soldiers. All she and Grace had to do was wander around until soldiers came upon them.

"If you don't want to do that part, you can always do my job instead," I said.

There was silence.

"Sorry," Jess said, more sympathetic this time. "But I'm absolutely terrified. I don't want to get caught. And I definitely don't want to die."

"I'm scared, too," Grace said. "We're in the same boat. But I trust you guys. You won't let anything happen to us... right?"

"Right," Levi said, giving Grace a reassuring smile.

"I know it sounds pathetic," Jess said, staring up at the low ceiling, "but I'm not ready to die."

"None of us want to die," Lizzie said practically. "But whatever way we look at it, there will be risks. Death is one of them."

"I've never done this before... and I don't want you all to feel awkward... but can I pray for us? Can I pray for protection?" Jess asked with hesitancy in her voice.

"Of course," Grace said.

"It can't hurt," came Levi's voice in the darkness.

"OK then," Jess said. We quieted, letting the unrelenting rain splash on the roof while Jess gathered her thoughts. "Dear Heavenly Father," Jess began. "Thank you for leading us safely through the war this far. I pray for your protection and guidance on this mission..." the words of her prayer were soft in our ears. Beckoning serenity. "...I pray, most of all, that we're doing all things in your will and aren't blinded by hatred and revenge. Amen."

"Amen," we all whispered in unison. There was nothing left

to discuss or say. I lay listening to the rain and felt peace. My shoulders relaxed, the knots loosened in my neck, and I let out a slow breath. I didn't know whether to call it God, karma, or destiny, but I knew ultimately, things would work out. Maybe it would work in our favor, or maybe it wouldn't. But right now, I was calm, and I knew no matter what happened, I had lived the best I knew how, and that was enough. It had to be.

I WOKE UP READY. My mind was clearer than it had been in days. Bright sunlight filtered through the flimsy makeshift door to our shelter, bringing a smile to my face. It was a beautiful day. The plan was going to work—I could feel it. I pulled the fern fronds to the side and peered out at the dewy morning.

"Dylan! What the hell, mate?" Levi yelled at me as he was abruptly awoken by the sunshine.

"Come on, Levi, nothing like some sunshine to wake you up with a smile," I said, still grinning.

"Is this some stupid ploy to make us enjoy life while we're still breathing?" Lizzie asked.

"Oh, come on, it's not that bad," I said, rolling my eyes.

Lizzie grabbed her pillow from under her head and put it over her face in response. Jess rolled over away from the light, muttering something about needing more sleep, and Grace simply made a moaning noise and told me to turn the lights off.

"Funny how the sun doesn't have a switch, Grace," Lizzie replied, her voice muffled through the pillow. "If it did, one of us would have broken it by now."

"I was dreaming about being back in the normal world. You guys didn't have to wake me," Grace huffed back.

"That was Dylan," Levi said.

"Guilty as charged. Guys, it's time to move. We've got to dismantle this whole thing before going." I gestured to the shelter. "And I'm guessing you don't want me to do that while you're all still in it," I added.

"I don't want to get up," Grace mumbled, tucking her head

into her sleeping bag.

"This could be the last sleep before we're killed," Levi groaned. "Let us have it in peace."

"Stop being dramatic, Levi," I said, resisting the urge to clock him one.

Lizzie sat up with a sigh. Her hair was tangled in knots, and she rubbed at her half-opened eyes. "You're not going to let us go back to sleep, are you?" she said, yawning.

"Nope," I said, standing up.

"At least put some water on to boil," Grace said, giving in.

"Sure thing," I said as I walked outside. I took the pot and strolled to the stream barefoot, letting the peaceful sounds of the waking forest surround me. The stream gurgled over the rocks, and I crouched down to splash water over my face. It was icy cold, but did its job. I filled the pot and stood, refreshed. I took one last look at our stream before carrying the water back to the shelter.

By the time I arrived, Lizzie and Grace had managed to drag themselves out of bed, and they sat moodily on the logs around the extinguished fire. I coaxed it back to life and set the water to boil.

Eventually, the water was ready, and Levi and Jess emerged from the shelter to the enticing smell of coffee. An hour later, the coffee kicked in, and the campsite was packed up. We buried everything we couldn't take in a shallow pit near the old Kauri tree. Everything else was loaded into two hiking packs. We'd managed to pack all the equipment into one bag. The other bag was stuffed with food and clothing. We had no idea how long we'd be gone for. Grace and Jess carried the packs while the rest of us were unburdened. Bags would weigh us down, and we couldn't take that risk. Especially when Jess and Grace's lives depended on us.

"We're ready, Dylan," Lizzie said. They stood waiting for me on the bare patch of ground where the shelter had been.

"I think we should say a few words... before we head off," I said.

"The world's not ending," Levi said. "We can skip the emotional speech."

"Actually," Lizzie said, "you never know. If one of us—"

"I know Jess and Grace are putting their lives in our hands," I interrupted, looking at Lizzie and Levi in turn. Lizzie seemed uncharacteristically nervous.

"Our very capable hands," Levi added.

I glared at him but continued. "And I promise we won't let you down. No one's going to fucking die."

"What a moving speech," Grace commented dryly.

"I guess it was emotion-free," Levi said.

"Let's hope you're right, Dylan," Jess added. She pulled at the straps of her hiking pack, hitching it higher.

"I am," I said confidently. I had to be. There was nothing left to say.

"Operation Dark Tower, roll out," Levi said with a goofy grin.

WE PUSHED THROUGH THE scrubby underbrush, our boots crunching on the dry sticks scattered over the ground. Apart from the chirruping of birds, only our quiet breaths and footsteps punctuated the serenity of the forest.

I looked at the others as they walked with extra purpose in their steps. We had been waiting this whole war to do something big. And that moment was finally here. Could Lizzie kill the soldiers when it came down to it? What if we failed? What if the soldiers overpowered us? The thoughts swirled in my mind and stirred me into a panic. My breaths came quicker, and I started sweating. Suddenly, the forest felt too small, and my heart threatened to beat out of my chest. I took a deep, shaking breath, trying to calm down. I hadn't had a panic attack like this since we were back in the US. Instead, I concentrated on putting one foot in front of the other. Lizzie met my eyes and gave me a nervous glance. Anxiety. Fear. Hope. I saw the emotions warring in her eyes, and I knew I had to be strong. For her, and for me.

Nothing we had done before matched this intensity—we'd never gone out on a mission with the sole intent of killing. It was stupid and selfish. But the saddest part was that we were all secretly looking forward to it.

My conscience had started out by screaming at me that what I was doing was wrong, but that voice was getting quieter and quieter as the war continued. Lately, another voice had spoken up. It whispered lies and told me killing our enemies would bring me some much-needed inner peace. It became so insistent I wondered if I was going mad. I no longer cared about the answer and embraced the feeling. It rewarded me with new strength.

I peered through the bush and could make out the edge of the forest. We stopped. I closed my eyes, listening to the sound of safety. A bird's laugh rasped through the trees. It was one of the many songs from a kākā, a New Zealand native. Dad taught me a lot about birds when I was a kid. He said if I wanted to learn to hunt, I had to know why I was killing the possums. These birds wouldn't survive without us. I opened my eyes and looked up. The big parrot stepped curiously out onto the branch of the tree above us and considered me with his beady eye. With a flap of his wings, he exposed his crimson belly and ran across the branch in an ungainly gallop, his voice now whistling a lilting melody, and then he was gone. Somehow, the kākā seemed significant. It was our call to action.

"Are you ready?" I asked, breaking the silence.

"Let's get it over with," Levi said, shrugging. Typical Levi, he always acted reckless and carefree when he was scared.

Grace and Jess were reluctant to leave us. I tried to picture what it would be like to do their job. It seemed easy enough. All they had to do was what we had been avoiding this entire war: get caught. But it wasn't without risk.

"What if—" Jess started nervously.

"I'm ready," Lizzie interrupted, tying her hair into a ponytail. "Levi's right. Let's do this."

"Don't worry, we've got your backs," I heard myself saying.

"You better," Jess said as she gave me a hug.

Grace looked at Levi, her eyes wide and scared.

"It's going to be fine," Levi reassured her, crushing her in his arms.

They pulled apart. "Be safe," Grace said to him. And, with one last look at the three of us, Grace and Jess strode out to the open road.

Lizzie, Levi, and I hugged the tree line. We stuck close together, Lizzie's breath hot on my neck as we lurked in the shadows, our eyes locked on Jess and Grace. In that moment, I envied them. They were out in the open, the wind messing their hair and blowing it in their faces. The sun beat down on them as they walked, unchallenged. I hadn't been in the sun like that, not since that first day we came back. But it was a hoax—they weren't really free. They were bait. And we were meant to save them.

It took maybe half an hour before the grumble of a distant truck interrupted the quiet buzz of cicadas. The knots in my stomach tightened. Lizzie met my eyes and nodded, tight-lipped. Go time. Together, we drew our knives and turned to face the road. The truck came into view. Khaki green, four-wheel drive, no bed cap on the back.

"I'll hang back here," Levi said as he crouched low behind the bushes, his hand curled around the rifle at his side.

Before we left, Lizzie clutched Levi's shoulder, her fingers white and her gray eyes serious. "If anything happens... don't hesitate," she whispered fiercely. Levi nodded, and we parted ways.

Lizzie and I dropped low, snaking through stalky grass. We belly-crawled as close to the road as we dared. The grass tickled my face as I peered through it, watching as Grace and Jess made a show of attempting to get away. But this was all part of the plan.

"Stop! Stop, or we shoot!" I heard a soldier yell over the wind as the truck drove slowly toward them. Jess and Grace obediently stopped and raised their arms in the air. At first, I couldn't see much, with the sun glinting off the dark windscreen of the truck. But then they parked up on the other side of the road. There, the road cut through a steep hill, a thin chicken-wire fence the only retainer. In the small patch of shade it created, I could finally make out three men sitting in the cab. Two of them aimed their weapons out the window, and they beckoned Jess and Grace to come closer.

It was time to act. Lizzie and I darted out of the dry grass, staying low. We scuttled across the road and around the back of the truck. I pressed my back up against the cold green metal and took a moment to catch my breath. Lizzie was right beside me, breathing hard, her eyes alert. I motioned for Lizzie to take the far side of the truck. She nodded and moved off. Instantly, I regretted my decision. Around the far side, Levi couldn't see her. Too late now, I thought.

Around the front of the truck, there was an audible commotion. One of the soldiers had left the truck and was interrogating Grace and Jess. I did my best to ignore it and focus on my part in the ambush. But it was impossible. The same question kept circling in my mind and causing me to lose focus: *What if one of them got shot?* There wasn't a choice to back out now, though. We were in this, no matter which way it went.

I wiped sweat from my clammy forehead as I inched toward the cab. The two soldiers were trying to radio in to report the incident to headquarters, and were apparently having a hard time of it.

"Give it here," the blond one demanded as his friend skipped through the channels, receiving nothing but static. The blond one took the radio from his friend and tapped it impatiently with the back of his hand, to no avail. "It's busted," he eventually admitted.

"Yeah, probably because you bashed the life out of it with your hand," the other one grumbled.

I couldn't work out what to do, and I assumed Lizzie was having the same dilemma. Until they got out of the truck, it was going to be impossible to get the jump on them. But just as I was considering changing tactics and trying to take down the boss guy first, the blond one gave up on the radio and swung open the truck door.

I took my chance and dove at him as he was getting out of the truck. He was still only halfway to the ground, and we went sprawling into dust and gravel. I had tried to swipe my knife at his throat but ended up only grazing him as we fell. His rifle clattered out after him as he tried to grab onto something to keep his balance.

Clumsily, I kicked the weapon out of his reach and under the chassis of the truck. There was no way I was letting him get it. But the soldier wasn't worried about that—his hands were fighting at my wrist, trying to tear the knife from my grasp. It was a battle of strength. An arm wrestle, where the loser dies, and the winner gets to stay in this hell.

There was a point where I thought I was going to fail. That this would be the end—my end. But the soldier's arms began shaking with effort, and I noticed him weakening. He was red-faced and panting, his blond hair slicked back with sweat. Eyes desperate. Panicked. I don't know what I looked like to him, but I imagined myself from his perspective. A merciless savage with no heart. Only the implacable will to send him to his maker.

It was sudden. His muscles gave way, and I all but fell on him with the knife. It sunk deep into his neck, and to my sick horror, his blood fountained upward. I thought that sort of thing only happened in the movies. I collapsed back, knife still in hand, and I stayed there for a moment, shocked and staring at what I had done.

Dimly, in the back of my mind, I recalled why I had done this. And that Lizzie was fighting her own battle. I couldn't leave her, or my friends. I knew if Lizzie wasn't here with me already, it was because she needed help. I crawled under the vehicle's chassis, hoping to take the soldier by surprise. Any remnants of courage quickly scarpered as I took in the scene before me. By the back wheel, I could see two pairs of legs. Lizzie's dirt-covered sneakers danced in front of me. She was on tiptoes, her feet barely reaching the ground, the truck rocking above me as the soldier held her pinned against the door. The soldier's solid black boots braced in the roadside gravel, feet spread wide. Then I heard her choking. Gasping for her breath. The worst sound I had ever heard.

I didn't think it through. If I had, I might have remembered the soldier's rifle still half-buried in the dust, only meters away from me, and forgone the plan. Instead, I lunged forward in a tackle, my shoulder ramming the soldier's leg. From where I was under the chassis, I could barely get any forward momentum, but the gravel was my saving grace. The soldier slipped and lost his footing. Lizzie collapsed in a heap beside me, clutching her throat and taking in long, ragged breaths.

The soldier was getting to his feet when I took my second try. This time I got him good, headbutting him in the stomach and winding him. As he doubled over, wheezing, I wrestled his sidearm from his grasp. But Lizzie grabbed my arm before I could take the shot. "Dylan... no... Grace and Jess," she managed to choke out. If I shot, the third soldier would hear it. So, I shoved the pistol at Lizzie and stumbled forward with my knife. If the other soldier had thought I was a savage, to this soldier, maybe I was some sort of demon, puffing and blowing with effort, fresh blood still dripping from my arm and congealing on the knife. He was still trying to catch his breath. He raised his arm in a half-hearted attempt to defend himself. I batted it aside and slit his throat like I had with the other.

Lizzie was still standing where I left her, holding the pistol slack at her side. "Come on," I said gently, taking the pistol from her and grabbing her hand. I pulled Lizzie around the front of the pickup, and we ducked down by the front wheels.

What we saw next scared the shit out of me. The soldier—a

thin, wiry man—was holding Grace at gunpoint, and Levi and Jess stood a few meters away with their hands on their heads. I didn't know how it had happened, but I could imagine: Grace and Jess had been in trouble, and Levi must have decided it was time to step in. And then the soldier had decided to use Grace as his personal safeguard.

We watched as the soldier yelled at Levi to kick his rifle away. Levi did it without question, his hands still on his head. You could tell the soldier was excited; he must have thought he'd get special treatment or something for bringing them in. He had an air of madness about him, and it made my stomach turn to see how his finger was resting, none too gently, over the trigger. The whites of his knuckles visible. Grace was pale white and trembling, and Levi looked defeated. Jess kept glancing over our way. I wished she wouldn't—I was worried she'd ruin any chance we had of saving them.

"Christ," Lizzie whispered beside me. I could feel her shaking, the skin of her arm cold against mine. And when I looked at her, I could see bruises beginning to purple on her neck. "Dylan, I can't. I can't," she whimpered. I knew what she meant. I didn't have the energy for another fight either. But we had to do something.

"Lizzie, listen to me." I actually gave her a shake of the shoulder, trying to get some sense out of her. Neither of us had the luxury of falling apart. Not now. "There's a rifle under the chassis. I need you to get it."

Her eyes were teary, but she nodded and crawled under. A minute later, she dragged the rifle out. I expected her to start lining up the shot, but she shoved it in my hands. Lizzie never let anyone take charge. Wordlessly, I swapped out my pistol and crawled forward with the rifle, trying to get a good angle where Grace wouldn't get hurt.

It was impossible.

With Grace at gunpoint, I couldn't take the shot. It was too risky.

"You're not doing yourselves any favors. I know you're all part of a rebel group… where are the others?" the soldier yelled at them. He stared up into the bushes, in the direction where Levi had come from. "Oi, Daniels, Pierce, get over here and start searching those bushes," he yelled over his shoulder.

When they didn't come, he turned. I knew what he was seeing: his comrades sprawled out on either side of the truck, cab doors flung wide open. Lizzie, crouched by the front wheel, the pistol I'd given her held loosely in her hand. And me, with a rifle aimed square at his head. I was close enough that I could see crystal clear in the scope, every detail of his face. I registered the shock in his eyes. The growing terror. In surprise, he finally slackened his grip on his sidearm. Grace scrambled away from him at the same time as I pulled the trigger. He was still staring at me as he stumbled backward—eyes wide open and frantic with the knowledge of his death.

My hands were still shaking as I dropped the rifle onto the tarmac. The image of that last soldier imprinted in my mind. It struck me as funny that out of everything I had done today, it was his death that stayed with me the most. Lizzie seemed to be equally frozen. I turned to her; she was all that mattered. I'd kept my promise. She was safe. My breaths began leveling out.

"Come on," I said, pulling on her arm. I tried to be gentle, but I was spent.

"I… I'm sorry, I didn't mean for…" Lizzie said, her voice choked with emotion, her face working, barely keeping her composure.

"It's OK," I said, trying to comfort her. "We did it. We're safe."

Lizzie finally swallowed her emotions, and her face stilled as she assumed her well-practiced blank mask. "You did it," she said. There was the faintest catch to her voice. "I did nothing."

Chapter Ten

Jess

Time was a scarcity we couldn't waste. Any moment, another truck could come barreling down the road, or worse, a whole convoy. Despite this, none of us made to leave. There was a strange sensation crawling under my skin. It flushed hot in some places, while in other areas—namely the back of my neck—a cold shiver snaked its way, vertebra by vertebra.

Seconds ago, the soldier in front of me had been alive. Now he was nothing but a lifeless body lying on the side of the road. I couldn't condone what he'd done. He'd threatened us, and he would've killed us. But I couldn't condone what we'd done, either.

"What the hell happened, Levi?" Dylan asked as he stood over the dead soldier.

"He had Grace," Levi said, his tone defensive. "What was I meant to do?" Grace clung to Levi, still trembling from the ordeal with the soldier.

"You getting caught wasn't part of the plan," Dylan said.

"And Lizzie almost being choked to death was?" Levi shot back, noting the dark bruises circling Lizzie's neck.

"I'm fine. We had it under control," Lizzie said. She balled her shaking hands into fists.

Guilt swam in Dylan's eyes. He lifted his hand, about to run it through his hair the same way he always did, but then he saw the blood caked thick on his hand and dropped his arm. He wiped his shaking, bloodied hands on his jeans. "That's bull," Dylan said to Lizzie. "But it's my fault, really. I should have done it on my own. Levi's right. You nearly died."

"Great." Lizzie threw her hands in the air. "So apparently, I can't be trusted. Perfect. My one chance to prove myself, and I fuck it up."

"No, Lizzie, that's not what I—" Dylan started. But Lizzie was already storming off. Dylan chased after her.

We had been lucky. Lizzie had always seemed so strong to me, but she hadn't been able to do it. If it hadn't been for Dylan... I couldn't bear to think about what would have happened.

"Whatever. What's done is done. At least we're all alive," Levi said as he watched them go. "We can argue about it later. Right now, we've got to clean this up."

Grace let go of him. "Do we have to? Can't we just go?"

Levi shook his head. "They'll work out the truck was hijacked, eventually. But if we don't clear the bodies off the road, they'll know a hell of a lot sooner."

I stared at the bodies littering the road as a terrible sense of guilt engulfed me.

Levi looked at me, sympathy spreading across his face. Or maybe it was pity. "Don't beat yourself up," he said. It sounded too casual.

"So what? You don't care about what we've done?" I said, biting my lip.

Levi's brow furrowed. He ran his hand through his brown hair and sighed. "Of course, I do. I care about who we're becoming. I care about the kind of people we're turning into. But right now, this is how we survive."

"What, kill or be killed?" I asked him, my lip trembling.

Levi didn't say anything, but we both knew that was exactly what he thought. I wasn't so sure. Levi tugged on my arm. "Come on. This one first."

Levi led me over to the man sprawled by the open cab door. The soldier looked young, maybe still a teenager like us. Blond hair and blue eyes were complimented by a refined chin and high cheekbones. He probably had a family: mother, father, girlfriend. I could imagine his parents learning of his death, holding each other in that desperate way people do when they are trying to stop each other from falling apart. I crouched down and placed my hands over his staring and empty eyes, closing them.

"Jess…" Levi tried again to reason with me, his voice softer this time. "At least they had a choice. They signed up for this. We didn't. They trained for it. They trained to kill, Jess. They chose their path."

I ignored him.

"Jess." Levi grabbed my shoulders and looked into my eyes. For a moment, I thought he was going to shake some sense into me. "Who knows how many people they've killed? They might have been the ones who killed Jennifer… or Leah. We don't know if our families are OK. They could be responsible for them, too."

"They might not be, and it doesn't make it right. The Bible says—"

"Thou shalt not kill. Yeah, sure, I've heard that's in there somewhere," Levi grumbled. He sighed loudly and removed his hands from my shoulders. "All I know is they aren't innocent in all this. If God wants to smite me… I don't care."

With that, Levi reached down and grabbed the wrists of the young soldier. With a grunt, he began to drag his body toward the forest. I did nothing and simply watched as Levi came back for the second one. By the time he got to the third, he was sweating heavily in the midday sun.

"Can I have some help here?" Levi yelled at us.

He was right. It wasn't fair he had to do all the dirty work. But I couldn't move. I was unable to will my feet to walk. Lizzie and Dylan were comforting each other over by the open door of the truck. Grace was still a mess after being held at gunpoint.

Finally, Lizzie pulled away from Dylan and stepped forward, saying, "I suppose I should do something useful."

She reluctantly went to help Levi. They dragged the last soldier to the trees, and I watched as they threw fern fronds over them. Lizzie kicked up some dirt for extra cover, and they walked away without a word. We all approached the truck.

"Are you OK to drive?" Levi said to Dylan.

Was he? Dylan's skin was pale, and just like me, I could see the guilt awash in his eyes. Tormenting him. But he nodded wordlessly at Levi. He had known what it would cost him to kill those soldiers. But he did it anyway. For us.

"I took these too," Levi said, dropping the soldiers' uniforms at Dylan's feet. "I don't know how far it will get us, and the third was a little too bloody, but..."

"I'm not wearing that," I said immediately.

Levi shrugged. "Wouldn't fit you anyway." Levi and Dylan stripped and hastily changed.

"Remind me why I'm doing this again?" Dylan muttered as he pulled the soldier's shirt over his head.

"Lizzie and I will sit in the back," Grace said, "there's not enough room in the cab."

"Make sure if any trucks come... duck," Dylan said, getting into the driver's seat.

"Yeah, whatever," Lizzie said. She was already using the back wheel to clamber into the tray.

"You're sure you don't mind?" I called after her.

"It's fine. Someone has to. Might as well be me," she said back. She sat in the tray with her arms crossed.

"Is she OK?" I asked Grace.

"I'm not sure," Grace said, glancing at Lizzie with concern.

"Maybe you should talk to her," I said.

"If she wants to talk. She barely tells me anything anymore," Grace said.

"But you're best friends," I said. I was growing used to being the odd one out now that Jennifer was gone, and I thought Lizzie and Grace talked to each other all the time.

Grace shook her head. "We were. We are, I mean," she said with a shrug. "Levi, can you give me a leg up?" she called.

Levi agreed and gave Grace a boost into the back before he shoved the packs in after them. I turned to the cab and opened the passenger door. Grabbing the inner door handle, I pulled myself up, scooching over to the middle seat. The safety belt clicked as I strapped it across my body. Levi and Dylan got in next to me.

Levi noticed an old stereo system and turned it on. Country music blared from the speakers. "What the hell is this?" he muttered as he rifled through a stack of CDs.

"Hey, leave it. I like it," I said, slapping Levi's hand away as he tried to silence the volume.

"I don't care what's on. But if you're going to bicker the entire way, I'll choose," Dylan said, throwing a sour look at us both.

"Fine," Levi muttered.

"OK, here we go," Dylan said. He started the engine and put the truck in gear. Then he pulled out onto the road.

The air in the vehicle smelled of sweaty men, but it quickly dissipated when Levi opened the window. Fresh air rushed in and blew around my face as we soared down state highway twenty-nine. Stalky, dry grass, yellowed from the sunshine, blew on the mountainous hills on either side of us. It felt daring and free to be traveling like this, but also strange. We were the only ones as far as we could see. Usually, this road was a trucking route, teeming with impatient drivers honking at logging trucks as they crawled up the Kaimai's. And before the virus spread, there were giant milk tankers. If you were lucky, they pulled over into the slow vehicle bays to let you pass.

Dylan looked like he was thinking about the same thing. "This road has changed a lot," he said after a moment.

"It hasn't, not really," Levi disagreed. "We're the ones who have changed. The world is what's changed. This road is still the same," he said.

It was true. We had changed. And I wasn't sure it was for the better. With all that had happened, I was at a point where I had lost all perspective. I knew God was testing us, but I wasn't sure if I was responding the right way. Sometimes, I didn't recognize the person I had become. I could feel the old me slipping away, and I wasn't sure I liked the new me. The new me might be stronger, but she had lost some of the soft edges, some humanity, and had become steeled to this new way of life. The worst part was that I was unsure how far she would go. The new me held secrets.

"We're the good guys, right?" I asked.

"Obviously," Levi said without a second thought.

"Seriously. Objectively speaking, are we?" I asked.

"We're the good guys," Levi said resolutely. "We didn't ask for this. We want what everyone else has—a shot at happiness and the right to freedom. Is that too much to ask for?"

It was true. We weren't asking for much.

"You'd think a human rights committee, or the Red Cross would step in," Dylan said. "We've been forgotten and left to fend for ourselves."

"No one wants to risk the virus getting loose," Levi commented. He was right, but it was a terrible excuse. The contagion had been gone since before the war, but the after-effects of it were still being felt. If it hadn't been for the virus, we might still be in London right now. "Plus, I guess the rest of the world has their own problems to deal with," Levi added as an afterthought.

"Problems that Marion made," Dylan muttered.

I had wondered about Marion's motives for a long time. Why turn on your own country? But, with Dylan's words, something clicked in my brain. I remembered being smothered in darkness on the luggage hold of Marion's private jet, terrified, while Marion and his cronies talked on the floor above us. Marion had said to his man, Joshua, *It's all about distraction.* We assumed he was 'distracting' Joshua before he brutally murdered him for disloyalty. But what if he was talking about something bigger than that?

"That's it. That's why he launched the rocket," I said with the realization hitting me full on.

"What do you mean?" Dylan asked, glancing sideways at me.

"The rocket was a distraction. To take eyes off our lonely little country, so no one would interfere, and he could continue his campaign. Whatever that is," I added.

Levi and Dylan were both silent. The only noise was the grumbling of the truck as we chugged onward. We still had no idea what Marion was planning, and the revelation that he would go so far to stop any other country from interfering unnerved me. Hopefully, no matter what happened with our mission, the Americans could help shed some light on the truth.

Finally, Levi snorted. "Well, it didn't work very well. He has the CIA breathing down his neck now. And us."

That made the nerves flutter in my belly again, thinking of what lay ahead. The more I thought about it, the more I realized it came down to one thing: We fought for basic human rights. Maybe it justified our actions, or maybe it didn't. But if we did nothing, we would lose more than our homes and families. We would lose ourselves.

Dylan had been thinking hard about it, too. Some of the guilt left his face before he said, "Anyway, we're definitely the good guys." There was an air of conviction in his voice that made me smile.

Outside the truck, the clear skies had quickly turned. A light drizzle began, and Dylan turned the wipers on low while Levi fiddled with the air-con, trying to clear the fog that was already creeping up the windows.

"It's not working," Dylan said. "Just turn the heat on."

Levi relented, and soon warm air was blasting into our faces. It was pleasantly cozy, our surroundings a smudging of green as the rain worsened.

"Do you think Grace and Lizzie will be OK back there?" Levi asked as he looked out the back. We could see Lizzie and Grace's backs leaning against the little window dividing the cab from the pickup's tray.

"Yeah, they'll be fine," I replied.

"Stop worrying, Romeo. Grace isn't going to get washed away," Dylan said.

"Who're you calling Romeo? Like you can talk," Levi said. He cleared his throat meaningfully.

"What?" Dylan asked.

"Lizzie, do you need help with that?" Levi said in a deep voice, mocking Dylan. "Oh yes, Dylan, thank you so much, you're so handsome," he continued in a high pitch that I supposed was his impression of Lizzie. I wanted to roll my eyes, but I couldn't help laughing. Levi was such an idiot.

"She doesn't sound like that. And neither do I," Dylan said uncomfortably.

"Na, you're right. She's more of the sarcastic type," Levi reflected.

Annoyance flitted across Dylan's face as he stared through the rain pelting the windshield. "At least Lizzie isn't moody and doesn't cry all the time."

So, this was what guys talked about in the car.

"No, you're right, Dylan," Levi said. "That isn't Lizzie's way. Instead, she makes bitchy comments that get on everyone's nerves."

"Lizzie is not bitchy."

"And Grace isn't moody."

"You two are ridiculous," I said as the song changed. "Have you forgotten those two are my friends? Stop insulting them. Maybe tell them how you feel instead. Unless either of you manned up and already did?"

I left the question hanging, but I was sure I knew the answer. Lizzie and Grace would have told me if anything had happened.

"Well, no, but I'm pretty sure she likes me back," Levi said.

"And what makes you so sure?" Dylan asked and looked across at Levi with a mocking grin on his face.

"Certain things have happened," Levi said vaguely.

I secretly began guessing what really had happened.

"So, you did sleep with her?" Dylan asked, only half-joking.

Levi snorted. "No."

"Bet you wish you did," Dylan said.

A playful smile danced on Levi's face.

I fell back against the faded gray upholstery and giggled.

"You can't tell Grace about this," Levi said quickly and glared at me.

"Of course I won't," I said to Levi with a reassuring smile before I turned to Dylan. "What about you and Lizzie?"

"I'm not even sure if she likes me back." Dylan stared blankly at the road ahead.

Levi laughed. "Seriously, are you blind?"

"She's never said anything," Dylan said naïvely. "And…"

Levi and I looked at him with anticipation.

"It's nothing," Dylan said, his face falling. "I don't know how she feels."

I looked up at him in disbelief. "If you weren't driving, I would slap you right now," I said to Dylan.

"What for?" he asked obliviously.

"For being a total idiot," I said. "You don't think she likes you back? It's so obvious it isn't even funny. She makes no attempt to hide it. Get a grip." I shook my head and let out another snort of laughter. No wonder Lizzie and Grace had been so keen to ride in the back. This wasn't a discussion between friends—this had all the hallmarks of a therapy session.

"So, she does like me?" Dylan asked, sounding childish.

"Get it through your thick head," I said. "She. Likes. You."

"Does she talk about me?" Dylan asked hopefully as we turned a sharp corner, and I leaned into Levi.

"You're pathetic." Levi and I grinned as we caught each other's eye. He was hopeless.

"Only as pathetic as Romeo over there," Dylan said, jerking his head toward Levi.

I started rifling curiously through the glove compartment in front of Levi's knees and smiled as my hands closed over a chocolate bar. "Snack?" I asked. I broke into the packet and shared around a couple of squares. Dylan held his between his teeth as he slowed the truck and crossed an intersection.

"I told you already, I'm no Romeo," Levi said to Dylan with his mouth full. He rolled the chocolate around his mouth. "You're Romeo. I'm more like Casanova. Smooth and suave."

Dylan snorted. "Keep dreaming."

"Don't even get me started with you," I said to Levi. "Dylan's right. You're just as bad."

"No, I'm not," Levi insisted.

I gave him a reproachful look.

"She knows," Levi said slowly.

"So, you've told Grace how you feel?" I pressed. I knew he hadn't.

"Actions speak louder than words," Levi said before staring out the window.

"So, you did sleep with her," Dylan said.

Levi shook his head. "That's not me, mate. I'm a gentleman. And that's why the ladies love me," Levi said with a smirk.

"Tell me what happened," I said, grinning.

Levi remained tight-lipped. I'd have to ask Grace about it later.

"You're right, though, Jess. I should tell her, you know, with words," Levi said.

"How eloquent," Dylan said, laughing.

"Finally. At least I've made one of you understand," I said.

"What about you?" Levi asked.

"What do you mean?" I said, feigning confusion. I didn't want to talk about myself. I pulled my hair up into a ponytail.

"I mean, obviously, our love lives are a mess. What about you? You know you can trust us," Levi said with a goofy smile.

"And tell you about my love life with who? My pillow?" I scoffed.

"She has a point," Dylan said.

"I wish I could meet someone," I said distantly.

"You will, one day," Levi said.

"If I survive the war first."

"We will survive," Levi said. But he didn't sound certain about it.

"Yeah, 'course we will," Dylan said in the same tone.

In silence, we all contemplated what it would be like if we didn't. Would anyone remember us? Would anyone care about the trials we'd been through? Or would it all be for nothing?

"I wish I could give Grace flowers," Levi said as he gazed over his shoulder at Grace's back through the grimy window.

"That came out of nowhere," Dylan commented.

"I thought we were having a quiet moment thinking about our life's purpose," I said, coming back to reality.

"What?" Levi said, totally clueless.

"Keep kidding yourself, Jess. Levi has a one-track mind," Dylan said and sniggered.

I rubbed my eyes sleepily before responding, "Don't be mean, Dylan. At least he had the thought."

A flash of lightning lit the darkened sky, and a few seconds later, a crack of thunder boomed in the distance.

"That is really unlike you, though," I added, looking at Levi.

"I know," Levi said and laughed nervously. "But they'd cheer her up. She's been really down lately."

"I think we all need cheering up," I said. Things had been tough, and it was hard to keep our spirits high when there wasn't really anything left to keep us going.

The truck rumbled steadily along the road, and I watched the familiar scenery race past. The lack of traffic was beginning to feel eerie, especially with the storm now raging all around us. I thought back to what Levi said earlier: The road hadn't changed. We had. But, like us, I no longer knew all its secrets. Behind every bend, there could be a surprise lurking. I closed my eyes and tried not to think about getting caught. Slowly my thoughts started tumbling into each other in odd disconnected ways, half dreaming, half awake. I surrendered to the strange scenes in my mind and let myself fall asleep.

THE TRUCK WAS SLOWING, brakes grinding, and I snapped my eyes open. "Are we...?"

"We're not there yet," Levi replied, tight-lipped. He nodded ahead. There was an army truck pulled over to the side of the road with its hood raised, and several soldiers were gesturing to each other. My breathing went shallow. There was nowhere to hide. They were already pointing at us, and I knew there was no escaping.

"What do we do?" I asked, my eyes darting between Levi and Dylan.

"I hope your good at acting," Levi said as I felt cold metal wrap around my wrists. I looked down to see Levi snapping on some cuffs. "Sorry, Jess," he added. I quickly pieced his plan together—it was only Dylan and Levi who had donned the soldiers' outfits. I was to be their prisoner.

Levi turned and rapped hard on the small window behind us. Grace and Lizzie peered through the dirty glass with confusion on their faces.

"Get down," he mouthed at them. They flattened themselves to the truck deck, and Lizzie flung the tray's soft cover over their bodies.

Dylan wound down the window as they flagged us down.

"What's going on?" Dylan asked with his arm casually out the window. He sounded confident. How was he so calm? And then I saw his hand shake as he changed the gear to park. He was just as terrified as me.

"We broke down," the soldier said, gesturing to the vehicle behind them. "Where are you headed?"

"We're taking this one to the prison up in Auckland," Dylan said, elbowing me in the side. I squeaked in pain. "They don't have the facilities to keep her back in Tauranga."

The soldier laughed. "She's only a girl," he said.

Levi glared at him. "A girl who killed a bunch of our comrades a few miles back. I wouldn't take her lightly."

"I see," the soldier said, looking more somber. He stared blankly at me for several moments before returning to the situation at hand. "Do either of you know anything about mechanics?" the soldier asked.

Levi and Dylan looked nervously at one another.

"You go. I'll keep an eye on this one," Dylan said to Levi, jabbing his thumb in my direction. Levi nodded tersely and jumped out of the truck. He wandered with the soldier over to the army truck. It looked like Levi was being given a rundown on what went wrong.

There hadn't been a sound from the back of the truck, and I assumed Lizzie and Grace were lying low.

"Fuck," Dylan murmured under his breath.

"Yeah. That about covers it," I replied.

Levi was working with a socket wrench on something under the hood of the soldiers' vehicle, and the soldiers looked on apprehensively, as did we. We stayed like that for half an hour, watching, waiting. The minutes agonized on. Every second I thought someone would work out Levi wasn't actually a soldier. I wasn't actually a prisoner. And there were two more of us hiding out in the back.

Finally, Levi called out for them to try the engine. It spluttered for a second and then leaped into life. The soldiers patted Levi on the back. He grinned briefly and waved them off, heading back toward us.

The lead soldier stopped him halfway.

"What's your name? I'd like to thank you properly when we get back to headquarters." I heard him say.

I held my breath. Surely this was it. We would be discovered.

Levi laughed and clapped him on the shoulder. "Honestly, the best thanks you can give is letting us get on our way. We'll be reprimanded if we're late."

"If you're sure," the soldier said, looking puzzled.

"I'm sure," Levi said firmly.

Dylan honked the horn.

"That's my cue," Levi said and grinned. He waved and then walked away without another look back.

Levi jumped into the truck beside me. "Drive," he muttered. He was still grinning, but the tone of his voice didn't match. Dylan honked once more, and we accelerated smoothly away.

As soon as we had rounded the bend, Levi and I looked back through the window.

"Are they OK?" Dylan asked. I still couldn't see them, and I rapped urgently on the window. Grace and Lizzie bobbed into view.

"They're OK," I said. We all let out a breath.

"What was wrong with their truck, anyway?" Dylan asked.

"Dirty spark plugs," Levi replied.

We drove on.

CHAPTER ELEVEN

LEVI

RAIN BUCKETED DOWN AS our truck roared along the road. On either side of us, dark green trees dripping with water washed away the essence of war. For a moment, it was like old times, driving down the twisting New Zealand roads with the music blaring. No war, just freedom and fun. Dylan drummed his fingers on the steering wheel. I watched the raindrops snake down the window.

"I can hardly see," Dylan commented, waving his hand frustratingly at the window. The rain was coming down hard, and through the gray, I could barely make out the road ahead.

"I'll slow down a bit," Dylan said.

With the torrential rain, it was impossible to tell how far we had to go before reaching Auckland. I glanced over my shoulder at the sopping forms of Grace and Lizzie sitting outside in the back. They had their arms hugged around themselves, trying to keep warm. I hoped they would be OK.

"Maybe we should stop and let Lizzie and Grace in here with us," I said aloud.

"And where would they sit? On your lap?" Dylan asked.

"Well…"

"They're going to be a little wet when we get to Auckland, that's all," Dylan commented.

Jess stirred on my shoulder and woke up from her nap. Her cheeks were rosy red from the stuffiness of the cab. "It's way too hot in here." She rubbed her eyes and then fumbled with the heat controls. "Damn, how do you work this thing?"

"I'll do it," Dylan said, reaching across toward the smooth black buttons.

"Dylan!" I yelled as a corner appeared through the rain.

"Shit," Dylan said, grabbing back onto the steering wheel. He swerved to the left, the tires struggling to find traction. Jess screamed as Dylan lost control, and we skidded across the tarmac. The wheels of the truck squealed as they locked firmly in place, the brakes useless. For a second, I thought Dylan was going to maneuver us to safety. But an instant later, we slid off the side of the bank.

A scream caught in my throat as we hung, suspended above the chasm below. From what seemed far away, I heard Dylan yell and Jess cry out. But all I could focus on was the ground coming to meet us as we plunged into the ditch. Then time shifted from slow-motion to break-neck speed, and the next few seconds were chaos: Crash. Screams. Airbags. Glass everywhere. Then there was only the sound of rain pinging against the roof of the car.

I opened my eyes. At first, the world was a haze of rain, broken glass, and steam. I tried to move, but my whole body was sore and stiff. My head spun as I tried to regain my breath. I felt someone shaking me. I managed to turn my head.

"Levi?" Jess wheezed from beside me. "Are you OK?"

"Yeah," I said, blinking my eyes a few times to clear my vision. Finally, the world came back into focus. I took stock of my body. I could move. That was a relief. And there was no blood. Also good. I took a few deep breaths that did nothing to ease the pain across my chest.

"We need to get out," Jess said, her voice quaking. "Grace and —"

Fear surged in my gut as I remembered Grace and Lizzie had been in the back. I tried to get out of my door. But our truck had slammed up against a tree, and my side of the door was completely scrunched in. I looked across at Dylan, who lay motionless on the steering wheel. The impact had buckled Dylan's door, which hung limply, attached by only one hinge. I ripped the airbags out of the way.

"Dylan, wake up!" Jess yelled hysterically, shaking him. Dylan didn't move. A pit of dread threatened to swallow me whole. Was he dead? Tears poured down Jess' cheeks as she shook Dylan harder. Finally, he moaned and lifted his head. He looked at me, dazed, and wiped a trickle of blood from his face.

"Grace and Lizzie," I shouted at him. "They were in the back." It took him a second to process what was going on.

"Shit," he said as our situation dawned on him. Dylan unclipped his seat belt and looked across at the door. It seemed to take all his effort to kick it open, but at last, the door fell off its remaining hinge and thudded to the ground. We followed Dylan as he eased himself out of the truck. He stood using the vehicle for balance, his legs trembling.

"Are you OK?" Jess asked as she clambered out after him.

"I think so," he muttered. "My head hurts like a bitch, though."

I couldn't care less about Dylan, who was clearly all right. It was Grace and Lizzie I was worried about. I searched frantically across the bank, stumbling through the long, wet grass, looking for any sign of them. A few meters ahead, the grass was crushed flat, and I spotted a body lying face down on the sodden earth.

"Grace!" I shouted as I ran over to her.

Grace whimpered.

I crouched down beside her. "Shhh," I soothed and carefully rolled her over.

She moaned in pain.

"Sorry."

"It's OK. It just hurts," she said, wincing. The old wound on her head dripped fresh blood down her face.

"Your head?"

"No." She shook her head. "My arm." Her arms were streaked with mud, bruises already erupting on her skin. One arm looked strange and crooked near her wrist. The other was gripping my hand tight. "I think my arm's broken," she said through her tears.

"Can you move your fingers?" I asked quickly. I was crappy at this first aid stuff, but anything was better than nothing. Grace wriggled them, crying out as the pain returned.

"You're going to have to sit up."

"I know," Grace said.

I wiped her tears off her face, wriggled out of the soldier's khaki jacket, and then peeled off my soaking t-shirt. Palming my pocket knife, I cut the shirt in half. Somewhere far off, I registered Dylan and Jess searching for Lizzie, but all my attention was on helping Grace.

"I'm going to help you sit up. Hold on to your broken arm for me," I said softly to her.

"OK," she said with a brave face.

I placed my hands carefully behind her shoulders and pulled her forward. She grunted in pain. A mixture of mud, blood, and tears streaked her face.

"That wasn't so hard," I said to her, gently thumbing her tears away. I fashioned the material from my shirt into a makeshift sling and looped it around her arm and neck as carefully as I could.

"Thanks," she said.

We sat there for a few moments as the freezing rain fell on us. We were both covered in dirt, and between us we had plenty of bruises. But we were still here. The full force of it hit and emotion threatened to overwhelm me. I gulped hard before saying, "Thank God you're alive." I pulled her into a hug, my chin resting against her head. Grace lay her head on my shoulder and cried. All that mattered was that she was OK. After several minutes like that, she quietened and pulled away from me. I tucked her sopping hair behind her ears.

"Levi!" Dylan called a few meters from me. "I need your help. It's Lizzie…" His voice was strained with emotion and he stood there with a look in his eyes that brought all the fear racing back.

I hesitated and looked at Grace. Dylan needed my help… but so did Grace."I'll be fine," Grace said. She put on a brave smile. "Go help Dylan."

Lizzie lay limply on the grassy slope. Dylan kneeled beside her while Jess paced back and forth, wringing her hands. I ran to them, panicking more with each step forward. I kept expecting Lizzie to sit up and wave off Jess and Dylan's fussing, but she didn't move.

"Is she…?"

Dylan already had her wrist and was feeling for a pulse. "She's alive," he managed to say, his throat thick with emotion.

"Lizzie, wake up!" I said, shaking her forcefully by the shoulder. She still didn't stir.

"Is she bleeding anywhere? Why won't she wake up?" Jess said with a sob, and she started to tremble all over. "Oh God, oh God," she said over and over.

"Hey, Jess, why don't you go and help Grace," I said, squeezing her shoulder and pointing.

"But Lizzie—"

"Grace is alone. She needs some help," I said, trying to keep my voice level.

Jess nodded as tears dribbled down her chin. I watched her walk over to Grace, who hugged her tight with her good arm.

"What now?" I muttered.

"I," Dylan was struggling to stay calm. "I don't know." His hands trembled as he looked down at Lizzie's motionless form.

Dylan's panic was infectious but I tried to keep my composure. We needed to save Lizzie, and right now I was the only one who could think straight. "There must be an injury somewhere," I said, crouching next to him. I tried to look past Lizzie's still body, and the rain snaking off her face.

"No, no, no," Dylan said as he reached a shaking hand towards Lizzie's head. I saw it too, dark blood pooling in the grass under her hair.

Dylan gently lifted the back of Lizzie's head. And the look on his face said it all. "It's here. She hit a rock." He pulled his hands away, and they were covered in blood.

"Use this," I said, throwing the other half of my t-shirt at him. He quickly coiled it and wrapped it around her head.

"Do you think she's bleeding anywhere else?" Dylan asked.

"I don't see any more blood."

"With all this rain and mud we'd never know," Dylan said, running a hand through his sopping wet hair.

"There's not much we could do about it out here," I said.

Dylan threw me a death stare. "A great help you are."

"I'm not saying we should give up on her," I hastily amended. "But until we get under some cover—"

"Give me a second to think about what to do," Dylan muttered.

"Dylan," I said, reaching for his shoulder. He was scared for her. And so was I.

"Levi, I said give me a second!" Dylan shouted at me. "Go help Grace or something. I need a moment. I can't think through this damn headache."

"OK...," I said, retreating to Grace.

"Is Lizzie OK?" Grace asked as I approached.

"She's alive, but she won't..."

"She won't what?" Grace demanded.

"She won't wake up. At least, not right now," I added quickly as Grace's lip began to wobble. Several tears slipped their way down her cheeks, and she wiped them away angrily.

"Grace," said Jess, who was now in better control of her emotions. "She'll be all right. It's Lizzie, after all. She's too stubborn to give up." Jess wrapped an arm around her shoulders.

"I hope so," said Grace, her voice thick.

"Shouldn't you be over there helping?" Jess asked me.

"Dylan said he needed a moment to himself," I explained.

"And you listened?" Jess said,. "He's panicking. He obviously needs our help."

She and Grace limped over to Dylan. I didn't know how she knew he needed it, but as soon as Jess gave Dylan a hug, tears fell thickly down his cheeks.

"Do you think she will be OK?" he asked as he tried not to choke on his tears. I didn't know what to say. I was no doctor, but I knew when something was serious.

"I'm sure she'll be fine," I said, trying to sound confident.

"Thank God," Dylan said as he cradled her in his arms. "Thank God," he repeated. He knew as well as I did that Lizzie was not OK, but he needed someone to tell him things would turn out the way we wanted them to.

"What do we do?" Jess asked. "We can't sit here. A passing truck will see the wreck and come looking."

"Maybe the truck still works." I suggested, hopefully.

The others looked doubtfully at it. It was totally wrecked, but we had to try. Grace was injured, and Lizzie was unconscious. Getting out of here by truck was our best option. I wrenched my way into the driver's seat and reached for the keys. They were still in the ignition. I tried starting it, but there was no answering click from the motor.

Maybe I could fix it? I looked doubtfully at the mangled metal of the hood. I flicked the switch for the hood and got out of the car. With a little effort, I forced the hood up.

The radiator was dead, and the oil pipe spewed its contents onto the ground. Unsalvageable. We weren't going anywhere in this truck.

"We've got to get out of here," Dylan said. He was right. We had no option but to leave the truck.

"Yes," Jess agreed, "but how?"

"We call the CIA," I said. "They'll tell us what to do."

The others perked up at my suggestion.

"Maybe they'll even help us if they know what state we're in. They might help Lizzie," Grace said in a brighter tone.

"Where are the bags?" Dylan questioned.

We hunted the surrounding area for the bags. They were scattered across the hillside. I found them near the road and hauled them back to where Lizzie lay.

"Which one was the radio in?" Jess asked.

"Mine," Grace said. Her face was white as she tried to ignore the pain in her arm. "That one," she said, pointing.

I dropped to my knees, and Dylan and I dug eagerly into the pack. My fingers gripped the little black box, and I dragged it up. We stared at it in dismay. It had taken a beating when it was flung from the truck. Some of the plastic casing had come apart, and several wires were visible.

"Maybe it still works?" Jess said, her voice optimistic.

I turned it on with a shaking finger. There was no answering static. Only muted silence. I tapped it against the palm of my hand, trying to coax it into life.

"Levi, can't you fix it?" Grace said with panic filling her voice. "You fixed that truck..."

"This is different, Grace. I have no idea how this thing works," I said.

"No! No, no, no!" Grace said. Her face screwed up into pain, and she bawled.

I couldn't blame her. Lizzie was close to death, and now the radio was broken. And we had no way of contacting the CIA. Not only were we alone, but if we couldn't get in touch with the CIA, they couldn't help us free our families. I wrapped Grace in my arms. Eventually, she cried herself out, and we were all silent.

"Maybe we should go back?" Grace suggested.

I shook my head. We had come too far.

Dylan still had tears coming down his face. He wiped them on his shirt. "Lizzie would want us to keep going," he said, his voice quivering with emotion. "Maybe..." he stopped.

"What?" Jess asked.

"No, it's stupid," Dylan said.

"Just tell us," she insisted.

"I was going to say, maybe the CIA will find us. They know we're heading to Auckland to destroy the Skytower. Maybe if we carry on and continue with the mission..."

It was barely a hope.

"Yeah. Maybe," Jess agreed. None of us really believed that.

None, except Grace, who perked up a little. "You're right. They found us before, after Jennifer died. They're hopefully still keeping tabs on us. I bet they'll come and rescue us." She sounded convinced the CIA would come.

"Grace..."

"Come on," she said, "the CIA will catch up to us. In the meantime, we can't stay here."

Dylan shrugged. "You're right about not being able to stay here. And there's really only one thing to do," Dylan said. He bent to hoist Lizzie's limp body up onto his shoulder.

"Dylan, it's too far," I said skeptically.

Dylan simply shifted Lizzie's weight to be more comfortable and took a few steps forward. "Are you guys just going to stand there?"

"Are you sure?" I said to Dylan.

"What other choice do we have?"

I carried Grace's pack, Jess shouldered the other one, and we trudged forward. Dylan began to walk the way we were heading before the crash, his biceps taut and his shoulders bunched as he carried Lizzie's weight.

I kept my eye on Grace. She seemed OK, but I couldn't stop thinking about how I had nearly lost her again. She could've died and never known how I felt. I thought about the almost kiss —it had been on my mind a lot lately. I had wanted it badly, and

I would've gone through with it if I knew she wanted it too. But something held her back.

Maybe she was waiting for me to say something? Give words to my feelings like Jess said. I could run up to her right now and spill my soul. But it wasn't the right time. Especially now, with Lizzie out of action.

Grace looked over her shoulder at me like she knew I had my eyes on her back. Her tears hadn't stopped, and the cut on her head oozed slowly. I caught her eye and succeeded in getting her to smile. Neither of us said anything, though. We just kept moving.

She put on a brave face, I thought. And though she had voiced so much hope of the CIA saving us, I was sure she knew they wouldn't be coming to our rescue. Not this time.

WE PLODDED ON STEP after step. Ferny ponga trees dotted the hillsides, and wild gorse spread unabated across the farmland, their tiny yellow flowers peeking out in a sea of green. On some bigger farms, sheep still trotted through the paddocks, the occasional bleating breaking the silence. I wasn't even sure where we were going anymore, but some internal compass kept us on track. No one was willing to say 'stop' or suggest we take a break.

Finally, it was Dylan who caved. "I can't carry her one more step," he puffed. I helped him place Lizzie gently on the ground as we paused for a rest. "I can't see clearly," Dylan said as he blinked a few times and rubbed his head. "Fucking car crash," he yelled loudly at the rain.

Grace carefully examined the gash on Dylan's head. "Does it hurt?" she asked, frowning.

"Of course, it hurts. And I'm dizzy." He sighed as the rain came down harder.

"What have we done to deserve this?" Jess said, her face desperate as she looked skyward.

"I don't think the rain cares about our problems," I replied as I let the pack drop to the ground.

"I wasn't talking to the rain."

"She isn't going to wake up, is she?" Dylan said. He bent down and rechecked Lizzie's pulse for the billionth time.

"You never know," Grace said with a brave smile.

Dylan scowled at her.

"I'll carry Lizzie for a bit," I offered.

"I think that's a good idea," Dylan said as he stalked off down the road.

Grace reluctantly grabbed my pack and slung it over her shoulder. Jess helped me lift up Lizzie, and we all followed Dylan. Lizzie was heavier than she looked. My back and arms quickly tired, but I pushed through. There was no point in complaining. If Dylan could do it, so could I.

After an hour or so, Dylan and I swapped again. It was a long, slow process. Dylan and I would alternate carrying Lizzie. She was heavy, but we ignored our screaming muscles. As long as we made it to safety and Lizzie recovered, it would all be worth it.

Jess and Grace offered to help, but I knew they were just being nice. There was no way I would let Grace carry anything more than she had to with her broken arm. I was surprised to see her makeshift sling still intact, but she moved awkwardly with it and struggled under the weight of the pack. When she thought I wasn't looking, she couldn't hide how much her arm hurt her. But as soon as she caught my eye, she pushed the pain down and looked back at me with concern.

"I can see you're tired," she said, her dark eyes accusing me as we walked side by side. "Isn't there something I can do to help? Anything?"

"I'm not tired," I lied. "I'm absolutely fine."

"I don't believe you. You should let me help," Grace kept pressing.

"I'm perky as hell. Besides, Grace, you've got a broken wrist. There's no way you're carrying anything more than you need to," I said, challenging her gaze.

She glared stubbornly at me.

"No. There's no way you can carry Lizzie, and you know it."

She squished her dripping hair and flicked it over her shoulder before marching off to Jess.

Dylan came up to me. "Let me take over for you. You've been carrying her for ages."

"Thanks," I said. My back and shoulders were crippled with pain, and the relief was instantaneous as I passed Lizzie to Dylan. I snuck a look at Grace, who gave me an 'I knew you were lying look'. I ignored it.

In the distance, I heard the rumbling of a truck.

"Seriously?" I muttered. "Why can't we catch a break?" We scattered and faded into the tree line, each of us scurrying for the closest cover. Dylan had Lizzie and hid somewhere on the other side of the road from the rest of us. I heard his heavy feet crunch over twigs, the sound loud against the background patter of the rain hitting leaves. Then, all was quiet except for the low growl of the approaching truck.

It was a light operational vehicle in green camo. Vomit green, as my mom would have said. It had three giant wheels on each side and crawled along the road. Maybe it moved slowly because of the crappy weather, but to me, it looked like they were searching for something. Or someone. I guessed they had seen the crashed truck.

Keep on moving, I thought as the truck crept down the road.

The headlights inched closer, and the windshield wipers' rhythmic beat synchronized with the rain. I could make out the shadow of a face in the window, peering out into the rain. Instinctively, I drew back farther into the tree line, hoping the truck would continue its slow procession. But, to my horror, it pulled in at the rest stop a few meters away.

The door squeaked open, and a man jumped out, jogging over to the trees near me. His shiny black boots with brightly polished buckles sank deep into the soggy mud, and he fumbled with his fly. I knew what was coming. I cringed as the pungent smell of urine wafted toward me, steam rising into the crisp air. His belt clinked as he readjusted his pants and buckled up.

"We have time for a quick smoko," the man called to his companion.

"I don't smoke, and it's raining," another soldier said from the truck.

The first man made a derisive noise. "As you please, Corporal."

I peered through the scrubby branches and watched the man hunch over to protect his lighter from the wind and rain. He flicked the lighter a few times and cursed as it failed to ignite. "Piece of shit," he muttered and shuffled closer to the shelter of the trees I hid behind. I drew farther back, hoping he wouldn't hear the scuffing of the leaves under my feet. The man grunted in satisfaction as the cigarette lit. A curl of smoke rose towards the canopy of trees.

How long was he going to stay here?

It took ten minutes—or maybe it was only five, but it felt like forever—before he let the butt of the cigarette drop to the forest floor. He ground it into the mud with the heel of his boot and let out a hacking cough. He was about to leave when the static of a radio sounded from his pocket.

"Harrison, you there?"

Harrison drew out his radio. "Copy," Harrison answered.

"Colonel Scott's been shot. They're taking him to zone twenty. They want you to report in. You're supposed to take over his assignment."

Harrison grunted. "Got shot, did he? Serves him right. He was always too soft for my liking."

"He has the Prime Minister's backing," the voice on the radio said.

"Marion's an idiot to trust him," Harrison commented.

There was a pause of static, and for a moment, I thought the connection had dropped. But the other man spoke again, "The

Colonel keeps his word. That's more than you can say for some."

Harrison grunted again. "We're still a way off. Be there in another hour or so."

"Better make that half, if you can manage it. We found a rebel trying to loot the barracks. Scrounging for food." The radio crackled as the man laughed. "Thought he was being smart, but he didn't make it far. We need you to sign off on him."

Harrison sighed. "We'll do our best," he said. He turned off the radio without saying goodbye and stuffed it into his pocket.

"You still hiding in the dry?" Harrison called to the corporal. "We have new orders."

He strode back to the truck. A moment later, the truck door slammed, and they sped away. I waited until the sound of the engine faded into the distance before crossing the road to help Dylan. Jess and Grace weren't far behind.

I found Dylan struggling to lift Lizzie into his arms. He gave me a grunt of thanks when I helped to lift her off the ground. "Are you OK?" Dylan asked. "That soldier must have been close to you."

"I'm fine. Guess I was lucky," I said.

"I was so worried," Grace said, looking at me with teary eyes. "From where I was, it looked like the soldier was almost on top of you."

"Like I said, I was lucky."

We staggered out of the wiry scrub and headed back up the road. Time dragged on, and Lizzie didn't stir. Our anxiety grew with every passing hour.

The hills gave way to flat plains and we knew we were close to Auckland when the freeway came into view. Now there was nowhere to hide, and all we could do was pray we wouldn't be seen.

We were all hurting. Grace whimpered each time she moved her arm. Dylan complained about his blurry vision, but he was too stubborn to stop for a break. Jess moaned about the purpling bruises that had begun to sprout over her stomach. There was nothing any of us could do about it. We had to push on until we reached safety.

As we walked, my thoughts drifted, and I started thinking about my dad. Like every time I thought of him since this war started, I wondered where he was now. Whose side was he on? If he was still alive, he was probably one of them. One of those soldiers. As much as I wanted to believe he was one of the good guys, it was easy to picture him behind the barrel of a rifle, gunning down an innocent civilian. It wasn't a big stretch to make—Dad was never 'father of the year'. More than once, he'd smacked me around in the name of discipline. But for some reason, I couldn't bring myself to fully believe he'd picked the wrong side in this war. For all his faults, I still hoped there was some good in him. Somewhere.

Dad always made a big deal about being the big protector and staying strong for the ones he loved. Mom used to say he must have been talking about his other family. His army one. Because he sure as hell wasn't talking about us. But as much as we scorned him for it, part of what he preached rang true.

I watched Grace struggle ahead of me. I would do anything to keep her safe. I carried Lizzie's motionless form. I was already doing everything I could to save her.

Perhaps this war would let Dad and I see eye to eye for once. I'd never been good enough for him, but maybe, finally, he would be proud of me. I looked down at Lizzie's blank face and then over to Grace's pained body. I was protecting those I cared about. I knew that much. And everything was going to work out OK.

Chapter Twelve

Dylan

Night had fallen by the time we finally made it to a settlement. Jess circled the house—a cursory check before I shattered the window to gain entry. Levi marched straight down the hall to the first bedroom he could find and laid Lizzie down. I followed and fell to my knees beside the bed. I desperately wanted to see Lizzie's determined gray eyes stare me down like they always did, but they remained closed. I put my ear to her mouth and felt the rise and fall of her breath against my cheek. She was still alive… for now.

"She'll be all right," Levi said and put a hand on my shoulder.

"This is all my fault." My stomach had been roiling with guilt ever since the crash.

"Don't think like that. We were all tired, and the weather was terrible. It was an accident," Levi said.

I wasn't convinced. "I crashed the truck…" My shoulders sagged.

"It wasn't your fault… I distracted you," Jess argued. Her face was flushed pink, and I could tell she was trying to hold back tears.

"It was an accident," Levi said again with finality.

Grace sat down on the other twin bed in the room and cried. Jess took a deep breath and forced away her own tears. "Grace," Jess said as she sat beside Grace and started rubbing her back. "It's going to be OK. Levi said she'll be all right."

I could tell Jess didn't really believe that either. Her green eyes roved upward, and her lips moved in a brief prayer to the heavens.

"We need something to eat," Levi said, taking command of the situation. "Jess, why don't you come and help me in the kitchen?" Jess nodded, dragging her pack laden with food and clothes with her as she exited after Levi.

Grace and I were left alone with Lizzie.

Grace hiccuped and wiped her tears away with one arm. She stood, walked over to Lizzie and me, and gently touched Lizzie's cheek. "Lizzie? We're going to look after you, so don't worry," Grace said, sniffling.

"She'd hate that," I said with a hollow laugh. "She hates to be looked after by anyone."

"I know. But that's why she needs to be. She might say she doesn't need you and act strong, but I've known Lizzie for a long time."

"Tell me something about her," I said. My heart ached to the point where it was almost a physical pain. It felt too big for my body as it beat against my lungs, forcing me to take shallow breaths. Lizzie would have said that was ridiculous, and it was all in my head.

"What do you want to know?" Grace asked. She sat on the ground beside Lizzie's bed and cradled her broken arm with her other hand.

I shrugged. "Anything."

"Before… before my family died, I was one of Lizzie's only close friends," Grace said. "She was bullied a bit as a kid because she was quiet and small. Some people thought she was weird. She grew out of that eventually, but she doesn't let people get close to her easily."

"Lizzie used to be quiet?" I said disbelievingly.

Grace laughed a little. The laugh sounded forced. "That's the thing. I think half the time she feels like no one's listening to her, and deep down, she's still that quiet little kid who can't make her voice heard."

I smiled and looked at Lizzie with tears forming in my own eyes. "There's no danger of that anymore."

Grace nodded with her eyes distant, still in the past. "I used to be the one who'd look out for her. She hated Jaden and me fighting her battles. But she was always her own person, you know? She never tried to be anyone else. Eventually, as everyone grew up, they started thinking she was cool because of that. And then... my family died."

Grace paused and took a deep breath. I remembered Levi telling me Grace hated to talk about her past. I thought Grace had finished her story, but she continued: "Lizzie was always there for Mom and me. She was at my house every day, helping with the washing... the cleaning... she went out and bought groceries for us when we were both too upset to make it to the store. I'd always looked out for her. But after that... she started looking out for me."

"I never knew that about her," I said. For everything I knew about Lizzie, I hadn't known who she had been before the war. It surprised me to learn she hadn't always been strong and opinionated. I took it for granted, but we all had a past.

I looked at Lizzie, and maybe for the first time, I truly saw her. Her heart-shaped face was untroubled by frown lines, and her skin pale and soft. The moon peeked through the blinds and lit her face. Dark streaks of blood through her blond hair were the only sign anything was wrong—she looked like she could be sleeping.

I thought back to when she got into the back of the truck. I shouldn't have let her. Just like I shouldn't have let her help me with the hijacking. She had been angry at herself, but she should have been furious with me instead. I was supposed to look after her, and here we were at her bedside. I didn't know whether she'd survive this.

Grace's eyes were bloodshot from crying, but she stared at me with sympathy. "Lizzie really likes you," Grace said eventually.

I shrugged. "She's never said anything."

"She said so to me back in the truck. And she's talked to me about it before." Grace turned her gaze back to Lizzie. Her lip wobbled, and she bit down to steady it before she said, "She was mad at herself for screwing everything up back there. She wanted to impress you."

The hollow feeling inside me filled up again with guilt. "She didn't need to do that."

"Of course, she didn't. But it's Lizzie we're talking about. You couldn't stop her if you tried," Grace said with another sidelong glance at me.

"Hey, food's ready," Jess said as she peeked back into the room.

"I'm coming," Grace said. She wiped away the last of her tears and walked out of the room.

"Are you coming, Dylan?" Jess asked.

"In a bit," I lied. I couldn't leave Lizzie alone—what if something happened?

"OK… well… the food's there when you want it," Jess said and left the room.

I was alone with Lizzie. With everyone gone, I let my emotions tumble out of me and sat beside her, silently crying.

Get a grip, Dylan. I could imagine Lizzie saying that to me and could almost see her rolling her eyes.

"Yeah, you're probably right," I said aloud to her. Too sensitive as always. "But, Lizzie, I don't think I can go through this war without you." My voice was barely a whisper. "Please, you can't die. Not after everything we've been through together. I haven't had a chance to tell you… how… how I really feel."

How did I feel about her? I knew I liked Lizzie, a lot, and

sometimes I wondered if it was more than that. Is it possible to fall in love with someone without them knowing? In the past, I would have said, no, it's not. That's not true love, only an infatuation. Recently, I was beginning to think that was wrong. I didn't know Lizzie before the war. But I knew her now—all her insecurities and flaws. And she knew mine. Christ, she probably knew mine better than she knew her own. She never judged me for them. She accepted them as a part of who I was.

"Besides… Grace needs you, too," I continued. "I think Grace would go crazy if you died. She's strong, but there's only so much one person can take."

Lizzie just lay there. Still. Motionless. Could she hear me? I remembered some movie I'd watched where they said people in a coma can still hear you.

"And, Levi and Jess would never be the same either. Who will tell us what to do if you aren't there? You're always the one who gives us a kick in the pants and reminds us we still have something to live for. You never give up… don't you fucking give up on me now."

Tears stormed down my face again, and I angrily wiped them away.

Don't you get it, Dylan? The Lizzie in my mind sounded exasperated. *If I die, then you can't fall apart. You have to do what we set out to do. The world doesn't care what happens to you, but I do. You have to make them see you.*

Grace had been right. All Lizzie had ever wanted was to be seen. To be heard.

"You're not invisible to me," I told her, my voice hoarse. I reached out and touched her face, dragging a finger across her soft cheek.

I didn't know how long I stayed there with her. At some point, Jess came back, and together we peeled off Lizzie's wet clothes and dressed her in warm, clean ones. Then, when Jess was gone, I lay down beside Lizzie and put an arm across her body, feeling comforted by the smell of her, and her soft breaths rising and falling under my arm. Her warmth meant the world to me. It meant she was still here. While she was still warm and breathing, there was still hope.

My head hurt from the crash, and my face was hot and puffy from crying, but I couldn't turn the waterworks off. I'd never cried this much before. My dad had taught me to be a tough kiwi bloke.

Once, at the university pub, some support group held an info night about depression. At the end of it, they passed out a bunch of pamphlets. There was even a little pin that read, '*Are you OK?*' My mates and I had made fun of it, and I'd tossed them in the garbage. I didn't need them. Not then, anyway. It was only now I was realizing what they'd been trying to tell me: I couldn't keep holding it all in. There wasn't any room.

I WOKE UP HOURS later, and dimly took in my surroundings. The sun was beginning to seep through the cracks in the blinds, falling across Lizzie's motionless body. It was dawn. Grace slept in the twin bed on the far side of the room. My head throbbed even worse, but I forced myself up, hoping things had changed for the better overnight. A gentle shake of Lizzie's shoulder was enough to tell me otherwise. Still no change.

"Hey," Levi whispered as he entered the room. "How's she doing?"

"She still won't wake up," I said. It had been almost twenty-four hours now.

"I can keep an eye on her for a bit if you want to go get something to eat," Levi said.

"I'd rather stay," I croaked. My throat was dry—it had been hours since I had last drunk any water or eaten any food. I realized I hadn't taken a piss for hours. My bladder was uncomfortably full, reminding me I was only human.

"Sitting here with her isn't going to make her wake up any sooner. You've got to look after yourself."

"But—"

"Seriously. I'll let you know if anything happens," Levi said, putting a hand across my shoulder.

"Who's on guard duty?" I asked.

"I've left Jess out there. She's keeping watch."

"Oh… thanks, Levi."

"It's no problem," Levi said. I took one last look at Lizzie before exiting the room.

After relieving myself, I found our meagre stash of food piled on the countertop in the kitchen. I grabbed some crackers, barely tasting them as I wolfed them down. I saw Jess curled in an armchair in the front living room. She stared out at the road with one of the AKs the Americans gave us lying across her lap.

"Jess, do you want anything?" I asked her.

"No. I ate half an hour ago," she said.

"How long have you been up?" I questioned her.

She shrugged. "I took over watch duty from Levi at around four a.m."

"Right," I said. "Do you need me to take over at all?" I didn't want to. I wanted to get back to Lizzie's bedside in case she needed me. But it seemed polite to ask.

Jess looked at me and smiled. "No, it's OK. I know you want to be with Lizzie."

I nodded and turned around before walking back into the bedroom. Grace was awake, and she and Levi were whispering to each other.

"Has there been any change?" I asked. Grace shook her head sadly at me.

"I want to wash her hair and change the bandage," I said. "Maybe it will help if we can see exactly how bad it is."

"I don't think there's anything we can do," Grace said softly.

"At the very least, we can give her some dignity," I said. Levi nodded. He walked away, and a few minutes later, he returned with some water, a bar of soap, and a towel. I slowly unwrapped the ragged t-shirt we had tied around her head the day before. Her skin was hot… too hot. There was a flush on her pale cheeks that hadn't been there the night before.

"She's burning up," I said.

Levi touched Lizzie's forehead and drew his hand away quickly. "Yeah, you're right. What do we do?"

Grace propped herself up against the headboard of the other twin bed, sucking air in sharply through her clenched teeth as her arm jostled in its makeshift sling. "She needs antibiotics."

"But there's no way we can get hold of antibiotics," Levi said hopelessly. He was right. Then I remembered what Lizzie had said last time about raiding a pharmacy.

"We're getting some," I said resolutely. "There has to be a pharmacy or something around here. Even some of that antibiotic ointment would be better than nothing."

I grabbed the towel and dipped one end of it in the water, and started gently trying to clean the blood from Lizzie's hair. The cool water quickly warmed against her flushed skin. I pulled the covers away from her body. "Her whole body is burning," I said. I soaked the entire towel in the cold water and lay it against her skin.

Suddenly, Lizzie thrashed against me, crying out in her sleep.

"She's waking up!" I said. But she continued to moan and thrash, and then, finally, she was still again. Her breathing seemed shallower than usual. I couldn't tell if this new sign was better or worse.

Levi and Grace looked on with scared faces.

Jess came running into the room. "Is she…?"

"She isn't awake. She was only thrashing in her sleep," I said, deflated.

"Oh. That has to be a sign of improvement, surely?" Jess asked.

I shrugged. I was on the verge of crying again.

"She has a fever. We think her cut must be infected," Grace explained to Jess.

Jess collapsed on the bed beside Grace with her face in her hands.

"We need to get her antibiotics," I said again. "Sooner rather than later." I didn't want to leave her, but I knew antibiotics might be her only hope.

"I'll go with you," Levi said quietly.

I shook my head. "What if the soldiers come?"

"I'll look after her," Jess said as she took her face out of her hands. "I can do it. I'm ready for this. I won't let you down. And Grace is here, too," she said, looking at me with fresh determination.

"We need to try and get her to drink something," I said.

"How?" Levi asked. "We can't exactly force it down her throat."

"If she doesn't drink something soon, she'll die from dehydration. Especially with a fever that bad," I said.

"I'll try my best. You and Levi go," Jess said. "…And, bring back some pain relief, too, if you can. For Grace."

"Yeah, that would help a lot," Grace agreed.

Levi walked over to a cupboard in the hall and grabbed a couple of guns, tossing a rifle to me and a pistol to Grace. He gave Grace a tender hug before he crossed the room and rested a sympathetic hand on my shoulder. "Come on, the sooner we get this done, the better," Levi said.

But I wasn't ready to leave. Not yet. I tucked Lizzie's wet blond hair behind her head. Reaching forward, I touched my fingers to her flushed cheek and clenched my jaw to stop myself from crying. I walked out without saying a word.

LEVI AND I CREPT through the empty streets. It was rare that we risked going out in daylight, but this time, we made an exception to our rule. If we waited until dark, by the time we got back, a whole day would have passed. I wasn't sure if we could afford to wait that long.

For once, it wasn't raining. It had been a wet summer, but this was how it always was in New Zealand. The weather had an agenda of its own. Today I would have preferred rain. The sun was beating down, and we ran through the streets in plain sight. We were somewhere in the outskirts of Auckland, and I wasn't as familiar with these streets as I was in the city center.

"Where are we? And what way do we go?" Levi puffed as we ran.

"I think we're in Manukau. And I don't really know where to go," I answered. We paused behind a house. "But we have to get closer to Manukau's town center. They'll have a pharmacy there somewhere."

"All I remember about Manukau is stopping at the mall on the way to the airport," Levi muttered.

"We can't go to the mall," I said. We both knew the mall was dangerous. Even if it wasn't a prison camp like the mall in Tauranga, it was bound to be heavily guarded, as it was a bright beacon for rebel groups like ours. Anyone who'd ever gone hunting knew the best way to find your prey was to lie in wait at the biggest food source. We'd already made that mistake once before, and we weren't about to make it again.

We followed our noses out to the main road and headed down it.

"This is a bad idea," Levi said nervously.

I was shitting myself too.

The road sprawled out in front of us, long and straight, stretching into eternity. Heat waves shimmered above it, and our shoes stuck against melted patches of black tar. On the fringes, palm trees were spaced about every fifty meters, but neither they nor the spindly lampposts offered any cover. Like Tauranga, it was now a ghost town. But I couldn't shake the feeling that there were eyes following us.

"I don't like this," Levi whispered, his gun held at the ready. "It's not good being in the open. Let's get closer to those houses." He nodded towards the dingy bungalows set back from the main road. An old gas station was set between the houses, a sign still showing the most recent fuel price: two dollars ten for the cheapest grade. The dusty windows of the station were pinned with faded adverts inviting people to the on-site cafe.

No sooner had we left the road, a low grumbling sent us fleeing for cover. We ran to the forecourt of the gas station. An army convoy trundled down the road, one truck after another. I was sweating heavily and tried to quiet my ragged breathing as I stood hidden behind a gas pump. Once they'd gone, we waited a few minutes and then set off again. The landscape was slowly changing from quiet rundown bungalows into shop fronts.

"There," Levi said, pointing. It was an old doctor's practice with an adjoined pharmacy. We ran to the building. The doctor's office had been broken into, and we pulled ourselves through the broken window, careful to avoid the shards of glass sticking out from the ledge. We were in the waiting room. Sunlight touched a faded red-upholstered chair as it sat behind an old wooden reception desk near the front entrance. Patient files were stored behind the desk in plain sight.

Levi walked over to the door leading to the pharmacy and tugged. "It's locked." He readied himself to lurch at the door.

"Wait…" I whispered to him. "Do you think the pharmacy alarm runs on batteries?"

"I don't know," Levi said.

We both stared apprehensively at the door.

"Let's look around here first and see if we can find anything. You keep watch, and I'll go see," I said. Levi nodded, and I moved off to look through the different exam rooms. I opened all the drawers in the room, but there was no medication in sight. I moved on. Then I found the plaster room, and I paused. Would we be able to plaster Grace's arm? I didn't know how, but maybe one of the others did. I looked suspiciously at dozens of packets of something that looked like plaster bandages before shoving a few of them into my bag. It couldn't hurt. I grabbed some soft rolls and a proper sling for good measure. Finally, I stuffed plenty of crepe bandages and a bunch of medical-grade Band-Aids into my pack. Maybe they would help with Lizzie's head wound. I met Levi back in the waiting room.

"Did you get any?" Levi asked. He was still nervously pointing his gun out into the street.

"I got some bandages and things, but there weren't any meds."

"What do we do?"

We looked again at the pharmacy door. "We throw a brick into the place, and if an alarm goes off, we run," I said with a shrug. It was the only way. We climbed out of the window again, and I hunted out a rock big enough for the job.

"Ready?" I asked as we hid behind a parked car on the street. Levi nodded, his muscles tense and ready to spring into action. I hurled the rock through the window. The loud crash was followed by a thump as it bounced across the pharmacy floor. We waited. There was no resulting wail from the alarm, so we ran forward. I put my arm through the hole made by the rock and opened the door from the inside. We were in.

"It'll be kept somewhere behind the counter," I whispered as we ducked behind several shelves displaying a variety of cosmetics.

We made it to the counter at the back of the shop and continued toward a small door. I opened it, and we stood with our mouths agape. There were thousands of medications, all listed from A-Z along the wall, stacked from ceiling to floor.

"Jackpot," Levi said.

"How do we know which is the right one?" I asked.

Levi shrugged. It was Lizzie who was usually good at this kind of thing. "Last time I needed antibiotics they gave me amoxicillin, I think. But, I can't really remember."

This was sounding more and more impossible. Then I spotted a book on a nearby shelf and grabbed it. It was some sort of drug reference book, and I looked up amoxicillin. "Dosage… 500mg every eight hours," I read aloud. Levi grabbed a couple of boxes and tossed them in the small rucksack I had on my back. "Oh… but does she have any allergies?" I asked as I continued reading down the page.

"I don't know," Levi said, "Grace might, though."

"What if she does? Then we've come all this way for nothing," I said. Levi grabbed the manual I was looking at and flipped through it.

"Maybe we should get two types. And then Grace can choose between the two if she knows anything about Lizzie's allergies. Here… what about this one. Gentamicin. It says here you can use it for septic infections."

"It's also for use by injection," I said doubtfully as I peered over Levi's shoulder.

"That might actually be a good thing," Levi said. "I don't know how we can get her to swallow tablets if she won't wake up."

"But we don't know how to give an injection!" I said, raising my voice. "No. We can't take that risk."

"Look… all we do is grab some syringes and needles, and we follow the guidelines in this book," Levi said, tapping the front cover. "It's simple. It's more of a risk not to give her anything." Levi walked over to the shelf and grabbed the gentamicin.

"OK. But only because I can't work out any other way to do it," I muttered. "Keep the amoxicillin. It might come in handy sometime."

"What do we get for Grace?" Levi asked.

We hunted around and found some tramadol. I remembered my aunt taking them after she had her gallbladder removed to help with the pain. We shoved the tablets in my bag along with the book. Levi found the syringes and needles in the storeroom.

So far, it had been quiet.

As we were about to leave, a shadow blotted out the midday sun. I instinctively pulled Levi behind the counter. We ducked low.

"I don't remember this shop being broken into yesterday," a soldier said, his voice drifting into the shop through the broken door pane.

"Probably happened last night. Some rebel group patching up

their battle wounds," another soldier replied.

"Should we check it out?" the first soldier asked.

The other one shrugged and looked at his watch. "Might as well poke about a bit. We've got time before the convoy leaves."

I cursed silently. We needed to get out of here. "This way," I mouthed at Levi.

Keeping low, we crouched around the aisles, using the display shelves for cover. To our right was the door to the doctor's office. From this side of the door, I could see the lock had a thumb-turn on the doorknob. I reached out slowly and turned the knob. The lock sprung back with a faint click, and I creaked it open as the soldiers entered the store through the front door. Levi and I crept into the doctor's office and shut the door quietly behind us.

"Let's go," Levi whispered.

I didn't need to be told twice. We pulled ourselves through the hole in the window and ran down the road, not daring to look back.

IT WAS MID-AFTERNOON by the time we reached our hideout, and we banged on the door.

"It's us," I said as I heard Jess cocking a gun from the other side. She opened the door, and we followed her in. She closed the door behind us, slamming home the bolt.

"Did you get the meds?" she asked as we attempted to catch our breaths.

"Yeah. How is she?" I asked as Grace came out to meet us.

"You're back," Grace said and fell into Levi's arms. "I was so scared you might have been caught."

"How's Lizzie?" I asked again, more urgently.

"She's... still alive. She woke up, kind of. She didn't really know where she was, though, or what was happening. She's pretty out of it," Jess said.

I ran into the bedroom and looked toward the bed. Lizzie's breathing was fast and shallow, the covers crumpled all around her. She'd twisted awkwardly onto her side, and her top had slid up halfway up her torso. I didn't know much about these sorts of things, but she didn't look like she was getting any better. Definitely worse.

"Grace, do you know if she has any allergies?" I asked.

"No… I don't think so…" Grace said unsurely.

I threw down my rucksack and shoved the book in Grace's direction while I grabbed the syringes and needles. "Are you any good at math?"

"Yes…" Grace said uncertainly.

"Look up gentamicin and tell me how much I'm supposed to be giving."

Grace flicked to the page and stared at it for a while. I watched her whisper to herself as she worked through the calculation.

"She's got to have 1.25 mL three times a day," Grace said finally. I joined a syringe and needle together and uncapped the syringe while Levi broke the glass vial. I shakily drew the liquid into the syringe. I held the injection up and then looked nervously at everyone else.

"In the arm?" I said. Suddenly, I wasn't so sure I could do this. But I didn't have a choice. I looked at Lizzie, and I knew there was no way I could live without her.

"It says intramuscular… so I guess the upper arm is fine. Is that needle the right one?" Grace asked. She bit her lip in anticipation. The needle looked long enough. I hoped it would be OK.

"Just aim and shoot," Levi advised. I took a breath and jabbed the needle into Lizzie's arm.

Lizzie woke up with a howl, but I'd already pushed the plunger. I pulled the needle out and tossed it to the side.

"Hey, Lizzie, shhh, it's all right," I said, cradling her in my arms. She thrashed against me, and her body was covered in damp sweat. But I didn't care. She wasn't lucid, and she screamed and cried. Finally, she was silent, and her body slumped back against the bed, spent. I sat there with her, still gripping her hand. The others left one by one until Lizzie and I were alone.

"Lizzie, you've got to get better," I said. "I don't just want you to get better. I need you to." My hand stroked her clammy cheek, and I bent and kissed her forehead.

I thought about the last few days and all that had happened. All I wanted to do was hit the rewind button. I wanted to rewind all the way back to before the war. Before I'd even met her. I didn't care if we never met, I just wanted her to be OK and live her life without all this horror. If I could do that for her, I would.

I would do anything.

That realization bowled into me with the strength of a wrecking ball, and then I knew without a doubt. This was love.

Chapter Thirteen

Lizzie

Darkness. The familiar comfort of my living room surrounded me. The curtains were pulled to block out the midday sun, and I stretched out across the sofa, my feet on the armrest. Mum hated me doing that, but that never stopped me. I pointed the remote at the TV as I surfed aimlessly from channel to channel.

"Lizzie. Lizzie."

My eyes left the TV and focused on Jaden. He was crouched beside me, shaking my shoulder. "What?" I mumbled, annoyed.

"Shove over," Jaden said. Unwillingly, I moved my legs and pushed myself upright. Jaden collapsed onto the couch next to me, wax clinging to his mousy-brown hair and slicking his fringe back from his face. His deep blue eyes were serious. "Mom says you need to go back."

"Go back where?" I asked, rolling my eyes. "School doesn't start for another week, Jay."

"Just… back. You don't belong here."

I ignored him and brought my focus back to the TV. I flipped through the channels, but the remote stopped working, stuck on this one scene. Buildings smoked, and fires ravaged through towns. Then it cut to the tranquil bush, but soldiers broke the peace, stomping through the undergrowth while people screamed out of sight of the camera.

"Jay… I don't understand…" I kept pressing the buttons on the remote. But the screen kept rolling. Now a group of teenagers were crying as they huddled together over a body lying motionless in a dark, unfamiliar room.

"You have to go back!" Jaden yelled. He pointed to the TV and grabbed my arm forcefully.

"Jay, no! You're hurting me," I yelled back with tears in my eyes. Jaden's nails jabbed painfully into my upper arm.

"You think this hurts? I'll show you what hurts, Lizzie!" Jaden pulled up his shirt and pointed dramatically at his chest. It had been flayed open, his ribcage shattered. Blood pulsed from his heart and oozed onto the floor at his feet. "It fucking hurts, Lizzie!"

I couldn't look. I closed my eyes and drew back into the soft couch. Jaden pulled me to my feet and shoved me hard. I grabbed at him as I fell toward the TV, but my hands clutched at thin air. I braced for impact and screamed as I hit my head. Then there was only pain. Hot, white pain.

My hand connected with something, and I opened my eyes in confusion.

"Lizzie, stop! Christ, can I have some help here," Dylan yelled. Dylan brought his face close to mine, his blue eyes full of concern. His lip was bleeding from a fresh cut.

"Lizzie, it's OK. Relax, I'm here, all right?" He licked the blood away from his lip.

"What… what's going on?" I muttered.

Dylan exchanged a look with Grace as the others stormed into the room.

"You had a nightmare," Dylan said. "Do you know where you are?"

I shook my head. The pain was still at the back of my head,

and my hand flew to the source. A bandage was wrapped tightly around it.

"This is the first time she's said anything that makes any sense," Grace said with a hopeful gleam in her eyes.

"What happened?" I asked again, but even as I did, fragments of my memory came flying back to me.

"How much do you remember?" Dylan asked, fretful.

"I remember the truck… tires suddenly squealing…"

"I crashed the truck," Dylan said shakily.

"It wasn't his fault," Levi said, with a sharp look at Dylan. It seemed like they'd argued about this before.

"I'm going to get you something to eat and drink," Jess said abruptly, and turned around to leave. She paused in the doorway with her back to us, and I saw her shoulders shake. She steadied herself against the frame before she marched off down the hallway.

"I should get back to guard duty," Levi said. He walked unsurely over to me and then patted me awkwardly on the back. "I'm glad you're feeling better, Lizzie."

Grace got up off the other bed and started walking out after Levi. She didn't say anything but just cradled her arm in a sling —I presumed she must have hurt her arm in the crash.

"Grace, wait," I said. She turned at the doorway, and tears were shimmering in her eyes.

"I'm really happy you're awake, Lizzie," she said with a catch in her voice, "but you need to rest right now, OK?"

"Come here," I said with a smile. Grace came and sat lightly on my bed beside Dylan. I took the hand that wasn't in a sling and squeezed it. "It's not like I was dying."

Dylan and Grace exchanged another look with each other.

"Was I?" I said uncertainly.

"You were pretty bad," Dylan said quietly.

"Whatever the case, I promise I won't scare you like that again, OK?"

Grace rewarded me with a weak smile. "You'd better not."

"Cross my heart."

Grace hugged me and then broke down into sobs. "I'm sorry, I'll be OK. It's j-j-just been s-s-so hard without you," she cried. She wiped the tears from her face, and I looked at her in concern. She took several deep breaths to get a hold of herself.

"Are you sure you're OK?" I said.

"Yes. Really, I'm fine," she added as I scrutinized her face. She gave me a pained smile and looked at Dylan. "I'm pretty sure Dylan wants his chance to talk to you," she said thickly and stood.

"I'm sure he doesn't mind," I said, looking at Dylan.

"No... I need to go help Levi anyway," Grace said. "We can talk later when you're feeling stronger."

Now she mentioned it, I was still pretty tired. "OK," I relented. Grace walked out, and I was left alone with Dylan. He stared at me with an expression I couldn't quite place.

"What did Grace mean?" I asked him.

Dylan's face went red. "I have no idea." He wouldn't meet my gaze.

"Whatever it is, you know you can tell me, right?"

"Lizzie," Dylan said and turned his gaze to meet mine. Dylan had changed. His face was charged with an intensity I hadn't seen there before. "Whatever I have to say can wait. You've been in and out of consciousness for nearly a week. You need to regain your strength."

"A week?" I said disbelievingly. "It's been that long?"

"Yeah. As I said, you were pretty bad."

Jess entered with some food and water, and Dylan helped me into a sitting position. A wave of nausea hit me. He helped me to drink some water, and I picked at the food Jess had brought, trying my best to eat as much as I could. I finished eating and lay back on the pillows, exhausted.

"I'll leave you to rest," Dylan said. He got up to leave.

"No, don't," I said. My stomach lurched in fear. What if I didn't wake up again? I remembered the nightmare I had, and suddenly it seemed too real.

"All right, I'll stay until you're asleep," Dylan offered.

I turned onto my side and tried to get comfortable. Dylan lay down next to me. He had puffy bags under his eyes, and rough stubble was growing around his mouth. He was asleep before I was. In his sleep, his face lost some of its fear, and he looked boyishly young. Subconsciously, he flung his arm over me and loosely hugged me to him. I wasn't sure what to do. Should I move? Or wake him? Eventually, I closed my eyes. His arm was solid and comforting, reminding me I was here. Alive. I let sleep overtake me and allowed Dylan to ward away my nightmares.

I WOKE SEVERAL TIMES throughout the day, and Grace filled me in on everything that had happened. In the afternoon, I gave myself another shot of the antibiotics Dylan and Levi had taken from the pharmacy, but I went to sleep again soon after. I didn't have much energy, and everything was an effort.

Now though, for the first time all day, my brain was fully awake. It was dark, and Grace was sleeping on the other bed, her breath quiet and steady.

Faint moonlight streamed in through the flimsy blinds. I lay there, thinking about it all. If it weren't for the crash, we would be initiating the first steps of our plan. Did we really want to go through with it? The CIA's plan was dangerous. Did it make sense to throw ourselves back into another terrifying fight after such a close brush with death? All the same, I didn't want it all to be for nothing. I wanted to strike the soldiers so hard they wouldn't know what hit them when it came. I wanted revenge for all I had lost and everything I would never have again.

I rolled over onto my stomach. My head wasn't feeling so bad, and I was possessed with the urge to get up and take stock of my injuries. I pulled back the covers and quietly, so as not to wake Grace, pushed myself to my feet. As soon as I did, I nearly wished I hadn't. I stood up too quickly and was so dizzy I almost fell back down onto the bed. I leaned my weight against the wall, feeling blackness cloud my eyes and waiting for the blood to come back to my head again. My sight returned, and I felt stronger once the dizziness had passed. My head throbbed more once I was standing, and there was a persistent pulsing pressure behind my left eye. I took a breath and ignored it. It was only a headache. It would pass.

I made my way out into the hallway and carefully began exploring the rooms. The next was also a bedroom, and I could see Jess curled up in a large double bed. Farther on down the hall, candlelight flickered, and I could hear Dylan and Levi talking in hushed voices to one another in the lounge.

I was torn between wanting to join them and crossing to the bathroom opposite the bedroom Jess was sleeping in. I would have liked some company, but I knew Dylan would send me back to bed to get more rest. As if I hadn't had enough rest in the last week. So I crossed to the bathroom.

There was a well-placed torch on the cistern of the toilet. I took it and flicked it on, staring at myself in the mirror. It was true, I had looked better. My hair looked greasy and unkempt from spending so long in a bed, and my face was unusually sallow and sickly. Unlike Grace's healthy glowing skin, I never had much color, but even for me, this was pale.

Carefully, I unwrapped the bandage and grabbed a handheld mirror from inside the medicine cabinet. I took a breath, preparing myself for the worst, and angled the two mirrors to get a good look at it. The bump was raised and an angry-looking red, but it wasn't as bad as I had expected. The wound was clean and even coming together at the edges, already mending. But if what the others had said was true, I was lucky. If Levi and Dylan hadn't risked getting those antibiotics, I might be dead now. I owed them big time, and I wasn't sure how I felt about that. I wanted to show Dylan I was strong. He could count on me. And as always, he ended up saving my life.

I reapplied the bandage to my head and clicked off the torch, placing it back on the cistern. I entered the hallway and headed to the lounge, where Levi and Dylan were still talking. They stopped abruptly when I entered the room.

"Lizzie, are you sure you're well enough to be up?" Dylan said.

"Definitely. If I thought I wasn't up to it, I would have stayed where I was," I replied defensively.

"I really think you should go back to bed," Dylan said kindly, with a warm smile.

"I'm fine," I said, standing straight and tall all on my own to prove I was healthy enough to join them.

Dylan sighed and rubbed his eyes. "OK, if you're sure, I guess." He was too tired to be bothered arguing.

I squeezed in between the two of them on the sofa. "What were you talking about?"

"We were saying, as soon as you're feeling OK, we should move from here and begin our mission," Levi replied. It seemed I wasn't the only one thinking about the crazy stunt we were about to perform.

"I thought you might have forgotten about our plan, considering the circumstances," I said as I leaned against the comfy cushions. "In fact, I'm surprised you guys didn't call the CIA and call it off already."

"Yeah, well… we tried," Levi said uncomfortably.

"I thought Grace said she filled you in," Dylan muttered.

I looked from Levi to Dylan, urging them to tell the truth.

"The radio broke in the crash," Dylan admitted.

"You can't be serious," I said. I drew my knees up to my chest and wrapped my arms around them. The news came as a shock. If the radio was broken…

"There's no way to contact them. Grace thought they might be keeping tabs on us, but it's been over a week since the crash, and we haven't seen them," Dylan continued.

"I guess we have to assume we're on our own then," I said, my voice stronger than I felt.

"Yeah," Levi agreed.

"Does everyone still want to go ahead?"

"I think so. There's still a chance, you know, that if we do this, the CIA will get in contact," Dylan said.

"There's a chance they won't, too," I pointed out.

"We don't have to do it if you don't feel up to it," Dylan said.

"No, I want to," I replied determinedly. "But… what about Grace?"

My injuries had been life-threatening, but now I was over the worst of it, I was on the up. On the contrary, Grace's arm was a problem. A break wouldn't miraculously heal, and she would be more of a hindrance than a help.

Levi studied me carefully, and I could tell he knew what I was thinking. "Grace isn't going to be a burden."

"But she isn't going to be the most useful." It was the wrong choice of words, but I didn't have a chance to explain myself.

Levi's face quickly showed annoyance. "What do you expect us to do, Lizzie? Leave her behind? Leave her for the soldiers to find her? We're all in this together, and there's no way we're leaving anyone behind."

"It's not about leaving her behind. It's about her safety. And ours."

"We could have left you behind," Levi pointed out. "But we didn't because you're our friend. I'd cut off my arm before I'd let soldiers find you."

"Lizzie, Levi's right," Dylan said sleepily from beside me. "Grace is going to be fine. You won't even notice her arm is broken. Leave it. Grace is coming, and that's final."

"Fine. But we've got to at least consider the implications. There's no way she's setting up one of the bombs alone when she only has one working arm."

"Jess can help her. There're only four bombs anyway," Levi said. "Plus, maybe it'll come right," he added optimistically, though he didn't sound too confident.

"Not in a few days it won't," I said.

"We got some stuff to plaster it with, but none of us know

how to use it. We'd do her more damage than good if we tried," Dylan said skeptically.

"I can do it. I know how," I said, my voice brightening.

"I don't know, Lizzie. Grace isn't some guinea pig you can practice your nursing skills on," Levi said, his voice wary.

"I know. But I really can do it. I've had it done to me before. And the nurse let me help cast Jaden's arm once too. Trust me, it's not too complicated."

Dylan and Levi exchanged glances.

"OK," Levi relented. "We can do it tomorrow."

We sat in silence by the flickering candlelight. My eye roved over Levi and Dylan. Levi's brown hair was flat and limp, and the tense way he moved made me sure he was sporting a few bruises. Dylan had a minor bump on his right temple. All four of them had looked after me the best they could, and now it was my turn to return the favor.

"How are the both of you?" I asked, finally.

"Fine," Levi said awkwardly.

"So, you're uninjured?" I asked.

"I have some pretty awesome bruises, and Dylan had a bit of concussion at the start," he explained.

"How bad are they?"

"I don't know, they're nice and purple."

Obviously, they hadn't been tending to themselves as much as they should have.

"Show me," I demanded.

"I'm not sure I want to," Levi said defensively.

"Show me," I said again.

Levi sighed and began taking off his shirt. He clearly felt awkward about it. He dropped his shirt to the floor, exposing his bare yet muscular chest. I was taken aback by the amount of bruising he had. His chest had a huge bruise across it which I assumed was from the seatbelt. I peered closer, choosing to ignore Levi's obvious embarrassment.

"That's not just bruising," I muttered to Levi as I cautiously poked one of the bruises in question. "It looks much worse."

"Then what is it?" Levi asked.

"I don't know. Maybe a hematoma?" I said. Jaden had one once from a pretty nasty sports injury.

"Is that bad?" Levi asked as he winced.

"I don't think it's too serious, it should go away eventually. But it's definitely not just a bruise," I explained.

"Should I do anything about it?" Levi asked as he tried to look at the hematoma in question.

"I suppose just leave it alone. There isn't anything we can do."

"So, you made me take my shirt off for nothing?" Levi said, only half-joking.

I blushed. "If there was something more serious, you'd want to know about it, wouldn't you?"

Dylan and Levi exchanged an awkward glance for a moment.

"What?"

"Nothing," Levi said hurriedly. "I've been fine for over a week. I don't think I'm going to die," he added.

I glanced over at Dylan, about to ask him about his apparent concussion. He seemed to be avoiding my gaze. "What aren't you telling me?" I said, getting stressed.

"Tell her, Dylan," Levi said, rolling his eyes.

"Fine. You know how you said we'd need to know if our injuries were more severe?"

"Yes..."

"When we got here, we were all wet through, and we needed to dry you off and check you for injuries. All over," Dylan explained. "Or Jess and I did. I sent Levi away." He was blushing furiously and judging by the heat in my cheeks, I was pretty sure mine were just as red.

"Why couldn't Jess and Grace..."

"Grace with her freshly broken arm?"

"Fine. Good. It was the right thing to do," I said finally.

An awkward silence followed.

I stared at the television even though it was a useless piece of junk without any power. It had been the right thing to do, but I felt a little violated all the same. My cheeks were still hot, and I took a few breaths to calm down. I should have been thanking Dylan. He had done so much to make sure I was safe. I looked over at him and noticed his eyes were softly closed and his breathing rhythmical.

"Is Dylan asleep?" I whispered to Levi, who was standing, pulling his shirt back on. He popped his head through the opening and looked over at Dylan.

"Looks like it." Levi sat back down on the couch, careful not to wake Dylan. "He was really worried about you," Levi said, nodding toward Dylan. "We all were."

"I know," I said, still looking at Dylan. He was always determined to look after me, despite the fact I always pushed him away.

"You know he likes you… a lot," Levi said.

"Yeah. I do."

"Then what's holding you back?" Levi asked.

I shrugged. This was getting more and more awkward by the minute. "Because I want Dylan to be the one to tell me that. When I was with Ryan, it was always me chasing him and I was never sure how he really felt. I want things to be different this time," I tried to explain.

We resumed our silence, and I watched the flame of the candle flicker and dance on its wick. A drip of hot wax slid slowly toward the base of the candle. Thinking about Dylan was confusing right now, and I pushed it to the back of my mind. Instead, I tried to focus on something else to keep me distracted.

I searched my mind and finally contented myself by going through how to brace an arm and fiberglass it. First, I would need some soft gauze to wrap Grace's arm. Then I would take some fiberglass—fiberglass was easiest and required the least amount of preparation—and soak it in water before wrapping it onto her arm. The trick was not wrapping it too tightly, or too loosely either, so it was comfortable. And getting it done quickly because fiberglass would completely set in less than half an hour. I felt sure I could do it for Grace.

I realized Levi had been watching me think about all of this with a strange expression. "What were you thinking about?" he asked me softly.

I shook my head. "Nothing, really. Just about how to fix Grace's arm."

At the mention of Grace, he turned away, a small frown visible on his face. "I hope her arm won't make things too difficult for her," he said at last, concerned.

"It'll be much better once it's set."

Levi nodded absently, a distant look in his brown eyes as the yellow candlelight flickered on his skin.

"What were you thinking about?" I wondered aloud to him. His eyes snapped back to me for a moment, and then he looked away into the distance again.

"Nothing, really," he replied without elaborating.

THE NEXT DAY PASSED slowly. I intended to cast Grace's arm for her, but my mind was foggy, and I kept battling the constant need to sleep. I didn't want to do a lousy job of it, so we decided to wait another day. Dylan and Jess had gone out to get some more food, and Grace and I moved our sickbay to the lounge so we could keep Levi company while he was on sentry.

Rain streamed down the windows outside as we sat on the couch playing 'President'.

"Looks like I'm president... again," Levi smirked triumphantly as he threw his final cards down onto the coffee table.

Grace glared at him. She had lost at least five games in a row. "How about we have a tournament of 'Speed' instead?" she suggested, sighing.

"But I won," Levi said. "Grace, I'm meant to swap my two worst cards for your two best cards. Hand 'em over."

"This game is so stupid. How am I meant to win when I have

to give away all my good cards," Grace muttered under her breath, flicking two of her cards at him.

"You'd probably lose 'Speed' if we played anyway because of your arm," I helpfully hinted.

"You're right. This is so unfair," Grace said, pouting.

"Hurry up," Levi said, "You're the bum, so you start, Grace."

With a sigh, she chucked down triple threes. Suddenly we spotted movement through the window.

"They're back," Levi said. He jumped up and started heading toward the door.

Dylan banged on it impatiently. "It's us. Let us in!"

"Hurry," Jess called urgently. The note of panic in her voice made my heart rate increase by several notches, pounding against my ribcage. Levi ran the last few steps, pulled back the bolt, and flung the door open. Dylan and Jess almost fell through it, exhausted and panting with flushed cheeks, and wet all over from the rain. I stood up nervously and moved toward them. Grace dropped her cards and got to her feet.

"What is it?" I asked.

"We have to leave, now," Dylan said, his breathing ragged. He wiped the rain from his face. A small puddle was forming on the ground where Jess and Dylan stood, soaked through.

"Why?" Grace asked as she joined us.

"Soldiers. Levi, grab all the guns. Lizzie, help me get the packs," Dylan directed. Levi made an impressive vault over the small settee in the open living room before sprinting down the hall. He flung open a cupboard under the stairs. I followed Dylan into the bedroom where we had been storing the packs. I grabbed one while Dylan shouldered the other. Back into the hallway.

"To the backdoor," Dylan said. The others were waiting. Levi took the pack from me, and he traded me a rifle.

"How long do we have?" I asked as I gave the rifle a cursory check.

"Minutes. If that," Jess said. Grace waited anxiously at the fringes.

Dylan opened the backdoor, and we fled out into the rain. I opened my mouth to ask another question, but Dylan roughly pushed me along with everyone else.

"There's no time," he said. We raced across the pavement, puddles of water quickly soaking my jeans. Mud squelched as Dylan diverted off the sidewalk, and we followed him across an expansive rugby pitch. The tall goalposts loomed above us and created shadows as lightning flashed across the sky.

"Where are we going to go?" I asked Dylan over the pouring rain.

"It's time to put the plan into action," Dylan replied briefly. "The soldiers chased Jess and me. They would have found us if we'd stayed."

I nodded, not wasting my breath asking any more questions. I felt bad for Grace. She held her arm awkwardly against her stomach. She bit her soft lips, defying the pain of her arm being jostled around. The rugby field gave way to more streets, and I blindly followed Dylan through the night with no clue where he was taking us. He seemed to have a plan in mind, though, as he darted from street to street with purpose.

We thundered down the pavement, wet shoes slapping the slick surface. The rain hadn't eased. My clothes dripped with water and clung uncomfortably to my body. They were heavy, too, dragging me down with every step. The bandage on my forehead slipped slowly down my face, and my eyes stung from the streaming water that ran unabated. It was the most exercise I'd had since my brush with death, and my breathing was ragged, my head pounding ferociously.

"Can we stop now?" Grace pleaded after a while. "I think we must have lost them by now," she said.

We slowed to a walk, Dylan still looking warily around in the darkness. "We're nearly there," he offered in comfort, seeing Grace and me.

Grace was unnaturally pale, and she was shivering with the

wet. I was pretty sure I looked just as pathetic. My teeth chattered. I had thought running was bad. Now we were walking, there was nothing to distract me from my splitting headache, and I was chilled to the bone.

"I'm fine," Grace lied. She looked like a drowned cat.

"We'll dry off as soon as we get there," Dylan promised us. He didn't seem to realize I hadn't the foggiest of where 'there' was.

CHAPTER FOURTEEN

GRACE

WE WALKED FOR ANOTHER thirty minutes through the downpour until Dylan pointed out a department store. Its iconic red paint was our beacon in the storm. Dylan picked up the pace, and we jogged the rest of the way. I couldn't stop tears from coming to my eyes as my broken arm jolted painfully in its sling. Just a few more minutes. A couple hundred meters to go.

Finally, the entrance to the store loomed in front of us. I hoped the glass sliding doors would automatically open, welcoming us, but they remained predictably shut. I crept forward to peer in. The expansive shop appeared deserted. Silent in the night. Lizzie walked up to the employee-only door and gave it a tug. It remained firmly shut.

"If only it was that easy," Levi commented with a bemused look.

I was unimpressed. My arm throbbed incessantly, and all I could think of was getting inside. Dry and warm.

"What do you suggest?" Lizzie muttered, wrapping her arms around herself.

Dylan and Levi eyed the glass doors.

"They don't call it breaking and entering for nothing," Levi said, cracking his knuckles.

"I don't know," Jess said, "that doesn't seem smart."

"Does anyone have a better idea?" Levi asked.

No one did.

"Let's get it over with," I said, wincing as I readjusted my arm. Surely one more building with smashed glass wouldn't give us away. Almost every shop had already been busted into, and it was a miracle the glass door was still intact. Levi looked around for something to use. He kicked up a chunk of cement from the crumbling curb and weighed it in his hand.

"Here goes nothing," Levi said, before hurling at it the door. A loud clang reverberated through the streets, and the offending concrete block bounced off. The door remained intact. I looked around instinctively, searching for the sounds of incoming soldiers. But the streets were quiet.

"That went well," Jess commented.

"Looks like you chipped it," Lizzie said sarcastically as she tried to fix the bandage around her head.

Levi frowned and started forward for a second go.

Dylan stopped him. "My turn." He grinned, palmed the rock, and lobbed it at the door. With a loud crash, the glass door exploded into thousands of tiny shards.

"I weakened it for you," Levi said, raising his gun and pointing it into the eerie darkness of the store.

"Whatever," Dylan said as he clicked the safety off his weapon.

We waited in silence for a few minutes, guns aimed at the blankness of the department shop.

"I don't think anyone's here," Jess said eventually. She took a hesitant step forward, her boots cracking the broken glass beneath her feet.

"We should still check," Dylan said, his voice echoing through the store. We automatically separated into two groups. I followed Levi, and we walked silently, aisle after aisle. But the place really was deserted. Boxes bound with blue plastic shipping straps stood silently, waiting to be unloaded. The checkouts were clean and empty.

"All clear," I heard Dylan call out.

"Same here," Levi responded.

I let out a long, slow breath and leaned against some shelving. The store was untouched, a relic where everything appeared precisely as it had been. And it brought memories flooding back. Shoe shopping with Mom. Retail therapy with my friends. And before Dad died, we'd sometimes shop as a family. When we did, Dad always spoiled me, and my siblings hated it. I smiled as I remembered the arguments with them. I'd give anything to fight with them like I used to.

"You should put some dry clothes on," Levi said, bringing me back to the present.

I'd forgotten he was still there.

"You're frozen to the bone," he said, gently touching my cheek with his warm hand.

I let him lead me to the women's clothing section. Jess and Lizzie were already there. I watched, faintly amused, as Lizzie and Jess combed the racks, pretending they were doing some retail therapy. Lizzie held up a cute floral top against her body before tossing it aside. We couldn't wear things like that anymore.

"Here," Levi said, thrusting some sweatpants and a black polyprop in my hands. This was about as fashionable as we got now.

"Thanks," I said. My eyes lingered on a light blue summer dress hanging on the rack beside me. It was strange to think there was once a time when I could wear stuff like that.

"It'd suit you," Levi commented as he noticed me eyeing up the dress.

"And these don't?" I joked, holding up the sweatpants.

"You look good in everything," he said. "Especially sweatpants."

My stomach fluttered.

"Do you need help?" he asked me.

"I can dress myself," I said, raising an eyebrow at him.

"Yeah... I know that... I didn't mean... I thought with your arm..." he said as he backed away, embarrassed.

"Some privacy would be nice," I said, hinting.

"Right," Levi said, turning and walking away.

I sighed. I had no energy to hunt for a changing room, so I ducked behind a rack, wincing as I peeled my wet clothes off one-handed. It was harder than I thought. I hated to admit it, but I could have used Levi's help. I pulled the polyprop awkwardly over my head with my one good arm and then struggled to get the rest of my clothes on one-handed, but eventually, I emerged fully clothed. My hair had escaped its ponytail during my clothing ordeal and hung loose down my back. I tried, hopelessly, to tie it back up with one hand. But I failed miserably. I settled for walking to the accessory aisle and finding a headband. At least now, it would be out of my face.

Levi returned a few moments later with some food. "Here," he said, handing me a muesli bar. "Are you doing OK?"

"I feel better now that I'm dry," I said with a weak laugh.

Levi nodded and gave me a compassionate smile.

"How's the arm?" He looked at me sympathetically.

Thanks to the rough journey here, my arm throbbed painfully. I pulled up my sleeve to get a better look at it. I looked past the marbling purple bruises and swelling that had spread from my wrist to my elbow. My wrist was still bent at an odd angle, and it hurt like hell. Lizzie promised me she would fix it, but I was worried there was nothing we could do to set it straight.

Levi grimaced at the sight of it. "That looks painful."

"It is." I covered my arm back up and eased it back into the sling.

"Lizzie will patch it up soon," Levi said.

"I hope it's fixable," I muttered, sitting down on the cold concrete floor. I struggled to open my muesli bar one-handed.

Levi watched on, a wry smile playing on his lips. After a couple minutes of struggling, I gave up and dropped the bar, still in its wrapper, in my lap. "Can you give me a hand?"

My broken arm was already a liability, but I knew I could overcome it. Once Lizzie set it, it would be good as new. I would be good as new.

Levi sat down next to me. "Sure," he said, picking it up and opening it for me, easily. He handed it to me with one of his goofy smiles plastered on his face.

"I'm not useless," I said to him.

"I never said you were," Levi replied as he watched me eat.

"You were thinking it."

"Not for a second."

"I can still help with the attack," I said. "I want to help."

"I know," Levi said, grabbing my good hand and giving it a squeeze. "We're not going to leave you behind."

"You guys have already talked about it… leaving me out?" I cast my eyes down. I should have known. The muesli bar felt dry in my mouth, and I struggled to swallow it.

Levi opened his mouth to speak but quickly shut it again.

"Tell me, Levi," I said, scowling. "I can handle it."

"It was hardly a conversation," Levi said.

I pulled my hand away from his.

"Lizzie brought it up. She was concerned for you," Levi added hastily.

"Of course she did," I muttered. Lizzie was always so concerned for me.

"But Dylan and I shut it down. We're a team. No matter what," Levi said. "No one needs to bring it up again. And you don't need to worry."

"You won't even notice I'm injured," I said defensively.

"You're a part of this group," Levi said, grabbing my hand again. "And we stick together no matter what." He gave my hand a gentle squeeze again before standing up and leaving me alone in the accessory aisle.

I watched him walk away and disappear into the depths of the store. My hand was still warm from where he had gripped it. A lingering memory of his touch. I liked him. Enough to admit it to myself. And enough to overthink it. If I liked him this much, why was I still holding him at a distance?

I thought back to the almost-kiss. I had wanted it desperately. But I held back, afraid one kiss might change everything. Afraid that I would lose him or he'd leave me. The thing was, this war had its own way of screwing everything up. We had no control over what happened. I didn't want things to change. But they were changing, regardless of what happened between Levi and me. I looked up at the expansive warehouse ceiling.

Why couldn't I let myself fall for him?

Maybe it was something to do with my ex. Sean'd hurt me. Just thinking about it now made me choke up. I needed him. I trusted him. And he left. And now, I was afraid open my heart to someone else. Levi was too good to be true, and I was too broken. Too damaged. This was why I struggled to get close to Levi. I didn't want to get hurt again.

I shuffled to get more comfortable. Pain shot up my broken arm as I accidentally moved it. I pulled my sleeve up, exposing my injured arm. With my good hand, I ran a finger down my injured arm. It was puffy, and an odd tingly sensation twinged along my arm as my finger crossed the suspected breakpoint. I shifted in my seat again, and was rewarded with shooting pain from my fingertips to my elbow. I shut my eyes and screwed my face up until the pain subsided. I needed my arm fixed. The sooner, the better.

I tried not to complain too much. I didn't need their sympathies. I could already see that they thought I was a liability, no matter how much Levi tried to reassure me. Maybe I was slower, clumsier, and weaker than the others. Why else were they seemingly impervious to injury? Or maybe I was simply unlucky.

And I wasn't the only one. Lizzie had her share of bad injury luck these past weeks. She was fortunate the burns from the fire had healed, and it was a miracle she survived the car accident at all. We had been afraid death might visit her quietly in the night and steal Lizzie away without giving us our chance to say goodbye.

I would never admit it out loud, but I almost gave up on her getting better. We had seen a lot of death throughout the war, and I had already lost so many people. The fact that Lizzie could be next seemed inevitable. I had already started trying to make peace with it, so the blow would be less crushing. When Lizzie's condition began to improve, I let myself believe she might survive. When she woke up, the relief was immense. I would get my best friend back.

"Grace!" Lizzie's voice echoed around the giant warehouse.

"Over here," I called out.

Lizzie's footsteps padded closer to me, and she appeared at the end of the aisle with her hands on her hips. Her blond hair was secured in a messy bun, and she had a determined look in her eye. "It's time to fix your arm," she said.

"You really think you can do it?" I asked, biting nervously at my lip.

"Absolutely," Lizzie said, her face softening into a reassuring smile. "Come on." She held out her hand to me. I grabbed it, and she helped me to my feet. I took a deep breath and obediently followed her to a small plastic folding table with all the necessary items. A kettle was heating water on a small camp stove to get the water to the right temperature for the plaster. She motioned for me to sit on a small plastic stool. Jess and Dylan were already there.

I hesitantly sat, my hands shaking as I thought about what was about to happen. A chill snaked its way down my spine, and I started shivering.

"Don't panic," Lizzie said, trying to be comforting.

"Saying that doesn't help," I muttered. I was panicking.

"It will be over in a second," Levi said, coming over.

"You'll barely feel it," Dylan added as he handed me a belt. I placed it on the little table in front of me. What did I need the belt for?

"That's a lie," I said to Dylan, who looked away sheepishly.

"Yeah… sorry," he muttered. "I was only trying to help."

"You aren't going to like this, Grace," Lizzie said, crouching down to talk to me.

"What?" I asked, dreading her answer.

"I have to realign the bone," Lizzie said. "There's no easy way to say this… it's going to hurt like hell."

"OK." That was all I could manage to say.

"You're sure you want to do this?" Lizzie asked.

"Do I have a choice?" I said. My pulse quickened, and my breaths came faster and shallower.

"It's up to you," Lizzie said. Her face was serious. "But I don't know if you'll get back much use from your arm if it heals… like that." She looked down at my crooked arm and grimaced.

"If there's no other option…"

Lizzie shook her head.

"Short-term pain for long-term gain," Levi said.

"You can say that again," I muttered.

Levi helped me take my arm out of its sling and rolled the sleeve up above my elbow. I couldn't bear to look at it. Instead, I tried to focus on Levi, who had a concerned furrow gathering on his brow. My stomach was queasy with nerves, and I closed my eyes, trying to mentally prepare myself.

"It will be OK, Grace," Levi said, squeezing my shoulder. He kneeled down next to me and grabbed my good hand. "Squeeze as hard as you want."

"And you should have this between your teeth," Dylan said, holding up the belt. I couldn't make myself let go of Levi's hand. Dylan gave me a sympathetic look before holding out the belt for me to bite onto. I did as I was told.

Lizzie instructed Dylan to hold my lower arm just below the elbow. Jess busied herself mixing the boiling water with cold water in a large bucket. I gripped Levi's hand tight and tried to focus on what Jess was doing instead of Lizzie.

Lizzie gripped my thumb and my other fingers in her hands, but I tried not to look. "Ready? On the count of three," she said. "One… two."

Lizzie never got to three.

She pulled on my wrist so hard I thought she might rip it in two. My arm exploded with blinding white pain that brought tears to my eyes. I screamed out, but the belt between my teeth muffled the sound. I bit down hard on the leather and squeezed Levi's hand with all my strength. A couple of seconds later, the eye-watering agony subsided slightly, and I could breathe. I spat the belt out from between my teeth and gasped in the stale air. I was breathing hard, fighting through the last of the pain.

"It's OK. It's OK," Levi repeated to me.

Finally, when the pain had diminished to a dull ache, I was able to look over at Lizzie.

"Good news," Lizzie said with a smile. "It's straight now."

"Thank God," I said as tears streamed down my cheeks.

"But you need to stay still until we get it plastered," Lizzie explained.

"OK," I gasped.

"You're doing awesome, Grace," Levi said.

I nodded at him wordlessly.

They applied the cast, and once it had set, Lizzie insisted on cutting a small split down one side in case my arm swelled any more. When it was done, my arm felt better and more secure. I finally let go of Levi's hand.

"You have a wicked grip, Grace," Levi complained as he massaged feeling back into his hand.

"Sorry," I said to Levi. "And, thanks, Lizzie… I think," I said shakily.

"I hope it wasn't too painful," Lizzie said.

"I'll survive," I said as the pain slowly abated.

I stayed sitting on the stool they had put me on, and Lizzie dragged over a beanbag. She collapsed into it and groaned.

"I'm so tired."

"Me too," I said, still trembling from the ordeal.

Now that my arm was on the mend, we could think about the plan again. "I can't believe we're going through with the mission," I said to Lizzie.

She didn't respond. I looked over at her, but she was already asleep. She had been sleeping more than usual since the accident. I supposed it was a normal part of the healing process. Especially since she had a head wound. I knew the tiredness that came with that kind of injury.

I looked at my arm and wriggled my fingers. It still hurt, but now the pain was bearable. The cast gave it more support and protection. I wrapped the sling back around my neck and gently lowered my arm into it. Definitely less painful, I thought. I took one more look at Lizzie, who was peacefully asleep. I didn't want to disturb her, so I quietly stood up and staggered to a couch I had spied earlier.

Once I made it to the plush two-seater, I sat and let myself relax. I leaned back and let out a big sigh. My stomach was churning with nerves. Not because of my arm. No. Now I was patched back up, we could carry out the mission. And it both terrified and excited me. It would have been easy to go back into hiding after the crash. We had lost contact with the CIA, and everything was going wrong. But we were stronger than we gave ourselves credit for.

Yes, we were behind schedule, but broken bones and Lizzie almost dying weren't enough to deter us from the plan. Operation Dark Tower was alive and well. And once we completed the mission, the CIA would help me find my mom.

I let myself drift in the memories of her, remembering her shiny black hair pulled into a loose bun, her brown eyes sparkling when she laughed. I missed her desperately. I missed all my family. But since their deaths, Mom had been my rock, and I had been hers. Lizzie had stayed at my side, and she had been a big help. But Lizzie was on the outside of our grief. She couldn't understand the pain Mom and I went through. We were all each other had left.

Mom had been inconsolable when the accident first happened. I had tried my best to be there for her. I pushed away my own pain as much as I could. I had to be strong. But the pressure was too much. Slowly, Mom picked up the pieces and started taking charge. And the more she got it together, the more I fell apart. Our roles reversed, and Mom stroked my hair. She told me I would be all right. On the days when I was so emotionally tired I could barely move off the sofa, she brought me meals. When the days got darker, and my shadows crept in, she showed me the light.

I hated to think about where she was now. Maybe a dingy cell crammed with other prisoners—that was the best-case scenario. Worst case, she was six feet under. Or perhaps, she wasn't given the dignity of a burial at all.

"No, Grace," I whispered to myself. I couldn't think like that. I had to hold on to the hope she was alive. Out there somewhere. OK without me. A tear rolled down my face and dripped onto my shirt. I needed the CIA to come through for us. Maybe if we completed Operation Dark Tower, the CIA would get in touch. I had to believe they would honor their agreement.

But... how likely was that? In the grand scheme of this war, we meant nothing to them.

The little hope I had left dwindled.

I WOKE A FEW hours later, curled up on the two-seater. Lizzie was busy putting food onto platters.

"Where is everyone?" I asked as I walked up to her.

"They've gone to do a test run with the microwave drills," Lizzie said. "I wish they'd let me go," she added with a scowl. "Apparently I need more rest."

"They're probably right," I said, smiling a little. I hated to be left behind too.

"That doesn't make it any less annoying," she said. "At least we won't be left behind tomorrow."

"Tomorrow? That soon?" Butterflies leaped in my belly.

"The longer we stay here, the more dangerous it gets. The soldiers will track us down here eventually," Lizzie said with a shrug.

"For some reason, I thought we might have a few more days," I said, readjusting my arm in the sling. Soon it would be too late to turn back, I thought.

Lizzie looked like she was thinking the same thing. "The guys say we can't risk it. And I tend to agree with them," she said as she portioned out a packet of jellybeans.

"It makes sense," I said. "But it feels like a whirlwind since the car crash."

"Do you think we're ready for this?" she asked me. I wondered the same thing.

I shrugged. "I don't know. I hope so."

Lizzie handed me a few jellybeans. I popped them in my mouth, savoring the sweet fruity flavor.

"Whatever happens tomorrow, you should know... I am really glad it was you with me the night the war started," Lizzie said.

"Thanks. Me too. I wouldn't have made it this far without you."

We stayed sitting silently for a moment, thinking about what tomorrow would bring. Then we spotted movement in the shadows, and Lizzie raised her gun. "Who's there?" she called into the blackness.

"It's us," Jess called out, and Lizzie let the gun relax by her side. They walked forward and dumped the packs down at our feet.

"Step one, complete," Dylan said with a grin.

"Step two, teach Grace and me what the hell to do with them," Lizzie said as she looked uncertainly at the packs.

"Sweet! Food!" Dylan said, rushing to the table and stuffing his face with several gummy worms. I looked at the plates Lizzie had been preparing. Gummy worms, jellybeans, chocolates, and some salami sticks.

"I feel like I'm at a kid's birthday," Jess said as she nibbled on a salami stick. A kid's party was an odd contrast to the microwave drills and the bombs that lay prepared in the packs.

"You don't mind if we eat first, right?" Dylan said, his mouth already full of gummy worms, as he saw the disapproving look on Lizzie's face.

She rolled her eyes. "Yeah, fine. It's not much anyway… this was the only edible stuff in the store."

"Doesn't bother me," Levi said as he chowed down some sort of toffee.

I picked at some sweets and then snacked on a bag of stale pretzels. As I looked at each of my friends, I wondered if this would be our last meal together. I hoped not.

"You're very quiet," Levi whispered to me. "Is everything OK?"

I looked up at him, my face worried. "What if this is the last time…" I let the words hang, unable to finish the sentence.

"If it's the last time, we better enjoy it," Levi said, offering me a toffee.

"Levi…" I thought about telling him how I felt. After all, this might be our last day together if the mission went south.

"Yeah," he said, looking up at me with a smile.

But my fear paralyzed me. I couldn't do it. I couldn't open myself up like that. I wasn't ready to let him in. Not here, not now, in front of everyone.

"Thanks for the toffee," I said instead.

Chapter Fifteen

Dylan

It was done. We were ready. The drums of war were rolling, and it was our time to march. I slept fitfully. It was a hot day outside, and the sun baked the outer cladding of the department store. With the air-con out, the place was a furnace. It was late afternoon, and the light was beginning to dim. I sat up against the bed's headboard and stared over at Lizzie. She had rolled right to the edge of the King bed she shared with Grace, and she'd shoved the covers toward her feet. Her mouth was slightly open, and her blond hair spread messily over her pillow.

Should I tell her I loved her? It was a question that continually circled my mind, and the closer we drew to carrying out our plan, the more the thought plagued me. I should. I mightn't have another chance. There were no guarantees we'd make it out of this alive.

But then again, maybe I shouldn't tell her. It would make things complicated, and now wasn't the time. We had enough trouble on our hands. Not to mention, if she turned me down, I didn't think I'd be strong enough to walk into battle. Or, on the off chance she felt the same, we'd both be too distracted to think straight. If anything happened, I couldn't have that on my conscience.

The afternoon lingered, and then dusk fell as the last rays of sunlight faded and died. Lizzie stirred and woke. Her eyes fluttered open, and she looked across at me.

"Morning. Or Evening. Whatever it is," she said, stifling a yawn.

"Shhh, the others are still sleeping," I whispered.

"Not anymore," Grace mumbled.

"What's the time?" Lizzie asked. Her whisper seemed loud in the stillness of the approaching night.

"Too early. We should go back to sleep," Grace muttered beside her.

Lizzie lay there silently, staring at the ceiling for several minutes, with worry on her face. "This is ridiculous." She let out a derisive snort, freeing the last of the sheets from her feet. "I couldn't go back to sleep now if I tried."

"What's going on?" Levi muttered groggily from his couch as Lizzie torpedoed past.

"It was Lizzie," Grace said to him, peeping out from her blankets.

I sighed. "I'll go after her, she looked pretty upset."

"Go kiss all her worries away," Levi said and smacked his lips together.

"Levi..." Grace flashed a warning look at him. Jess giggled from her bed.

Great, so I was a laughingstock now.

"It's not funny," I said.

Jess giggled more.

I dropped my feet to the cool concrete floor and jogged dispiritedly in the direction Lizzie had taken off in.

Eventually, I found her sitting in a giant crate of stuffed toys in the children's section.

"Really?" I said, a smile pulling at my mouth. I climbed in after her, and there was a loud squeak as I sat on a giant teddy bear, and we both laughed.

As the smile slowly faded from Lizzie's face, she turned to me and said, "I miss it."

"You miss what?"

Lizzie gestured around her. "This. Innocence. We'll never get that back."

"You know," I said with a grin, "people say that about sex, too."

Lizzie punched me in the arm and gave me a reproachful look. "That wasn't what I was talking about, Dylan," she said with her cheeks going red. "Trust a guy to turn every conversation into one about sex," she muttered with a dramatic eye roll.

"I'm serious. People think it will change them, and somehow they'll wake up and be a totally different person after they lose their virginity. But it's not like that."

"And you would know?" Lizzie said and stared at me. It was my turn to blush. My cheeks reddened under her intense scrutiny.

"Maybe," I said awkwardly. "My point is, I don't buy into that whole 'losing your innocence' crap. Everything that happens is another experience that layers over it. It doesn't mean you're not you anymore."

"I can't tell whether or not you're right," Lizzie said. She collapsed back onto the pile of soft toys. "All I know is once we do this, we can't turn back. Why are we doing this, Dylan?" Lizzie asked with a sigh.

"You know why," I said, becoming serious. "Because even if the CIA never helps us, we have a chance to make a difference in this war and gain some ground against the soldiers."

"What you say makes total sense, but... I'm scared, Dylan. I don't want to die," Lizzie admitted. I studied her as she picked up a plush toy elephant, turning it over anxiously in her hands. Tears glistened in the corners of her gray eyes. It was rare Lizzie ever admitted to being scared.

"You won't die, Lizzie. I know you think you always have to be strong, but you don't. I don't care if you want me to, but I promised to keep you safe. And I don't intend to go back on that."

Lizzie looked at me. One glance from those gray eyes of hers was enough to make my heart pound. Ever since I'd realized I loved her, I couldn't get her off my mind. I reached out and tucked a strand of hair behind her ear. She had an unfamiliar look on her face. Vulnerability. I wanted to tell her. But was she ready for it? Was I ready for it? I opened my mouth, but somehow, I couldn't form any words.

"What?" Lizzie whispered softly. My hand was still behind her ear, her soft hair tickling my fingers, and she didn't turn away. I leaned closer to her. I was only inches from her face, and I could see a very light dusting of freckles across her nose that I'd never noticed before.

"What are we doing?" Lizzie said, her breath soft against my cheek. Her eyelashes fluttered down shyly. I ran my fingers slowly down her cheek and lifted her chin, willing her to look at me. She opened her eyes, and I drifted in their depths.

"I don't know. But I'm tired of dancing around each other. Aren't you?" I asked her. I leaned my forehead to hers and cautiously brushed my nose against hers… nuzzling… closer.

With my eyes now closed, I let the feeling build within me, a deep ache rippling through my body. I opened my mouth and tasted her lips. My hands slid to her waist. One of Lizzie's hands combed through my hair, and her other slid across my back. It felt like sparks were shooting off her fingers everywhere she touched me. I blindly followed my emotions, my heart soaring. Breaking away from the kiss, I pressed my mouth into the curve of her neck.

"Dylan, wait," Lizzie said breathlessly.

I drew back.

"I don't want to go… too fast."

I nodded, and we collapsed back into the soft toys. Lizzie gave me a coy smile, her face flushed pink. I grinned back. If this was our last moment alone, at least it was one to remember.

We lay there for a long time, watching time slip by. I traced little circles with my finger on the skin of her arm.

"I don't want to go," Lizzie said as she stared distantly at the ceiling. I knew how she felt. I would give anything to stay in this moment. But time would never stand still for us. There was a war to fight, and I didn't want to be hiding in a department store all our lives, either.

"I know. But we'll be OK."

"Do you really think that?" Lizzie sat up, tying her hair away from her face in a messy ponytail.

"I hope so. I don't want to lose this so soon," I admitted. I brought my eyes up to hers.

A ghost of a smile passed over her face. "Me neither."

"There you guys are," said Jess as she wandered down the aisle. "We've been searching the entire store for you," she said, annoyed.

Lizzie jumped over the edge of the crate, and I stood and stretched.

"Sorry, Jess. We were just talking," Lizzie said.

Clearly, Lizzie wasn't ready for our new relationship to be public knowledge. Jess stared at us suspiciously, trying to deduce what had happened.

"OK, well… it's nearly time to go," Jess said and didn't push the matter. Lizzie trailed after Jess. They rounded the corner, and I stood alone atop the mountain of stuffed bears and animals. Lizzie and I were together… finally. My heart was bursting with happiness, and not even the soldiers could take it away.

I caught up with the others back in the furniture section. They were checking through their bags in a state of urgency and paranoia. I grabbed mine and started doing the same.

"Are you OK?" I whispered aside to Lizzie.

"I'm fine," she said, "but please, can we drop it for now? We need to focus."

Lizzie was right. I continued rifling through my bag and checking everything was there. We'd reorganized our gear into four large hiking packs we had taken from the hunting and fishing aisle. Grace was the only one who didn't have a pack, and she glanced back and forth between Lizzie and me.

Was it that obvious? She said nothing, though, and after several minutes, we were all ready. We stood, nervously looking at one another.

"Everyone knows how to get here again, after we escape, right?" Grace asked for the fiftieth time.

"Yes," we all replied in unison.

"And if we get split up, we wait here till three a.m., no later, for everyone to regroup," Lizzie warned us, her gray eyes alight with determination. I wanted to say something to her. But we never said goodbyes. We had to believe we were going to come out of this alive. I had to have faith I would see Lizzie again. Goodbye wouldn't be required. Lizzie's gaze lingered on me. She wanted to say something too. That was enough.

"We know, Lizzie," Jess said calmly. We all knew the plan. We were ready.

As we walked bravely onto the footpath, I tried to shake off the feeling of impending doom. Though I didn't hold out much hope, like Grace, I still had a whisper of a dream where the CIA would help us reunite with our families. If nothing else, at least we could get revenge for everything Marion and his soldiers had put us through. I didn't realize, as I stepped out onto the footpath, that while revenge can taste sweet, eating it can also rot your insides.

We walked close to an hour before we saw much beyond the odd grouping of soldiers patrolling the streets. All the while, the Skytower loomed in the background, urging us on and taunting us with its powerful silhouette. Was it even possible to bring it down? The knot in my stomach grew larger with every step I took.

We paused outside a covered parking lot on Federal Street and shrank back in the shadows of the ticket office.

"It's not much farther now," I whispered to the others.

They were relying on my internal compass. I had walked this street a thousand times in the last year as I made my way about Auckland City. I had a part-time job to help fund my study that was only two blocks from where we were now. I took time to wonder what it looked like. Had any of my co-workers escaped? I stopped my train of thought, pulling my head back into the present. I needed to focus. "The dangerous part will be getting to the pillars at the base. Once we get there, we can use them for cover," I said. The others nodded wordlessly.

A thunderous buzzing filled the empty streets, and the bright lights of a helicopter beamed out as it lifted from the Skycity Hotel. The search beams flicked across the ground surrounding the Skytower.

"Can they see us? Do they know we're here?" Grace said, panicking.

"No, there's no way," Lizzie whispered. The helicopter hovered until it reached adequate height before it took off into the night.

"What if Marion's in there?" Levi said. "Is there even a point in continuing?"

"We don't know that. We don't know anything about that helicopter. We can't turn back. Not now," I argued.

"Dylan's right. We can't turn back. We've made our decision. It's only fear that's playing in our minds," Jess said.

"So we continue," Grace said. She pursed her lips nervously.

"Are we ready?" Levi asked. In reply, I clapped Levi on the shoulder. He looked as scared as I felt. The others nodded a solemn vow. We were in this neck deep.

"Good luck, guys," Lizzie whispered beside me.

"Good luck," we echoed.

Taking a deep breath, I scouted out some columns evenly spaced down the sidewalk and took off, crouching low. They were barely wide enough to offer much cover, but it was better than nothing. We had traveled in the dark so often I was beginning to feel I was part of the night, a looming shadow growing as the moon rose in the sky.

We moved closer to the junction between Federal Street and Victoria Street West. Several raised garden beds containing scrappy-looking trees obstructed my view. I peered past them and was surprised to see how close we were. I could see the base of the tower. The CIA were right. There was no way we could approach by road. Soldiers swarmed the street like they were expecting us to attack. But that was impossible.

I turned my attention to the Chinese restaurant next to us and eyed up our planned route. A series of interconnecting porticos fanned above the cluster of shops at the Skytower's base.

"The roof starts over there," I whispered quietly to Lizzie, who was closest to me. She nodded, and we all started silently forward. Levi gave Jess a leg up first. We cringed as she thumped loudly on the roofing, but there was no time to check whether we had been made. Until we were all in position, we were too exposed to stop.

Levi gave Grace a boost, and Jess aided her from above. I helped Levi and then Lizzie. Now was the hard part. I pushed a pot plant standing by the restaurant's entrance closer and used it to stand on. I reached out and found a grip. So far, so good.

Then halfway up, I kicked the pot plant over.

It smashed into pieces, and I was left hanging from the roof, my legs swinging through the air. Shouts echoed from the direction of the road, followed by the crunching of boots. My hands sweated as I gripped the roof's edge, struggling to pull myself up. My arms burned with effort. Levi gripped my wrist and helped to heave my body onto the rooftop as a flashlight shone in the direction of the pot plant. I rolled onto the roof and flattened myself against the tiles.

"Have you seen this?" one of the soldiers yelled.

I held my breath, waiting to be discovered.

"It'll be a feral cat. They're everywhere these days," a voice replied.

The torch shone away. I relaxed a little, and we started inching forward on our bellies. We moved excruciatingly slowly, but we were still too noisy. I felt exposed—all the soldiers had to do was look up. And if they caught a glimpse of movement, we would be dead.

We paused as Jess reached the part of the portico closest to the tower. She began planning her drop. It was higher than we had expected, and my nerves kicked in. What if one of us broke a leg from the fall? What if they heard us drop? We couldn't control our noise level while jumping one story with a pack on our backs. My clothes felt too tight, and I pulled at my collar as I broke into a sweat.

Jess crawled to the edge and I shimmied alongside her to help. Her eyes widened and she shook her head. *No good.* I peered down at the base of the Skytower and immediately saw the problem. Only meters away, there was a guard. We'd come so far. It was impossible to give up now because of one soldier. But none of us knew what to do. Lizzie silently brought the rifle slung across her shoulder in front of her. She rested it in front of her, sniper-style. Once she had the soldier in her sights, she looked over at me: *Should I shoot him?*

I shook my head. There was no way. We'd be dead in minutes, and never complete the mission. We were still there five minutes later when a whistle blew, and the guard moved away. His shift was over.

Now was the time.

"Here I go," Jess mouthed to the rest of us before dangling down and dropping several feet to the ground. She disappeared quickly into the darkness. Levi was next and stayed to help Grace down with her broken arm. In an act of total trust, she let herself drop, and Levi caught her safely and quietly. Lizzie followed, and finally, it was just me. I peered over the edge. I could no longer see the others, and I had to breathe to stop the panic from returning. What if that was the last I had ever seen of them?

I dismissed the thought. I had to act now before another guard came. I took a deep breath and swung myself over the edge. I landed with a small thud on the balls of my feet and fled to the cover of the broad pillars. Once there, I leaned against the cold concrete and counted breaths in and out to calm myself. We had made it. There had been no gunshots, no shout of discovery, so I assumed the others were all OK.

I turned my attention to the pillar in front of me and placed the bag down gently at my feet. For our bombs to cause maximum damage, it was essential to embed them in the pillars. I stealthily drew out the thing I had started referring to as 'the contraption'. When we first tested these microwave drills, we found they were silent, but it was slow work.

I placed the drill against the pillar and turned it on. It took me almost half an hour, but centimeter by centimeter, the hole grew. When I was sure it was large enough, I stuffed the explosive into the hole, hooked up the detonator, and stared at it for a moment. It was unbelievable to think such a tiny thing could have such a massive impact.

We'd unanimously agreed on the timing: The bombs were due to go off at 0100 on the dot. Our getaway was timed, too. It was 0032. Eight minutes before we made our escape. I checked the bomb. I checked the leads. I checked the timer. And then I waited.

I thought about a lot of things in those eight minutes. Would we survive? Would our attack have any real impact on the outcome of this war?

And then my thoughts drifted to Lizzie. I couldn't help it. What would it be like when the war was over, and it was just us? Would we still be together at the end of the war? I bloody well hoped so. I didn't want to screw this up.

I snuck a peek at the pillar beside me. Lizzie was supposed to be there, somewhere. I thought I could faintly see her shape in the dark, but I wasn't sure if my mind was playing tricks on me or if it was really her. I looked at my watch again and counted down the minutes.

When it seemed I couldn't wait any longer, my watch ticked over to 0040. There was no way to go back the way we had come. Even if we'd been able to get back onto the roofing, it would take too long to escape. We had to cause a distraction and make a run for it.

The grenade Levi lobbed across the road detonated in one of the shops, causing a bright flare that lit the night. Nice throw, I thought. The bored-looking soldiers, who'd been peering out toward the road, yelled out. With their guns raised, a whole bunch of them stormed the shop.

It was now or never.

I moved around the pillar to where Lizzie had been moments before and could see my escape route. There was an abandoned bus not far down the street, and I used it for cover. I found Lizzie hidden around the other side of it, panting and looking triumphant. She held her gun firmly by the barrel in both hands.

"We're not away yet," I whispered to her as I readied my rifle.

A moment later and Grace arrived beside us.

"Where are Jess and Levi?" I whispered.

"I thought they were right behind me," Grace replied as she fiddled with the safety on her handgun. We waited for a minute, and then two. But Levi and Jess didn't show.

"We did say…" Grace began looking uneasy. Her eyes darted around, looking for any sign of Jess and Levi.

I risked a look around the bus. Smoke billowed onto the street, shrouding everything in a haze. Through the fumes, I saw nothing but soldiers swarming out onto the street. If Levi and Jess weren't here by now, there was no way they were getting past that many soldiers.

"We've got to run," I whispered.

Lizzie shuffled anxiously from foot to foot.

"But Levi—" Grace said.

"No time," I said. I was already on my feet with my gun pointing ahead of me. "This place is crawling with soldiers."

Grace and Lizzie reluctantly followed me down the street. Lizzie kept looking back for the others, but she didn't say anything, so I knew there was still no sign of them.

"Is this far enough?" Lizzie said anxiously, looking backward again. She was worried, and to be fair, so was I.

"They'll be OK," I reassured her again. But it was empty comfort, my voice uncertain. I looked at my watch. There were five more minutes before the bomb was due to blow. "I think we can walk now," I said.

We walked away in the shadows, still nervously looking around, expecting Levi and Jess to appear at any time. I glanced at my watch and turned to look at the Skytower.

"Any second now," I said in response to the unasked question on Lizzie's face. We all watched with bated breath.

The sound was ear-splitting. First, there were a series of bangs from our explosives. The ground quaked under our feet, thick grey smoke mushroomed out around the base of the Skytower. In the seconds that followed, I worried we hadn't used enough explosives. It looked as if the Skytower would live to see another day. But I had judged too soon.

In slow motion, the tower began to lean. A low rumbling grew into a thunderous roar as the Skytower toppled. The tower hit the ground, and the earth groaned. Floor by floor, the tower disintegrated, and a rising black cloud consumed everything in its path. Windows shattered around us, the clear night sky hazy with dust. Several buildings near us cracked as their foundations shifted. Concrete bricks were shaken loose and fell to the ground.

Lizzie pulled on my sleeve and hauled Grace and me into a nearby shop. I ducked under a doorway while Lizzie and Grace took cover underneath the cashier's counter.

Finally, it was all quiet again. I looked out into the chaos. A red glow lit the sky, illuminating the ash that had started to fall like snow around us.

"God, I hope Levi and Jess weren't in that," Grace said with a sob.

"They will have gotten out," Lizzie said. But her eyes searched for mine and held my gaze. She was as worried as I was. I went to them, putting my arms around them both. We sat there for a while, Grace crying onto my shoulder and Lizzie staring dumbly out onto the street.

The magnitude of what we had done was beginning to hit me. I felt the guilt growing like it always did after an attack. Ever since that first soldier I killed back at Lizzie's house. But this time, I had underestimated the guilt, and it washed over me. Each wave crushing me under and leaving me spinning, trying to catch my breath. Because this time, we had gone out to kill, unprovoked.

I wasn't religious, but I prayed. I prayed Jess and Levi would be all right. I prayed everything we had done was for the greater good. I prayed we would be forgiven for all the destruction we wreaked on this city.

"We should go," Lizzie said finally.

I pushed the rising guilt back down into my gut. I could fall apart later. Right now, I had to keep Grace and Lizzie safe and find Jess and Levi. We rose, walking out into the smoky streets. Three a.m., we had said. There was still time to find the department store before we fled from Auckland for good.

"We did it," I said as we stared in shock all around us. We'd destroyed the Skytower. We'd won this battle, and so far, we were still alive. I thought I'd feel triumphant, but I didn't feel anything like that. I'd called this city home once, and now I'd torn it down with my own hands. As we marched forward among the debris, I tried to comfort myself. If nothing else, we'd made the soldiers take notice of us. We'd done something to be remembered. Ironically, all I wanted was to forget.

Chapter Sixteen

Jess

I LOOKED DOWN AT my watch. It was 0040. Go time. Grace hovered at my shoulder, ready to take off into the night. I could just make out Levi standing behind the pillar next to ours, and his shadow moved as he lobbed a grenade at the shop across the road.

A second later, the grenade exploded, showering the street with glass and debris. Soldiers shouted, running through the smoke to examine the scene. As their bodies disappeared into the dust, Grace made her move, darting away into the black. I was about to make a run for it when Levi arrived next to me, breathing hard.

"Come on," he mouthed. I followed him out into the street and looked ahead. But there was no sign of Grace. I started wondering if we had gone the wrong way.

My eyes darted around frantically, searching for an escape route, but I was disorientated. Levi motioned for me to keep close to him. We stumbled toward an abandoned car that straddled the footpath and road. Levi and I crouched behind it, peering through the smoke still billowing from the shop.

"We need to get over there," Levi whispered, pointing at a bus parked about thirty meters away down the street.

The soldiers were still inside the shop, but shouting was coming from up the street. More soldiers were on the move.

"We've got to go soon," I said. "I can hear more soldiers coming."

Levi nodded. "On the count of three, we make a run for it."

"OK," I said. I readjusted my position, ready to sprint to the bus.

"One, two—"

Soldiers burst from the Skytower's convention center. A stream of thirty men ran past our hiding spot and flooded the street.

"Shit," Levi whispered.

We weren't going to make it to the bus.

"Now what?" I asked as I clicked the safety off my handgun. Levi checked his gun was loaded and glanced at his watch.

"We're running out of time," he said as he peeked around the car to check out the street. "There are too many soldiers."

"We need to get out of here," I said. Our explosives would blow in fourteen minutes.

"We're going to have to go around the block," Levi said, looking around for a safer route.

"But the others—"

"We'll have to meet them at the department store," Levi said. "We don't have a choice. Come on."

We checked the soldiers were still preoccupied before emerging from our hiding spot. I followed Levi up the road a few meters, but the rhythmic pounding of boots up ahead forced us to duck down a small alley between buildings. We pressed our backs against the rough brick wall as a couple of squads of soldiers jogged toward the exploded shop. Once the soldiers passed, Levi motioned me to continue after him up the street. We ran to the next intersection and took a right, sticking to the shadows.

Again, the shouts of soldiers heading to the scene of the explosion forced us to hide.

Levi looked down at his watch anxiously. "We don't have long," he whispered, running his hand through his hair.

He was right. We had less than ten minutes to get far away. I looked up at the Skytower. *Too close for comfort.*

"Let's go," Levi said as we moved from our cover and sprinted alongside the high-rise buildings. After a couple minutes, he turned sharply, another right, and we dashed along a side street. It was narrow, and the tall buildings blocked out most of the moonlight.

The narrow street opened onto another main road a few minutes later. Levi and I slowed to a walk to make sure the coast was clear.

Levi whispered to me, "Looks clear to—"

A thunderous boom rocked the city.

Levi and I looked at each other. We were still too close. The ground trembled beneath my feet as Levi and I ran for cover. We found refuge in a bus shelter as the base of the Skytower was consumed by flames. For a couple of agonizing seconds, the Skytower teetered on the brink of falling. Then, the remaining pillars gave way, and the tower crashed into the city below. The surrounding buildings shook as a wave of ash and dust consumed the streets. I covered my face and cowered against the back of the bus shelter as the fallout from our explosion engulfed us.

Levi shook my shoulder. "We've got to move!" he yelled.

I coughed as acrid smoke filled my lungs.

"Come on!"

We staggered out of the bus shelter and onto the road. As I looked around, it felt like the end of the world. Maybe it was.

Debris and glass crunched underfoot as I walked, dazed. A cloud of dust obscured the city in a murky haze while thick smoke choked the air. Ash fluttered down from above and covered the ground in a blanket of gray.

"Look," Levi said, pointing.

One of the Skycity buildings had erupted into flames, adding plumes of black smoke to the already smoggy sky. Whatever material the roof was made of was degrading with the fire and polluting the air with the toxic odor of burning rubber. I coughed violently as a wave of smoke blew through the streets.

"We need to keep going," Levi said as he grabbed my wrist and pulled me along.

"Lizzie! Grace!" I shouted through the fog, hoping they were nearby. I walked forward slowly, my hands shaking as I realized all this devastation was because of us. Our success had left me with a strange feeling of triumph blighted by the fear we had possibly killed innocent people.

I glanced at a soldier who lay on the ground, groaning and clutching his leg. Should I stop and help him? After all, this was our fault. He was in pain because of me. I stood rooted to the spot and stared at him with growing revulsion.

What had we done?

Then the soldier saw me. "Rebels!" he screamed as he grabbed for his rifle at his side. I stared at him, too shocked to move. My handgun hung limply at my side.

A gunshot erupted next to me, and the soldier slumped sideways, dead.

I turned my head and saw Levi lowering his weapon. "Come on, Jess," he said. There was a tremble in his voice. "We've got to get out of here… we've kicked a fucking hornet's nest." He set his jaw, and his dark eyes lingered on the dead soldier in front of us. "It's only a matter of time before another soldier sees us."

Levi broke into a jog, and I ran to keep up with him, jumping over small chunks of concrete. Through the eerie stillness, I heard the scuffling of boots and the cracking of glass.

"Levi, down here," I said and hurriedly grabbed his arm, pulling him into a dark alley. We watched with bated breath as more soldiers marched past, their faces painted with murderous rage. Rifles raised at eye level, bullet chambers scouting the streets with hungry eyes.

"That was way too close," Levi said.

We made our way through the rubble, alternating between short sprints across the bare ground and hiding amongst the wreckage. The soldiers searched relentlessly, and I lost count of how many times we ducked for cover. Every soldier had the same rage burning in their eyes. They were out for blood. Our blood.

Half an hour passed before we were finally free from the downtown district. There were fewer soldiers out here, and Levi and I could make faster progress. We sprinted along the dark streets toward the department store.

Ahead of me, I saw a flicker of movement as several people darted between a tree and a building.

"Levi." I tapped his shoulder.

"I saw it," he said back as we slowed to a walk and crept forward.

We raised our guns, ready. As the shadows moved to another building, the moonlight silhouetted them. I recognized Grace instantly. Athletic frame, long hair, arm in a cast.

"Is that them?" I asked as I lowered my weapon.

"I think so," Levi said, grinning.

We sprinted toward them. We were now far enough away from the Skytower that the streets were clear of debris, but still, I sensed the dark watching us and whispering our location to the soldiers.

"Grace," Levi called.

They spun around in surprise.

"Oh my God, Levi!" Grace called back. She flew to Levi so fast she barely seemed to touch the ground before she leaped toward him and crushed him in a one-armed hug. "We thought you were…" She trailed off, overcome with emotion.

"Soldiers got in the way," I explained.

Lizzie crossed her arms and leaned against the glass front of the shop beside us, her gray eyes darting anxiously around.

"Where do we go now?"

"Back to the store?" Grace asked.

Dylan shook his head. "No. We're together now. Maybe we should head towards—"

Something thumped across the portico of a nearby building.

"What was that?" I whispered.

"I swear I saw someone over there," Levi said.

I peered through the hazy darkness, took out my gun, and aimed it nervously toward the disturbance.

"Do you think it was a soldier?" Grace asked, with fear edging into her voice.

A black cat sprang out from the shadows, and I breathed a sigh of relief, lowering my gun and tucking it into my waistband. The cat skirted around a rubbish can next to the building and disappeared into the night.

"Come on, let's go," Levi said.

We turned to leave, and I paused as I heard another noise. Lizzie heard it too. She looked over her shoulder.

"Run!" Lizzie screamed.

The soldiers came up on us so fast, monsters advancing from the shadows. One of the men gave a shout of discovery, and they stormed toward us. Everyone turned to flee, but I stood frozen with fear as a hulking soldier appeared before me, his gun shimmering in the faint moonlight.

"Jess! Run!" Dylan yelled at me.

I gasped in the cool night air and came to my senses, following Dylan's back down the street. But there were more soldiers at the intersection ahead. We were hemmed in. Lizzie was out front, and she darted into the closest building, a lawyers' firm. We ran in after her, and I slammed the door shut. The others had their guns raised, checking the office was clear.

"Where to now?" Grace whispered. She had her back pressed against the wall, out of sight of the soldiers on the street.

Lizzie ran to the other side of the small office space and tugged at what looked like a back door. "It's locked."

A dead end. I grabbed my handgun from my waistband and slid down against a desk.

A megaphone blared into life. "Come out. We have you surrounded. Surrender your weapons and come out with your hands raised."

Did they think we were idiots? If we surrendered, we'd be dead as soon as we stepped out the door.

"What do we do, wait them out?" Lizzie hissed as she dropped down beside me.

"They know we're the ones who set off the bombs. We can't surrender," Dylan replied from the opposite side of the room.

A loud bang brought our attention to the backdoor. Lizzie and I aimed our weapons at the back while Levi and Dylan covered the front entrance.

"Maybe it's the CIA!" Grace said hopefully. "They've come to save us!"

"Grace, I don't think—" I began to say. I was interrupted by another bang, and then a crunch as the door-locking mechanism gave way.

"We're armed," Lizzie said forcefully to the figure who stood framed in the doorway.

"Yeah? I'm assuming you're not idiots. Aim that thing away from my face, and let me help you. I'm not a soldier."

I squinted. I could barely make him out, but he looked... like us. Lizzie switched on her pocket flashlight. His eyes were a bright clear blue, and his contrasting dark brown hair was flattened to his forehead with sweat. Dirtied jeans hung slackly from his waist, and his plain black t-shirt wasn't quite loose enough to hide his muscular physique. He wasn't dressed like a soldier... but that meant nothing after everything we'd seen.

"I don't believe you," I said.

"What do you mean, you don't believe me?"

"Who busts down a door to save people they don't know in the middle of a war?"

"You have one minute to surrender your weapons and come

out of the building," the voice on the megaphone blared loudly, cutting through our whispers. "Surrender, or we will enter the building."

"We can get to the 'why' of it later," Levi muttered. "This guy's our only hope."

The guy held open the unhinged door, and we each stepped cautiously through, half afraid we would face a firing squad of soldiers on the other side.

"You'd better not be lying," Lizzie said as she passed him.

I exited last, and the guy closed the door behind us. "This way," he said and took off into the night.

We followed him through a maze of streets. I was soon out of breath, and I struggled to keep up. We had been running all night, and I wasn't sure how far I could go. We didn't know this person, we didn't know where we were headed, and we didn't know if we'd even be alive tomorrow.

"Stop, stop. Can we slow down now?" Grace wheezed.

We had made it to a large park, and the trees gave us a feeling of safety.

"What's stopping us running off and leaving him?" I heard Lizzie whisper to Dylan as we slowed at Grace's request.

"We still can. But let's hear him out first," Dylan said. "Hey," he said louder, though his voice strained with the effort. Dylan was tired too. "Dude, whoever you are, we need some answers."

We paused by a tall oak tree, and Grace leaned against it, clutching her arm against her chest and trying to slow her breathing. I placed my hands on my knees for support and leaned forward, waiting for my breath to come back.

"For starters, what's your name?" Levi asked.

"Kyle." He held out a hand.

Levi didn't shake it. "Levi," he said in return. "This is Grace, Jess, Dylan, and Lizzie," he said, pointing each of us out.

"OK. So everyone knows everyone," Lizzie said, rolling her eyes. "Let's skip the life bio and get down to it. Why are you helping us?"

"You guys are suspicious as hell," Kyle said, crossing his arms. "Where's the thank you? You'd all be dead if I didn't step in."

"He's right," I muttered to Lizzie. Perhaps we had grown too suspicious, and we couldn't even be thankful when someone saved our lives. We had lived in fear of the soldiers for so long that we treated everyone and everything with fear and paranoia.

"You never know who you can trust out here," Levi said.

"Fair. I was scrounging for food. The suburbs where my crew live have gotten pretty lean. I was in the city when the tower came down. I saw the soldiers all hitting up this one building, and to be honest, I thought you might have been a friend who disappeared from our group a couple of weeks ago," Kyle said. He dropped his eyes, and I could feel his disappointment. "I mean, I guess I knew it probably wasn't, but we never found out what happened to him, and you always kind of hope, you know?"

"Yeah," I said softly. "We've lost people too." I thought about Leah and how much her friendship had meant to me. I missed her, and thinking about her too much was still painful. I still wished she would show up with her peppy smile and sassy attitude, even though I knew she was gone. I had seen her die with my own eyes. And as hard as that had been, I could only imagine how much tougher it would be if we had never known Leah's fate.

"Next question then," Lizzie interrogated. I shuffled uncomfortably from foot to foot, embarrassed for her. Sometimes I couldn't understand how Lizzie could be so callous. "Where are you taking us, and how many of you are there?"

But Kyle didn't seem offended. "Four of us managed to evade the soldiers," he answered. "We have a house out in the suburbs. It's pretty safe there, but like I said, we're short on food. The others will kill me if I go back empty-handed and with five more mouths to feed."

"Maybe we can save you that problem by splitting up," Lizzie said. "I mean, thanks for your help and all, but we can take it from here." She turned and began to walk away.

Grace gave a little shrug to the rest of us and wandered after her. Levi and Dylan took an uncertain step in her direction.

I was rooted to the spot. Undecided. On the one hand, we had done well by ourselves, and a larger group would draw attention. But on the other hand, we needed them. Kyle had risked his own neck for us and was giving us a place to stay. He clearly knew Auckland better than we did, and we needed to find somewhere safe to bunker down, fast. Soldiers would be searching high and low for us for weeks. If they caught us... I hated to think what would happen.

And, there was the defiant part of me that resented being told where to go and what to do. Why did Lizzie always get to dictate our actions? She forced everyone to go along with whatever she wanted. She knew no one would call her bluff.

But that was about to change.

"Hey, wait a sec. We don't know Auckland. Soldiers are crawling all over the city, and you're going to ditch the one person who has offered to help us?" I called after them.

"Since when did you start swallowing all his bullshit? We can take care of ourselves like we always do," Lizzie said.

"Then leave me here." I held my ground and crossed my arms in defiance.

"You're being childish," Lizzie said.

I wanted to scream at her that she wasn't always right. My opinion mattered too. Instead, I said, "This is the right choice, and you know it."

"What's got into you?" Lizzie's voice was cold.

"Look," Kyle said, taking a step back. "I was excited to see some other people around because I didn't actually think there was anyone left except for us. But you know, if you don't want to come, that's your choice." He put his hands up in surrender. "I'm not going to force you to come with me."

"I'm coming," I said to Kyle, looking him directly in the eye. I was sick of being pushed around by Lizzie.

"Jess," Lizzie snapped.

"What? I can make my own choice, Lizzie."

Lizzie stared at me with pursed lips, fighting to keep her temper under control.

"We don't leave anyone behind," Dylan said to the group. "If Jess is staying, then…"

Lizzie looked torn, and I was glad I was forcing her hand for once, instead of the other way around.

"Then I guess you're all coming too," I said.

THE STREETS WERE DANGEROUS, and we made the unanimous decision to bunker down in a nearby house while we waited for the day to pass. We were exhausted and, as much as we all wanted to get out of the city, we were at our limit.

We chose a single-story brick house in a state of disrepair. The orange and red bricks were worn and chipped, and a few had crumbled off the exposed corner nearest to the carport. The bricks lay scattered across the driveway, along with a couple of tiles from the roof. The house had obviously been through a few wild storms and now needed some serious TLC. But it was a good place to spend the night—no one in their right mind would choose to stay here, and I hoped the soldiers would think the same. Kyle and I stood guard outside while the others checked if it was all clear.

"Thank you," I said after the silence became too much.

"For what?" Kyle replied.

"For helping us. We'd be dead if you hadn't come when you did."

Kyle shrugged. "I didn't do much. I'd have done the same for anyone."

"Maybe, but still. I'm glad you came."

"It's all clear," Dylan called as he creaked open the front door, stiff from disuse.

"Coming inside?" I asked.

"Yeah, sure," Kyle said. His troubled face suddenly brightened. "I wonder if they have any beer," he said with a grin.

"Don't let Lizzie see it," I said.

"She's got drinking problems?" Kyle asked as we headed indoors.

I laughed. The thought of Lizzie as some dysfunctional alcoholic was so out of character, I could barely imagine it. "More like she has a problem with drinking."

"Oh, right. Drinking is irresponsible. Imagine if soldiers came," he said in a girlish whiny voice. "We have a girl back at our camp… Charlie. She's kind of like that too. Still, no one can be responsible one hundred percent of the time."

"What is it like… drinking alcohol?" I asked curiously. I had come from a family who walked the straight and narrow, and being underage, I'd never even had a sip.

"You've never?" Kyle said, incredulous.

"Never."

"It's like… if someone gave you a pill. That pill doesn't make you care any less about what's happening around you, but it makes you all right with it." My expression was skeptical, so he continued. "It makes it OK that nothing is the same anymore, and it makes it OK that your friends died because it makes you feel everything has a plan, and you're just a tiny insignificant speck in a great big world." He laughed. "I suck at explaining it."

"I don't know, it sounded convincing enough to me," I said wistfully. It would be nice not to question every action I made in this war and to go with the flow for a while.

"Would you guys get in here and help?" Lizzie bossed from the kitchen.

I rolled my eyes. "Coming, mother," I called back.

Lizzie and Grace had busied themselves, laying out all the non-perishables on the table to see what we could make.

"Is there a can-opener in here?" Lizzie asked as she grabbed a tin of chopped tomatoes. I tossed her one from the drawer next to me.

"The house runs on gas. We might actually get a cooked meal for once," Grace exclaimed as she tested the oven.

"Good. Jess, can you give me those noodles?" Lizzie asked. She filled a pot with water.

I handed her the noodles, and Dylan slapped a hand over Kyle's shoulder.

"I think they've got it under control. We should leave the girls to it."

"Sounds good to me," Kyle said and walked out with Levi and Dylan.

Maybe things would work out with a bigger group, I thought. I knew I had made the right choice, and I smiled to myself as I grabbed some plates from one of the cupboards. Things were going to work out fine.

CHAPTER SEVENTEEN

LEVI

Joining another group came with risks. I couldn't tell if it was the right decision. On the one hand, it was nice to know other people were still free. On the other, could we trust Kyle?

I sat across the dining room table from Kyle, eyeing him suspiciously. Lizzie and Grace had cooked up some pasta, and we ate in tense silence.

"Chill out, guys, you're so serious," Kyle finally said. "Someone smile… or something."

"We've been through a lot," Lizzie snapped back. She looked shiftily around the room, clearly anxious a soldier might discover us.

"What she means is it's hard to trust someone we don't know," Jess said. Her gaze lingered for a moment on Kyle before returning to her meal.

"It's totally safe here. The soldiers never come this way," Kyle said, flicking his floppy hair back.

"We just blew up the Skytower. Soldiers will be everywhere," Lizzie said.

Kyle grinned. "That was so badass."

A smile pulled at the corners of Dylan's lips. "It was pretty badass."

"How'd you pull it off?" Kyle asked, leaning back in his chair.

Lizzie gave us a warning look: Don't you dare mention the Americans.

"It was no big deal," Dylan said, boasting. "We stole some equipment, and after that, it was easy to rig up the explosives."

I groaned inwardly. Dylan always got weird around new people.

"We should toast to that," Kyle said. He strode into the kitchen and began rummaging through cupboards. "I found the good stuff," he called out.

Lizzie crossed her arms and glared.

"Give him a chance," Dylan said, with a calming hand on her back. "He might be a good guy."

Kyle returned with a bottle of vodka and a stack of shot glasses. After generously filling them, he slid them across the table to each of us. I looked down at mine. The old, carefree Levi urged me to drink, but it had been a long time since I'd been that guy.

"To explosions and retaliation," Kyle said, lifting his glass before knocking back the shot.

"Cheers," Dylan and Jess said, downing theirs heartily.

Grace had a distasteful look on her face and pushed her glass away. Lizzie had no interest in taking part in anything involving Kyle. Dylan gave her an encouraging look, but she shook her head adamantly.

"Go on, mate," Kyle said to me.

It was only one shot, after all. I tipped it back and felt the familiar alcohol burn. It seemed like years since I had done this. For a split second, it brought memories of happier times. I had forgotten I used to party with friends and have fun. It was like this one shot was a brief look in a mirror of my past. Now, looking around me, I was with friends. But this was hardly a party. Everything about it felt wrong. Disgusted with myself, I stood up from the table and walked to the kitchen, dumping my plate unceremoniously in the sink. Grace shadowed me, precariously balancing her plate and cup with one hand.

"I'm getting bad vibes from Kyle," she whispered as I helped her with her plate.

"We don't really know him yet," I said, hiding my doubts about him. No use worrying her yet.

Grace's brow furrowed, and she readjusted her sling.

"He's probably stoked to find some other free people," I said.

"Maybe," she muttered, unconvinced. She leaned back against the cupboards as a look of worry crossed her face.

"Are you all right?" I asked. I knew she wasn't.

Darkness clouded her face, and she looked up at me with tired eyes. "I think the Skytower was a mistake," she said so quietly I had to lean closer to hear her.

"But it worked," I said back.

"I know… but I think deep down…" Grace trailed off.

"You didn't think we'd actually do it." I had thought the same thing.

She shook her head slowly. "We killed a lot of people."

There was no denying it.

"They deserved it," I said, stepping closer to her so the others couldn't eavesdrop. "They took our friends from us."

"I thought the revenge would make me feel better. But I feel… sick. And dirty with their blood," she whispered. "I should have known… when does revenge ever solve anything?" She was on the verge of tears, but managed to keep it together.

"Levi, are you making out with Grace in the kitchen?" Kyle called.

Grace rolled her eyes. "See."

"He's a typical guy," I said. "It's harmless."

"I don't like him," Grace whispered.

"Well, it looks like we're stuck with him for now," I said to her with a shrug.

I turned to face the dining room. "Man, I wish," I said to Kyle with a casual laugh. I walked away, leaving Grace alone. But I couldn't help but wonder if she was right. It had been bothering me, too. Just like that. Bang. We had killed dozens of soldiers. I had seen them lying injured or dead on the road, caked in dust and blood. It was like London after the rocket hit; death, pain, and chaos in the streets. Were we as bad as them now?

I tried to tell myself it was revenge—they deserved it. Our friends were dead because of their regime. And some of us had lost family members. Jess' uncle. Lizzie's brother. Not to mention the hundreds of unsuspecting civilians in London. Our Skytower attack was nothing compared to that. It wasn't mass murder like the rocket. It was a targeted strike against a real enemy who had killed innocent people. With that final thought, I tried to engage back in conversation with the others.

Grace was still in the kitchen, looking contemplatively out the window. She nursed a cup of tea as she watched the world outside. Kyle was deep in conversation with Jess, who appeared to be hanging on to his every word, clearly swept up in his carefree charm. She deserved to find someone, I thought. Maybe Kyle was that guy.

"We should get some bags packed," Lizzie said, interrupting whatever Jess and Kyle were discussing.

"We've got hours," Kyle said. "Don't panic."

"Don't worry, Lizzie," Jess said with a friendly smile. "It's only a few cans of food. We've cased places in minutes before. We'll be fine."

Realizing Kyle and Jess would be no help, Lizzie turned to Dylan and me.

"Guys, we need clothes and food," she said, exasperated.

"I'm on it," I said instantly. I wasn't too interested in hanging out with Kyle at the moment, especially when there were more important things to get done. Dylan watched Kyle and Jess for a moment without responding to Lizzie.

"Come on, mate," I said to him, pulling him up. "Kyle looks busy."

"Man, you guys are intense… like a group of elite soldiers," Kyle said, tearing away from Jess and laughing.

"You know it," Dylan said, pointing at Kyle and winking.

Kyle's comment struck a nerve with me. Was I a soldier now? Anyone else would say yes. I was a real soldier, fighting for my freedom and my people. This is what Dad would have wanted. He had trained me for this my whole life, and I didn't know how to feel about it. I hated my dad and everything he stood for. Was I becoming him? That thought sent waves of panic through me. I needed to know. I looked at Grace. She would tell me the truth.

"I need help packing some clothes," I called to her.

"Sure," she said as she followed me toward one of the bedrooms. Once we were safely out of earshot in one of the bedrooms, I shut the door and turned to face her.

"Levi, what's wrong?" she asked me, alarmed. Apparently, my inner conflict was clear on my face.

"Am I good?"

"What?" she asked, confused.

"Am I a good person?" I repeated.

A bewildered look passed over her face. "Of course you are."

"Good," I said.

"I don't understand. You're acting weird," she said, looking at me with uncertainty.

I took a deep breath. I hadn't talked about Dad much. "My dad's a horrible guy. He was a soldier… and I hated him."

"You're worried you'll become him."

I nodded. "Yeah."

She looked at me sympathetically and moved closer before crushing me in a comforting hug. "Don't worry. You'll never be like him," she whispered in my ear. I hugged her back with everything I had. When I finally let her go, she stood within arm's reach of me. "Usually, it's you comforting me," she said with a weak laugh. "This is a first."

"Guess it is."

We stood staring awkwardly at each other. Things hadn't

been the same between us since the attempted kiss. We both wanted it to happen, but…

"So, about those clothes?" she said with a sheepish smile.

"Yeah, right," I said. "Find some stuff that will fit you girls."

She rummaged through the chest of drawers. "Everything in here is massive." She held up a shirt she could wear as a dress.

"You'll have to make do."

"I'm going to check another room," she said, flicking her hair over her shoulder. "These clothes won't do."

She walked purposefully to the door. Before leaving, she turned around. "You're not your dad, Levi. You never will be."

"Thanks," I said as I watched her back disappear. I hoped she was right.

THE REST OF THE afternoon passed quickly. We packed up clothes and as much food as the house had. When the sun finally sunk below the horizon, we were ready to go.

"We're about an hour from our base," Kyle said, Jess close by his side.

"Lead the way," Dylan said.

Kyle took charge, and we followed him through the maze of suburban streets, sticking to the shadows like always. I felt safer outside the confines of the house. Here, we could run if we had to. But it was an uneventful journey to Kyle's base. We didn't see any soldiers, and by the time we arrived, everyone was in good spirits, even Lizzie.

To Kyle and his crew's credit, the house they had chosen was unassuming—a typical 1930s bungalow set back from the road. The gray paint was faded and peeling, exposing patches of dark timber underneath. We walked down the cracked concrete path and crowded onto the small veranda.

Kyle rapped on the front door. "Open up, Charlie, it's me," he said through the door. We heard the door-chain slide and a heavy lock turn. The door creaked open, revealing a girl my age with strawberry blond hair.

"Who are these people?" she asked, hands on her hips. She was a little heavier than Lizzie and Grace, but she had a pretty face, fair features, and alert green eyes.

"I found them. They're OK," Kyle said. "Let us in."

Charlie stepped aside. "Nice to meet you," she said with a smile. I followed Kyle in, stepping over the threshold and into the dimly lit home. Kyle led us down the rustic wooden hall and into the living room, where he threw his pack to the ground. Two guys lounging on threadbare sofas looked up at us newcomers.

"I found some stragglers," Kyle said to them with a laugh. The lanky Asian one with large, thick-framed glasses came up and shook my hand.

"I'm Ollie," he said.

"Levi," I replied.

The other guy refused to move from the couch. His lumbering frame was hanging off the small two-seater. He brushed his long dark fringe off his face and gazed up at us, beer in hand. "I'm Knox," he finally said, before letting out a low wolf whistle. "You finally found some more chicks, Kyle." I chanced a look at Lizzie and Grace, who looked horrified at his comment. I laughed to myself. Like Kyle, this guy knew what buttons to push.

Dylan had already decided to befriend our new companions. He had seated himself next to Ollie and was laughing at something one of them had said. Knox threw him a can of beer, which he cracked open.

Lizzie stood staring at Dylan, not sure what to think. "You're going to drink that?" she said to him.

"You can have one too if you want," Dylan said, apparently oblivious to Lizzie's growing annoyance. "Come sit," Dylan said to her. She moodily stalked over and perched uncomfortably on the armrest.

Grace wanted no part in the party and began lugging the packs with her good arm to the kitchen. I gave her a hand. No one was going anywhere, and I could chat with the others later. She began unpacking the food we had taken.

"Knox seems like a creep," she commented as she began stacking tins of food.

"Clearly, they've been alone here for too long," I said. The kitchen was filthy with dirty plates, and rubbish overflowed from the bin. The counter was grimy and covered with empties.

"It seems they like their liquor," Grace said sourly as she picked up a can and let it fall to the floor.

"More likely they're slobs," I said, picking up a few cans and moving them into a pile in the corner.

Grace continued to unpack our bags. "Levi," she said, concerned, holding up two bottles of whiskey she had pulled from Kyle's pack.

"Don't worry about it," I said. It wasn't a huge deal. Teenagers drank. So what?

"We're at war…" she said, her eyes pleading with me. "What if soldiers come and they're stumbling around wasted?"

"It's only alcohol," I said. "I'm sure they only drink occasionally."

"Are you defending them?" she asked, raising her voice. Her hand that held the whiskey bottles started trembling.

I tried to defuse the situation. "No. All I'm saying is we don't know anything about them."

"I don't like it," Grace said as she bit at her lip.

"You've got to calm down and give them a chance," I said, taking a step forward to comfort her.

At that moment, Lizzie stormed into the kitchen. "Honestly, what's their problem?" Lizzie said, fuming. "And what does Dylan think he's playing at?"

"Don't tell me to calm down," Grace yelled at me, slamming the bottles down on the counter. One of the bottles tipped over and rolled along the bench before smashing on the floor. Grace looked at it with malice in her eyes. "Good riddance," she muttered.

"Grace, you should clean—" Lizzie began to say.

But Grace blew right past her.

Lizzie raised her eyebrows at me as Grace stormed off into the house. We heard a door slam. Lizzie grabbed a tea towel and tossed it onto the spilled liquor. I wanted to go after Grace, but I had no idea what I had said or done to set her off.

"Should I go after her?" I asked Lizzie, who was now hunting for a broom.

"I don't know what you did, but give her a minute to cool off," Lizzie suggested.

"Do you need help?" I asked.

Lizzie shook her head. "I can finish this. I can't stand being around the others. Like… what the hell's their problem?"

I sighed. "I don't know, Lizzie. I haven't had a chance to talk to them yet."

"Well, go talk to them, and maybe talk some sense into Dylan while you're at it," she said, crossing her arms and looking up at me impatiently. "I'll finish this off."

I edged my way out of the kitchen and into the hallway. Boisterous laughter beckoned from the living room. I poked my head around the door.

"Levi," Dylan said with a massive grin on his face. "Where'd you get to?"

"Helping Grace."

"Grab a seat," he said, dragging me to a chair.

"And have a bevvy," Knox said, lobbing a beer across the room to me. "Where'd the other girl go?" he added.

"You mean Grace…?" I said as I leaned in to catch the beer and cracked it open. My thoughts were still with her. I should go after her. But what would I say? I didn't even know what I had done wrong.

"The blonde."

I glanced at Dylan, but he was already caught up in conversation and didn't seem to notice. I didn't know if Dylan had made a move, and I didn't want to interfere. "She's… um, having a quiet night," I said eventually.

Knox shrugged. "She doesn't know what she's missing," he said, before turning his attention to the others.

Lizzie and Grace weren't missing much, I thought. I could do with a quiet night, too. I was drained from the Skytower attack and not really in the mood to talk. But it seemed rude to ignore these new people. Kyle had saved our lives, after all. Yes, they were all drinking right now, and heavily, by the looks of it. Knox had a decent stack building up next to him. So did Kyle. Jess was sitting beside him giggling, her cheeks flushed, and a cheap vodka mix gripped tight in her hand. Charlie sat on his other side, silent and eyeing Jess with dislike. Meanwhile, Dylan was re-enacting our adventures in the US and UK.

"We broke into the Pentagon. It was fucking insane. We had fake IDs and everything," he said, his eyes glazed from the booze.

"That's sick," Knox said lazily.

"The fucking Secretary of Defense even tried to smack me in the face," he continued. I rolled my eyes. He always swore and exaggerated when he tried to show off in front of new people. I held my drink limply in one hand and took a swig. It was a cheap, warm beer. There was a time when I wouldn't have given a shit about that. But now, it felt like life was too short to spend it getting blind drunk with strangers. Staying alive was way too important.

"Levi, where were you while Dylan was about to get his ass kicked by the Secretary of Defense?" Knox asked, a lopsided smile spread across his face.

"Getting the hell out of there," I said with a laugh.

"Man, you guys do some crazy shit," Kyle said. He was pretty drunk now, and his hand slipped onto Jess' thigh. I felt a strong urge to protect her come over me. How dare he touch her. I stood up to get at him.

"Levi," Jess said, raising her voice. "It's fine." Kyle was so smashed he didn't notice me.

"Are you sure?"

"Yes. You don't need to protect me," Jess said, blushing.

"If he ever—"

"I'm fine, Levi," she said with finality. She returned her gaze to Kyle and shifted closer to him. I couldn't sit there and watch it go any further. It was like she was my little sister.

"Is there a spare room somewhere?" I asked Kyle. "I'm shattered."

"First door on your right," Ollie said. "I'll show you."

"Thanks," I said.

Ollie got up and led me down the hall. "In there."

"Do you guys drink like this every night?"

Ollie shrugged. "Not every night."

I pushed the door open and noticed Grace curled up in the corner of the room, asleep.

Lizzie leaned against the opposite wall, staring distantly out the window at the moon. I pulled the door shut, and she looked toward the door. "Is that you, Levi?" Lizzie whispered.

"Yeah," I whispered back. I made my way across the room, and sat down on the floor next to her, resting my head against the wall.

"So, what do you think of them?" she asked, shuffling to get comfortable.

"Ollie and Charlie seem all right."

"I don't trust Kyle... or Knox."

"I'm not surprised," I said with a weak laugh.

Lizzie's face was conflicted with emotions, and she was silent for a moment.

"Do you think Dylan's acting weird?" Lizzie said eventually.

"What do you mean?"

"He's usually responsible. Reliable."

I wasn't sure what to tell her. Dylan was always like this around new people. He had a compulsive need to fit in and would transform into someone unrecognizable.

"I wouldn't worry," I said. "He's... coming to terms with the

Skytower attack. I'm sure that's all it is."

"But what if it's not?" Lizzie turned her face away. I couldn't quite tell through the hazy dark, but she looked embarrassed. "What if it's about something else?"

"What else would it be?"

Lizzie faced me and opened to her mouth to speak. "Forget I said anything." She looked away again.

"OK," I said. "But if you—"

"Before we left the department store, Dylan and I kissed," she blurted. "And now I'm scared he's acting weird because he regrets it. Maybe he doesn't want to be with me after all."

"Um, OK," I said, raising my eyebrows in surprise. "I mean… I don't think that's why. He always does this. But he's not an idiot. He would never put us… you in danger. He's just blowing off steam."

Lizzie sighed loudly and turned to face me. "Maybe you're right. But either way, I'm worried, Levi. Drinking is dangerous in our situation."

"Me too," I said absently. I was worried I was about to lose my best mate.

Chapter Eighteen

Grace

I WOKE WITH THE rising sun. Its weak rays shone through the dirt-encrusted window, casting hazy morning shadows on the dusty carpet. I sat up and pulled the shabby blanket tight around my shoulders. The mornings were cooler now, and with everything that had happened in the last few weeks, the departure of summer had gone unnoticed. Autumn was here.

Through the dim early light, I could make out Dylan lying on his stomach in the middle of the floor, snoring unglamorously. Meanwhile, Lizzie was asleep in the corner, curled up in a ball, and Levi lay on his back, staring at the mildew-covered ceiling.

Condensation dripped down the windows and pooled on the windowsills, blackened with mold. A peculiar damp odor hung stagnant in the air. It wasn't the nicest place, but at least there was a roof over our heads.

Quietly standing up, I tiptoed to the living room. It was in the same state I imagined Dylan was in when he finally retired to bed in the early hours of the morning: trashed. I half-heartedly picked up a few empties. But once I realized there was no rubbish bin, I gave up and settled for piling them in the corner out of the way.

When the lounge finally resembled something civilized, I sat on the tatty two-seater. It was nice to have a moment alone. The house was too small for all of us. Our tight little group was accustomed to living outdoors, where you could wander off into the forest to get away. I wasn't used to being confined with them, let alone stuck with a group of strangers.

My ears pricked as a droning sound whined outside. I padded to the bay window and cracked the curtain open. My eyes were drawn skyward to the formation of fighter planes swooping low over the suburbs. Probably searching for us. I watched them bank over the city to the east before circling back toward me. I pulled the curtains shut and took a deep breath to stop my hands from shaking.

If I had it my way, we'd be hiding out in the forest by now. And I wouldn't feel like my life was on the brink. Instead, the entire war was crashing down on me at once. Suffocating me, encircling me. And the strength I had to carry on was ebbing away, leaving me vulnerable to my ghosts.

We were trapped here, and I struggled to make sense of anything anymore. I was overwhelmed, and my emotions were spiraling out of control. All the people we had killed. The fear of being caught and the disappointment of the Americans not coming for us. All my hopes of finding Mom were pinned on the CIA. With the loss of the radio came the realization that, for now, Mom was still lost.

My eyes drifted to the stack of empties I had piled in the corner. The drinking brought back my buried memories of Dad and my siblings, and Sean, my ex. I tried to keep them suppressed, but my grip on the situation was slipping. I wanted to walk away from the house, wander the streets, and let my tears loose. It sounded pathetic, but it was how I coped with life. It was the only way I knew to get control back. But, with soldiers after us, I couldn't leave. It was too dangerous to venture out, and there was nowhere inside to get a respite from anyone.

This house felt more and more like a prison every minute. And I couldn't shake the feeling that this place was going to be the end of us. Of me. But nothing could be done about it now.

"Grace?" Levi whispered from the doorway.

I was still angry with him from last night and didn't feel like talking to anyone. What I wanted was to be alone.

"I'm sorry," he said, and took a few hesitant steps into the room.

I took a deep breath to help compose myself. Levi didn't understand. That night before the Skytower attack, I was so close to breaking down my walls and letting Levi in. He was different from other guys, and I liked him a lot. The trust between us was building, and I was even starting to see a future with him in it. But for some reason, I couldn't let go of the past. The pain of Sean leaving after Dad died lingered. Sean betrayed me the moment things got tough. What was stopping Levi from doing the same thing?

"I should have come after you last night," Levi said as he cast his eyes down. "I got trapped talking to Lizzie," he said, walking the length of the room and sitting next to me. He put his hand over mine.

I knew I had to say something. "Have I ever told you about what happened to my family?"

"They died in a car crash," Levi said.

"A drunk driver killed them. It was a straightway, and he was going too fast. He crossed the centerline right in front of my dad's car," I said as the tears began to well. "There wasn't even time to brake. Dad, Tristan, and Mallory died before the ambulance got there. The drunk driver walked away unhurt."

"I'm sorry," Levi said.

"The driver was a teenager, barely sixteen… almost the same age as me at the time," I said. I expected Levi to put his arm around me like he always did, but it didn't come. Was this information scaring him off? It was too confronting, and for once, it seemed Levi didn't know what to say.

"So, that's why you hate drinking," he eventually said.

"When you say it like that, it sounds stupid."

"That's not what I mean… the drinking reminds you of your family," Levi said.

Wrong again. I was frustrated. "It reminds me of that day and all the shit that came after it. You don't get it, do you?"

"Maybe I don't. Help me understand," Levi said to me, gripping my hand. "You can tell me."

Should I tell him about my shadows? Or, once he knew, would he run off for good?

At that moment, Kyle sauntered into the lounge and flopped onto the other couch. "What a night," he said before stifling a huge yawn.

I stood up to leave and looked over at Levi, whose eyes were shimmering with unshed tears. A part of me wanted to stay with him. His presence alone made me feel safe, but I didn't want to be around Kyle.

"Yeah, you guys partied hard," Levi said with a forced smile.

Without another look behind me, I left the room. All I wanted was to find somewhere to be alone. I headed down the hallway and bumped into Jess as she came out of Kyle's room. Her face morphed from one of embarrassment to one of concern when she saw my face.

"Oh my gosh, Grace, are you OK?" she asked. Her usually bright eyes were bloodshot, and her hair was disheveled.

"Everything's fine," I said, choking back tears.

"Do you want to talk about it?"

"I think I've talked enough. I need some time alone." I walked away toward the kitchen, leaving her staring after me. I put a pot of water on the camp stove to boil and made myself a mug of tea. That never failed to calm me down. I was relieved to see a frosted-glass door, which led out to the back garden. I pushed it open and found myself on a deck in an overgrown yard. A large sycamore tree grew tall at the back.

Weather-worn outdoor chairs had tipped over and were

strewn amongst the knee-high weeds. I pushed my way through the dew-soaked grass and resurrected a forlorn-looking chair. I dragged it awkwardly with one arm to a secluded corner, sat down heavily, and cried.

I let all of it out. The memories of the past, the deaths on my conscience, and the fear the Americans had abandoned us. The thought of seeing Mom again was the only thing that kept me going. Losing the radio when we crashed had severed our link with them. We were alone and had done their dirty work.

Between my sobs, I heard someone walking through the grass.

"You can't walk out on me like that," Levi said from over my shoulder. He put his hand gently on my back, and I melted into a pool of tears. "What's wrong?"

All I could do was cry. I couldn't get the words out.

Levi stood behind me, silently, letting me cry myself out. "I want to help," he eventually said.

"Y-y-you ca-ca-can't," I said, gasping for breath between my tears.

"Please," he said.

I shook my head. "You won't understand."

"Try me."

It took a few minutes to compose myself enough to talk again. Levi waited patiently beside me in a chair with a broken seat. Once I calmed down, I turned to face him. I was so confused. On the one hand, I liked him a lot. On the other, I was terrified he'd leave when things got tough.

It had taken Sean all of two minutes to find someone more fun than me. When we first got together, he'd told me nothing could ever separate us. No one would come between us. We were meant to be together. It turned out nothing was a devastating car crash and no one was my archrival on the swim team. I guess they were meant to be together.

Levi was different. I knew that much. But I couldn't expel the nagging fear our relationship was a sequel to the same old story. He'd move on as soon as someone better came along. Especially if he ever found out how screwed up I really was.

"Let's start with something easy," I said with a strangled laugh.

Levi didn't find it funny. Instead, he looked at me with deep concern. He was worried about me. I could tell. "I know the drinking—" he started.

"Forget about the drinking." It was dredging up memories from my past I had spent all of last year trying to bury. But I was starting to crack, and they were beginning to drip through. I didn't want them to pour through, though. I knew how depressed I had gotten back then, and now wasn't the time to slip into that misery again. The war had made me stronger, and if I tried hard enough, maybe I could defeat it.

"The Americans abandoned us," I said.

"We lost the radio," Levi agreed. "It was our only communication with them."

"I know. I hoped after we blew the Skytower up, they would find us," I said, my voice measured.

"How?"

"I don't know," I admitted, defeated. "We did what they wanted, and now we'll never find our families."

"You wanted to find your mom," Levi said.

"Of course, I wanted to find her," I said, tears welling in my eyes again. "She's all I have left."

"You have me."

It was a sweet thing to say, and I desperately wanted it to be true. But I wasn't ready to believe it yet. After all, that's exactly what Sean said.

"I told you I would always be there for you, and I still mean it," Levi added.

"You said that, but how can you be sure?"

"What do you mean?" Levi's brow contracted.

"I mean, what if something happened to change that? What if —"

"I'll always be there, Grace. As long as I'm still breathing."

This conversation was all too familiar and momentarily transported me back to our almost-kiss a few weeks back. I chanced a glance over at him. He sat hunched forward, elbows on his knees and hands clasped. His face turned toward me, and our eyes met briefly. I could feel the connection between us and knew I had to change the conversation before he tried to kiss me again. This time I wasn't sure if I would be strong enough to resist, or if I wanted to.

"We did the American's dirty work for nothing," I said, pulling my eyes away from his.

"It wasn't for nothing," Levi insisted, sounding dejected.

"We did it to find our families, but now all we've done is commit bloody murder."

"Our names will be cleared," Levi said. "The world will know we didn't launch the rocket. We're not terrorists."

"That hardly matters here."

"It matters a lot. We're the good guys."

"Maybe."

"Only maybe? Grace, before you were angry that they thought we did it. What happened?" he asked, sitting upright and looking at me.

"I knew you wouldn't understand," I said, tears falling afresh. I stood up and marched off.

"Grace, come back," Levi pleaded. I kept walking back into the house. I managed to hide for a few hours in one of the bedrooms. Levi didn't come looking for me again, and no one else bothered me. For a while, I was able to calm down and focus. I didn't know what was happening to me. Before the Skytower incident, everything was fine. But now, I was falling apart and questioning everything I thought I knew. I blamed this house and these new people. It was the only explanation. The sound of the door opening made me look up. It was Charlie.

"I made some lunch if you want some," she said.

"Thanks. I'll be out in a minute," I said, affixing a well-practiced smile on my face.

"That Levi guy seems pretty worried about you. He said to force you to come now," Charlie said.

I blushed a little. "Why would he say that?" I mused out loud.

"Clearly, he's into you," she said, coming in and shutting the door behind her.

"I know that," I said.

"He seems really great. Please tell me you've hooked up with him." She was so direct I couldn't help but laugh.

"Wow, subtle," I mused. She checked the door was firmly closed and came closer, sitting down next to me.

"I'm stuck in this house with three guys," she said. "I need any girl talk I can get."

It must have been frustrating living with Knox, Kyle, and Ollie. I looked over at Charlie, who stared at me with eager eyes. I sighed and readjusted my arm in its sling. I needed to get this stuff off my chest for my own sanity. Jess was obsessed with Kyle, and Lizzie was hating on everyone in the house. Even if I talked to Lizzie and Jess about it, they would tell me to go kiss Levi and be done with it. I needed someone on the outside, so I decided to spill.

"I haven't told Lizzie or Jess any of this," I said to her.

"Even better," she said, looking at me with anticipation.

"What did you want to know?" I asked her with a sigh.

"Have you kissed him?"

"No. But almost. I don't know." I said, stumbling over my words. "It's complicated."

"Why not? What happened?" she asked.

I grimaced, thinking back to that day, "I backed out."

"So, he initiated? How?" she pressed.

"One minute I was crying, the next, his hand was on my cheek and our faces were so close."

"Why the hell didn't you go through with it?" she asked.

"I'm an idiot," I said. "I was worried things would be awkward."

"Relationships are always awkward. If it doesn't go well,

you'll both get over it," Charlie said, rolling her eyes.

"You're probably right," I said, looking down, a little embarrassed. "But it's not only that."

"What is it then?"

"I think I'm afraid," I whispered.

"Afraid of what?" she asked.

"That he'll leave if things get tough. My ex…" I hesitated and took a breath. "My last boyfriend cheated on me. My dad had just died and…" I cleared my throat to compose myself as all the emotions came flooding back. The betrayal. Heartbreak. The pain, like my soul was being wrenched in two. "I don't know if I can trust someone that way again."

"Shit." Charlie winced and put her hand on my shoulder. "Your ex sounds like a dick."

"You can say that again." I looked up at the mould-covered ceiling and sighed. I hadn't even told her about the darkness I plunged into after. My life was so messed up.

"But it could be different this time." Charlie offered me a smile. "Levi doesn't seem like the kind of guy who'd do that."

"Neither did Sean," I said.

"Have you talked to him about this?" Charlie asked.

"Sort of," I said. "No."

"That's the first thing you have to do," Charlie said. "Tell him all of it."

"I don't know." Was I ready to open up to Levi that much? Was he ready to hear it? Once I told him about Sean, I'd have to tell him everything else. He'd know how damaged I was.

"What do you mean? He seems like a real decent guy." She gave me a wink. "Plus, he's hot. You have to give it a go," she said. I remained silent, thinking about what she said. "Or just get with him. A little fling isn't a bad thing."

"That's not me," I said. "If I commit, it's for the long haul."

"Oh, come on, go for it," she said, a playful smile pulling at her lips.

"We'll see." I couldn't help but think maybe she had a point.

Was I overthinking this whole thing? Maybe I should just jump in.

"At least you have a guy who notices you," she said.

"I can imagine it's tough living in a house with a whole group of them," I sympathized.

"It's not so bad," she said. "They treat me like I'm their sister, though."

"What's wrong with that?" I asked. Dylan, Jess, and Lizzie were like family, the siblings I had lost.

"I don't know," Charlie said, averting her eyes from mine. She was definitely into one of them.

"They only want to protect you," I said, "like any friend."

"I'm sick of being treated like one of the gang. I'm a girl with feelings, too."

She definitely liked one of them.

"I don't know if I'm the best one to give advice. Clearly, I've made a mess of it with Levi."

"A kiss would fix everything," she said.

"A kiss would make it complicated."

"By the sounds of it, it's already complicated." She was absolutely right. "Come on, let's go have some lunch. It's going to be cold by now. And Levi's waiting for you," she teased. We both stood up and headed to the kitchen.

The first thing I noticed was the open beer in Kyle's hand. *Here we go again.* Why did everything have to remind me of Dad? Kyle and Jess were laughing together. She pushed her hair behind her ear and giggled before briefly brushing her hand against his thigh as she walked over to talk to me. Kyle stared after her.

"Are you sure you're all right?" Jess asked me, her eyes glazed from the alcohol.

"Yeah, perfect," I said with a smile.

"Good. I'm so glad. You looked terrible before. Like you were crying. I was so worried," she said all at once. She took a swig from the beer she was holding.

"How many have you had?" I asked her.

"Oh, a few. I'm not counting. It's too hard," she said with a giggle.

"Want one, Grace?" Kyle offered. I shook my head. "Sure? It looks like you could use it."

"Grace, you should have one. It will help you relax. It's helped me so much," Jess said, hiccuping.

"Grace is fine," Levi said, cutting in.

"She can speak for herself," Kyle said.

"No, thanks," I replied with a polite smile. Charlie pushed a bowl of rice into my hand as Dylan traipsed through the kitchen, looking terrible.

"The best way to get over your hangover is to start drinking," Kyle said to him, holding up a beer. Dylan shrugged, accepted it, and walked out.

I watched Kyle offer Levi a drink, which he casually turned down. Kyle and Jess were too much for me to handle. I took my bowl and escaped to the living room. Lizzie was there, uncomfortably seated next to Knox, who was eyeing her up. Dylan was sprawled out on the other couch. Lizzie looked upset and kept glancing at Dylan and then away again. Had something happened between them?

"I feel like shit," Dylan complained.

"It's your own fault," Lizzie pointed out.

"Seriously, loosen up, Lizzie," he said in reply. It was a bad move.

"Loosen up? Dylan. Look at yourself! If a soldier walked through that door right now, would you even be able to defend yourself?" Lizzie shrieked, pointing dramatically toward the front door. "And what about me? Did you really mean any of what you said about keeping me safe?"

Something had definitely happened between the two of them.

Dylan glared at Lizzie. "I did, actually. I meant every word. You have no idea," he said, shaking his head.

"Then man up and prove it. You're acting like a child."

"And you're acting like a bitch," Dylan argued back. I stared awkwardly at them both. This was the biggest blow-up I'd witnessed between them. Knox looked on with amusement on his face. There was a long, tense silence.

"Screw you, Dylan." Lizzie stood up, blazing in anger, and fled the room.

Knox laughed. "She's a feisty one."

If Dylan cared that he'd upset her, he didn't show it.

"Take a seat, babe," Knox said to me, patting the couch next to him.

"Dylan, are you going to check on Lizzie?" I asked, ignoring Knox.

"She needs a minute to calm down," Dylan said.

"What's gotten into you?" I asked him.

"She's too high maintenance for him," Knox said.

"Stay out of it, Knox," I snapped back.

I walked over to Dylan and kneeled next to his couch. "I think she's really upset. You should talk to her," I whispered. Dylan didn't bother to open his eyes.

"She'll be fine," Dylan dismissed.

"But you care about her, Dylan. And she's not fine."

"Back off, Grace. This isn't your battle," he said back.

Angry tears came to my eyes. I got up and stormed toward the door. What was his problem?

"You're pretty hot when you cry," Knox called after me.

I found Lizzie in our bedroom. She looked up as I came in and quickly wiped away some tears, but it was too late to hide them from me.

"Dylan's being—"

"A jerk," I said.

She laughed bitterly. "Yeah. Does he not see how stupid he's being?"

"Apparently not," I replied. "Those guys drink a lot."

Lizzie looked up at me, concerned. "I know."

"Did something happen between you two?" I asked.

Lizzie shrugged. "I don't want to talk about it."

"OK. I understand," I said.

We sat in comfortable silence together. It felt like so long ago when we sat in the back of the pickup truck driving up to Auckland. That was the last time we were able to talk properly.

"The memories are coming back," I said to her eventually. Lizzie knew what I meant. She stuck with me after Dad, Tristan, and Mallory died. She was there when Sean and I broke up. She knew how bad it got.

"You're stronger now," Lizzie said, looking over at me.

I shrugged. "It doesn't help when Jess and Dylan are stumbling around drunk."

"It's another reason we need to get out of here," Lizzie said.

"I feel like this whole house is full of bad vibes. I was fine. I honestly was, back in the bush. But I'm struggling here."

"It's a rough patch," Lizzie said. "Once we get out of here, you'll be so much better."

"I hope so."

"You have Levi to rely on, too," she said with a smile.

"I don't think he understands. He tries, but there is this distance—"

"Stop it," Lizzie said harshly. "Levi isn't Sean. Don't even try and compare them. He looks at you like Sean never did. I was there. I know."

"Maybe."

"Maybe? Definitely," Lizzie said. "Don't shut him out."

"OK, OK," I said. I looked down at the threadbare carpet and took a deep breath.

"You're going to get through it," Lizzie said to me. "I know it."

I hoped like hell she was right.

CHAPTER NINETEEN

LIZZIE

SEVERAL DAYS HAD PASSED since our Skytower attack. We hadn't seen any soldiers in our area, but helicopters searching the suburbs for us constantly buzzed in the sky. And it had me on edge.

I sat by the window in the living room, watching two helicopters fly around the neighborhood next door. Anxiety knotted my stomach. There were no two ways about it. Soldiers were going to find us, eventually. And given the drunken, carefree state of our new roommates, we were well and truly screwed. Except for the assorted guns we'd arrived here with, I doubted there were any other weapons in this place. We wouldn't last in a shoot-out. Our only hope was to get out of this house before soldiers came upon us.

I sighed and pulled my eyes from the sky, looking instead toward the forlorn street. It was easy to imagine what it had been like here before the war. And, if it weren't for the little telltale signs, you would never know a war was happening. Without knowing what to look for, you might mistake the neighborhood as a little quiet, a bit poor and rundown, but you would never guess the truth.

For me, I knew what New Zealand had been like before the war. And although I had never lived in this city, I could see where civilization ceased and where the war began. A tendril of ivy had snuck into a broken window of the house across the street. The rubbish bin by the local park had spewed onto the road, and trash stuck to the pavement. Paper fliers dated pre-war were pinned under doormats. A dead dog lay encaged in a narrow dog run. My heart broke for the poor animal that had clearly starved to death.

"It's sad, isn't it?" Charlie commented as she saw me looking out.

"Yes, it is," I agreed absently. My guard came up again. I didn't feel comfortable admitting I was hurt over seeing a dead dog. It seemed weak, and I quickly changed the subject.

"We should have a guard posted. It's dangerous here. Even if the streets seem sleepy, that could change at any time."

"No one has come here before," Charlie said, looking confused. She swept her strawberry blond hair over one shoulder. "And even if they did, we have a bolt-hole."

"Right," I muttered.

"See, we have it all planned out. No need to worry," Charlie said with a smile.

"I'll try not to," I said. I tried to hide the sarcasm in my voice, to no avail.

"Whatever," Charlie said, looking sharply at me. "I'm not worried. You shouldn't be either." She stalked off toward the kitchen.

I knew I should try harder to befriend our new roommates, but I couldn't embrace our situation. I was miserable. And it didn't help that no one seemed worried about soldiers finding us.

Dylan wasn't making my life any easier, either. Before we'd carried out the attack on the Skytower, our relationship had seemed perfect. I thought I'd finally found someone who got me.

I didn't have to pretend to be someone else around Dylan. He liked me for me, flaws and all. And I could rely on him. Our joint hijacking of the truck had shown me that. This entire war had taught me that. But, since the fight we'd had a couple days ago, I'd been avoiding him. He was a different person around these new people. The Dylan I thought I knew was AWOL. The way Dylan was acting reminded me of how terribly things had ended with Ryan, my last boyfriend.

At first, Ryan seemed like he'd stepped right out of a romance novel and into my life, but it wasn't long before he showed his true colors. No more bringing me flowers. No more dates. No more anything. The only times we would hang out was at school, and he seemed uninterested. He spent more time with his mates playing rugby than he did with me.

Had I figured Dylan all wrong, too? Was our entire relationship a lie? Or perhaps Levi had been right. Maybe Dylan needed time to blow off some steam, and then he'd be back to his usual sensible self. I hoped so.

Raucous shouting came from the kitchen, and I inwardly cringed. I was sure soldiers would hear and come storming into the house. I turned away from the window and walked over to the kitchen, where Dylan and Kyle had put together a toy racetrack and were competing. Dylan whooped noisily as his car sped into the lead, only moments from the finish line. Jess was cheering Kyle's car forward before Dylan celebrated again as his car won. I rolled my eyes.

It was hard to believe Kyle and his friends were older than me. Like Dylan, they were in their first year of university. Yet they acted immature and were woefully shortsighted when it came to the risks they were taking. Then again, apparently, I'd misjudged Dylan's level of maturity. He wasn't exactly acting his age at the moment, either.

Levi leaned casually against the kitchen bench, watching on amused but declined to join after Dylan's win. Grace was nowhere to be seen, and I hoped she was OK. She couldn't stand all the drinking, and I didn't blame her one bit. Kyle always had a beer in his hand, and something about him made me uneasy. Jess gave Kyle a consolatory kiss for his loss, and I turned to leave. I'd seen enough. I wandered into the hallway and eventually found Grace in one of the bedrooms. She looked… lost.

"Are you OK?" I asked, sitting on the side of the bed. Her eyes flickered thoughtfully to me, and she shifted her arm uncomfortably in its sling. I could still hear the helicopters roving outside.

"I'd be better if there weren't helicopters circling above us day and night," she muttered as she tucked her long hair behind her ear.

"Me too," I said.

"Soldiers are going to find us," she said, standing up and peeking out the window.

"Those planes and helicopters are incessant," I agreed.

Grace stood wearily with her good arm wrapped around her waist. She looked over at me with bloodshot eyes. I couldn't tell if they were red from crying or tiredness. "We're going to die here," she said, pursing her lips together. "Trapped."

I wanted to tell her she was wrong, but I was equally afraid. She met my eyes with hers, and she knew I was thinking the same thing.

"We never should have come here," Grace said, shaking her head and walking away from the window.

"Are you sure you're OK?" I asked her again.

"Yeah, I'm fine," she said brightly. The fakeness in her voice was painful to listen to. Something was going on. And it was more than just fear of soldiers finding us.

"That's bull," I said, scrutinizing her face. She bit at her lip, and her hand trembled as she gripped her baggy sweatshirt tightly.

"I was thinking about Tristan and Mallory." She paused, but I didn't interrupt. Grace barely ever talked about her dad or her siblings. But lately, they had been on her mind a lot. And I didn't know if that was a good thing. "When it was rainy, and we were stuck indoors, we'd always make up these ridiculous games."

"Yeah, like what?" I asked.

"One time, we built up a giant stack of cushions, and one of us would have to sit on top of the pile and answer pop quiz questions from the others. If they got it wrong, we'd push their tower over," Grace said with a hollow smile.

"Pop quiz questions? Only your family would come up with something so geeky," I said, laughing.

Grace laughed too, but it was short-lived and inauthentic. I knew it was painful for her to think about her family. I thought about losing Jaden and how that had hurt me, and I completely understood. She still missed them so much.

"You should join everyone in the kitchen," I encouraged. "I feel like I've barely seen you the last few days."

"There're too many people," Grace said, her face immediately closing off. "And they're probably drinking."

I couldn't argue with that. The house was not meant for nine of us and felt far too cramped. If it weren't for Jess, I'd have left long ago. I still considered leaving. If Jess thought she was better off with Kyle and his group, then so be it. That didn't mean the rest of us had to stay, and I was sure Dylan, Levi, and Grace would feel the same with time. It would be hard to see Jess go, but it was her decision.

"OK," I said to Grace. "But you know you can always talk to me if you need to, Grace."

"Thanks, Lizzie," Grace said with a fake smile fixed on her face. I knew that smile well. It was the same smile she would plaster on her face as she comforted her mom after the accident. "Seriously, I'll be fine," she insisted.

I didn't believe her for a minute, but Grace knew I was there for her when she wanted to talk. I walked away.

The hallway was eerily quiet. I wandered toward the kitchen and poked my head around the corner to check where everyone had gone. Dylan was the only one there, leaning against the counter and looking out the window. A part of me wanted to walk away and pretend I hadn't seen him. But I needed to confront him about our fight. I had to know what was going on and where we stood.

"Hey," I said in a voice that didn't sound like mine.

"Hey yourself," Dylan said, looking over at me with a warm smile.

I walked hesitantly into the kitchen and leaned back against the fridge. Dylan was immediately standing in front of me, studying me with his ice-blue eyes.

"What the hell is going on with you?" I asked him, trying to keep my voice level. Better to be direct about it, I thought.

"Coming right out with the tough questions, huh," Dylan said as he ran a hand through his hair.

"Dylan," I said, pleading with him to open up.

Dylan cast his eyes down and frowned.

"Seriously," I said, grabbing his hand. "This person you are right now… is… it's not you."

"I know," Dylan said as he moved closer to me. He took a deep breath. "I wanted to apologize. Levi said I should talk to you. I've been struggling, you know, after the Skytower attack. It's nothing to do with you or us. I needed to forget the destruction we caused. I needed to feel like a normal guy again."

"But we can't be normal here," I said. "Soldiers are hunting for us. They could storm in here and—"

"I know, Lizzie," Dylan said, embracing me in a tight hug. "I know. I've been reckless. I'd never let anything happen to you. You know that."

I melted into his embrace. He was saying exactly what I needed to hear. "I'm sorry, too," I muttered into his shirt as tears gathered in my eyes.

He pulled away and looked down at me. He wiped a tear away with one of his thumbs and brought his face close to mine. "I've been a jerk," Dylan said simply.

"It's OK," I said, even though it wasn't. He was right—he had been a jerk. But admitting it meant there was hope for us, after all. "Just promise me, no more drinking," I said.

Dylan held one hand up, palm flat, like he was swearing an oath. "I promise, no more. I already decided that earlier this morning: I'm turning over a new leaf."

I breathed a sigh of relief. He was back to the old Dylan, the one I knew and trusted. He caressed my cheek before kissing me long and slow. The bitter taste of alcohol flooded my mouth.

"What happened to turning over a new leaf?" I asked, pulling back.

"I am," Dylan said, apparently bewildered by my reaction.

"Do I have to spell everything out for you? Usually, when someone quits drinking, they don't celebrate the choice with cheap beer, Dylan."

"Lizzie, chill out," Dylan said, trying to keep me calm. "I had that beer before I decided."

It was only now I noticed the half-empty can perched on the countertop behind him. The gentle hiss of carbonation proved it was freshly opened.

Dylan followed my gaze. "That's not mine," he added. It was a weak excuse.

"Don't tell me to chill out, Dylan. I thought you cared about me, but I was wrong," I said. I barely noticed the shrill tone of my words. "You don't care whether we survive this war. You're drunk, Jess is infatuated with a stranger, Grace is depressed, and Levi is—"

"I'm what?" Levi asked as he walked into the room. Levi was the only friend I had, was what I was going to say. Levi quickly assessed the situation, his warm brown eyes lingering on the beer can that stood between Dylan and me. "Maybe you and I should go for a walk, Lizzie," Levi suggested. He didn't try and say anything about calming down or that I was unreasonable.

"Levi, bugger off. I've got this," Dylan said. "We need to talk through some stuff."

I stared at Dylan, still furious with him. I snorted. "Honestly, Dylan, maybe us being together was a giant mistake. You can apologize later. For now, get out of my face." I pushed past him and walked out the backdoor with Levi following.

"Where are we going?" Levi said.

I shrugged, but after a moment, I saw a giant sycamore tree in the backyard and made a beeline for it. I always found nature calming, and trees were like old friends to me. I dug my fingers into a crevasse and pulled myself up. Levi didn't say anything and followed my lead. Eventually, we were high enough to get a decent view of the neighbors' backyards. I took a deep breath. And another. Levi didn't even say a word. He knew me well enough to let me talk first so I wouldn't end up a screaming lunatic.

"I'm OK," I said finally as we sat together on a branch.

"No, you're not."

I looked at Levi. His face was stressed, and he ran his fingers through his short-cropped hair like he always did. His brow was furrowed in thought as he stared down at the back gardens below us.

"You're right. Maybe I'm not OK," I admitted.

"It doesn't take a genius to work that out," Levi said.

I gave him a sour look.

"Seriously though, what happened?" Levi asked.

I swung my legs uncomfortably. "Um, OK. It's not just Dylan. It's everything, really."

"What do you mean?" Levi asked. He rubbed a graze on his leg he had obviously acquired while climbing.

"Well, to start with, Grace… something's wrong," I said, frowning. "And, I'm worried."

"I know. I've noticed too," Levi said distantly. "She's not herself. She won't talk to me."

"The alcohol brings up a lot of memories for her," I explained. "She told you her dad and siblings were killed by a drunk driver, right?"

"Yeah, she only told me a few days ago," Levi said.

"I'm worried she's living in her head too much."

"I tried talking to her. But she's given up trying to explain things to me. She must think I'm too useless to understand," Levi said. He sounded down, which was unlike the cheerful guy I had come to know. "And now all she does is cry."

"She doesn't think you're useless. I know that for a fact," I said.

"I hope you're right," Levi muttered.

"She needs time and patience," I said, squeezing his arm.

"I don't know what to do for her. One minute she's fine, and the next…"

"Grace is strong. She'll be OK," I insisted. I hoped I was right. If I was wrong… I didn't want to think about it.

"Yeah. I hope so," Levi said, sighing. He stared out at the fading sunlight. "Anyhow, I was here to cheer you up, not the other way around. What else has been eating at you, Lizzie?"

I scoffed. "Take your pick," I said as I cracked my neck and tried to massage out the knot. "I mean, Jess and Kyle is another thing. I don't trust Kyle at all, despite Dylan becoming his best mate," I said, glowering.

"Yeah," Levi said, looking equally frustrated. "I don't trust him either. I met some of Dylan's university friends once when I went up to visit him."

"And?"

"Here," Levi said, moving my hand away and massaging my neck for me. I closed my eyes and breathed.

"You think he knows these people?" I pressed.

"Nah, but he's acting the same way around them as he did when I visited him at Uni. I think he feels like he has to show off. Dylan always wants to be liked by everybody."

"Right," I said. "So, Dylan's on an ego trip while those of us who actually care about surviving this war are struggling to make sure everyone is safe?"

"Yeah, pretty much," Levi muttered. He stopped massaging

my neck, and we sat in silence for a moment. It struck me how much this must be affecting Levi, too. He had always been Dylan's best friend, and now Dylan had new ones.

"It sucks," I said. The branch we were sitting on creaked as the wind blew through, and I took another breath of the fresh air. It felt good to be outside. I had been cooped up indoors for far too long, convinced the best way to stay under the radar was to stay hidden. My eyes drifted around the scenery before they were drawn to a flash of movement a few houses over.

"Did you see that?" I asked Levi.

"See what?"

"I thought I saw... it's probably nothing." My heart started beating fast.

"It's never nothing," Levi said, concerned. "Where?"

I pointed to where I had seen the movement. But I was already doubting myself. It looked quiet. Maybe I hadn't seen anything. Then, a black cat leaped onto the fence between two houses, his back arched as he stalked along the narrow ledge.

Levi visibly relaxed. "There's your culprit," he said with a laugh.

I laughed too. "I swear that's the same one we saw after the Skytower attack. Maybe he followed us here."

"Of course, it's not," Levi said with a smile. "Could be an omen, though."

"I hope not." The heaviness in my chest returned. I hated it here, and the last thing we needed was more bad luck. "Do you think we should leave? That we should gather our group and go?"

Levi didn't answer right away. I could tell the question bothered him. Maybe he had been asking himself that question too.

"I think... it would be pretty hard right now to do that," he said finally.

My heart sank.

"Don't get me wrong," he said, seeing the disappointment in

my eyes, "I want to. I even think we need to leave. But Jess won't come with us, at least not now. Maybe if things don't continue between her and Kyle, she would listen to reason."

"We've been here long enough," I argued.

"We owe it to Jess to give her a chance," Levi said, more to himself than to me. "All she wants is to find someone."

"Kyle's not the guy," I said. "Surely, she can see that."

"We can't tell her who she can be with," Levi said with surprising insight. "It's not fair to Jess. We've been to hell and back with her. The least we can do is let her see Kyle's true colors before deserting her."

"You're probably right," I admitted.

"But we can't stay here forever. The city was swarming with soldiers, and I don't think they'll stop searching for us any time soon."

"And Dylan?" I asked.

"I think Dylan could be convinced. Don't give up on him yet, he's an idiot right now, but he's still—"

The backdoor burst open, and Grace stood there, panic wild in her eyes. She said one word. "Soldiers."

I reached for my rifle. My hand grasped at air. I'd left it inside.

"Where?" Levi demanded, already climbing down the tree. His automatic gun was slung across his back. I wasn't far behind and jumped the last bit to the ground.

"Two houses over," she whispered, her voice shaking. She held her handgun tightly. "They're searching the houses."

So it hadn't been only the cat that I'd seen. My heartbeat sped up again, going as fast as my racing thoughts. This was the trouble in this war, I thought as we sprinted into the house. It was either all go or all nothing. There was never any middle ground.

We screeched to a halt in the kitchen. It was chaotic. The others stumbled around, panicking.

Levi and Grace immediately ran to the windows to check where the soldiers were.

"Where's my gun, Lizzie?" Dylan asked me.

"How the hell should I know," I said dismissively.

"What do we do?" Charlie asked, desperately pacing the kitchen.

"You're the one who said there was a plan," I snapped as I retrieved my gun from the living room.

"Under the house," Kyle said, holding on to the bench to keep his balance.

"We should fight," Dylan said, his face determined. "Screw the soldiers."

"Yeshhh," Jess slurred. "Screw 'em."

"No way in hell," I said. "You guys are in no state to fight."

"We've got to do something," Levi called out. "They're coming. A whole squad by the looks of it."

Grace flicked the safety off her gun and stood facing the front door. Levi was at her side, his weapon aimed.

"Guys!" Grace said. "Do something!"

"Lead the way, Kyle," I ordered. "Now!"

Kyle nodded and stumbled down the hallway. I followed. A full-length Manchester United flag hung down on one wall, with the bathroom across from it. Knox fumbled with the flag, pulling it aside to reveal a door. He yanked the door open and started down the stairs. Everyone else followed. I stood at the top of the stairs and looked over my shoulder to see Grace and Levi slowly backing away from the front door toward us.

"Grace, Levi, come on," I said.

They kept their gaze fixed on the door as they ran toward me. They darted past me and down the stairs. I carefully closed the door and hoped the flag would drape down to conceal our escape route.

I walked down the stairs in total darkness. I had to duck to avoid hitting my head on the beams above. A damp earthy smell filled my nose, and my bare feet stepped down onto cold dirt. As my eyes slowly adjusted to the dark, I noticed the support posts that held up the house. The underside of the grimy wooden floorboards hung over our heads, faint slithers of light streaming through the cracks. The others were huddled as far from the stairs as possible, stooping under the floorboards and waiting with bated breath. I stood hunched in front of Ollie and Knox.

"Hey, hot stuff," Knox whispered to me.

"Shut up," I hissed at him as the front door opened and footsteps pounded on the wooden floor above our heads.

"Move, move, move!" a male voice shouted at the soldiers who ran through the house.

"Clear," a woman yelled.

"Clear, sir," another gruffer voice called.

"Kitchen's clear."

"The place is empty," the woman said.

"Looks like rebels have been squatting here. They probably took off when the Skytower fell," the man I assumed was in charge said.

"They can't have gone far," the woman said.

"They're probably days gone," the man in charge said with a sigh. "Goddamn it."

I could see their shadows blocking out the light directly above me. I held my breath as the floorboards creaked.

Knox shuffled behind me, inching closer. His breath was warm on the back of my neck and reeked of alcohol. I cringed away from him. But even as I backed off, he moved forward.

"Move on to the next house," the man ordered. "Maybe they're on the run."

"We should go upstairs and celebrate as soon as they leave," Knox whispered in my ear. He reached out with his hand and gave my ass a fond squeeze. My immediate reaction was shock. I froze up, my face hot and skin prickling.

"Are you for real?" I hissed. I gave Knox a shove. The blood was boiling so loud in my ears that I barely remembered why I couldn't clock him one. That was probably why he chose this moment, I thought. There was no way I could kick up a massive fuss with the threat of our enemy so close by.

"Hey, you were the one rubbing up against me. I thought you wanted it," Knox whispered with a smug smile. I bristled with anger. He had some nerve, I thought. He was still staring at me with that cocky look on his face when the soldiers' footsteps stomped directly over our heads. The door slammed as they left. I looked over at the others, but everyone was distracted by the soldiers.

"In your dreams. It's never going to happen," I whispered back. Knox shrugged carelessly and finally gave me some space. My cheeks were flushed hot pink, and tears pricked at the corners of my eyes. I was still trembling. I hated the way he looked at me. I was angry, most certainly, but was it fear, too? He was just an idiot, I thought. A perv with no sense of boundaries. He wouldn't actually do me any harm… would he?

"Man, that was close," Kyle finally spoke.

"I'm still shaking," Ollie added.

"Do you think it's safe to go back up?" Jess asked in a quiet voice.

"We should play it safe," Dylan said, his voice sober, "and wait it out for a few minutes in case they come back."

I wiped the tears from my eyes and tried to breathe. I wanted to go to Dylan and confide in him. But Dylan wasn't himself anymore. Instead, I leaned against one of the support posts away from the group and crossed my arms as we waited in silence. The minutes ticked by without another sound from the soldiers.

"It's gotta be good now, right?" Knox said.

"Probably," Dylan said.

"I'm getting out of this dungeon," Knox commented.

I watched Knox, Kyle, and Jess head up the stairs.

"Come on, Lizzie," Dylan said to me. He reached out and put a hand on the small of my back, gently nudging me forward. My skin was still burning, hot all over.

I squirmed away from Dylan's touch, trying to hide my tears. "Give me a minute."

"Fine. Have it your way," Dylan said, walking off. Fresh

anger burned my cheeks.

Grace and Charlie followed him up the stairs. Only Levi and I were left under the house.

"You don't have to stay down here, Levi," I said to him. He was sitting against the outer wall with his legs outstretched.

"You're clearly upset," Levi said. "I can tell from all the way over here."

I took a few deep, steadying breaths. Now that Knox had gone, I felt like I had blown it out of proportion. "It's nothing, really," I said and marched up the stairs.

"Lizzie…" Levi chased after me, taking the steps two at a time.

We found the others in the living room. Night had fallen, and Charlie was trying to light a candle on the coffee table. I immediately headed to the window and peeked through the curtains, checking for any sign of the soldiers. But the streets were empty and silent. I rested my gun across my lap and looked at the others. The mere sight of Knox made my skin crawl. But I tried to ignore his presence and clear my head. I had to think smart if we were going to get out of this mess. First, we had to get out of this house before the soldiers came back. It wasn't a question of if. It was a matter of when.

"We should leave," Grace said, her eyes wary, glancing from side to side. She stood at the entrance to the lounge with her handgun tucked into the waistband of her jeans. Levi was now beside her, leaning against the doorframe.

"No way. Not now," Dylan said, avoiding any eye contact with me.

"Why the hell not?" I asked. I crossed my arms and glared at Dylan. Leaving was the best option, and he knew it.

"Who knows how many soldiers are out there searching," Kyle said as he gulped a glass of water. Jess curled up next to him on the two-seater, her head resting against his shoulder.

"Exactly. They think this place is empty. We may as well stay until the streets are quieter," Dylan explained.

Anger rose in my chest. I attempted to stay calm, but all I wanted to do was get the hell out of here. Away from Knox, away from these people. Not wait around for the soldiers to find us again. I looked over at Levi. "Levi?" I asked, trying to gather support. I knew he agreed we should leave.

"Dylan has a point," Levi said slowly. "It's too risky to go now. The soldiers will be on high alert."

Grace gave Levi a pleading stare, but he shrugged. "I'm sorry," he whispered to her.

"And then there are the helicopters. Don't forget those bad boys," Knox added. He was squashed between Charlie and Ollie on the other sofa. "They'll spot a massive group of us running a mile off."

I scoffed and gave Knox a disgusted look, ignoring his comment.

"He has a point, Lizzie," Dylan said.

"I'm sure he does," I said icily.

"I don't want to go out there," Charlie said in a high voice.

"You won't have to," Ollie said. "We're staying here, right?"

"Looks like it," Grace said, her voice empty. "Majority rules."

"It's the right choice," Levi said to her, "I promise."

"It's going to break me," she said in a low voice.

I could yell and scream as much as I wanted, but Grace was right—majority ruled. I swallowed my protest and covered up my anger by looking out the window again. If this was what everyone else was choosing, then so be it. When the soldiers found us again, I'd be the one to say I told you so.

"We at least need someone to keep an eye out," I muttered. If I couldn't convince them to leave, at least I could try and give us a heads up if soldiers came knocking again. "We got lucky Grace was looking out the window at the right time."

"Lizzie's right," Levi said. "We need warning if soldiers come this way again."

"And a better plan," Grace added.

"And a better plan," Levi agreed. "There's no guarantee

soldiers won't find the bolt-hole next time."

"We aren't fighters like you," Charlie said. "I'm fine with hiding again."

"Well, I'm not," I said, as fresh frustration surged through me.

"It worked this time. It will work again," Knox said.

I felt anger flush my cheeks. These people were going to get us killed.

"I'll take the first shift on lookout," Dylan blurted out before I had a chance to launch into Knox. I studied Dylan's face. His eyes were downcast, and his forehead was creased with frown lines. He ran a hand through his hair and looked up at me, waiting for an answer.

"I don't know…" I said.

"Better you than me," Kyle said, stretching and yawning.

"You're still drunk, Dylan," I added. What was Dylan trying to prove? That he was back to his old self?

"I'm fine," Dylan said. "Really. Let me do this."

I didn't know if I could believe him, or trust him, for that matter. I looked to Levi for answers.

"Just don't let us down, Dylan," Levi said, shoving his hands into the pockets of his jeans.

"You can trust me," Dylan said, trying to keep his voice even.

But could we really?

"I sure hope so," I said as I stood up. I walked past Dylan and dropped my gun into his lap. "Don't screw up."

Without another look behind me, I stalked off to the kitchen. I heard Levi come after me. He pulled out one of the kitchen chairs and flopped down onto it.

"They're going to get us killed," I said, trying to stop myself from exploding in anger.

"Lizzie," Levi said calmly. "What's wrong?"

"Nothing is wrong," I said, turning away from Levi and staring out into the back garden as tears pricked at the corners of my eyes.

"Is it the soldiers? It was a close call," Levi said. "Real close."

"I wish it was just soldiers," I said under my breath.

"Then what is it?"

Should I tell Levi? Would he think I was overreacting?

"Knox made a pass at me," I said, feeling my cheeks redden. For some reason, it was awkward talking about this to Levi. I expected Levi to laugh it off and tell me Knox meant no harm.

"What?" Levi said angrily. "He tried to kiss you?"

"No, he grabbed my ass," I said, turning to face Levi. It sounded so pathetic, saying it out loud.

"I'll kill that asshole," Levi said, getting up and making a move to run back into the lounge.

"No, Levi. Stay here, please," I begged. "I'm pretty sure Knox is the kind of guy who would try and hit on anything that moved."

Levi relented and sat back down across from me. "That doesn't make it OK. He needs to know that. When did this happen?"

"Just before," I said.

"What? Under the house?" Levi asked.

"Yeah, when the soldiers—"

"What the hell is wrong with that guy? He needs some sense knocked into him," Levi said, getting riled up again.

"Thanks, Levi, but I don't need my honor protected," I said. "I'm not a defenseless maiden, you know."

"Fine. But if he does it again…" Levi said threateningly.

"If he does it again, I'll punch him myself."

"I guess that's fair," Levi said as he shoved his hands into his pockets. "So, are you going to tell Dylan?"

I didn't respond.

"I'll take that as a no," Levi said.

"I haven't decided yet," I replied.

"Give him another chance," Levi said.

I shook my head and hugged my arms around my body. I wasn't ready to let him in again. Not yet. "He's got to earn another chance."

Chapter Twenty

Dylan

By the time the first rays of light spilled over the horizon, I could barely keep my eyes open. My head throbbed incessantly, and I rubbed at my temples to try and alleviate the hangover pain. But I didn't move from my seat. I couldn't risk soldiers sneaking up on my watch. I wouldn't let Lizzie down. Not again. She deserved better.

Even the thought of Lizzie made guilt curl in my stomach. She had been right all along. Since the Skytower attack, I had been an idiot. That first night of drinking had taken away all of it: The pain. The fear. The guilt. It had taken me back to better times, partying with friends and competing to see who could hold their liquor best. It felt good to let go. So, I had more. But we couldn't relax here. We couldn't relax until this war was over. I knew that. It took soldiers breaking into this house and Lizzie putting the brakes on our relationship to make me see it. And now I had to fight an uphill battle to win my way back into Lizzie's heart.

My eyes pricked with tiredness, but I kept them open, glued to the lightening sky outside the window. Lizzie would see I was still me. She could trust me like she always had.

Footsteps padded down the hallway, but I was too tired to look and see who it was.

"No soldiers?" Lizzie said from behind me.

"It was quiet," I said, stifling a yawn.

"Good," Lizzie said in a tone that shut down any future conversation. She left to boil some water in the kitchen.

"Looks like you managed to keep us alive," Levi said as he walked into the lounge.

"Glad you have confidence in me," I said sarcastically.

"I never doubted you for a minute," Levi said with a smirk as he sat heavily on the couch and put his feet up on the coffee table. Lizzie returned with a mug of coffee that she shoved in my hand.

"Thanks," I said.

Lizzie ignored me.

"I'll take one of those," Levi said.

"Sure," Lizzie said with a smile. "Sugar?"

"Yup."

Lizzie bustled off to make Levi a coffee.

Another door in the hallway opened, and Knox emerged. He lumbered into the living room and flopped down onto the other couch. "Morning," Knox said.

Lizzie came back with two mugs. She handed Levi his coffee and sipped at her own.

"I can take over," Lizzie said to me.

"Thanks," I said, stiffly getting up from the chair and stretching my legs.

"I'll keep you company," Knox said as he got up and began dragging a chair over.

Lizzie looked over at him, and with a sudden spasm of her hands, she spilled the best part of her coffee onto the floor. "Shit," she cursed.

"I'll get a towel," I said with a tired sigh.

Lizzie grabbed onto my arm to stop me. "No, Dylan…"

"What?"

Her eyes begged me to stay with her. Anyone was better than

Knox, apparently. But I was exhausted and couldn't bear the thought of another minute on watch. Plus, Knox wasn't that bad. He was good for a laugh.

"Don't worry, Knox," Levi said. "I've got it, mate." He grabbed the chair from Knox and carried it over to Lizzie.

"You sure?" Knox said. "You guys do all the work around here. Not that I'm going to complain about that, though."

"I'm sure," Levi said. "Lizzie and I need to talk, anyway."

Knox shrugged and wandered into the kitchen to find some food.

Levi pulled his eyes away from the spilled coffee, which was seeping into the worn carpet, and looked up at me. "We'll clean this up. Get some sleep, Dylan. You look terrible."

I felt terrible. "Thanks, I think I will."

I walked from the lounge and headed toward my room. I quietly opened the door so as not to bother Grace. But I realized I had left my gun by the window. I wasn't going to let that gun out of my sight. I turned around and went back to the living room to retrieve it. As I approached, Lizzie and Levi's hushed voices drifted into earshot.

"I owe you one," Lizzie said.

"Anytime. The offer still stands… if you want me to tell him to back off," Levi said.

"Thanks, Levi. But I'm good. I can handle it," Lizzie said.

"Are you sure? Because—"

"I'm OK. I'm fine." Lizzie had a catch in her voice, and I could tell she was upset. But about what? "Thanks, though. I do appreciate it. I don't know what I'd do without you," she added.

"I'm here for you whenever you need me," Levi said in a comforting tone. Then his voice dipped into a whisper, "But honestly, Lizzie, this is getting out of hand."

What the hell were they talking about? I crept closer to continue listening.

"Like I don't know that," Lizzie muttered.

"You need to tell Dylan. He has to know what's going on. You owe him that much."

Tell me what? Lizzie didn't answer.

"Lizzie," Levi prompted.

"I know, I know," Lizzie responded. "But Dylan's going to flip when he finds out."

"He might. But it wouldn't be without reason. Just make sure you tell him."

Lizzie sighed. "I will. When the time's right."

Why were they being secretive? Was this all about me? Had I upset Lizzie so much she had run off with Levi? No. That was ridiculous. Levi would never do that to me. We'd been friends for too long.

Maybe they were both mad at me for the drinking. That was it, I thought. I turned away from the lounge and headed back to the bedroom, forgetting all about the gun.

Grace pushed past me in the hallway. I caught a glimpse of her teary eyes and tired face. "Morning," she muttered.

I was too preoccupied thinking about Lizzie and Levi to acknowledge her. Grace headed toward the kitchen, and I shut myself in the bedroom. I flopped down on one of the mattresses and closed my eyes. I wanted sleep to overtake me, but I couldn't shake the feeling something was going on between Lizzie and Levi. The more I thought about it, the more I realized they had been spending a lot of time together.

But I knew it couldn't be true. Only days ago, Lizzie and I were in a relationship. We were happy. How could something so good slip away so fast?

"It's because you're an idiot, Dylan," I whispered to myself.

I pulled a blanket over me and closed my eyes, willing sleep to overtake me. But the thought of Lizzie and Levi together tormented my sleep, and I tossed and turned for hours.

I must have fallen asleep at some point, though, because when I opened my eyes, it was past midday. I groggily sat up and rubbed at my tired eyes. The headache was gone, thankfully. But the nausea accompanying my hangover had stuck around.

I dragged myself out of bed and walked to the bathroom. I

splashed cold water over my face and felt refreshed. I ran my fingers through my hair to make myself presentable before shuffling to the kitchen and collapsing onto one of the kitchen chairs. Kyle lounged across from me, studying me with perceptive blue eyes.

"Thinking about Lizzie, huh?" Kyle asked.

"How'd you know?" I muttered as I drew circles in the dust covering the tabletop.

"Lucky guess," Kyle said with a shrug.

"I don't understand it," I said. "Lizzie and Levi, I mean, they've always been friends, but it's not like they were close. And now they're inseparable."

"Obviously, they're an item now," Kyle said with a shrug.

Kyle had given my fear words.

"It's probably why Grace is crying all the time, too. You need to get over Lizzie, dude."

"Levi wouldn't do that. Neither would Lizzie," I said, shaking my head. "That would never happen. Lizzie's mad. That's all. And Levi's probably furious with me, too."

"Justify it however you want," Kyle said. "But I'm telling you as I see it. They're together."

I hated to admit it, but if Kyle saw it too… maybe they were together.

"I'm such an idiot," I said out loud. "Getting drunk during this war. The soldiers could have caught us, and I was too buzzed out to notice."

"I've never seen anyone more responsible than you, Dylan," Kyle said with a broad smile. "And you weren't drunk. You'd only had a few."

"Tell that to Lizzie," I said under my breath. "Two drinks or ten—it's all the same in her eyes."

"Speaking of, it's beer o'clock. Want one?" Kyle said, reaching down and grabbing a beer from the box by his feet.

I shook my head. "Seriously, Kyle?"

"I'm not compromising in this war. If today's my last day in this hellhole, I'm going out on my terms. If I want a beer, I'll bloody well have one."

"Cheers to that," Knox said as he walked into the kitchen. Kyle grinned and tossed a beer to Knox. Charlie and Jess entered the kitchen. Jess walked up to Kyle, wrapped her arms around him, and pecked him on the cheek.

"Want a drink, Jessy?" Kyle asked.

"Yes, please, one of those pink vodka thingies," Jess said.

Kyle rummaged in the beer box and pulled out Jess' request.

"Don't I get one?" Charlie asked petulantly.

"I thought you never wanted it," Kyle said.

"Maybe I want to try," Charlie said. From what I had noticed, Charlie always seemed to be hanging around Kyle and Jess. She clearly had a thing for Kyle, who wasn't into her.

"Fine," Kyle said and tossed Charlie a beer. She went to catch it the same way Knox had but fumbled, dropping it on the floor. Kyle and Jess laughed as Charlie blushed. I got up and picked it up for her. I opened it over the sink. Half of it fizzed and overflowed. I wiped the stickiness off it and gave it to Charlie. She caught my eye and gave me a look of complete gratitude.

"Woah, did you see the look she gave him?" Kyle grinned, winking at Knox. "Careful, Charlie, you do know Dylan's on the rebound."

"What?" Jess asked. "Dylan, what happened with Lizzie?"

"Nothing. We're not together anymore."

I left them and walked out to the veranda at the back of the house. Levi was there, sitting on a deck chair, but didn't say anything. I had been right. Levi was pissed, too.

"I'm sorry," I said at last.

"Good. You should be. You put us all at risk."

"Is it so wrong to want to blow off a little steam?"

"In this situation… yes."

I sighed and sat on the deck. It was still warm from the sun. "I know. I haven't been acting like myself."

"You're not the only one. Everyone's struggling. Lizzie and I were talking, and we think we should leave as soon as it's safe," Levi said.

"In a couple of days, once everything's calmed down."

"What about Jess?" I asked.

"We wait to see if this thing she has with Kyle sticks, and if she'd rather be with him than us, then so be it."

"You can't be serious. After everything we've been through together as the five of us, you would leave her here?" I replied angrily.

"That's the thing, Dylan. There is no 'five of us' anymore. There's a group of crazed teenagers in the middle of the most dangerous city in New Zealand."

"Levi, stop being dramatic," I said. He was sounding a lot like Lizzie.

Levi shot me a dark stare. "Do you even know why Lizzie was mad?"

"I get it. I made a mistake, and I said I was sorry. Both of you need to lay off. All her nagging is enough to drive anyone away," I bickered.

"If that's what you think, then why do you want to be with her?" Levi said.

"Maybe I don't anymore," I huffed childishly.

"Well, good. She deserves someone better than you," Levi countered.

"Who? Someone like you?" I said before I could stop myself.

Levi looked like he was about to laugh. And then he looked like he was about to punch me. "Is that how little you think of me?"

"Sorry," I muttered.

Levi stood up harshly, and the deck chair grated loudly against the wood veranda as he kicked it away and stomped indoors. I watched him go and thumped down into the chair he had been sitting in. Everything was a mess. A bloody mess.

GRACE WAS IN THE kitchen when I finally came back indoors. Her eyes were bloodshot, and her cheeks flushed. She had pulled her long hair into a messy bun on the top of her head. It felt like I hadn't spoken to her in days, and a fist of guilt curled in my stomach. I'd been neglecting my friends.

"Hi, Grace. How are you doing?" I asked. She was getting dinner ready, and I pulled some plates from a shelf to help her out.

"I'm fine," Grace said. She didn't seem certain of that. Her hands shook, and she dropped a whole lot of extra salt into the dish she was trying to make and cursed herself for it.

"Are you sure you're OK?" I asked. "Can I help?"

"Why does everyone have to keep asking me that?" Grace shrieked.

"I'm sorry," I said. Sorry was becoming a habit. Seemed like I couldn't do anything right.

"I can't believe I've ruined this," Grace said as she stared at the bubbling pot. She burst into tears and stormed out of the room just as Lizzie came in.

"What did you do, Dylan?" Lizzie snapped at me, seeing Grace and running after her. I was left alone with the boiling pot. There was nothing else to do but stir the pasta Grace had started cooking.

"All hail Dylan, the domestic god," I muttered sarcastically. I went to look for some sauce and realized the pantry was almost entirely bare. We needed to get some food. Tonight.

Lizzie wandered back into the kitchen.

"Come to yell at me again?" I asked moodily.

"No. I'm sorry," Lizzie said a little stiffly. "Grace told me it wasn't your fault she was upset." Lizzie turned to leave.

"Is that all you came to say?"

Lizzie stopped and audibly sighed.

"Why is Grace upset, anyway?" I asked, trying to change the topic and make Lizzie stay.

"She's having a rough time. All the death and the war bring back memories of her family," Lizzie explained.

"Oh," I said, stirring the pot. I hadn't realized she was so upset. "Will she be OK?" I asked.

Lizzie shrugged. "It's a burden she's been carrying for a long time. It'll never go away entirely, but I think in time, she'll be OK. It would help if alcohol wasn't shoved in her face all the time."

"What do you mean?"

"A drunk driver killed her family. Surely you knew that?"

"No. I didn't," I said. "So, I suppose Grace feeling upset is my fault for being drunk yesterday?" I asked. This was clearly what Levi had been talking about when he had asked me if I knew why Lizzie was mad. Now it all made so much sense. Lizzie, the overbearing, protective friend. This sounded more of a likely story than Kyle's version. It even explained why Levi was talking to Lizzie so much now. They were both worried about Grace.

"Yes, Dylan, because everything is all about you, and this is all your fault," Lizzie retorted. Her lip quivered, and I hoped she wouldn't burst into tears the same way Grace had.

"Hey," I said, lightly touching her arm in what I hoped was a caring way. "I'm sorry about yesterday." Even though we both knew it wasn't my fault, maybe an apology would help ease some of the tension.

"I needed to talk to you. Not this other Dylan. You!" Lizzie said.

"But I failed you." The guilt kept eating away at me.

"Yes," Lizzie agreed. She sounded like she had simply accepted that fact.

"It's not going to happen again," I promised.

Lizzie peered into my eyes like she was trying to decipher my soul.

"I won't let you down," I said.

Lizzie's gaze softened. "I miss you, and I still… I care about you, Dylan. But I need the real you back."

I felt a flicker of hope awaken and ease some of the guilt.

"I'm back. This is me."

"I hope so," Lizzie said, turning her attention to the pot boiling on the stovetop, which was bubbling furiously.

There was a chance. I could feel it. Lizzie and I weren't over.

"You know we need more food tonight. Maybe we should go together. Just us. I don't think Kyle and his mates are up to it anyhow," I said, thinking of the beers they were already drinking.

"What about Levi?" Lizzie asked. She moved closer to me and took over stirring the pot before I let it boil over.

"We argued," I admitted. "I'd rather it be just us anyhow."

"OK then," Lizzie said. "We'll go after dinner."

DINNER CAME AND WENT. Lizzie ate in the front room, accompanying Grace, who had taken over sentry duty. I wolfed down my small portion and threw the dishes into the sink. My stomach was beginning to churn at the thought of Lizzie and my plan to get food. I wish I could say it was just the fear of facing the streets again, but that wasn't it. I had to try and fix things. And tell Lizzie how I felt. That was what had my stomach in knots.

I left the kitchen to get Lizzie. It was now, or never.

"Where are you going?" Levi stopped me.

"Lizzie and I are going to get food."

"Alone?"

"We won't go far," I said. I resisted the urge to tack on the word 'Dad'. I knew how Levi felt about his own dad, and it would be a pretty low blow to turn it into a joke.

"It'd be safer to go with three," Levi said. Lizzie came up behind Levi. She walked over to the sink and deposited her plate and cutlery into it.

"We'll be fine, Levi," Lizzie said in a tone that closed the subject for comment.

I could tell she was still mad at me, but she was trying to give me a chance, and that meant something.

Lizzie marched to the door. "You coming or what?" She waited by the door with a handgun tucked into her pocket.

"Yeah, I'm here," I said.

"You haven't lost your gun again?" Lizzie asked pointedly.

"No," I said. It was still in the lounge. Shit. "But I need to go grab it." I darted into the living room and snatched the gun from the floor by the chair Grace was sitting on.

"Be careful," Grace said to me as she kept her eyes fixed on the window.

"I will be."

"You better not be drunk," she warned, her voice icy. "If you get Lizzie killed—"

"I haven't had a drink since yesterday," I promised her as I ran from the room to join Lizzie, who was standing by the front door with her arms crossed.

"Let's go," Lizzie said as she opened the door. I slung the gun over my shoulder, and we set off at a jog down the road. It would be hard to find a place Kyle and his group hadn't already raided. They had been here a long time, and it seemed certain that food was scarce.

We wound through a maze of streets, and I noted each turn in my head. I didn't want to get lost on the way back.

"Which way?" Lizzie said, puffing.

I glanced in the direction of the city. If yesterday was anything to go by, the search for us was still too hot for my liking. "Away from town. Best let sleeping dogs lie."

"OK then. I guess we go this way, right?" Lizzie replied, pointing. I nodded, and she turned down the next street, which led to a path by the water. Lizzie jogged up the path before we slowed to a walk, looking around us.

It was beautiful, with the moon glistening off the velvet water, and I could see why there were dozens of luxury houses dotted all along the path. In another time, I might have taken Lizzie here for a romantic walk while we watched the sunrise over the water. It looked familiar. I'd been here before.

"This is Pakuranga. I think we're near Half-Moon Bay," I said.

"Great. And that helps us how?" Lizzie asked.

"We don't want to end up at the marina. It's not big, but I'd rather not stumble onto some huge operation we don't know about."

Lizzie shrugged and pulled out her small handgun. She vaulted over a small hedge onto someone's back lawn. "Let's try these houses then."

I nodded and followed her across the lawn and toward the back door. The door was unlocked, and finding food here didn't seem likely, but we went in anyway. We did a search first to make sure we were alone. And then we started checking out the kitchen. The floor-to-ceiling windows brought back my anxiety. It felt like there were eyes on us, but I knew we had checked the area thoroughly. Lizzie went straight to the butler's pantry while I walked over to some drawers underneath a smooth granite countertop.

"I kind of wanted to talk to you while we're alone," I said as I pulled open a drawer. Nothing but some pots and pans. I pulled open another one and found some rice. The one thing we didn't need, but I took it anyway.

"About what?"

"I want to know if you've forgiven me," I asked her.

She stopped what she was doing and turned to face me. "I'm trying, Dylan, but you don't always make it easy, you know."

"I don't make it easy? You're the one blaming me for making Grace upset. I had no clue that was how she would react to us drinking."

"I thought you got it, Dylan," Lizzie said, turning away and grabbing some items that she quickly shoved into her bag. "It's not about Grace."

"It's not?" I was confused. I walked over to her and grabbed her arm to make her look at me. The slight glow from the moon lit her blond hair.

"I needed *you*. This has always been about you."

"I'm here now," I said softly, "and I'm sorry I wasn't before."

"Right now, you're the one who's making me upset, Dylan," she said, sighing and pulling her arm out of my grasp. "Our group is falling apart, and you act like you don't care. I've been struggling to hold it together for days with everyone constantly commenting on what an uptight bitch I am, you included, all while I'm trying to keep us safe. How do you think that feels?"

Her words hurt, and I had no idea this had been how Lizzie was feeling. The guilt came rushing back.

"Lizzie, I didn't mean to… tell me, what I can do?"

"I need you to have my back, Dylan, instead of trying to be Mr. Nice Guy who wants everyone to like him. I don't want to have to tell you how to be responsible." She turned away and wiped a tear. "Come on, let's get this over with," she said. She stuffed some canned food into her bag.

"I don't want to leave yet."

"I'm done here," Lizzie said, holding up a full bag. I took the bag away from her and stared into her gray eyes.

"Lizzie," I said. I lifted a hand and touched her cheek. "You know how sorry I am. I need you to forgive me. There's something I didn't tell you before… when we were in the department store. I didn't want to scare you off, but I've known ever since you were injured in the car crash. I… I love you, Lizzie." It felt good to admit it out loud to her. She needed to know I was here for her, and I wanted this to last.

Lizzie looked at me, lost for words. I wasn't sure what that meant, but I was in deep now. There was no turning back from this. I closed my eyes and leaned in to kiss her. Her hair smelled like flowers from the shampoo she used, and I breathed it in as I leaned closer, my lips only inches from hers. Then she turned her face away, and my lips bumped awkwardly against her cheek.

"I can't forgive you yet, Dylan," she said with a tear slipping down her face. "You still don't get it."

"Then tell me," I said, fully exasperated now.

"I thought you talked to Levi. Didn't he tell you what happened?" Lizzie huffed.

"Something happened between you and Levi?" I said

furiously. "I can't believe Kyle was right."

"What?" Lizzie exclaimed with her cheeks turning red in anger. She took half a step back from me. "Nothing happened between Levi and me. I can't believe you would accuse me of that, Dylan!"

"Then what the hell are we arguing abou—"

I stopped talking as I noticed Lizzie's eyes widen in fear, and the fine hairs on her arm rose in the moonlight.

"Lizzie—"

"Dylan! Get down!"

The breath was knocked out of me as Lizzie tackled me to the floor. At the same time, gunshots exploded through the night. The windows behind me shattered, showering us with glass. Bullets smashed into the kitchen cabinets above our heads. They ripped into the floor, tearing up the tiles. We crouched behind the kitchen island, unable to move as the soldiers shot up the house. The instant the gunfire stopped, we made a run for the door. But soldiers beat us to it. Three men burst through the front door. Lizzie had her handgun ready and emptied her magazine into the first one before he made it past the threshold. Lizzie's gun clicked empty, and she shoved it back into her waistband. The remaining soldiers fired back, and we ducked back behind the counter.

"I'm out of ammo," Lizzie said desperately as she rummaged through the drawers beside her.

"What the hell are you doing? You won't find ammo in there," I whispered as bullets continued to strike the cabinets behind us.

"I've got to do something." Lizzie pulled out a long butcher's knife and grasped it with white fingers.

Silence. The soldiers were reloading.

I stood up and aimed at the soldiers who'd taken up residence in the lounge. I pulled the trigger, to no effect. The safety was still on, and I had wasted precious seconds. I flicked the safety off, and a spray of bullets pelted the open-plan living. Puffs of dust and stuffing erupted from the sofas, and an opulent chandelier came crashing to the ground. When my gun was empty, I ducked back down, expecting return fire. But there was silence.

"Did we get 'em?" I whispered to Lizzie.

"No idea," she whispered. "But let's get the hell out while we still can."

We gunned for the door. I didn't make it far. Something caught my trousers and sent me nose-diving onto the glossy tiles. I hit the floor hard and tried to kick at the soldier trying to grab me. He was badly wounded, but not so bad that it stopped his hands from locking tightly around my ankle in a death grip.

Lizzie screamed as I struggled to squirm free. His vice-like hands found my neck. I clawed at his fingers as they closed around my windpipe. This was it, I thought. We'd survived the truck crash. We'd destroyed the Skytower. But I was going to die here, in some townie's souped-up villa. I'd never get a chance to prove my worth to Lizzie.

And it might have been the end if it wasn't for her.

Lizzie lunged toward the soldier with the knife. Fighting two of us now, the soldier had no choice but to release me. He grabbed at Lizzie's arm as she drove the knife towards his chest. I drew back, coughing and spluttering. But I couldn't take my time to recover. Lizzie had the knife pointed at the soldier's chest, and he was holding her back. How long before the tables turned and he gained the upper hand? I could see the fire in his eyes—the burning will to live. And Lizzie was weakening, her face pink with effort.

I had to do something. But I felt the walls closing in, my heartbeat throbbing in my eardrums. The suffocating heat. My mouth dry and chalky. Another one of my panic attacks. In desperation, Lizzie shoved her knee into the soldier's throat and pinned him to the ground, plunging the knife into his chest. She fell back on her outstretched hands, panting.

Finally, I came to my senses. I grabbed Lizzie's arm, and we sprinted out onto the street. We zig-zagged down the suburban streets to throw the soldiers off our trail. I kept glancing over my shoulder, but the streets were empty, and it seemed the soldiers weren't giving chase.

After thirty minutes, I was sure we'd lost them. I hadn't seen or heard any sign of them, so we slowed to a walk. It took me a minute or two before I got my breath back.

"Thanks," I said to Lizzie.

The look in her eye told me she was still pissed at me. If she'd considered forgiving me before, there was no chance of it now. I'd failed her again. I froze at a critical moment, and she could have died.

"Let's get the hell out of here," Lizzie said coldly.

We walked in silence the entire way back to the house. When we got back, she slammed the front door in my face as she marched inside.

"That went well," Levi said sarcastically as I opened the door and followed in Lizzie's wake. The candle had blown out when Lizzie charged through, and a wisp of smoke trailed into the air, extinguished as quickly as our relationship. "What the hell happened? You look like you've been dragged through a construction site."

I brushed the dust and glass from my clothes. "Soldiers found us."

"Did you lose them?" Levi asked, immediately concerned. He stood up to warn Grace, who was still keeping watch.

"We lost them over an hour ago," I muttered.

"You sure?" Levi asked, sitting hesitantly back down.

"Of course, I'm bloody sure," I growled.

"OK, OK," Levi said, leaning back against the wall. "Is Lizzie all right?" Levi asked.

"Ask her yourself," I snapped back.

Levi scowled but didn't leave.

"It's my turn to ask you what the hell is going on with Lizzie," I said.

"I have no idea," Levi said.

"Don't lie to me, Levi," I said, feeling anger flush my cheeks. "You've been talking to her a hell of a lot. She seems to think you know."

"Oh, that," Levi said vaguely.

"So, you're not going to tell me?" I said after another moment's silence.

"If she really wanted you to know, she would have told you herself," Levi replied. I threw him a dirty look and Levi amended, "It's not a huge deal, really. But I guess I can fill in the blanks. Knox grabbed her ass. I offered to punch him for her, but you know Lizzie. She said she'd lay one on him herself if he ever gets the nerve to try anything again."

I tried to hide my instant rage and took a moment to process it before I said, "Sounds like she's got it all well in hand."

Levi looked at me as if I was thick. "If he had tried it on with Grace, I would have knocked his teeth out. And Grace and I aren't even together yet."

"Yeah, well. Lizzie and Grace are different," I pointed out.

"You know Lizzie always puts on a brave face. She might say she's fine with it, but I'm not so sure."

"I presume you know everything that's been going on between us," I said as my face reddened.

"Yeah. I do. And I know it's not only your fault—Lizzie's not always the easiest person—but you've been a pretty crappy boyfriend so far."

"I know," I mumbled.

"Lizzie's strong and smart. She'll get through it, and she'll forgive you in time," Levi said confidently.

"I'm not so sure," I said, shaking my head. "It gets worse. I couldn't work out why she was mad at me, so I accused her of being together with you," I said apologetically to Levi.

"Why would you say that?" Levi asked with a groan. He didn't seem pissed off at me, though he had every right to be.

"Just something stupid Kyle said to me that screwed with my

head," I explained.

"Mate, you're an idiot," Levi said, shaking his head.

"Thanks. Nice to know you think so highly of me, too," I said.

"I'm gonna get some shut-eye," Levi said.

I nodded and mumbled, "See you in the morning."

I thought about what had happened and what Levi had said. Disappointment swirled in my gut, coalescing with a healthy dose of self-loathing. Everything that had happened in the last couple of days had been a total shitstorm, and most of it was my fault, if I was honest with myself. I had been scared of failing Lizzie, and somehow, I had done just that. I walked over to one of the bedroom doors and knocked.

"Knox, are you in there?" I called.

Knox opened the door and stood there, looking at me thickly. "What is it?" he asked. I drew my arm back and threw a punch that hit him squarely in the face. His nose made a horrible crunch and started bleeding badly.

"Don't fuck with Lizzie," I said as he brought his hands to his face, whimpering in pain. It wasn't his fault, but he wasn't exactly innocent either. Maybe I had overreacted, but I was sure of one thing: It felt damn good.

Chapter Twenty-One

Jess

Lazily, the clouds floated outside as I watched through the kitchen window. My legs were crossed as I sat on the rickety chair, with Kyle right beside me. I let out a contented sigh. Since I met Kyle, the days had gone by in a happy haze. I couldn't remember feeling this good since before the war, and even then, I wondered whether I had ever known this kind of joy.

Kyle had this way of making me feel special. He looked out for me, and he knew exactly how to lift my spirits when I was down. I had struggled internally to find peace after blowing up the Skytower. I was sure a lot of people had died. I tried to tell myself it didn't matter—we had killed soldiers, and it was retaliation. They deserved death for what they did to Leah, Jennifer, and Evee. Our friends had finally been avenged. But a part of me knew that an eye for an eye never solved anything. Instead, it made me question the person I was turning into. Kyle saw how it was eating me and gave me an escape route.

"Hey, what are you thinking about?" Kyle asked me with a gentle nudge.

"Everything. So much has happened over the last few days," I said. Soldiers had nearly found our hideout, I thought with unease. But we had cheated death again, and I pushed the worry from my mind. It wasn't helpful to dwell on the past.

"I'm glad I found you, Jess," Kyle said. "My friends… they're good people. But I always felt like I was missing something from my life, and if I'm honest, I was scared I was going to die without knowing what… or who," he said, smiling at me.

I gazed helplessly into his dreamy eyes. It was impossible not to notice how good-looking Kyle was. His immaculate white teeth grinned behind his parted lips, and his crystal blue eyes had a boyish twinkle to them. His head had masses of shiny black locks that curled at the tips and made me want to run my hands through them. My eyes roved over his shirt that stretched over his muscular frame. He looked like he'd stepped off a movie set.

As Kyle looked expectantly at me I realized he was after some sort of response. "That's exactly how I feel, too," I said. I thought about the others and everything we'd been through. I had gelled quickly with Kyle's friends. They were all a little weird, but in a good way. They had the same hang-ups and insecurities as any of us, and the fact they weren't scared to let it show made me like them.

At the same time, it had been a while since I'd had a decent conversation with Lizzie and Grace, and I was itching to talk to them about how amazing Kyle was. But somehow, it didn't feel like they approved of Kyle, and that frustrated me. Who were they to judge?

I expected it from Lizzie—she judged everyone harshly—but I didn't expect it from Grace. She moped around the house and barely talked to anyone. It was hard to see her miserable, but I had learned that the difference between being miserable and happy was a choice. You had to choose to be happy. Grace was the one who taught me that, so if she was choosing to be miserable, I wasn't sure I could help her. I had finally found a tiny piece of happiness, and although it felt a little selfish of me, I didn't need her dragging me down.

Dylan and Levi were so wound up in the saga of Lizzie's life that it put me off approaching them. All the drama only emphasized the reason I'd felt so lonely since Jennifer's death. I used to have Jennifer to talk with, and we'd roll our eyes whenever Lizzie went off in a huff with Dylan chasing after her, or whenever Grace and Levi went off on their own. Now she was gone, it felt good to have new friends and new people to talk with. A little bit of my aching soul was slowly healing.

"You look like you're overthinking," Kyle said. "Too much thinking will drive you up the wall, you know."

"You're not wrong there," I said with a laugh.

"I have the perfect cure," Kyle said. He winked at me and hunted in the cabinet above the fridge. "I found this right at the beginning of the war, and I've been saving it for a special occasion," Kyle explained as he pulled out a bottle of scotch.

"I've never had scotch before," I said curiously. We usually drank beer or vodka mixes—they were light and didn't give us a huge hangover.

"Here, hang on to this," he said, passing me the bottle. He walked away and pulled out a couple of glasses from one of the cupboards. I sat cross-legged on the chair and pulled out the cork. It made a faint thunk as it came free. I cautiously sniffed the heady aroma and found it at least smelled good. If it tasted as good as it smelled, it couldn't be too awful.

Kyle took the bottle from me and poured out a generous measure into each of the glasses. He clinked his glass against mine.

"Cheers to you," he said.

"Cheers to us," I replied.

He downed his in one while I sipped at mine, trying to decide whether I liked the taste. A few drops burned the back of my throat and I fought the urge to cough. It would be embarrassing if I spluttered all over the floor. I continued to sip it in silence before I finally brought up a subject that had been preying on my mind.

"Kyle, there's something I want to tell you," I said. But was it too soon? We had both talked of the people we lost along the way. I felt sure he would understand me.

"What?" Kyle asked.

I anxiously clutched my glass and stalled by taking another sip. I wanted him to know me, all of me, including my past. But I also didn't want to scare him off.

"Jessy, you know there's nothing you can tell me that I would judge you for," Kyle said. He squeezed my hand.

"Yeah. I know. Which is why I want to tell you. A little while ago, when my friend Leah died"—I took a breath—"I tried to commit suicide."

It was terrifying to admit it aloud to someone. I waited for him to suck in his breath or check I was OK. To ask me how I could think of doing such a terrible thing, but he just shrugged.

"I've been there too," Kyle said. "This is how I know we're meant for each other, Jess. We've both been to that dark place and come out the other side." He rolled up his left sleeve, and for the first time, I noticed a fine web of white scars that crossed up his left arm. "What matters is we both made it through, and because of that, we were able to meet and be together. See Jess, everything happens for a reason."

"Do you believe in God?" I asked him.

"I don't know," he said thoughtfully. "Maybe there's someone looking over us. Maybe not. But I believe we're destined to be together."

Dylan wandered into the kitchen with a sour look on his face. "What, you're not going to share?" he demanded, holding out his hand.

"I guess your trip with Lizzie didn't go well yesterday?" Kyle asked as he passed over the bottle. Dylan collapsed into one of the kitchen chairs but didn't reply. The chair creaked as he swung back on its legs. A dark expression soured his features as he reclined precariously in the chair. It didn't take a genius to work it out: There was a brand new episode to the Dylan and Lizzie saga. I rolled my eyes, hoping Dylan wouldn't see.

It was probably Lizzie's fault, I thought. Dylan had been the only other person in our group who was open and friendly. Of course, Lizzie had to go and ruin that, too. I felt a pang of sympathy for Dylan as he held the bottle of scotch, deciding if he should take a swig.

"Mate, it's for the best," Kyle said kindly.

"You have no idea what we've been through together. I can't see how it's for the best," Dylan said, shaking his head. He gave in and took a swig of the scotch. Kyle got up and grabbed another glass for Dylan.

"You drink it that way, and you'll be sloshed in no time," Kyle said, offering the glass.

Dylan threw Kyle a dirty look. Getting wasted was all Dylan wanted right now. But he took the glass anyhow and allowed Kyle to pour him a drink. Kyle topped up our glasses, which were already empty, and set the bottle back down beside Dylan. Absentmindedly, Dylan swirled the scotch in the glass. He was about to take another sip before he changed his mind again and shoved it away.

"It will feel better," I said, "and Lizzie will come around in time."

"She won't," Dylan said with an air of finality. "Oh, by the way, Jess, great advice," he said, turning against me.

"What do you mean?" I asked, confused.

"You told me to tell her how I feel. That turned out well."

It took me a minute before I finally remembered the conversation we'd had in the truck when we were driving to Auckland. It felt like an age ago.

"You're blaming all of this on me?" I asked incredulously. I didn't understand why exactly, but with Dylan acting the way he was, I felt like our group from before was lost to me. I had simply reached out to someone else, and they couldn't take it. They had turned on me and made this an 'us' versus 'them' thing. They had forced me to choose, and now there was no way to go back. They would never again accept me with open arms. Not while I was with Kyle.

A tear tracked down my cheek. Though I had lost so much in this war, my friends were closer than family. Had been, I corrected myself. Now, they, too, belonged to the past.

I stood up furiously, marched forward, and took the bottle from beside Dylan. "I'm not the one to blame. Blame Lizzie, or blame yourself. I don't care anymore. But don't drag me into this to absolve you of everything that's going wrong in your life." I smeared my tears away with one hand and stormed out of the room. I stopped in the hallway and took a swig of the scotch.

"Hey," Kyle was at my side in an instant. That same instant, I knew I had made the right choice. Kyle was there for me in a way none of the others were. If I had to make a choice between our group and Kyle, I would choose Kyle every time. "Come on, Jess. Don't mind Dylan. Let's party with our friends. They're awesome at cheering people up," he said, smiling and wiping a tear from my face.

"OK," I said and took a deep breath.

Kyle took my hand and led me outside to the veranda. We'd often sit out here. The property was screened from the outer world with towering fences, so it wasn't easy for soldiers to see in. As long as we kept our voices down, no one knew we were there. I breathed in the crisp air outside and managed to calm myself. Kyle left to find the others, and I relished a moment to myself.

I was here, I was alive, and I had to live to the fullest. I wouldn't waste my life, not when so many people had theirs cut short.

"Hey!" Charlie said brightly as she came out on the veranda, her round face dimpling as she smiled at me. I liked Charlie. She was always cheery, even though the others teased her sometimes.

"Hi." I smiled at her as she came and sat in one of the old

chairs.

"Kyle said you needed cheering up. Dylan was bugging you?" Charlie said, looking at me kindly through her grassy green eyes.

"That guy sure has some anger issues," Knox said as he came out and joined us. I offered him the bottle, and he took a generous gulp.

"Oh my gosh, what happened to your face?" I asked. His nose was swollen, and one eye was purpled.

"Like I said. Dylan has a few anger management issues," Knox repeated.

"That's awful." I was lost for words and felt embarrassed by my old friends. Kyle came through the door with Ollie and shrugged.

"He probably deserved it," Kyle said, grinning and elbowing Knox. "I wouldn't worry about it, Jess. Dylan had a score to settle, and Knox is big and ugly enough to look after himself."

"Here, have another sip," Kyle said as he took the bottle off Knox and handed it back to me. "Today's all about having fun," Kyle announced, and gave me a playful squeeze at my waist. I took another sip, but it was hard to force myself to relax. My parents would be horrified by how much drinking we were doing, but that was their job—to keep me safe from the outside world. There was no one to protect me anymore. Now, I was my own protector. Right or wrong, the decision was mine. And mine alone.

"I think… I feel… a little—," Charlie started. We had been laughing and trading stories for over an hour now, and the bottle of scotch was half empty. Knox and Kyle had started on a line of empty beer cans that ran along the veranda.

"Not here!" Ollie yelled as Charlie's face turned as green as her eyes. Ollie pulled her to the side of the veranda, and she hurled onto the grass below. Ollie helpfully held her strawberry hair out of the way. Dylan, Levi, Lizzie, and Grace all remained inside. The lines had been drawn now. I wondered how long it would take before they left me.

The roaring of a plane overhead made us all stop in our tracks. It was frightening in a way I hadn't known before. When we were in the bush, it was easy to forget about the army up above us. They didn't fly over the bush as often as out here in the suburbs. Kyle and the others quickly went back to talking and seemed to settle very quickly, but I found it unnerving.

What if they had seen us?

I was paranoid. It was too easy to think of the soldiers as an omniscient, all-seeing power when you let fear into your heart.

Lizzie appeared in the doorframe.

"Did you not see that plane?" she shrieked at us. "They could have seen you. And what the hell is all of this?" she marched forward and grabbed the beer straight out of Kyle's hand. Defiantly, she poured it out onto the grass in front of him.

"You really are a pain in the fucking ass," Kyle said.

Lizzie had left the back door ajar, and it creaked as Levi swung it wide open. His eyes roved over us as he took in the scene. His lips drawn into one long, thin line. And though he appeared calm, there was tension exuding from his core.

I knew the look too well and spoke before he could. "Soldiers?" I said. Quickly, I forgot all about our party.

Levi gave me a jerky nod. "They're a couple houses over, and they have a dog."

"Shit," Lizzie said.

Shit was right.

"Those soldiers from last night probably tracked you here," Levi said to Lizzie.

"I told you this was going to happen," Lizzie growled at us as she shouldered her weapon.

"You and Dylan are the idiots who went looking for food yesterday," Knox said.

Lizzie could have murdered him with her stare.

"What do we do?" I asked.

"We can't hide," Levi said.

"This is why we needed a better plan," Lizzie said. She unslung the rifle from her shoulder and gave it a quick once over.

"The dog," Charlie said as fear spread over her face.

"It'll sniff us out easy," Kyle said as he caught onto our predicament.

"Grace and Dylan are out front keeping watch, but they'll need help soon," Levi said.

"We're going to fight them?" I asked. My stomach flipped nervously. Lizzie disappeared inside and came back a few seconds later with our meager supply of weapons. There wasn't enough to go around all of us.

"Here." Lizzie tossed me a gun and gave another to Ollie. The others were left empty-handed.

"What about me?" Kyle asked angrily.

Lizzie shrugged. "That's it. I'm not Santa Claus. Besides, you're so drunk you'd shoot yourself in the foot."

"What do we do?" Charlie called after Lizzie with terror in her voice.

"Try and stay out of the way," Lizzie replied coolly. She walked indoors, and the others followed her unsurely.

"Stay away from the windows," Levi directed.

Dylan and Grace were flattened on either side of the front door with guns at the ready. I took the back door while Kyle grabbed a knife from the kitchen. Charlie and Knox followed Kyle's example, looking scared.

"Can you see them?" I called out to Dylan.

"Yeah," he said.

"How many?" I asked.

"Five… no… six," Dylan replied.

I kept trying to focus, but my mind kept drifting. As much as I hated to admit it, I knew Lizzie had been right. The combination of alcohol and fear had my stomach churning. I didn't want to kill anyone. We'd been in gunfights before, but there had never been this moment of waiting. Impending doom closed in around us.

"Let's get them," Ollie said. He was standing off to the side of the window with his face pressed up against the rifle sights.

"No! Not yet," Levi said, frustrated. "We have to wait until they're close enough. Hold it until they get to the door."

All was quiet except for the barking of a dog coming closer and closer. I looked at Kyle, and he looked back at me. We were both terrified.

"It will be OK," I whispered to him.

"Jess, whatever happens, I promise we'll get through it together," Kyle said. "I won't let you go."

"I know." He was here for me. I cocked my gun.

"Now!" Dylan yelled. Shots rang out, and the glass in the front room shattered. Something came flying through the window, landing not too far from where Dylan and Grace were. It rolled along the floor and rested against the wall.

"Grenade!" Dylan screamed. He and Grace dove away just as the grenade detonated. The explosion rocked the floor and blew the door off its hinges, flinging plaster and dust around the room.

"Jess!" Kyle yelled, pointing out the backdoor. A soldier was rolling over the top of the fence. I took aim and fired, but my arms shook, and the shot went wide. I missed my chance, and the soldier dropped to the ground on our side of the fence. I took aim and fired again—another miss.

"Here, take this, Jess," Kyle said, pushing the knife into my hands and taking over with the gun. I glanced down at the knife with tears in my eyes. I had used one in hot blood when Leah died. Back then, I had been torn up with grief over Leah, and I hadn't cared about the life I took. But I hadn't escaped the guilt entirely—that soldier had haunted me ever since. I couldn't do something like that again. Knives were too personal, looking your victim dead in the eye.

I felt sick. I should have never let myself drink as much as I did. My mind was too far from the present moment, and it made me feel useless and defenseless. A soldier made it through the front door and came running at me. Lizzie popped up from behind the kitchen counter, and there was a burst of gunfire. The soldier fell.

I stared at Lizzie with my face full of fear. The soldier in the backyard had made it to the door, and still, Kyle hadn't managed to end him.

"Haven't you been in a gunfight before?" Lizzie yelled at him. "Pull the damn trigger, Kyle!"

I looked at Kyle and realized Lizzie was right. Asides from running from the soldiers when they went on supply trips, Kyle had probably never killed anyone. Compassion welled deep in my heart. I knew how hard it was to pull the trigger. Pulling the trigger changed you forever, and struggling with that choice didn't make Kyle weak in my eyes. It made him strong.

The soldier strode forward and ripped the gun from Kyle's hand. He clearly felt secure knowing we were amateurs. Lizzie raised her weapon again with determination shining through her gray eyes, but Levi came up to her. He put a shaking hand over the barrel of her gun and pointed it away toward the floor.

Levi looked at the soldier, his body trembling all over, and said, "Dad?"

CHAPTER TWENTY-TWO

LEVI

IT WAS A MONTH before the war started. Dad had his feet up on the second-hand coffee table, watching the news. I lounged on the couch nearby. Mom forced me to see him at his flat. If I had it my way, I'd never visit.

"There's still time, Levi," Dad said, his eyes fixed on the TV.

"I'm not joining you," I said. "We've been through this."

He shook his head of short, dark hair. "If you come with me, you'll make it in time for basic training."

"No, Dad. I'm not keen," I said, keeping my voice level. "Sorry."

"That's disappointing. This isn't how I raised you."

"I don't care how you raised me. I'm not joining the army."

"Where's your honor?" he spat at me. His face twitched with the effort of trying to contain his rage.

"My honor? This isn't about honor. This is about not turning into you," I said.

That pissed him off. His face morphed into a look of disgust as he launched himself at me. I leaped over the back of the couch before he got to me.

"Coward," he growled.

"I'm not going to fight you, Dad."

We stood across the couch from each other, fists clenched.

He stormed over to me, grabbed my collar, and pulled my face close to his. "Fine, don't join. But don't say I never tried. I hope you get what's coming to you."

Dad let go and shoved me away. I walked out his door, determined to never look back. But his face had haunted me ever since. The look of rage. The anger in his eyes.

That was the face I stared at now.

"Levi, get out of the way," Lizzie yelled, snapping me out of my thoughts. But I couldn't move. My dad's face stared back at me. The crack of gunfire melted into background noise. The dust from the grenade washed out my surroundings into a surreal haze. But Dad stood in front of me. It was him, all right.

Did he know who I was?

His face stayed blank, but a flicker of recognition glinted in his dark eyes. Shit. This wasn't real. Was it?

"Behind you!" Jess screamed at Lizzie. Out of the corner of my eye, I saw Lizzie spin and shoot, but my eyes were fixed on Dad.

He stared at me, cold and calm. He wouldn't kill me, would he?

A yell came from over my dad's shoulder. Knox charged forward with a kitchen knife. I tried to say something, but I couldn't get the words out. In one swift motion, Dad pulled out a handgun, turned around, and shot Knox twice, square in the chest. Knox fell with a strangled scream. I managed to will my arms to move. With shaky hands, I aimed my rifle at Dad.

He watched me, amused. "Go on, shoot me, son," he said. His voice was too calm.

With trembling hands, I tried to pull the trigger, but I knew I couldn't do it.

"You're still pathetic," he said before lunging at me and smacking the gun from my hands.

"So what? You're going to kill your own son," I managed to

say as he pressed his gun against my stomach.

"You're not my son anymore," he growled in my ear.

I looked Dad directly in the eyes. If he was going to shoot me, I wasn't going to make it easy. He tore his gaze away from me.

"Cease fire!" Dad shouted and spun me around, the gun firmly at my back. The steady gunfire continued. "CEASE FIRE," Dad roared.

His men looked up and hesitantly lowered their weapons. The dog handler restrained the ferocious German Shepherd at the front door. It snarled with saliva oozing from its bared teeth as it pulled against its harness.

Lizzie, Grace, and Dylan looked around, unsure if they should continue shooting. Lizzie took aim at a soldier close by.

"If you shoot my man, I will kill him," Dad said as he pressed the gun painfully into my back. I couldn't bear to look at Lizzie. She would be so disappointed in me. Lizzie lowered the gun to her side.

"Good girl. Now, drop your weapons," Dad ordered. Grace and Dylan slowly placed their guns on the floor. Lizzie glared at my dad before letting hers fall to the floor with a clatter. The rest of our crew stood, terrified, around Knox, who moaned on the floor.

"Stand down," he said to his men. They looked at him, confused. "Stand down," he repeated firmly. He hauled me around to face him. "You have twenty-four hours," he said to me. "Then I'll hunt you down. Do you understand me?"

I stood up to my full height, took a deep breath, and steeled my face. "Yes, sir."

"No mercy next time," he said as his face briefly softened, and I saw a glimpse of the man he used to be.

"No mercy," I repeated.

He looked up at his men. "Move out." They turned around and marched from the house. "Also, put your friend out of his misery. He's going to die anyway," Dad said to me before turning away and walking out the front door. We watched in stunned silence as they marched away. Grace was immediately at my side.

"Are you OK?" she asked me, her voice wavering. I was too stunned to say anything back. She gave my hand a comforting squeeze.

Lizzie instantly took control. "We need to stop him bleeding," she said, running to Knox, who was gasping for breath on the floor. "Someone, find something to stem the bleed." She pressed her bare hands over the bullet wounds, but the blood seeped between her fingers. "Get me a towel, now!"

I stood, paralyzed with shock and unable to help as my mind raced. Dad was here. He knew about the war and never tried to warn Mom and me. We were abandoned, left at the mercy of Marion and his soldiers.

Jess stumbled into the kitchen, grabbed some grimy towels, and tried to compress Knox's wound. But it was no use. The towels quickly soaked with blood. Jess looked around frantically for someone to help. Knox started violently coughing up blood while trying to gasp for air. It was clear he was going to die.

Lizzie stood up, wiping her bloody hands on her jeans. "I don't know if we can save him. He's losing so much blood."

Jess continued in vain to stop the bleeding.

"What do we do?" Charlie asked, her voice shaking. "He can't breathe."

Lizzie looked lost and, for once, unsure what to do. "Help me put him in the recovery position," Lizzie eventually said as tears slipped down her cheeks. "I don't think there's anything else we can do."

Ollie began helping Lizzie roll Knox on his side. Jess stood and let the blood-soaked towels fall to the ground, defeated. She moved toward Kyle and held his hands in hers. We all knew what was about to happen. Knox was dying.

"This is Levi's fault," Kyle suddenly accused. "Your Dad pulled the trigger!" He pulled away from Jess and ran at me. Dylan charged forward and stepped into Kyle's path.

"No, it's not," Dylan said calmly. "Kyle, we're all upset."

"I'm going to fucking kill you for this," Kyle yelled at me as he tried to get at me.

Dylan grabbed him and stopped him from reaching me. "Calm down, mate."

"Get your fucking hands off me!" Kyle screamed at Dylan. They struggled, and Dylan eventually wrestled him to the ground.

"Don't listen to him. It's not your fault," Grace said to me.

Then the rage came.

"Leave me alone, Grace," I said as calmly as I could.

"But—"

"Fuck off," I yelled at her, roughly shoving her away. She stumbled backward with a yell and fell over an upended chair. I stormed from the kitchen, running in blind anger to the bedroom. I slammed the door shut and yelled in frustration. Dad was one of them. One of those fucking soldiers.

"Fuck!" I shouted, turning around and punching the wall. My fist smashed through the flimsy plasterboard. I looked down at my bloodied knuckles and punched again and again. It was all too much. Overwhelmed, I sank down against the wall to the floor and cried.

How could Dad do this? He was the reason for my suffering before the war. Now, he was a part of our whole country's suffering. And I felt responsible. He was my dad. It was like his mistakes were mine. I furiously wiped at my tears. God, I hated him.

After a few deep breaths, I managed to stop crying. The last thing I wanted was for everyone to see me weak. Dad would be embarrassed by me.

A few minutes later, there was a faint knock at the door. I wasn't in the mood to see anyone now. But the door creaked open, and Grace's tear-streaked face peered around the corner.

"Knox is dead," she whispered. "I thought you might want to know."

I looked up at her. There was fear in her eyes. Was she afraid of me?

"Dylan and Ollie are digging a grave in the backyard." She turned to leave.

"Wait," I managed to say.

Her face reappeared. But I couldn't get any words out. I wanted to apologize for pushing her. Her eyes roved from my bloody fists to the holes in the wall. She stood at the door, waiting for me to ask her to come in. But I wanted her to come in on her own and sit next to me. I wanted her to tell me everything was going to be OK. All I wanted was her. But there was something in her eyes that wasn't there before. Distrust.

"Levi, you should come out," she eventually said. "You'll get lost in your thoughts here."

"I'd rather get lost alone," I said defensively.

She took a hesitant step into the room.

"Maybe you should leave," I said.

"I don't think you should be alone," she said weakly and took a few steps closer.

"I don't need your help."

"At least let me wrap your knuckles."

"I don't need your help," I repeated.

"But I know how you feel," she said, coming and kneeling next to me. She lightly put her hand over mine.

"No, you don't," I said, pulling away from her.

"My dad—"

"Your dad's dead." Why did I say that?

She worked to keep her face compassionate, but cracks were beginning to show. She bit at her lip and wiped her teary eyes. I should apologize, I thought.

"I don't know what you want me to do," she said eventually. "I want to help you. Talk to me. Please."

"I want you to leave."

Grace refused to move and looked at me with concern. "You don't mean that," she said eventually.

I didn't mean it. I wanted her to stay with me. But I couldn't find the words. So, I looked away and didn't respond.

"If that's what you want," Grace said quietly. And then she left.

I leaned my head back against the wall. I was taking my anger out on Grace. It was unfair to her, but I couldn't help myself.

I couldn't understand why Dad would've gone along with Marion's plan. I knew he was a callous man, but I thought he had a conscience. Clearly, I was wrong. My mind wandered back to before the war, searching for clues. He had been so adamant that I join the army. Sometimes angry enough that he flew into a blind rage.

Any normal dad would try and keep their family safe. Not mine. He was never normal. Fresh anger boiled inside me. I wanted to punch and yell. Instead, I tried to calm myself down. I stood up and began pacing. Anger was always Dad's problem. It would never be mine. I tried to never let anything bother me. Until this moment, it had worked. But I could feel myself slipping into the uncontrollable. I couldn't let it happen. I refused to be like him.

Soft footsteps pattered down the hall, and the door swung open. Lizzie stood there, holding some bandages. "I'm going to wrap your knuckles," she said.

"Get out," I said to her.

"No," she replied as she marched over. Her face was red and puffy. She'd been crying too. "I couldn't help Knox, but I can fix your stupid hands," she said, sniffling and affixing a brave smile to her face.

I glared at her.

"I'm not going to make you talk. But sit," she ordered. I obeyed. She got to work quickly. She roughly washed my cut-up and bruised fists with some alcohol. It hurt, but not enough for me to care. Then she wrapped them tightly in gauze.

"How'd you know about—" I began to say.

"I heard you punch through the wall earlier."

"I upset Grace," I said.

Lizzie sighed and looked up at me. "I think she'll forgive you. You have other stuff on your mind. She knows that."

"Everything's fucked up," I growled, getting up and pacing again. My hands shook as I tried to contain the rage at my dad that burned inside me. "We never should have come here."

"It was a mistake," Lizzie agreed. "Let's hope it's not a fatal one."

"We need to leave. The soldiers will come back, and we don't have the weapons to fight them," I said, pushing the thoughts of Dad from my mind. Maybe jumping into action would help.

"We have to discuss it with the others."

"Screw the others. I'm not fighting Dad. I won't sink to his level. If he wants to fight me, he'll have to find me first."

"I agree with you, Levi. But we have to talk to the others," Lizzie said. She was standing close to me now and looking up at me with understanding.

There was a knock at the door, and Grace came in. A look of confusion passed over her face at seeing Lizzie there. "We're going to bury Knox. You two should come and pay your respects," Grace managed to say.

"I don't want to," I said stubbornly.

"Come," Lizzie said sternly. She grabbed my wrist and pulled me past Grace toward the backyard. Grace trailed behind us. We skirted around Knox, who still lay on the floor, covered with a blanket. Lizzie pushed the backdoor open and deposited me on the deck. Charlie and Ollie stood off to one side, crying together.

"Give me a hand," Dylan said to me. "We need to get Knox." His face was flushed with the exhaustion of digging, and his hands were grimy with dirt. More importantly, he was acting like himself. He jumped up onto the deck, and I followed him back into the kitchen.

"Fuck your dad," he said to me quietly as he looked over his shoulder. If anyone knew what I was going through, it was Dylan. He had known my dad and hated him like me.

"Why did he have to be one of them?" I asked, almost pleaded with Dylan.

"Cause he's a shit person. Always has been," Dylan said as he pulled off the blanket covering Knox, and we bent down to carry him. I lifted his legs while Dylan gripped his arms.

"I know," I said. I tried not to look at Knox's face, which was now pale and waxy. I cringed as we lifted his lifeless body off the floor. It wasn't the first time I had done this, but it was the first time doing it to someone we knew. Dylan noticed the look on my face.

"We were bloody lucky it wasn't one of us," he said.

"Yeah," I muttered.

"I will say this for your dad. He kinda saved us. He gave us another chance."

I was silent.

"If it was any other group of soldiers, we would have been dead," he said as we lugged Knox out to his makeshift grave. Kyle and Jess were there now. Kyle glowered at me, but Jess seemed to have him restrained. Grace stood alone at the edge of the group. Her face was blank, but it seemed to take all her energy to keep it that way. The trembling lip and empty eyes were enough to give it away. Dylan and I carefully set Knox into the hole. I stepped back, and Lizzie was at my side.

"Does anyone want to say anything?" Dylan asked awkwardly. We never had the chance to bury our friends that the soldiers killed. They were taken from us without a goodbye. Weirdly, this felt like a way to let go of everyone we'd lost. Kyle cleared his throat and stepped forward.

"Knox, mate. We've been friends since kindergarten," he said as he swept his hair behind his ear. He spent a moment composing himself. Jess was immediately next to him, whispering encouragement in his ear.

"I was going to say something meaningful… but this sucks," he said through tears. He broke down and cried again before anger flared in his gaze. "You didn't deserve to die," he eventually said. "I'm going to get them back for this. I promise you. Whatever it takes."

Lizzie caught my eye. Kyle was going to do something stupid.

Kyle walked up, grabbed the shovel, and started scooping dirt over Knox. When emotion overcame him, I came forward and took the spade from him. Jess led Kyle away. I looked down into the hole at Knox's motionless body as tears of anger began to spill from my eyes. My dad had done this.

"I'm sorry," I whispered to him as I tossed a scoop of dirt over his face. Just like that, Knox was gone; a patch of upturned earth in the back garden.

Chapter Twenty-Three

Lizzie

Sycamore seeds went flying as the cool autumn breeze rustled its fingers through the branches of the tree. The little helicopter wings twizzled through the air and landed gently onto Knox's freshly dug grave. If I had known this would happen, only days ago, after Knox had made the pass at me, I would have said good riddance. Now, I wasn't sure how to feel about it. I couldn't feel sad. But I did feel guilty, like it was my fault. I had wished this on him. And despite my best efforts, I had been too weak to save him.

I pretended to know a lot about first aid. But having taken a first aid course to add weight to your high school diploma is a hell of a lot different from knowing how to deal with a bullet wound. Had I done everything right? Could I have saved him if I had known more? Maybe one day, if I ever became a nurse, I would find out the answer to that. For now, I was left staring at a mound of dirt. There was nothing to mark his grave.

"Lizzie." Dylan came and sat down beside me on the deck. I tensed. It seemed Dylan and I couldn't be near each other without arguing at the moment, and I wasn't sure I had the energy for another fight.

"Look," Dylan said. His blue eyes were distant as he tried to think of what to say. "I know I tried to tell you I was sorry before, but this time, I really mean it."

I was silent. I didn't know what to think about Dylan anymore. It seemed pointless now, all this fuss and drama when people were dying. Of what consequence was our messy relationship?

"Please," he begged, "if you would just listen to me?"

My heart ached. I wanted to tell him we could put it all behind us, but in truth, I wasn't sure anymore. I wasn't sure about anything.

"I'm listening," I said and turned my gaze to him.

"I was stupid, and I wasn't thinking clearly, and I hurt you. But with everything that's been going on, we can't hold grudges. We've got to stick together. Otherwise, we'll end up like Knox… buried in a stranger's backyard," Dylan said, speaking from his heart. "I don't want to end up that way, and I don't want to see you end up that way either. We've come too far for that, Lizzie."

"I know," I said heavily. "I was confused because you weren't yourself. You were the one person I could count on, Dylan. And then everything changed."

"Nothing changed, Lizzie. I'm still me. I hit a rough patch, but that isn't an excuse. It's no defense for the way I treated you. For the way I treated all of you. I love you, Lizzie. I think I always will," Dylan said honestly. I pulled my gaze away from his and stared awkwardly at my knees. I wasn't sure I could say the same back. Not yet, anyhow. Surely Dylan would understand? Wind swooped over the fence, and I clutched tighter at the thin cardigan I was wearing.

"Thank you… for apologizing, and for being open. It means a lot." I paused for a second longer than I intended, and Dylan's face fell.

"But?" Dylan said.

"But… I think I need time. I don't know how to feel about us at the moment. Or anything," I said. "You're right, though. To get through this war, we all need each other. And for what it's worth, I'm sorry, too. We said some pretty shitty stuff to each other."

"Do you think you'll ever get past it? That you'll ever trust me again?" Dylan asked.

I sighed. "I trust you to have my back in this war, and maybe… someday…" I trailed off awkwardly.

"So, I can still hope?" Dylan said. He looked at me earnestly, and for a moment, I could see the Dylan I met at the beginning of this all. A sensitive, loyal guy who I could count on to be there, my life-raft amid a sea storm. Maybe I had already forgiven him, after all. Despite everything, it hit me: There was no one I trusted more. Thinking this, my heart swelled, and I felt lighter than I had in weeks. Yes, there was hope. Not that I was going to admit that right now, though.

"You can hope," I agreed. "You can hope for a quick death if you ever accuse me of cheating again. I mean, seriously. Aside from the fact you and I weren't exactly official, you thought Levi and I were a thing?" I said with a snort.

Dylan grinned. "Yeah, I was way off base."

"You bet you were," I said, punching him lightly in the shoulder. "I can't think of any situation where that would ever work out," I added. Levi had always been a good-looking goof by my books. If Grace and Levi weren't an item, would I have looked twice? I tried to imagine it but couldn't quite get there. Yet, over the last few weeks, I'd learned there was more to Levi than met the eye.

"That would be weird," Dylan said.

"Definitely," I agreed.

We sat in silence for a bit, just the two of us, each alone with our thoughts. Neither of us were willing to go back inside and face the chaos. As the wind picked up, Dylan finally stirred to life. "Well, we'd better go back inside," Dylan said, "the others need us."

I nodded and stood. Brushing off the dust that stuck to my jeans, I followed Dylan indoors.

Grace was sitting on the only remaining kitchen chair. The soldiers' grenade had smashed a few, and Kyle had thrown a couple around in fury when he'd come back in from burying Knox.

Grace looked broken and small. I wanted to stand up and shield her from everything that had made her life so miserable, but I was only one person. And there was a whole world out there trying to rain hurt down on us. Dylan sat down on the couch.

"Can I help?" he mouthed at me. I shook my head.

"Grace?" I said quietly. "Are you all right?"

She turned to face me with her face crumbling, and then she crushed me in a hug, sobbing loudly. "No, I'm not. Nothing's all right. Levi... he won't let me help... he won't t-t-talk to me."

"Levi is going through some stuff right now, just like you are," I said, patting her gently on the back. I pulled back with my hands on Grace's shoulders. I waited until she managed to take a few deep breaths and calm herself. I looked into her deep brown eyes. "Grace, things are going to work out. I'm not saying the road ahead won't be tough, but so long as we all stick together, we'll be OK. How about you go sit with Dylan? I'll go get the others. We need to decide on what to do."

Grace nodded and wandered over to the living room. She sat down sadly beside Dylan like a deflated balloon. Just then, Levi stormed out of the bedroom and marched out through the broken front door toward the street.

"Levi, where are you going?" I yelled at him. When he didn't reply, I ran out down the concrete stairs after him. He was already on the road when I caught up with him and pulled on his arm. "Stop. Levi! For Christ's sake. Stop!"

He turned around and wrenched his arm out of my grasp. "We're wasting time. We should go now. They could come at any minute."

"Your dad said we have twenty-four hours," I said. "There's still time."

"And you think he keeps his promises?" Levi bellowed at me in anger. "Do you know how many promises he's broken, Lizzie? Do you!"

"No, I don't. But you can't walk out on us. We deserve more than that," I said angrily. Levi paled and stood there in the middle of the street, looking lost.

"Fuck, I am like him. He was never there for Mom and me, and now I'm walking out on all of you," Levi said as the realization hit him.

"You're not him, Levi. I know Grace has told you this before. You're better than him. It's not something that's written into your soul. You get to choose how to live your life." I pulled him over to the shade of a small tree in the next-door neighbor's backyard and sat on the grass.

Levi hesitated for a moment and then sat down beside me. "I can't fight him, Lizzie. I can't do it. I know it makes me seem weak."

"It's not weak, Levi."

"Dad expects me to run. I've been running from him all my life, but if I turn and fight him, then I will have become exactly the person he wants me to be. I don't want to give him that satisfaction," Levi tried to explain.

"Sometimes, the strongest decision a person can make is to say no, and walk away without a fight," I said.

Levi's almond-brown eyes met mine. "You've changed, Lizzie," he said.

"We're all changing." I looked out at the street. It was empty and silent. In the park down the road, some children's swings swayed in the wind. The weather was changing too, and it was time to get the hell out of here.

"You know I agree with you," I added after a moment. "You're right about not fighting. Putting aside the complications with your dad, we don't have the weapons. They know exactly where we are and how many of us there are. It would be suicide to try and fight them. But we have to talk it over with the others. We can't just lay down the law and get up and go."

"I know." Levi pushed himself up and looked skyward with a sigh. Then he brought his gaze back down to me. He ran a hand through his brown hair. "Let's go then. I don't want to leave this to the last minute," Levi said and held out his hand.

I grabbed his hand, and he pulled me to my feet. We walked together up the driveway to the house and climbed the old concrete stairway. I stepped through the broken door. It lay in splinters on the floor. In the lounge, Dylan and Grace were still sitting, waiting for us. Grace looked a little calmer.

"Are you all right?" Grace said to Levi.

"Yeah," Levi said quietly, embarrassed. Jess and the others were nowhere to be seen. I wondered if they had left without us, but then I heard voices down the hall, and my heart calmed. While they were still here, there was still time to reach Jess.

But first things first. I had to inject life into our group. We would never convince Jess to come with us if we were in pieces. I looked around me, and it was a dismal sight. Dust caked the surfaces, and the worn two-seater sagged under Dylan and Grace's weight. The TV had a bullet through it, and the bookshelf in the corner tilted worryingly. Levi dumped himself down onto the other sofa, but I stayed standing, staring at the three of them.

"We can't stay here," I said. The others looked at me, exhausted. "We're tired. We've been through a lot lately, I know. But we need to pull together. The soldiers will come back, and though I know we'd all love to give them hell, it wouldn't be a smart move," I said strongly, trying to force some life into them. I couldn't save Knox, but I could do this. It was a different kind of CPR.

"This is a first," Dylan said. "I never thought I'd see the day where you'd be convincing us to run and hide."

"Honestly, neither did I," I said. "But our lives are too

precious to throw away. This doesn't mean we're giving up. But I think we need to choose our battles… and this is one we can't win."

"I think you're right," Grace said. "I don't know about you guys, but I can't take much more of this."

"Who's going to talk to Jess?" Levi said. The conversation felt eerily familiar, but it was all backward. Last time, we had convinced Jess to fight with us. This time, we were standing down.

"I don't want to bully her into doing anything," I said, "but I think it needs to be all of us. She needs to see we all care for her."

"Should I go and get her?" Dylan asked.

I shook my head and sat on the other sofa with Levi. It groaned sadly.

"No. Give her time. She'll come to us. She would never do anything without at least saying goodbye," I said. I hoped I was right. Jess was one of us, and we couldn't leave her alone to die. We owed her more than that.

After everything we had all been through together, I knew without a doubt we had to have each other's backs. I had thought when this war started, if I had to do it alone, I would. If I had to fight, I would die for my ideals. But everything over the last few weeks had convinced me otherwise. What point was there to fighting if you were the only one left standing? What kind of reward would that be? Like Levi, I refused to fight this battle. But I would give my all to convince Jess to side with us because, in the past, she'd given her all for us. I only hoped it wasn't too little, too late.

Chapter Twenty-Four

Jess

The night was quiet and still outside Kyle's bedroom window, with no sign of the soldiers who would be combing the streets in a few hours. I sat on Kyle's bed with my elbows on the windowsill, peering into the darkness. So much had happened in the last few hours, and I needed time to think.

My friends wanted to flee, and I was half inclined to join them. Levi was right when he said we didn't have enough weapons and weren't prepared for the number of soldiers who would come. But I finally had someone for me. Kyle and I were so close now, and it felt like what we had was real. We understood each other. And Kyle was upset after Knox's death. Knox meant so much to him, and I couldn't leave when he was in this state, even if I wanted to.

"Jess," Kyle said, touching my shoulder.

"Sorry, I was thinking," I said, looking over at him. His face was blotchy with anger and tears. His other hand rested on the remnants of the bottle of whiskey we were drinking before the soldiers came. We hadn't had any more.

"I want to fight, and I don't care what the others think," he said stubbornly.

"You've never fought before. You still haven't even shot a gun," I said gently.

"So what? You guys do it all the time."

"I'm not sure fighting's the best idea," I said, pulling away from the window and shuffling up next to him.

"What? So, it's OK for you guys to wage war, but not me? You blew up the Skytower. All I want to do is shoot up some soldiers."

"That's not what I mean. We're not prepared for a battle," I said.

"Levi's dad killed my best mate," Kyle said, standing up. "Am I supposed to sit here and do nothing?" Fresh tears came to his eyes as he ran a shaky hand through his dark hair.

I was immediately by his side. "Of course not." I wrapped my arms around his waist and pulled him close to me.

"I'm fighting back," he said. "I'm going to put a fucking bullet in that man's head."

"Are you sure that's what you want to do?" I asked, burying my face in his shirt.

He pulled me away from him at arm's length. "You're either with me or not. I'm going to stand and fight, even if it's just me."

"Kyle..." What was I supposed to say? I hadn't felt this way about anyone before, and I couldn't leave him. It was certain death to face the soldiers alone. At least he would have more of a chance if I was with him. But it would mean leaving my friends.

"I need you with me, Jessy," Kyle said softly. "I can't do anything without you." He gently kissed my forehead.

"I'm not going to leave you. Never."

"I knew you'd understand. We're the same, you and me," he said as a watery smile came to his lips. I secretly hoped Kyle would change his mind. There was still time.

"Always," I said.

"We're like Bonnie and Clyde," Kyle added with a wild glint in his eye.

"I guess so," I said with a weak laugh.

"And we'll go out like they did if we have to," he said.

"It won't come to that," I said confidently.

"I'll do anything to get back at them."

"I know you will."

"But we can't let this go to waste," he said as he tightened his grip on the whiskey bottle and picked it up. "Knox would be disappointed in us." He unscrewed the lid and took a hearty swig. "Here, have a sip," he said, offering the bottle.

I took the bottle from him, and he caught me by surprise as his arm snuck around my waist. I put my hand on his cheek, which was still wet with tears, and then ran my fingers through his thick, dark hair. He leaned down and lightly kissed my lips. Everything about him was right for me, and I was going to stay with him for as long as I could. Lizzie and the others wouldn't be able to change my mind.

Kyle and I spent the next thirty minutes finishing the bottle in his bedroom. By the time it was empty, I still felt sober. This time, the drink wasn't strong enough to take away the pain. Kyle didn't look drunk at all. His eyes were alert, and his face was tear-free.

"We should talk to the others," I said. "Try again to get them to fight with us."

"We don't need them," Kyle said. "It can be just us."

"Yes, we do. The two of us can't take down an entire army."

Kyle sighed. "All right, let's give it a go." He trudged from the bedroom.

We found the others in the lounge talking in hushed whispers. Everyone except for Grace, who sat away from the group, lost in her own world. She looked pathetic, with her broken arm still wrapped in a filthy cast. Her head wound hadn't healed entirely, and an ugly scab clung to her hairline. The grenade had covered her and Dylan in a thin layer of dust, which they hadn't managed to shake loose.

"We're going to stay and fight," Kyle said.

"No," Lizzie said, shaking her head. "It's suicide."

"I'm telling you, Jess and I are staying. We're going to kill Levi's dad and the rest of his men."

I looked over at Levi. He sat defeated on the couch, lines of stress etched into his forehead. Both his hands were bandaged but bleeding through. I thought he might jump up at the mention of Kyle wanting to kill his dad, but it seemed he had lost the will to fight. I knew then—they weren't going to help.

"Jess, surely you can see this is a stupid idea," Lizzie insisted.

"I'm not going to leave him. You wouldn't leave Dylan. It's the same thing," I snapped.

Kyle turned and looked at Charlie and Ollie. "Help us. For Knox's sake," he said to them. Charlie was holding back tears and looked on the verge of collapsing in grief.

"Sorry, mate," Ollie managed to say. "Charlie and I have been talking. We think it's best to head to another house, far from here… hide out there for a bit. You should join us. All of you," he said, looking around at everyone.

"So, you're going to run, too," Kyle said. "Some friends you are."

"We don't know how many soldiers will come," Charlie said. "I just want to get through this war in one piece." She broke down into tears.

"You two are pathetic. Cowards," Kyle spat at them.

"If that keeps us alive, you can call me whatever you like," Ollie said.

"I thought we all had each other's backs," Kyle said.

"We do," Ollie insisted. "Come with us. We can hide out somewhere until this shitstorm blows over."

Kyle was shaking his head in anger. "No. The soldiers are going to pay."

"Dylan, Lizzie, are you guys going to come with us?" Ollie asked, ignoring Kyle's outburst. "Charlie and I have already packed. We're ready to leave."

The others looked torn. Dylan and Lizzie looked at each other and then back at me.

"We can't leave you, Jess," Dylan said.

"I'm staying with Kyle," I repeated.

"You two go without us," Lizzie eventually said to Ollie and Charlie.

"Suit yourselves," Ollie said with a shrug.

"We're not leaving without Jess," Lizzie said, looking directly at me.

Ollie and Charlie moved off to get their packs.

"I don't think you're listening to me, Lizzie," I said, frustrated. "Get it through your head. I'm not leaving Kyle."

"But you can't stay here," Lizzie said. "Don't you see?"

"You should go with Ollie and Charlie. Save yourselves because I'm not changing my mind." They were continually trying to break us up, and I was sick of it. It was so unfair, like they didn't want me to be happy.

"Jess and I are fighting back. We don't care what you do. Leave or stay. We really couldn't care less," Kyle said as he stood protectively next to me.

"We aren't going to let you stay," Lizzie said desperately.

"I'll drag you out of here myself," Dylan said.

I felt anger burning up inside me. They didn't understand and never would.

"Get over yourself, Lizzie," I said. "You don't rule my life. I can do whatever I want, and I don't need your permission."

"Jess," Lizzie said.

"No," I said, storming to Kyle's room as tears sprang to my eyes. Kyle was right behind me.

"They've had a problem with us right from the start," Kyle said. "Some friends they are."

"They're trying to protect me," I said, slamming the door shut. "But I don't need it. I'm not a child."

Kyle put his arm around my shoulders and pulled me close to him. I melted into his warm embrace. But worry still swirled in my stomach. Staying in this house to fight... maybe Lizzie was right. It was suicide. I had to tell him how I felt, and maybe there was still a chance we could all get out of here together.

"Kyle," I said, looking up at him. "We can't fight them. Not here," I admitted to him. He avoided my gaze. "I want to help you. But this isn't the way." I felt embarrassed sharing this with him. He desperately wanted to avenge Knox, and I wanted him to succeed. Kyle's happiness mattered to me, more than I cared to admit.

"I know," he eventually said. Finally, he was starting to see clearly through the fog of his grief.

"What do you want to do?" I asked him.

"I want it to be you and me," he said. "Not your friends, not Ollie or Charlie. Just us."

"We could run away together," I said, but deep down, I didn't want to leave the others. We had been through so much together, and they were the only family I had left.

"No. I still want to get back at the soldiers. I want revenge, and I don't care what I have to do to get it." A shadow of vengeance passed over his face, and then he turned away from me, walking over to the window and staring down the street.

"Kyle, what are you saying?"

He remained silent, clearly thinking over some sort of plan.

"Kyle?" I urged.

"Don't freak out," he said, glancing over his shoulder at me. "Dad was a helicopter pilot, and he took me flying all the time."

"Where are you going with this?" I asked, confused, and worried.

"There's a small airfield out in Ardmore. If we can get to it, I know there are a bunch of helicopters there. I reckon I could fly one no problem—"

"You can't seriously be suggesting flying a helicopter," I said.

"I know I can do it, Jess. I've flown them a million times with Dad. We can take the guns and shoot the soldiers from the air."

Was he crazy? Out loud I said, "That's never going to work."

"It will work. I know it will," he said, turning to me.

I wasn't so sure. "How will we get to this airfield?"

"Steal a car. It shouldn't be too hard," he said with a shrug.

"And what about the weapons?"

"We take some of those automatic guns the dead soldiers had. Easy." This time, his face was inches from mine. I caught a whiff of the smoky whiskey on his breath. He was drunk. That explained it. I probably was too, but why didn't I feel it? My head wasn't light, and I saw everything clearly. But I must be, I'd had enough whiskey to make sure of that.

"This is the whiskey talking," I said to Kyle.

He shook his head adamantly. "It's not. I'm not drunk at all. In fact, I've never thought so clearly."

"What if we crash?" I said. "This plan is crazy."

"We won't crash. I know how to fly. Once we've shot up the soldiers, we can fly away and be together."

That piqued my interest. If Kyle really knew how to fly, maybe once we were in the air, I could convince him to abandon his revenge plot, and we could escape to freedom. The chances of it working were slim, but if we could get up in the sky... we had every chance of escaping.

"What do you say?" he asked.

I hesitated. I knew I should say no, but the chance to be free now sat enticingly in front of me. We could fly to one of the islands off the coast and hide until the end of the war. I closed my eyes and imagined a new life without fear of the soldiers. More importantly, I thought about the life Kyle and I could have. Everything I hoped for could come true if I could convince Kyle to fly us away. It was a chance worth taking.

"I'm in."

Kyle's tear-streaked face broke into a smile. This was a much better plan than waiting around for the soldiers to find us.

A soft knock at the door interrupted our conversation. "We're leaving," Charlie said shakily through the door.

Kyle opened it, revealing a teary Charlie and Ollie standing with packs strapped on, ready to go.

"You're sure you don't want to come with?" Ollie asked.

Kyle shook his head.

"I guess this is goodbye then," Ollie said, sounding disappointed. He readjusted his glasses and stepped forward to give Kyle a hug. "Take care of yourself, mate."

"I will," Kyle said.

"Don't get yourself killed. I want to see you again when the war's over," Charlie said through her tears. She rushed forward and crushed Kyle in a hug. I managed to hold in my emotions. It was going to be tough leaving my friends, too.

"Bye, Jess. Hope to see you soon," Ollie said.

Charlie glared at me, and then they left. I sat down dejected on the bed and tied my wild locks back in a ponytail.

"What are you thinking about, babe?"

"I should talk to my friends one more time," I said to Kyle.

"Suit yourself. But they're going to upset you. They don't understand what we have," he said.

"I have to try."

I found Lizzie sitting outside on the deck, alone. She looked contemplatively out at the overgrown yard and Knox's grave. I wanted to talk to her once more. They were my friends, and we had been through so much of this war together.

"Lizzie," I said quietly, trying not to surprise her.

"Jess, I'm so worried about you," she said.

"You shouldn't be," I said with a weak smile.

I sat down next to her, facing the garden.

"Remember when we found you and Leah when the war started?" Lizzie asked.

"Of course, you and Grace held us at gunpoint. How could I forget?"

"Who knew this is where we'd end up?" she commented. "Think how far we've come since then."

"We're different now. The whole world's different." My mind started replaying everything we had been through: Leah's death, the warehouse attack, and our escape to the US. Then Jennifer's death not so long ago, and our attack on the Skytower. It was strange to think back to the beginning of it all and see how far we had come. Tragedy had struck. Our entire world had changed, but we had stuck together through it all. It was true. We were different now. Stronger, and closer. I would miss them.

"We're a family," Lizzie said.

"And we always will be," I said. "But I need to decide what's right for me."

"Please come with us. We can't leave you behind."

"I'm sticking with Kyle," I said.

"You're going to get yourself killed," Lizzie pleaded with me.

"I'm old enough to make my own decisions," I said defiantly.

"See some sense… please. Fighting the soldiers here, you can't win," she said. "Leave with us. Bring Kyle if you have to."

"You always want to fight. What's happened? Now it's not your idea, you don't want to?" I said back.

"It's nothing like that. I know we're in over our heads. You should too."

"I'm not an idiot. That's why Kyle and I have a new plan," I said, clenching my fists to stop them from shaking.

"So, you are going to join us? You've changed your mind?" she asked hopefully.

She still didn't get it.

"No. Kyle and I are escaping in a helicopter, and you can't stop us." I didn't mean to bring up the helicopter, but what harm could it do? It's not like they could stop us, even if they tried.

"Wait, what helicopter?" Lizzie asked.

"It's none of your business."

"Don't do it, Jess," Lizzie warned. "He's drunk. Does he even know how to fly?"

"He's barely had any," I said defensively. "And yes, his dad taught him."

They were always complaining about drinking, but nothing bad had happened.

"I can smell it on him. And you, for that matter," Lizzie said.

"He's smashed."

"Why do you hate him so much?" I yelled at her.

Lizzie flinched at my outburst, but when she looked at me, her eyes were blazing. "He's a bad influence. You don't need him."

"That's rich coming from you. You would never leave Dylan. Imagine if I said this to you," I said.

"This isn't about Dylan and me," she dismissed. "Don't you hear yourself? You're not thinking clearly."

"Actually, for once, I see everything for what it is," I said. They didn't care about me, they never did. "If you were my friends, you'd be happy for me. Not trying to break us up."

"Jess—"

"No, Lizzie. Get off your high horse. You don't know what's best for me. I'm going to Ardmore with Kyle, and there's nothing you can do to stop me." With that, I left Lizzie sitting alone on the deck. I don't know why I even bothered trying to talk to her. None of them understood what Kyle and I had.

"Jess," Dylan said as I came into the kitchen.

"Fuck off, Dylan," I said, blowing past him. I had to find Kyle, I wanted to leave now. I found Kyle grabbing the assault rifles.

"Let's go," I said to him.

"What, now?"

"Yes. I don't want to see the others anymore," I said, holding back tears.

"If that's what you want," he said.

I nodded. "Yes."

Kyle quickly got to work, throwing anything useful he could find into a pile. I sat on the bed, watching him frantically search the wardrobe for a decent-sized bag.

Was I making the right choice? It didn't matter anyhow. I was leaving with Kyle, and we would be happy together. He'd had a bit to drink, but not that much. And our decisions weren't rash; we were proactive, unlike the others. I wanted to go and say goodbye to Grace and Levi. They were always so nice to me, but

I knew they would try and convince me to go with them instead of Kyle. I had made up my mind now. Kyle and I would be together until the end.

Kyle stood silhouetted with the window behind him. "Come on," he said as he extended his hand to me. "Let's do this."

We walked hand in hand to the window. He opened the latch and swung the window open, letting the cool night air into his room. We snuck out the window and took off into the streets. I looked back at the house one last time. Was this the last time I would see them alive? I prayed not.

"I'll hot-wire the next car we find. It needs to be an old one, though," Kyle said.

"Over there." I pointed to a crappy-looking station wagon parked on the street. Kyle looked around for something to break the window. He settled on a piece of plywood, which he swung at the driver's window. It exploded into tiny shards of glass. He unlocked the car and pulled a flathead screwdriver from his backpack, and started uncovering the wires in the steering column.

"How do you know how to do this?" I asked.

"Knox was always in trouble with the law," he said. "Actually, he'd be pretty chuffed seeing me do this."

After fishing through bundles of wires, he found the right ones and began stripping them down. A few minutes later, he had the wires sparking together, and the car jumped to life. He dusted the glass off the seats and sat, revving the engine a few times.

"Let's roll," he said with a grin. I hopped into the passenger seat, and he shoved the car into gear. We sped off down the dark streets to our freedom.

Chapter Twenty-Five

Grace

THE NIGHT SLEPT PEACEFULLY outside the kitchen window, oblivious to the wicked invading the world beneath its protective wing. A gentle breeze swept through the unkempt grass, except by Knox's grave. The little cross Charlie put up looked so lonely. Was he doomed to be a forgotten casualty of this war? Were we all? We had to hope someone would make it to the end, or we would be lost forever.

I pulled my eyes from the window as flashes of our efforts to save him came back to me. He was the first person we had the chance to save and the first one we failed. My eyes were drawn to his blood, still smeared across the beige linoleum. How many more would die before this war ended? I couldn't handle another death.

I leaned back against the dust-covered kitchen bench and wiped at my eyes with shaking hands. It took all my energy to keep the shadows from my past at bay. They lurked and pulled at my mind, willing me to fall into their open arms. This house and the people in it brought the painful memories of the past to the surface.

Soon we'd be back in the forest. The alcohol would be gone, and I'd be able to push the pain down. Everything would be back to how it was. A shuffling sound at the doorway to the kitchen caught my attention, and I looked up to see Levi standing there, his eyes downcast.

"I didn't mean to push you," he said at the ground. I subconsciously rubbed the large bruise on my back and readjusted my arm in the sling. It had gotten pretty beat up after the grenade blast, and it broke my fall when Levi pushed me. The painful throbbing moving up my arm worried me. Was it broken again? I hoped not, but there wasn't a lot I could do about it if it was.

"It's fine," I managed to say. I desperately needed Levi right now. He was the only person who could help keep me afloat. But he wasn't himself. Something changed when his dad showed up. There was a restless darkness in him, and it made me uneasy. He was living in his own hell, and couldn't help me. No one could.

"No, it's not. I'm angry… and I can't control it," he said. "I don't want to hurt you."

"It was an accident," I said.

He looked up at me, eyes glistening with unshed tears. I wanted to go to him, but I didn't have the strength. And, it seemed, he didn't have the will to come to me. We stood in tense silence across the room from each other.

"I'm sorry," he eventually said. I wanted to rush forward and collapse into his comforting embrace, but he couldn't give me that. Not right now, not with everything going on.

"He really means it," Lizzie said as she came into the kitchen and placed a hand on Levi's arm. Since when were they close? "He was worried he hurt you," she said with a lopsided smile.

I was stuck, staring at Lizzie's hand still on Levi's arm. I was reading into this too much, right? Lizzie and Levi were friends. They always had been. And when I saw them standing close after Lizzie fixed his hands… that was nothing as well. My mind was playing tricks on me, and I was overthinking it. Levi wasn't Sean, and Lizzie was my best friend. She'd never betray me.

At that moment, Dylan came sprinting into the room. "Jess is missing," he said breathlessly.

"What?" Lizzie asked, a wave of panic washing over her face.

"They're gone. Jess and Kyle," he said. His eyes darted around to each of us.

"Have you checked their room?" Lizzie said as she ran from the kitchen. We chased after her and came to a halt at Kyle's open door. The window was wide open, allowing the chilly night breeze to swirl around. Lizzie rushed up to the window and peered into the dark.

"I can't see them," she said, pulling the window shut.

"They can't have gone far," Levi commented.

"No, they can only be… ten minutes ahead of us," Lizzie said with a glance down at her watch.

"We have to go after them," I said.

Lizzie and Dylan looked at each other, uncertain.

"Jess was pretty adamant she wanted us to leave her alone," Lizzie said. She tucked her tangled blond hair behind her ear and sighed.

"Plus, who knows where they've gone off to," Dylan said as he paced back and forth.

Lizzie looked sheepishly at the ground. Something was up.

"What do you know, Lizzie?" I asked. I couldn't let Jess leave with Kyle. He was a bad influence and would end up getting her killed. I didn't trust him.

"She was talking nonsense before… at least I hope it was nonsense," Lizzie said.

"Lizzie," Dylan said. "Spill."

"Jess said something about taking a helicopter in Ardmore," Lizzie said as she bit at her lip. "But she can't possibly be that stupid."

"Kyle's that stupid," I said. A helicopter? What sort of suicidal plan were they dreaming up?

"And they're both smashed," Levi added.

"What are they going to do with a helicopter?" Dylan asked.

"Fly away? Kill soldiers? Who the hell knows? He's so wasted, it could be anything," Levi said, leaning moodily against the doorframe.

"Jess never said," Lizzie said quietly.

"Why don't any of you seem concerned that Jess is gone?" I asked, outraged. Kyle was drunk. He was going to get her killed. I could feel it, and panic began to rise within me. We had to save her.

"I think we should take the hint," Levi said. "She doesn't want us anymore."

"Don't say that," I said, my voice breaking with the effort to control my emotions.

Levi shrugged. "It's pretty clear to me."

"Lizzie, we have to go after her," I said.

"I want to, Grace, but at what point do we admit she's a lost cause?" Lizzie said to me. "I tried to talk to her, but she wouldn't listen."

"We have to try. It's Jess. We can't abandon her," I pleaded with them.

"She seemed pretty happy to desert us," Levi commented.

"Would you give up on me?" I asked, looking at Levi. "Would you?"

"It's not the same thing," Levi eventually said. "You're different."

"She's one of us. We have to try," I said.

A heavy silence filled the room.

"Lizzie, you know as well as I do we need to stick together. What you said before about showing Jess how much we care for her—this is how we do that. If we turn up there, all of us, and help her see how much we love her… well, that's got to count for something, doesn't it?" I tried to keep the waver out of my voice. I had to get through to them.

Dylan scratched the back of his neck. "Grace is right," he said eventually. "There's no way we can leave her. I've been just as guilty of being caught up in the new crowd as Jess has, but that doesn't mean I'd ever want you guys to leave me behind. I say we go after her."

Lizzie's expression softened as she looked at Dylan. "OK," she said. "I'm in."

We looked at Levi for a unanimous vote. "I don't like that she went off without telling us. But I can understand it. If Lizzie didn't stop me, I was ready to walk out of here myself," he said.

"Let's go then," I said, eager to get going.

"One problem. Do we even know where Ardmore is?" Lizzie asked, always the pragmatist. "I've never heard of it."

"It's a small airstrip an hour's drive out of the city," Dylan said.

"An hour's drive? There's no way they're walking all that way," Lizzie said.

"I bet he stole a car," Levi said.

"Then we steal a car, too," I said.

"That's not going to be easy," Levi said, reluctant.

I was determined to save Jess. I had to. "We have to find a way. I can't lose someone else," I said shakily. "I can't."

I looked up at Levi, who avoided my gaze. He was still upset about his dad. That's why he wasn't himself. Usually, he had my back. He always had my back. I knew none of them meant for me to feel this way, but looking around at the apprehensive faces of my friends, I had never felt so alone, not since my family died.

The three of them stood together, leaving me as the outsider. Maybe Jess thought she didn't have a place in our group, but she was wrong. Jess was the glue holding us all together. If an argument cropped up, she was the one person you could count on for unbiased advice. The peacekeeper. Without her, we were already falling apart. We needed to save her, no matter what. Even if Jess didn't want to be saved.

"Does anyone know how to hot-wire a car?" Lizzie asked eventually. Finally, someone was taking the lead. "We'll never catch them on foot."

Silence.

Levi averted his eyes.

"Yeah," Levi said resignedly. "Dad taught me a bunch of car stuff."

"Dylan, do you know how to get to Ardmore?" Lizzie asked.

"I can probably wing it," he said.

"All right, grab the guns and the rest of our stuff. We need to hurry if we're going to catch them," Lizzie said. She looked over at me, her eyes sympathetic with understanding. Maybe I felt alone, but they did care about me. And they cared about Jess, too. Now we had to prove it to her.

We dispersed through the house, gathering anything useful. Regardless, we wouldn't be returning here.

"The AKs are gone," Dylan called from the lounge.

"They must have taken them," Levi said. This wasn't a good sign. What were she and Kyle planning?

Dylan, Levi, and Lizzie armed themselves with the hunting rifles while I took our remaining handgun. It was all we had left. Then, we stepped onto the street.

Levi led the way as he searched for an appropriate car. Eventually, he selected an aged hatchback. Dylan used the butt of his rifle to smash the window. Levi reached in, unlocked the driver's door, and jammed a butter knife into the ignition. He beat it in a few times with a brick he found strewn on someone's lawn. Then, with a grunt, he twisted the knife and broke the ignition open. After pulling out a bunch of wires, he separated two of the wires and scraped off the plastic-insulated coating. Bright sparks erupted from the tips as he touched the wires together, and the car sprang to life with a satisfying rumble.

"Get in," Levi said. Lizzie and I jumped into the backseat, dumping our weapons between us. Dylan climbed into the passenger side. "Where to?" Levi asked as he shoved the car into gear.

"The motorway," Dylan said, pointing. Levi floored the

accelerator, and we sped away. We skidded around the suburban street corners and eventually made it to the motorway.

"I hope we have enough fuel," Levi said, worry edging into his voice. I peeked over his shoulder at the dash. The fuel gauge hovered at a quarter tank. It would have to be enough.

"Fuel's the least of our worries. We need to make up some serious ground if we're going to catch them," Lizzie said.

"I'm trying but I can't get this piece of shit to go any faster," Levi said as we drove along the abandoned highway, the speedometer struggling to creep above 120 kilometers per hour.

"Surely the soldiers will hear us," I said, feeling anxious about the noise our chosen car was making. It protested loudly with Levi's incessant attempts to get it to go faster.

"You're the one who wanted to steal the car," Dylan commented.

It was a risk we had to take to save Jess, I decided.

"So far, no soldiers," Lizzie said, looking over her shoulder into the darkness behind us.

Levi was driving almost blind, using only the parking lights. The road raced under our car. How far ahead were Kyle and Jess? I felt like we were making good time, but was it fast enough? I prayed we weren't too late.

Clearly, my concern was painted across my face because Lizzie said, "It's going to be OK." She grabbed my hand and gave it a tight squeeze, reminding me I wasn't alone in this war.

I closed my eyes and took a breath. "God, I hope so."

"And if it's not, we'll get through it like we always do." Lizzie sounded so confident.

"How can you be so sure?" I asked, opening my eyes and watching the stalky shadows of unlit streetlights whizz past the window.

"Because I think we all see what's important now," Lizzie said. She still hadn't let go of my hand.

Dylan looked over his shoulder and caught Lizzie's eye. "We only have each other," Dylan said. "And for what it's worth, I wouldn't have it any other way."

"We're stronger together," Lizzie said.

Stronger together. I let that thought steel my mind. We would deal with whatever we found at Ardmore the same way we had dealt with everything else—together.

"Turn off here," Dylan said about thirty minutes later. Still, we hadn't seen a trace of Jess and Kyle. I supposed it was a good thing. At least they hadn't crashed… not yet, anyway. Memories of my dad's wrecked car flashed into my mind, and I felt my breathing quicken. It wouldn't happen to Jess. It couldn't. I tried to push the memories away.

"I think it's a right up ahead," Dylan said.

"There's a sign," Lizzie said. "Faster, Levi."

"I'm trying, but this car's a piece of crap." Levi momentarily flicked the lights to full beam to make the turnoff.

"There, there, I see the airport," I said. It was pretty small, a collection of little hangars and buildings in the distance.

"Hurry, Levi," Lizzie yelled.

"It doesn't go any faster," he yelled back.

"There's a car on the tarmac," Dylan said. "It must be Kyle and Jess."

"Drive out there," Lizzie ordered. Levi screeched around the corner and sped out onto the runway. Our high beams illuminated an old station wagon, but Jess and Kyle were nowhere to be seen.

"We've missed them," I said, dejected. Levi parked the car, and we all jumped out, peering into the darkness, trying to see across the airfield, but we couldn't see much.

"Can you see anything?" I asked desperately.

"No," Levi said. Two bright lights flashed on about three hundred meters away as the familiar sounds of helicopter blades cut through the night.

"Shit," Dylan said as we watched a helicopter rise unsteadily off the ground.

"What do we do?" Lizzie asked.

Jess was in there. We had to get her out. Levi and Dylan were already running across the tarmac toward it. But a loud droning sound overpowered the noise of the helicopter that was now hovering a couple of meters above the concrete. Lizzie and I looked up to see two fighter planes speeding toward us.

"Hide!" Lizzie screamed. We dove behind our car as the planes swooped low and opened fire, strafing the airfield with machine-gun fire. The vehicle we sheltered behind exploded into flames and blew Lizzie and me backward. I lay dazed for a moment as I tried to shake the grogginess from my head. I got to my knees, with my ears ringing from the blast. I eventually struggled to my feet and helped pull Lizzie to hers.

"Are you hurt?" I asked shakily, trying to keep my balance.

"I'm fine," Lizzie said breathlessly. Soot covered her face, and her clothes were singed, but otherwise, she seemed unhurt. We looked out over the airfield that was now foggy with smoke and torn up by bullets. The helicopter was still intact but wobbled thirty or so meters in the air. Levi and Dylan were nowhere to be seen.

"Come on," Lizzie said as she grabbed my wrist. We ran together toward the helicopter. We didn't know what we would do when we got there, but maybe Jess would see us and come to her senses. Halfway across the airstrip, the deafening drone of the planes was back. On their approach, they opened fire, this time directed at Jess and Kyle. Lizzie and I watched, horrified, as bullets smashed into the tail of the helicopter.

"Run!" Lizzie screamed. But I was transfixed as the helicopter began to spin out of control.

"It's going down," Lizzie yelled. "Get out of the way," she said as she dragged me. I couldn't get my feet to move. I watched in slow motion as the helicopter crashed into the ground with the ear-splitting sound of twisting metal.

"Jess," I screamed as hot tears burned down my cheeks. I wrestled free from Lizzie and ran toward the wreck.

"It's going to catch fire," Lizzie yelled at me. I didn't care. All that mattered was finding Jess. I approached the mangled helicopter and peered through the cracked window. I could make out Jess, her eyes closed, and blood streaked across her face.

"No, Jess," I cried as I kicked in the glass window and squeezed into the cockpit.

"Grace, get out of there," Lizzie yelled at me as she followed me.

"I have to see if Jess is OK," I said, crying and choking on the smoky air. "Jess," I yelled as I finally managed to get to her.

No response.

I reached forward and tried to find her pulse with my shaking hands. Nothing.

"No, no, no," I said, sobbing. "Jess," I screamed at her through my tears. "Wake up. Please wake up."

"I think she's gone," Lizzie said, crying.

I put my hand on Jess' cheeks and tried to wipe the blood from her face.

"Come on, wake up," I begged. But she was still.

"Help," a voice said weakly. I was so focused on Jess that, for a moment, I thought it was her. But my hope died as quickly as it had come. I had forgotten about Kyle. I looked over at him as he weakly tried to get out of his seat. A fierce rage rose within me.

"Help me, Grace," he wheezed with pleading eyes. I noticed a piece of metal stabbing through his side. He was going to die. "Help."

I glared at him. He had done this to Jess.

"Grace, help him," Lizzie said tearfully. "But hurry. We need to get out of here."

I stared at Kyle's helpless form dying in front of me. He struggled for breath, gasping. Jess was dead because of him. He was drunk and reckless. If only he had been thinking clearly, maybe she would still be alive. I couldn't bear it. He deserved this.

I felt around on the ground and found a long shard of glass. I gripped it tight in my good hand. It cut through my skin, but I didn't care. Warm blood dripped down my fingers as I crawled toward Kyle. Jess didn't deserve to die like this. She didn't deserve to die at all.

Lizzie saw the glass in my hand, the look in my eye. "Grace! What are you doing?" Lizzie was panicking as she tried to get into the cockpit through the broken window. But I had made up my mind. Plus, he was going to die, anyway. It was his fault, and he would pay.

In a swift motion, I stabbed the shard of glass into his neck. I pulled it out and let it fall to the floor. Kyle's eyes widened as he tried to gasp at the air.

"No!" Lizzie screamed. "Grace, what have you done?"

"He ki-ki-killed Jess," I managed to say through hysterical tears. Lizzie was now crouched next to me, trying to stem the bleeding from Kyle's neck. I looked away and back toward Jess' motionless form.

"We've got to go," Dylan said as he came up to the helicopter. "Soldiers are coming." His face fell as he saw the grizzly scene in the cockpit.

"Come on," Levi said, his voice thick with emotion. "There's a convoy approaching. And those planes might be back."

"He's bleeding out," Lizzie said, crying. "I can't stop it."

"Lizzie, get out of there," Dylan said sternly.

Levi wrenched open the busted helicopter door. He charged inside and dragged me out.

"Jess!" I cried. "We can't leave her."

"We have to get out of here," Dylan yelled. "Lizzie, come on."

Lizzie crawled from the helicopter on her own, her hands covered in Kyle's blood. "You killed him, Grace. How could you do that?" she sobbed.

"Run!" Levi yelled as he pulled me, stumbling, away from Jess. The rumble of the approaching army convoy broke through the night.

"Come on," Dylan said as he sprinted forward.

I followed Levi through the dark, away from the pursuing soldiers. What had I done? Jess was gone, Kyle was dead, and I was broken inside. I wiped at my eyes as soldiers began to shoot. Bullets whistled past my ears and crashed into the concrete up ahead. The darkness was enclosing me all around. Fear rose within me; my shadows were coming for me. Nothing could stop them now.

ACKNOWLEDGMENTS

This book wouldn't have been possible without the help and support of a number of people. Firstly, thank you to Dr Melodie Lindsay from Doclins for proofreading and editing this book. It has been incredibly helpful, and we are grateful for all your hard work. We'd also like to thank our amazing cover designer Lance Buckley. We are absolutely thrilled with how the cover of this book turned out.

First, I want to thank my husband, James. You've always supported my writing even when it meant taking on extra baby-watching duties. Thank you for giving me the time and space to write when I needed it.

Thanks to my writing group – Sue, Shan, Nick, Jade, Jess, Mayur, and Claire. Our frequent sessions have, without a doubt, made me a better writer. I've learned so much from your critiques, and this book wouldn't be as good as it is today without it. A special thanks goes to Sue for being our number one supporter. Thanks for the encouragement and writing sessions over the past year with TJ in tow. Without your friendship and support, this book would still be a rough draft on my laptop.

Finally, I have to thank Sarah. Our lives have changed so much over the past two years but through all of it, our friendship has remained strong. Thank you for being so understanding when life got in the way of writing. I know wouldn't be where I am today without your friendship. I still find it hard to believe that those stories we dreamed up together back in high school are out there for the world to read!

~ Ashley

Thanks to Dan, my husband. It is too easy to let the business of everyday life get in the way of writing. You remind me of the importance of doing what we love, allowing me time to write, even when there is barely any time to be had. Your dependable support is my anchor during times of change (and boy have we had a lot of changes these past few years!).

Thanks to my family and friends, especially my mum, who told me a long time ago, "No one can ask for more than your best". Because of you, I know as long as I am trying my hardest, that is enough. Those words give me comfort on the days when I doubt my ability, whatever my endeavors may be.

And to Ashley. The word 'friendship' barely scrapes the surface of what we have. You give me strength, patience and understanding when I struggle to give it to myself, and challenge me with every word, every paragraph, and every chapter to improve. It is strange to think that all those years ago when we decided to start a book together, we didn't really know each other all that well. We were brought together by our love of books, oblivious to the long journey ahead. But, I couldn't have chosen a better person to walk this road with me.

~ Sarah

ABOUT THE AUTHOR

Sasha A. Linderson is the joint pen name for collaborative authors Ashley Lindsay and Sarah Anderson. Ashley and Sarah grew up together in the small city of Tauranga, New Zealand, and in high-school they began co-authoring the first draft of the Black Skies series.

Soon, their lives took some major plot twists—Sarah moved halfway across the world and is now an operating room nurse in Canada, while Ashley remained in New Zealand and completed a PhD in Chemistry. Ashley now applies her knowledge in the fields of sustainability and innovation.

Despite the distance, after a hiatus of several years they returned to the Black Skies series with fresh eyes and new determination. Their passion for writing and co-authoring has remained strong, and along with the Black Skies series, they have a number of other writing-related pursuits in progress.

For writing tips from Ashley and Sarah, visit the blog at www.lindersoncreations.com, or tune into their podcast by the name of *Dear Writer*, available on your podcatcher of choice. Or, join the tribe and sign up for new blog posts, and be the first to learn when the next installment of Black Skies is expected.

COMING SOON:

BLACK SKIES: BOOK THREE

DARKNESS, SET US FREE

Sometimes the hardest battles come from within.

After the devastating helicopter crash, the teens struggle to deal with the aftermath. Not even the serene New Zealand bush is enough to vanquish the shadows of the past.

But the war will wait for no one. Something is brewing—the Prime Minister's troupes are on the move. And when teens get word about what the Prime Minister has planned, they realise they are running out of time to save their families…